the morningstar

Book 5 of the Morningstar series

LJ FARROW

ISBN: 978-0-578-85401-4

This one is just for me.

Contents

And now, the giants, who are produced from the Fallen Angels and flesh, shall be called evil spirits upon the earth, and on the earth shall be their dwelling.

Evil spirits have proceeded from their bodies; because they are born from men and from the holy Watchers is their beginning and primal origin; they shall be evil spirits on earth, and evil spirits shall they be called.

And the spirits of the giants afflict, oppress, destroy, attack, do battle, and work destruction on the earth, and cause trouble: they take no food, but nevertheless hunger and thirst, and cause offences.

And these spirits shall rise up against the children of men and against the women, because they have proceeded from them. From the days of the slaughter and destruction and death of the giants, from the souls of whose flesh the spirits, having gone forth, shall destroy without incurring judgement...

-First Book of Enoch, Chapter 15

The Dragon's scales are merely her physical armor; it would be unreasonable (indeed, reckless) to assume that her defenses are shed when she is in her human form.

1

SUMMER WAS COMING TO AN end in the southern hemisphere, the days long and perfect, without any of the hectic activity brought on earlier in the season, when the crowds are still hungry for the novel good weather and it is impossible to get into the best tapas bars in the Plaza de Mayo. The light in the late afternoons was changing, the shadows lingered longer ahead of cool, romantic dusks, the first hints that autumn was around the corner.

But these portents could be ignored on this mid-March afternoon in Buenos Aires, where the sidewalk cafés still did a brisk business, and the breeze sailed gently inland, pushed from as far away as Uruguay, across the mouth of the Río de la Plata. A golden-haired exotic beauty with equally golden eyes made her way along the boulevard, and her passage did not go unnoticed by anyone along the street, both because she was so exceptionally striking and apparently so obviously distressed.

No one watched her more carefully than the handsome priest in the doorway of the *quiosco de periódicos* across the street, with a vulpine curiosity that betrayed his religious vocation. He had marked her flight from the hotel Algodon Mansion on Montevideo, occurring, as it did, at about this same time each afternoon for the past four days.

Kedron was fascinated with this creature, and having nothing new to divert him here in the city while he waited to make contact with his new operative, he indulged his wonder about such a profoundly gorgeous being. He could not know that his every move was catalogued in its own right, and when he stepped off the curb to follow the woman it was noted.

"He's on the move," *Ku* said quietly, alerting Azuma and *Ichi* who were seated around the corner at the end of the block. *Hachi* paused and glanced briefly over her shoulder to signal she had heard, and even this subtlety was enticing.

"Doesn't mean he's taking the bait," Azuma spoke casually, and she and *Ichi* moved their heads closer like two women discussing some very juicy gossip.

"If he doesn't, he's an idiot," *Jūichi* observed. "*Hachi* is a walking thirst trap."

"She can hear you," *Ni* reminded him from her position beneath the hotel awning. She sounded both amused and sympathetic.

"He wanted me to," *Hachi* replied.

"Vote of confidence," *Jūichi's* tone was wistful, and it sounded altogether as though the trap were working on *him*.

Hachi then proceeded to push the issue farther than she had on any of the previous days, when the priest had noticed her and clandestinely followed, but had failed to initiate any contact. She slowed her pace, allowing him to get within half a block of her while she appeared to stop and get control of herself, taking out a handkerchief and dabbing her eyes, checking her makeup in a small mirror she fished from her purse and reapplying gloss carefully to her full lips.

Let's just give you something to think about, she thought to herself as she turned in at the doors of *Secretísimo,* where she was greeted warmly by the matron on staff within, and proceeded to begin perusing expensive lingerie that left little to the imagination.

Kedron expertly blended in with the patrons outside the ice cream parlor next door, taking a seat at one of the sidewalk tables and pretending to focus on his newspaper, but it was clear that he was registering *Hachi's* every move through the enormous show windows of the shop. *Hachi* obliged him and everyone else who could see by fondling and displaying a number of lacy unmentionables, stroking them covetously, and pretending she was trying to decide what might be the most flattering purchase.

It worked. Kedron stood up as she accompanied the clerk to the registers to make a purchase, stretching as though he were getting ready to continue his journey. It was obvious he was planning to approach her when she exited, cleverly poising himself to make it seem accidental.

"Are we allowing contact?" *Ni* asked.

"Not yet. Let him suffer another day," Azuma's reply was swift. "*Roku*, you're on."

On cue, three sharply dressed Japanese businessmen exited the hotel and passed behind *Ni* on their way across the street, *Roku, Jū,* and *Ku* in character. They managed to look as menacing, dangerous, and forbidding as the *Akai* generally were.

"Why does *Roku* always get to be the darkly handsome antihero?" *San* asked, giving a bit of gentle ribbing.

"Because he looks most like a Karate Kid villain," *Shi* quipped.

"That's not racist at *all*," *Roku* murmured without breaking stride as he stepped onto the far curb. He and his companions moved quickly down the block, reaching the doors of the lingerie boutique just as *Hachi* was emerging, before the priest could step forward and speak to her. Indeed, Father Kedron seated himself quickly once more and made as though he were looking over his newspaper with renewed interest. It was clear he wanted to avoid a confrontation with the men, worked to avoid their notice.

Hachi, for her part, managed to look frightened, and *Roku* gave her his most predatory smile and gripped her upper arm, hard, yanking her through the doorway. Her gasp of pain was loud enough to be heard without earbuds. *Roku* spoke several words of Japanese in the harshest tone he could muster and managed to smile rather fetchingly at his male companions as he took the small bag that she carried out of her hands. He glanced inside with a roguish nod and passed the bag to *Ku,* then roughly shoved *Hachi* at him as well.

Ku nodded in turn and smiled without any sympathy for his charge, and all but dragged *Hachi* back down the street under protest, ignoring her struggles all the way back to the hotel. *Roku* merely capped off his performance by smoothing his hair and checking his reflection in the shop windows before sharing a laugh with *Jū* while they proceeded off down the sidewalk.

Kedron watched them until they disappeared in the distance, with a thoughtful expression, all while glancing back at the progress of *Hachi* and *Ku* as they vanished into the hotel lobby.

"I believe we have him, *Aijin,*" *Ni* remarked.

"I hope you're right," Azuma replied. "Don't let him out of your sight, *Shi.*"

"*Hai, Aijin,* he's all mine."

M

We were once ethereal beings, light and matter, but when condemned, locked into these earthbound forms. These fleshy prisons, the anchors that dragged us from the heavens. It took some time for us to devise a way to escape them again, and go out into the world, but to do so we had to pay a steep and humiliating price.

We had to leave our wings behind.

2

"I'VE GOT ANOTHER PLAYER," *Shi* made his report to *Ni* later that evening.

"Go ahead," she encouraged, stepping away from the table where the others were sharing a meal.

"Young man, poking around. Not sure what he's on about. He's painfully obvious, and seems to be alone." There was something in *Shi's* voice that *Ni* couldn't fully decipher.

"How young?"

"Young enough that I wonder where his parents are," *Shi* said. "And there's something else, but...it's probably not...well, just a feeling."

Ni said nothing, signaling that she was listening, and she was obliged when *Shi* made his next observation. "He's not Argentine, but speaks the language impeccably. He sounds – and looks like – Iara. Brooding, slouchy, pouty lips and everything."

"She had a brother," *Ni* confirmed, but then felt distressed. "But he wasn't even out of school."

"Then I think this is he," *Shi* lamented. "He's woefully out of his depth. He's about as subtle as a sledgehammer. He's probably looking to be noticed, and this Kedron will likely disappear him if given the chance. Instructions?"

"Just keep the primary in focus for now," *Ni* replied, making eye contact with Azuma, who had picked up on the subtle distress in her priestess' posture and tone, and perhaps could even hear the particulars of the communication from her seat at the table. She wasn't relishing the thought of dedicating someone to this detail; the *Akai* were not a babysitting service.

"Before you go, there's something else," *Shi* sounded apologetic. "Not to further complicate things, but there's another priest."

"He travels with a secretary, a younger priest, sometimes two or three of them," *Ni* reminded him.

"This is someone else, I think. He's dressed like them. But he wasn't with them. He was watching the hotel when Kedron arrived. Then he just disappeared. I didn't see his face. Big guy. Looks dangerous."

"Dangerous how?" *Ni* asked, and Azuma watched her forehead wrinkle.

"He's built like an assassin, not a priest. Massive, even by Western standards," *Shi* sounded worried, and *Ni* trusted his instincts as well as her own. The *Akai* did not spook easily, and his tone concerned her. If he identified this man as a threat, it needed to be taken seriously.

"Did you see his face?" she asked.

"Negative, but I could probably ID him if needed," *Shi* sounded confident about this, at least. "Something familiar about him as well, just can't put my finger on it right now."

"Maintain your current objective; I will discuss this with the Mistress."

"*Hai.*" He gave his acknowledgement and ended the transmission.

Before *Ni* could finish returning her phone to her jacket pocket, Azuma was at her side.

"Complications?" the Dragon asked.

Ni looked over her shoulder at the group at the table and nodded toward the bar, entirely unsure how Azuma was going to react to any talk of Iara. *Ni* remembered the verbal carnage in the hotel the day Iara died, when their typically stoic mistress was ready to eviscerate anyone in her path.

Azuma joined her there and ordered plum wine for the two of them. The bartender was alone, cleaning glasses. It was too early for the crowds, the sun was just below the horizon, and it was quiet here outside their private dining room.

Speaking in a voice too low to be picked up by human hearing, *Ni* relayed the essential details of *Shi's* report to her mistress. Azuma maintained a stiff composure when she heard Iara's name, but her expression was one of worry.

"The boy's name is Iago," she said. "He can't be more than fifteen or sixteen years old."

"It appears the parents are not around, but how did he get here?" *Ni* wondered aloud.

"Their father travels extensively on business throughout the Americas, and I am pretty sure the family has money. From what Iara suggested, he was far less controlling with his son than he tried to be with her. It isn't impossible that he could have learned of the priest from Iara at some point. They were close; she was closer to her brother than anyone," Azuma explained.

"We can't ensure his safety if he gets between us and Kedron," *Ni* reasoned.

"Then we'll need a dedicated contingency plan." Azuma considered carefully. "I think this is a task for *Ichi*. Iago needs to fall asleep here and wake up safe in his bed, at home. I'll talk to her."

"And what of the other priest? Any instructions?" *Ni* inquired.

"He will declare his position with his actions," Azuma told her. "We will take the battle as it comes to us."

3

THEY CHOSE A QUIET BAR, one that served tapas in the evenings but was otherwise dim and deserted, private until the magic hour when throngs of patrons descended upon it, and piano music was played, and food and fellowship transformed it. It fronted a quiet street several blocks away from the Plaza de Mayo, on a corner, which provided an advantage for surveillance. The big windows didn't hurt.

By mid-afternoon, the tall buildings cast shadows over that side of the street, giving the place an even more hollow, lonely appearance, and it was here that *Hachi* came, at the midpoint of the traditional *siesta*, for fully three days in a row, apparently alone, damaged, in distress. The bartender, when clandestine inquiries were made, noted only her sadness and his surprise that one so small could consume such quantities of *anejo*. He did not know her story because she said nothing, made no calls, and no one ever came to meet her.

And on that third day, at a time when they were just about to abandon the ruse for another day, Kedron arrived, a spring in his step, wearing the dark priest's uniform without his collar. He looked neither left nor right, and to an uninterested observer behaved as though he belonged there.

"*Hachi*," *Roku* said her name only, knowing she would understand it was a signal.

"What did we decide about listening in on him?" *Hachi* asked. "The device is ready." She spoke in a tone so low it would be hard for the bartender, indeed any human, to hear. They had debated planting a small microphone on his clothing that attached with a special adhesive, a tiny dot less than a quarter centimeter in diameter that disappeared when adhered to fabric.

"*Aijin?*" *Ichi* asked, when there was no response from their mistress, and for several seconds there was only silence.

"I've decided against it," Azuma finally spoke. "It will be easier to remain dispassionate and get this done without having to listen to his innermost depravities. We know who he is."

Hachi didn't acknowledge that she had heard, because the priest had entered the bar and was approaching. She communicated more directly, and more painfully, by activating the listening device briefly and immediately crushing it between her fingernails; as it died it shrieked in everyone's ear, including her own, but she didn't wince. *Ku* was watching through the scope on the second floor of the building on the opposite corner diagonal, and he jumped when the mic was killed but *Hachi's* expression never changed. Classic *Hachi.*

"Girl, we need to send you to finishing school when we get home," *Ichi* complained, though she sounded mostly amused.

"She's perfect as she is," Azuma responded, losing patience. "You all are. Now shut-up and listen."

Hachi sat quietly, sipping her tequila, staring off at nothing in particular, watching the play of the light and shadows through the multicolored bottles stored at the bar back. The mirror behind them created interesting prisms. She was perfectly content to be with herself, and was a master at ignoring people, or seeming to, while she sized them up like any other mark.

Kedron took the stool next to her, ignoring the twelve or so others that stood empty along the bar. *Hachi* thought this a bold move, and it told her quite a bit about who he was. One would expect a priest to be unassuming, avoid intrusion, and she knew enough of his religion to understand its general misogyny. On the other hand, perhaps a priest would wish to appear inclusive, signal fellowship, or telegraph loneliness.

Altogether, she felt this one was entitled, arrogant, and dangerous. She glanced in his direction, and it was apparently enough of an encouragement for him to speak to her.

"*Buenas tardes, senorita,*" Kedron said, offering his hand with a small nod and smile.

Hachi made looking confused and lost a work of art, tilting her head and looking at his hand before grasping it briefly, softly, the way she assumed a demure, ladylike woman might do it. She shook her head, just a quick movement that made her hair move alluringly and dispersed the scent of her perfume. It had the effect she intended, his grey eyes flashed with appreciation, his pupils dilating.

He liked what he was seeing, and she watched as he made the connection between her confusion and his use of the language, realizing she did not speak it. And her performance was meant to make him believe she was vulnerable, so it pleased her when, just for a moment, she saw that lizard thing in him in those eyes, the monster beneath the surface, before he shuttered it, making his gaze guileless and attentive.

"I am sorry," he said, touching his forehead in a gesture of self-admonishment. "English, perhaps? I should not have assumed."

Hachi nodded, and he was about to say more when the bartender appeared to take his order.

"*¿Puedo tomar un vaso de Lacrimi Cristi?*" Kedron asked, and the bartender nodded, shooting a glance of concern at *Hachi*. It was clear he was letting her know that she should not hesitate to ask for his help if she needed it.

Kedron was silent until the glass of wine was set down before him. He swirled the dark liquid gently, and said, "Do you know, the name of this wine means 'tears of Christ?'"

Hachi watched him carefully, examining the scars on his knuckles as he held his goblet to his lips.

"It is a lovely color," she allowed, letting him hear and identify her accent.

"Ah, you are Japanese." Kedron said this with some satisfaction, as if pleased with himself. "Would you like to try it? I would be delighted if you would allow me to-"

"Thank you, no," *Hachi* gestured her gratitude at the offer, and then said, "I don't drink wine."

"*Cliché*," coughed *San* softly in her earpiece. She tried to master her amusement, which caused her mouth to waver slightly. Kedron read it as something emotional, and introduced himself.

He made small talk, asking her what she thought of Argentina, specifically the city when she had admitted she was here because of her husband's business travels. He saw that as his opening.

"There are many amazing things to be learned about Argentina that have little to do with this city," he told her, regaling her with a folktale about the gauchos of the Pampas, and their tradition of poetic songwriting, as well as the ways in which their cooking of meat over open fires had become a lauded tradition in both Brazilian and Argentine cuisine.

Hachi listened attentively, as she guessed, correctly, that he would respond most favorably to her rapt focus on him. His eyes took too many liberties, his gaze lingering in particular on the flesh of her inner thighs, which was no less than she had intended, having hemmed up her dress herself.

So caught up was she in her inventory of his repulsive shortcomings that she almost missed his question to her. "Now you. Tell me something of your Japan," he asked, as much to test whether he could compel her as to make her believe he was actually interested in her.

"Have you been there?" she asked, watching him carefully.

"Alas, my travels have taken me through Europe and the Americas, but I have not had the pleasure myself. A close…associate of mine was there recently, and I was envious of the reports I heard of your beautiful country."

"Perhaps I will trade your folktale for one of ours," *Hachi* murmured, speaking softly and shyly, pleased when he leaned in toward her. "Japan is a very magical place, our stories and traditions just as heroic as any other country, but there are many tales of the *yokai*, or night demons, that capture the imagination.

"In particular, a group of forest demons, called the *Tengu*, who capture those who are abandoned or lost. If a human infant is left to die in their forests, they take it up and spirit it away, often training it in the deadly art of combat, hoping to unleash it on its own kind once it has grown."

Kedron was enthralled, but could not have known that *Hachi* had picked this tale purposefully. First, had he been paying attention to anything other than his own lust, he would have heard the foreshadowing in it. Second, she preferred to discuss things that were true, even in a situation where subterfuge was needed, because she knew it made her come across entirely authentically, in a way that one cannot appear if one forces a topic of conversation.

Only Azuma knew that the story's truth came not only from the faithfulness of the retelling, but from *Hachi's* earliest memories. She, unlike the others, had been found by the priests of Akenomyosei's sect as she wandered lost in the mountain forest near her home. Unlike the others, she was not abandoned or stolen as an infant; she was four years old when taken in by their order.

Her mother had sent her from their house, having raised her there in secret, knowing that if they were found, *Hachi's* father had sworn to kill them both. His child, born with albinism, for being an aberration that he felt could only be the result of his wife's infidelity, and his wife for dishonoring him and his family.

Hachi's mother had escaped his initial judgement, climbing high into the mountains, taking shelter in an abandoned woodcutter's shack and making it a home for herself and her beautiful daughter. And there she raised the little girl with love, telling her nothing of the danger they had left behind, teaching her to forage, showing her how to honor the beauty of their mountain home.

Until the night *Hachi's* father had found them, and *Haha* had pushed her out the window, whispering to her to run and not look back, that she would come after. But little *Hachi* had heard the screams as she ran, stumbling over obstacles, wanting to get as far away as she could, knowing her mother would not be coming, would not ever come for her.

The terrible priests of Akenomyosei had found her, half-starved, dehydrated, wandering aimlessly in the mists. They had claimed this bounty the mountain offered, and had begun their cruel tutelage, the same torture that all initiates were subject to, on a path to become worthy of the ultimate honor, a chance to become one of the *Akai Hogo-sha*, those who were guardians of the Dragon.

It was there that she had learned to manipulate those priests with the only weapon she had, her astounding physical beauty. And although Azuma knew the story, had learned it during the ritual, when she had first tasted *Hachi's* blood, her young priestess had never spoken of it aloud, and Azuma silently kept her secret.

The predator in Kedron could not resist the story of the *Tengu*, seeing it as an invitation only he could recognize, something to use against her. He was by training an Inquisitor, a master of manipulation, and he had twisted it into an artform, a weapon of subtlety and ruthlessness.

He said, in a voice too low to carry, "How interesting that this is what you choose to share with me. It seems, to my reckoning, that it must be somewhat autobiographical. I must confess that while you were talking, I remembered that I had seen you before, on La Avenida Montevideo." His tone was conspiratorial, the tone of a confidant, the tone of a would-be lover.

He leaned back, finished his wine in one greedy gulp, and fished a small business card from an inside pocket of his jacket.

This he slid gently across the bar, wedging it beneath the edge of her handbag. She glanced at it.

KEDRON CALAVERAS Y VACAMONTE, OP, M.DIV., BISHOP
VATICAN OFFICE OF THE PROMOTOR FIDEI
PAPAL EMISSARY TO CENTRAL AND SOUTH AMERICA

The card itself was printed on expensive paper, thick cream-colored cotton, laminated. The print was authoritative and somewhat antiquated and there was a complicated crest of some sort, embellished in gold and repeated on the cardstock as a watermark.

The *camarero* was listening, from his place at the other end of the bar, being subtle about it, polishing glasses ahead of the evening rush. *Hachi*, who was not given to sentimentality, found it sweet, albeit entirely unnecessary in her case. But Kedron noticed it as well.

So when he stood to leave, he leaned in behind her, putting some of his weight against her, improperly leaning into her back, bringing his mouth down beside her ear, enjoying the feel of her hair against his face. She noticed that he placed his right hand on the bar, the large cross on his signet ring in plain sight so that the bartender would know him to be a priest, and assume nothing was amiss, here in this Catholic country where they were so revered.

Kedron closed his eyes to further the illusion that he was only praying over her, whispering to her as his other hand rested insolently on her thigh, the tips of his fingers brushing against her bare skin. *Hachi* held her breath, masking her revulsion, swallowing her rage, knowing the destruction of this bag of blood would more than repay the insult. "Your husband must be a very cruel man, but I think a part of you enjoys that domination, likes it when he punishes you. I believe you think him a monster, like your *Tengu*, but I also think you chose him, subconsciously, for that reason, that subjugation which gives you pleasure. I think you provoke him just to taste the pain, just to feel. If I am right, I must tell you that my card is a key that will open many doors. And if I am wrong, I *must* say that this encounter has been a singular enchantment."

He stepped away from her then, letting his fingers slide off her dress slowly, like an emphasis to his little speech, and then completed the illusion he wanted to create by sketching a blessing in her direction and stepping out the door.

The bartender, for his part, was gratified, thinking that the chance encounter with this unknown priest had brought his forlorn patron some peace, mistaking her smile for newfound hope, not the homicidal warning that her fellow priests knew it to be.

4

WHILE *HACHI* WAS STILL GATHERING herself to leave, Azuma slid onto the stool beside her, not shying away from seating herself where the priest had just been. *Hachi* felt her mistress' fingers brush against her fist where it rested on her lap. Azuma felt the subtle trembling in *Hachi's* hand but did not mention it.

"I heard it all," she confirmed, soft enough that it wouldn't carry. She reached over and picked up the card that Kedron had left, turning it over on a whim. He hadn't disappointed, and it made it even more clear he had been watching *Hachi*, as they had wanted him to, and that he had planned this encounter some time ago. On the reverse of the card he had written the name of his hotel, including his room number. Azuma grimaced involuntarily; it dredged up a memory of Iara and what she must have suffered at the hands of this man.

Hachi glanced over at the bartender and signaled for another drink. He came over promptly to deliver it, leaning on the bar expectantly, looking from one woman to the other, and deciding it was safe to flirt.

"Sisters?" he asked, which both women guessed was the lamest attempt at small talk they had ever heard, and Azuma had to school herself not to cringe, fully aware that the rest of the *Akai* were hearing everything, knowing it would be a source of ongoing in-jokes for the rest of the trip. She could already hear an assortment of snickers and commentary as the rest of the group reacted.

So Azuma just looked at him like he was an idiot, an unwanted idiot, and let the Dragon out in her gaze. He abandoned his futile position, shoulders slumping slightly, and reverted to a professional demeanor, asking whether she would like something to drink.

"No, thank you." The words were more courteous than the tone, but he felt slightly less defeated when she dropped ten thousand Argentine pesos onto the bar. It was enough to soften the insult, but not so much that he wouldn't forget them just as fast as any other tourists. He made the money disappear and made himself scarce, which was exactly the result Azuma was looking for.

Hachi tossed back her tequila with one swallow, managing to make even this loutish gesture appear poised and alluring, and then slid off the stool and gathered her purse. Not waiting to see if Azuma followed, she said, "I need a shower."

Azuma understood perfectly. It felt like they all did.

5

"SOMETHING IS WRONG, *AIJIN*," *Shi*'s voice betrayed his distress, an ominous signal to Azuma and her other priests.

"Talk to me," Azuma's voice sounded unnaturally calm and surprisingly clear, as though she were in the car with them, rather than on a rooftop two blocks away, watching the entrance of the hotel.

"The asset isn't just late, she is missing entirely," came the steady response.

"Is it possible she took an alternate route?" Azuma asked, already knowing what the response to her question would be. She knew her priests would have covered every contingency.

"All potential approaches are covered, *Aijin*," *Ichi* assured their mistress with calm confidence. Yet Azuma detected some anxiety in her tone as well.

"Has the boy been secured?"

"By now, Iago should be in the departures lounge at the airport, enjoying an illicit cocktail, I'm sure," *Ichi* replied. "The Dominican consulate representative will see to it that he is put on the plane home. The father was insistent upon it."

Azuma said nothing more, they had their instructions, and the worst part of any operation was the waiting. She knew *Hachi* was going in without any communications device, in the event that she could be searched by Kedron's thugs, three formidable priests that occupied the rooms adjacent to his suite on either side and the one directly across the hall.

This didn't bother Azuma in the least; *Ku* would have eyes on *Hachi* until she entered the lift in the hotel lobby; after that he would take up a position on the floor where the target was staying, but *Hachi* was supremely capable of defending herself from the four known adversaries; either singly or together, the odds were in her priestess' favor.

The sun was slipping rapidly over the edge of the world, and the streets below Azuma had been in deepening shadow for most of the afternoon. She watched the crowds begin to grow, fairy lights in the trees came on, the magical hour between day and night had come.

"Mistress?" *Nana's* voice was suddenly in her ear. "I think I have located the asset. She's in a sidewalk café with an unknown male, appears to be early middle age with dark curly hair. My position is tenuous, if I betray myself they will know I have been watching. Location is southwest corner near your current position, near the rear entrance to the hotel. I'll keep eyes on until you can confirm."

Azuma didn't like the description of the man *Nana* was looking at, so she sprinted to the opposite corner of the roof and peered carefully over the crenellated parapet. Her angle was better than his, and the lanterns only assisted her preternatural night vision, illuminating the patrons of the café as though they were spot lit by stage brights.

A raven-haired beauty of less than two dozen years sat with an urbane gentleman of apparent means. His suit was crushed velvet, despite the heat, midnight blue this time if Azuma were not mistaken, his silk shirt unbuttoned just so, silver to match a pocket square with tiny lapis fleur-de-lis, and impossibly immaculate matching velvet loafers with silver adornments, no socks of course, in deference to the mild weather. Akenomyosei at his finest.

She thought her sigh of frustration inaudible, and perhaps it was, but the Monster knew she was there nevertheless, glancing upward with a graceful tilt of its head, those shiny, unfathomable eyes meeting hers directly. It gave the slightest nod of acknowledgement and returned its diabolical attentions to its companion.

"*Ane*," came a whispered voice in her ear, a familiar one, calling to her, not by name but by reference. *Elder sister.* Tatsuo Tomo, on the corner opposite the café, his hand on the shoulder of a young boy, clearly recognizable as Iago.

Azuma backed carefully away from the edge, looking around for an escape, needing to be on the ground, not having time to descend through the building. She considered her options, not wanting to risk being seen engaging in any supernatural feats, but having no other viable option.

"Get *Hachi* out," she commanded, the last thing she could say, because the change was upon her. She took a running start toward the opposite end of the roof and then she leaped off, windwalking, floating downward into the alley, landing gently on her feet and immediately sprinting to the opening onto the street opposite, hoping that her stunt maneuver had not been seen.

From her vantage point at street level, she could no longer see Tatsuo Tomo, but she put him out of her mind for a moment, because she *did* have a perfect line of sight to Akenomyosei, who hadn't moved at all. Indeed, it appeared it had settled in, its fingers moving slightly, caressing the delicate handle of the demitasse that held its handcrafted coffee, sharing a moment of mirth with its young companion.

But she could also clearly see the staff entrance to the hotel, and the neat figure who bounded easily up the steps to the door was so identical in form and mannerism to the Monster that she had to look at both of them twice. But no, her eyes did not deceive her, what she saw was real, a dual manifestation, although the Dark Twin wore a suit of charcoal black, with a shirt to match, and a white pocket square. Its shoes were different somehow, incongruous with its otherwise pristine haberdashery, but she couldn't quite say what was so singular and recognizable about them.

This one turned its head at the last moment, confirming what she had feared. It did indeed wear the Monster's handsome face, and as it took a last glance over its shoulder before disappearing through the door, its gaze seemed to rest on Azuma.

"Acknowledge my last communication," Azuma said, suspecting that she would never get anywhere near that door.

"Confirmed. Extracting *Hachi*," *Ku* responded immediately.

"The rest of you abort," Azuma told them. "Do not engage subject or asset should you encounter them. Everyone but *Hachi* and *Ku* to rendezvous point in ninety seconds and do not be seen."

This time, Azuma resumed her position on the roof by retreating into the alleyway and climbing up a concrete drainpipe, finding it amusing that if someone saw her doing so it was less disturbing than witnessing a windwalk. The edge of the parapet was embedded with shards of glass, a common way to discourage both thrill seekers and thieves, but she vaulted over it without a scratch.

Within seconds, the others began arriving, black clad figures all, some in tactical gear, others in street clothing, depending upon their roles in the operation. But as Azuma took count, she discovered one too many among her priests, so she surveyed their faces, half recognized and accounted for before she came to one with its back turned, near the front parapet, a shadow in stark relief against the false façade.

And then, not one, but two figures were discernable, the one of slighter build just beyond the closer, and she saw Tatsuo Tomo. Behind him, Iago, looking scared and confused.

"Sister," the demon spoke, and the response of the *Akai* was immediate.

"*Teki*," *Ichi* said sharply, and they dropped back several steps and into position, protective of their mistress, moving as one as Azuma stationed herself behind their ranks, keeping pace with her forward progress and placing themselves between the Dragon and the threat.

They rotated in deadly synchrony, betraying their inhumanity so aligned and symmetric was this warlike dance they did, ensuring that Azuma was not vulnerable from any angle, not compromised by the lack of two of their number.

"Impressive display," Tatsuo Tomo said, sounding bored and amused at the same time. Not to be outdone, he said, in rapid succession, snapping his fingers following each name, "*Ichi, Ni, San, Shi.*"

But whatever he had expected would happen, he was thwarted, thinking that by calling out each of them in turn, he named them, intending them to drop dead where they stood, a demonstration of the Death Bringer's power. He was so angry at this failure, he hissed aloud, shaking in his umbrage.

Azuma said nothing, recognizing the mistake he'd made, but *Roku* spoke up, a taunt of his own at the ready. The *Akai* did not forget that this one had engineered much of their own torture during their initiation in the ways of the Temple of Akenomyosei, and they hated him as Azuma did for being the architect of much endured and creative cruelties. "It won't work, those aren't their true names."

"Unlike, *Iago?*" Tatsuo Tomo sneered delicately, almost whispering it to the wind, and Iago's head came up, strangely and unnaturally attentive suddenly.

"*No,*" Azuma's whisper was inaudible to all but herself, and perhaps her evil twin.

Tatsuo Tomo gestured impatiently at the boy, who moved, somnambulant, to the edge of the roof, bending his face gently toward the ledge, smiling as he pressed it against the glass shards and began to walk, slowly and deliberately. His handsome face ripped and shredded against the sharp pieces, alternately abraded by the rough concrete. He turned to the Death Bringer, torn and bleeding, now missing an eye, the other rapturous, seeking approval from this diabolical puppet master.

Unmindful of her clothing now, Azuma hurled herself at Tatsuo, changing, winding herself about his fleshly figure. Too late she realized he was changing himself, becoming as ethereal as smoke, disintegrating, escaping her deadly embrace, only to reappear once more in another place, now embracing the bloody broken boy who was marked with the results of his infernal order.

He opened his mouth gently, allowing an unnaturally long forked tongue to unfurl against Iago's bloody cheek, tasting the blood, his expression one of ecstasy. He looked at Azuma, looked at her priests.

"Anyone want to share?" he offered, entirely sincere now, and Azuma saw with horror that the manipulation was real, she recognized the changes in the posture of the *Akai*, the bloodlust in their eyes at this offering, the blood of this, of any pureflesh child too enticing for a blood drinker to resist, enough to distract them from any duty to protect him.

Azuma positioned the Dragon directly between the *Akai* and Tatsuo Tomo, shrieking with anger and rattling her scales menacingly, advancing on her enemy, hoping to distract him from the boy. She made eye contact with Iago, trying to draw his attention to her gaze, feeling a moment of hope as she captured it, one second, and then two, trying to stretch out the enchantment long enough to divert him from his reality, lure him away, hoping her greater control could keep her from feeding on him.

Although there was no safe position on this roof, the *Akai* were successfully compromised, and too late she saw her twin becoming something else, serpentine, and sinister. It laid its own claws upon Iago's form, forcing her to watch, to face her own failure in this, ripping him apart for the sport, the satisfaction, the malice, or most likely, no particular reason at all. Still, Iago kept to his feet, so Tatsuo Tomo whispered something in his ear, something too soft for even Azuma to hear, and the boy turned, walked to the edge of the roof, leaned out over the void, and was gone. The screams of horrified passersby floated up to the roof, and Tatsuo Tomo closed his eyes for a moment, swaying drunkenly, as if this were a symphony to be savored.

"Sister. Goddess. Twin. Pupil," its sibilant hiss she felt in her bones, penetrating even her grief, augmenting her guilt, sensing her priests awakening around her, alert to the death, alert to their inability to stop the inevitable. "Your concern for these worthless beings is beneath you, it is interfering with your reason.

"It was not for you to save Iara, not for you to mourn her enough to rouse the Dragon in anger. Whatever you hoped to learn from this errand, it is lost. Or was never for you to find, or to know. You may have thwarted my emergence in you, but you fail to recognize that you cannot supplant me at our Master's side. I alone have the power of death over life, no matter what gift of the blood you grant your minions or any other you choose to love, they will all taste the sweetness of my embrace, and I shall endure beyond the time of the Dragon."

"*By all means, embrace me now, Dear Brother,*" the Dragon spoke, surprising them all, making the invitation clear and unambiguous. "*Why wait? Or have you forgotten my importance to our Dark Father? You cannot take a thing from me unless you have permission. I forget not my place in this world or the next, and it remains to be seen who shall prevail and who shall fall. Neither do I forget the insults of my enemies, and I bear the responsibility to chase them hence to the ends of the earth.*"

Tatsuo Tomo merely smiled, declining her challenge as she had known it would, disintegrating, like the spent ash of a dark star, carried away on the breeze, leaving carnage and chaos behind. The Dragon had no difficulty holding onto its pain, cementing the memory, adding it to the inventory of sins it had no intention should go unanswered.

6

AS KEDRON MADE PREPARATIONS FOR the evening ahead, he did not even realize that in his contentment and excitement he was humming beneath his breath. Alone in his lavish hotel suite, there was no one to comment upon it. Humming not a sentimental tune, not for comfort, but rather something akin to what the executioner might do, passing the time as he sharpens his blades, or the inquisitor, heating the brands in the forge.

He looked around the room, pleased as always with the surroundings, comfortable, with an air of businesslike efficiency that was a hallmark of hotels everywhere, but with an underlying sumptuousness that could not quite discourage seduction, should such be required.

His stoles, books, and other religious paraphernalia were packed away, out of sight, as he preferred it, whether alone or entertaining a lover. He was a calculated being, he understood the allure of the cloth, so he was wearing his collar at present, but he disdained the cassock, its red piping was, he found, a bit cumbersome for the imagination to hurdle.

A studied Catholic, one who would otherwise find a priest attractive, can willingly overcome certain obstacles but not others. A simple black cassock is mysterious and inviting, and he knew he had always cut a gorgeous figure in the tailored frock. The buttons invite the fingers to engage, undressing a priest a forbidden pleasure, a Pandora's box, a rebellious act, the crossing of a delicious boundary. But the addition of the red accents, the sash, were like a warning, danger, a reminder that the sanctity was greater, and perhaps, too, the sin. Even the damnable buttons were red, and the soutane, which he was normally vain about, made the wearer seem older, less loverlike, more authoritarian, geriatric even.

And when meeting a new asset, it was best to acknowledge his vocation, to do otherwise might seem suspicious. They were meeting a priest, some understood why they had been chosen, and most could be convinced that an audition was warranted; after all, many doors that were formerly closed to these individuals would now be opened. Their lives changed. They were doing God's work, never mind that it was essentially Kedron's discretion that determined what form that work would take.

He stepped into the marble bathroom to take one last look at himself in the mirror, pleased as ever at what he saw there. He felt that his looks were even more finished in his middle age, that he had lost some of the prettiness and uncertainty that he used to feel were at odds with his internal sense of authority; his face now matched his sentiment.

A slight movement at the corner of the glass drew his attention, and he gasped, seeing the priest reflected back at him. Weston, but how?

Kedron whirled around to confront this intrusion, not understanding why his young, misdirected protégé would be here. And how did he get in? But the room, and indeed the suite beyond, were empty.

"Are you losing control so easily?" the voice behind him now, cultured, accented, and amused. Kedron turned to find the gorgeous being leaning against the vanity. What he had initially thought a black cassock and white collar, he now saw was a fine black suit, dark and depthless, snowy white shirt, and a pristine white pocket square. The material of the suit was interestingly the identical weave and weight of his own cassock, and this detail was momentarily distracting. Kedron blinked carefully, examining the man. Not Weston after all. The Other.

"*Ehyeh Asher*," the man who was not a man spoke, ironically not completing the phrase, but Kedron guessed it was purposeful. Instead of *I am That I am*, why would the Devil not say, *I am That*. Cleverly distinguishing itself from the Maker.

Kedron smiled, acknowledging its statement, believing he had rightly identified it. Still not understanding the reason for the visit.

"Your command of the ancient languages is improving, at least those sanctioned by the Creator," the man remarked bitterly, moving past the priest into the rooms beyond. It looked around approvingly. "I see you've embraced your station and disdained your vows of poverty. So useless anyway, I never understood to what end insolvency made anyone closer to the Almighty."

"It only ever made me more desperate, more willing to do anything to avoid it," Kedron remarked unnecessarily.

"It taught you to barter flesh, and the manipulative power of desire," he remarked softly, as if proud. "But trafficking sex for the Church – you took it to another level. How you've come up in the world."

"My superiors know-" Kedron began, unable to resist defending himself for some futile reason. His arrangement with this creature was satisfying, but even he was too egotistical to listen to much criticism.

"Know of your appetites for sexual degradation? Know you to be a rapist, a sodomite, a defiler of those who have no recourse against you? Your superiors may know that you use ill means to obtain your ends. Those ends satisfy the Church's need for information, so She has been a lax mistress in overseeing your occupations on Her behalf. They ignore or perhaps are unaware of the money these men pay you for satisfying their appetites, men you would otherwise root out in the interests of the *Dei Gloria*. But the

Jesuit sees much more, and is not willing to turn the other cheek. You are being watched. And not just by the Church."

Kedron felt a cold finger of fear along his spine. Who would dare spy on him? Not the Church, surely, for he and his priests were their eyes and ears. None were left to look in upon him.

"You've angered someone. Lost an asset that would be missed. Invaded a house so sacred you could not comprehend the danger of even attempting such a maneuver. Where is Iara? How long since you've heard from her? The one who seeks you must never know your secrets, and she is at your door. Not the Wolf, but the Dragon." The being's dark eyes were knowing, his expression a living thing that Kedron felt crawling over his skin. The man turned away from him, toward the ornate French doors that led to the balcony, where the sun was descending rapidly in the western sky.

"I have your protection, it is promised me, Senester," Kedron argued, appealing to him, yet understanding the bargain.

He shook his head, those dark curls moving gracefully, alluring against the broad shoulders. Turned to confront Kedron. "You mistake me for another, Brother. I thought you recognized me in the mirror. You rely wrongly on these visions of the Devil, my friend, *do not be wise in your own eyes; fear the Lord and shun evil.*"

"No. It cannot be you, I won't accept it," Kedron gazed in disbelief as the man approached him, and tried, vainly, to hold him off, but he was too strong, pushing Kedron's hands away almost gently, as if he were a child.

"It is he, and he is I, but we are we," the man proclaimed, tilting his head slowly to one side and twisting sharply, making the bones pop, much like a bodybuilder would, or a bruiser ahead of a fight, without laying a hand on his opponent. But then Kedron felt it, with a dawning horror, as a rivulet of blood ran from his nose. His own neck, popping outward, violently, and so quickly that he had time to understand his death, before his body failed, no longer in communication with his distant brain. Down he went, down and down, into the depths of a darkness much different than what he had bargained for, all for listening to the Devil he desired over the one he already knew.

7

HACHI CROSSED THE LOBBY, AWARE as always of the many eyes following her progress. She had never let her looks define her, nor was she particularly interested in attention for attention's sake. She put her appearance to use when it was useful, but otherwise disdained exploiting it, understanding its worthlessness while taking advantage of those who upheld it as a virtue. They were often as bankrupt as the thing they sought.

Her silk kimono dress had elaborate frogging, and she had secured her blond hair in place atop her head with *kanzashi* that were as sharp as they were beautiful, both as a nod to her heritage and a concession to the expectation that violent expenditures would be needed on this errand. She particularly looked forward to it this time, if she had been irked about the situation with Iara, she was now personally invested by the repugnant behavior of their target.

For once, *Hachi* was happily waiting for him to cross the boundary and touch her. It was the point at which she gave herself permission to unleash the pain he deserved. She gave it very little thought, sure her creative tendencies would kick in when the opportunity presented itself. She had no doubt it would.

As in most luxury properties, she barely had to wait for an available elevator. She rode the lift to a high floor, but not the highest, and she surmised that Kedron considered this a purposeful expression of his humility. The textiles used in this place were of the finest quality, on par with that of the property where the *Akai* were carrying out their pretense of being a group of Japanese businesspeople, with one or two spouses along for the adventure.

The carpet was deep and quiet beneath her feet, purposefully chosen to allow for discreet movement of the guests, and the guests of the guests, she assumed. It was certainly engineered for clandestine affairs, none would recall hearing footsteps at odd times of the night, and even the wallcovering was a thick burnout velvet, which would dampen the more subtle sounds of premature assignations at as-yet-unlocked doorways.

She was alone, and walked self-assuredly down the center of the hallway, oblivious to the events occurring outside the hotel. She approached the doorway, turning coquettishly to look at the door opposite, knowing that perhaps she was watched even now, making it seem as though she were double-checking the room numbers to be certain she had the correct one.

She listened, and frowned, feeling as though she should hear at least some industry taking place on the other side, as the priest made his arrangements for entertaining a beautiful young woman, never mind that *Hachi* was not the young woman he expected to discover at his door. She assumed he would handle it with aplomb, perhaps his secretary bodyguards were poised to intercept the asset should she show up close behind this unexpected visitor.

No. She listened to her instincts, and it was too quiet on the other side of the door, although she felt someone was there, had the oddest sensation of being watched through the fisheye mounted slightly above her line of sight.

She sensed movement behind her, almost too late to turn, the figure large and substantial, catching her briefly in shadow, and a large hand came over her mouth, surprisingly gently, not over her nose, while simultaneously she was lifted into a strong embrace, pulling her in, her spine against a firm male torso. Her surprise too great to avoid one reflexive struggle, inadvertently her heel connected with the door of the room with a hollow boom, but her captor was unnaturally quick, withdrawing with her around the corner and pushing through to the stairwell landing.

Even the door here slipped closed behind them with a barely discernable whisper of air, its pneumatic hinge also calibrated for discretion in escape. They sheltered out of view of the glass transom in the fire door, huddled in shadow.

Her captor placed her carefully back on her feet, and she slipped out of her heels.

"I didn't mean to scare you." *Ku's* whisper against her ear, his mouth on her hair completely different from Kedron's same gesture a few days prior, this almost sensual, and certainly affectionate.

"I knew it was you," she said. "If you wanted to scare me you would have covered my entire face with your hand, at least my nose, make it hard to breathe," she told him.

"Thanks for the advice," he said, ironically. "Something's up. They told me to pull you out."

"Something's wrong," she said, easing out of his arms. "It was too quiet. But someone was in there. It felt like I was being watched."

Then they both heard something. The doors to the rooms were not as quiet as the one to the stairwell. From the location of the sound, it had been the door to Kedron's suite. They looked at each other. The stairwell was the best escape, closer than the elevator, and it would let out on the alley behind the hotel.

"Up or down?" *Hachi* asked, thinking they could at least cover both possible routes.

"My money says up," *Ku* reasoned. "Less expected."

"Then I will go up," she replied, resisting the urge to laugh at his expression.

"Rock, paper, scissors," he said, not planning to let her have all the glory, but she won, as she so often uncannily did, her hand, paper, closing over his, rock. Her smile was satisfied and mischievous, and she handed him her shoes, tiny, strappy, size 5 Louboutin's. He was puzzled.

"Go ahead and go up," she whispered. "He's going down, which is where I will be. Logical. Escaping, because who has transport waiting on the roof? You've seen too many movies."

"Why do I have to carry your shoes? What if I have to fight?"

"You won't. He's going down the stairs, towards me. And I am not leaving them. Those are Louboutin's. Have you lost your mind?!" she asked, and then slipped silently down the stairs, leaving him standing there a beat too long, hearing the latch engage from the outside before he remembered himself and leapt silently up the central opening to the landing above.

Ku listened as someone stepped into the stairwell; a large man based on what *Ku* could make out of his shadow. The man seemed to pause there, reflecting, or more likely listening, and *Ku* readied himself, but whoever it was, he had turned away, his footsteps pattering softly and quickly downward. *Ku* waited several moments and then turned to follow, ensuring that their quarry would not be able to retreat when he saw *Hachi* waiting below.

On the fifth floor landing he caught the sounds of a struggle somewhere ahead, a brief break in the pattern of the footsteps, a sharp gasp, and a thump he didn't like, the sound of something compact connecting with something immovable. *Ku* jumped the rail, dropping all the way to the bottom, and found *Hachi* slumped in the corner opposite the alley door, which had just banged shut, no need for quiet egress here.

He pushed it open, unmindful of the force he used in his distress, and it banged against the outer wall, bouncing back to him. He caught and held it, looking both ways, but the alley was clear, no one in sight. The sounds of the evening crowds on the sidewalks at either end of the passageway betrayed no unusual disturbances.

Ku turned back to check on *Hachi*, who was already trying to sit up on her own.

"Did you see him?" *Ku* asked, knowing it was a waste of time to fuss over her. He could see the look on her face, read the anger in her eyes.

"Not really. He threw his jacket at me and then jumped me. It wasn't Kedron though," she replied, beyond furious.

"*Aijin,*" *Ku* called out to Azuma. "When you get a moment, could you join us at the alley door?"

"Let's meet at the room," Azuma recommended, and there was something dark in her own voice. "I heard everything. We're on our way."

The suite door was unlocked, and they found Kedron, dead of unbelievable forceful injury, with very little evidence of violence. A drop of blood, essentially. Nothing broken. Nothing disturbed.

The *Akai* scoured the rooms but found nothing of interest, nothing of value, and were gone before those who attended this criminal of his church could discover anything was wrong. Perhaps, Azuma thought, they had been sent away to allow him to enact his evil. There was nothing to suggest any other person had been in the room, although given the mortal injury the priest had suffered he had not been alone.

The others withdrew, each taking a different route back to the lobby. *Hachi,* for her part, scoured the stairwell once more, pushing out through the alley door, following the path of the unknown assailant. She searched the alley pavement for any items of use, but all she found was a discarded piece of soft white rubber emblazoned with a single blue star, sloughed from the sole of some kid's raggedy Converse shoe.

W

I am changing somehow. It started before we left New Orleans. My dreams are worse, if that is even possible. Thus I fear they may not be dreams.

These things I am given to know, these echoes of the Other, the diabolical path through the world. It moves through a veil of time, just on the other side, and when I sleep it is as though I am reaching through, piercing that membrane, carried along on errands I cannot recall. Oh, I am so weak that I dare not try to recall them, the greater part of me does not want to know what or whether I have been manipulated to do.

But I seem to be losing waking time now. And because I have been so much alone, both as a child and an adult, there is no one to turn to and ask about it. Seemingly no proof of these fugues. I am aware I do not remember what I should, and some of what is at the very edges of my memory I cannot piece together, though I know I should try. I will learn too much, so I push it away. It threatens to be too ugly to bear.

I woke screaming this morning. My heart was pounding, and I could taste fear, but it was not my own. How I knew it I have no idea. A part of me, too big I think, liked it. And my arms were sore, muscles screaming like at the middle of a deadlift, my hands shaking.

Amaoke came on the run. His expression both sympathetic and suspicious. He was a comfort, but what he sees, or thinks, or knows, I cannot guess. I read his concern for me, but it is tempered with a larger worry.

We leave for Africa in a week. I need him, need the Beast at my side. I hope the prophecies don't indicate that he is a facilitator of my evil. I feel safer with him; not because I expect him to protect me, because I need him to undertake the needful task of intervening, even if I am to be destroyed in the balance.

Perhaps it is not I who have broken through. Perhaps it is the Morningstar, successfully crossed over, slowly completing its possession.

I see that its destruction is not possible without mine. I am afraid, but I am certainly willing. I know that evil won't disappear from the world. It will simply falter without a conductor to lead the dissonant symphony.

Humanity must do the rest.

8

ALETA WAS ALREADY SKEPTICAL OF the genetic reports on Amaoke, so she felt justified in remaining suspicious when RSI representatives reached out to her to apologize.

"Dr. Himura is in the States to address other client concerns, but she has asked whether it would be possible to set up a meeting for the two of you," the woman told her, after Aleta's office staff had taken a message for her.

"Is it her practice to privately meet with every physician who uses the company's services?" Aleta inquired, not bothering to mask the incredulity in her tone.

"Of course not," the woman continued, undaunted. "But she has an investor meeting in Dallas on Thursday, and was hoping that you would consider joining her for dinner on Friday evening in New Orleans."

"Dinner?" Aleta found this even more curious. There was a possibility that it was all true, but dinner sounded a bit informal for a clinical discussion.

"Yes. Those were her instructions." The receptionist paused to let Aleta speak, but when she remained silent, she added, "While Dr. Himura does not formally have clinical responsibilities, she understands the demands of it. She felt it would be disruptive of your practice schedule to try to see you during office hours on such short notice, so she suggested something more casual, hoping that dinner would better suit the demands of your work."

"I can't make it before eight o'clock," Aleta sighed, looking at her calendar. "I would prefer Delachaise to something in the Quarter."

"I can make a reservation," the voice on the phone suggested smoothly. "Do they have a private dining room?"

"They do, but you won't get in on a Friday on short notice, no matter who you are," Aleta warned her. It was what she intended. She wanted a public venue, and a situation that could not be controlled in any way. If she was paranoid, so be it. She was trusting her instincts. Amaoke and Weston had gone; she had to. "They won't take a reservation for the main dining area that night. We'll have to meet and perhaps wait for a table in the bar."

"I will pass along the information," came the crisp reply. "Thank you for your time, Dr. Madison."

Aleta made two calls after she hung up, one to her sister that was surprisingly answered. She spoke quickly for about thirty seconds, then paused and listened for a few more before thanking Alaina and ringing off. She was forced to leave a message for Carter at Our Lady with the convent switchboard, hoping against hope that it was passed along.

***

On Friday evening, Aleta arrived at Delachaise right at eight, and breezed in through the doors behind a starry-eyed pair of college co-eds, likely here to fuel up before a night of partying. She crossed to the hostess stand and caught a movement out of the corner of her eye and turned toward the bar where Alaina was signaling her discreetly. She looked at her shoes and glanced left under her lashes, noting a lovely trim Asian woman in a charcoal grey pantsuit. She wore nothing under the sharply tailored jacket, was about Aleta's height, and had a fall of dark hair over one eye.

The woman stood with the straight posture of perfect deportment, confident, powerful, gorgeous. But it was Friday night, and the beautiful were a dime a dozen here, so she was able to blend in with the crowd awaiting entry.

The college couple gave way, and Aleta gave her name to the hostess, who smiled and nodded, picking up a couple of drink menus and gesturing to the Asian woman, who stepped forward with a nod of her own. The hostess led them onward, seating them at a four-top near the windows, which was miraculously available in the crush of humanity.

Aleta swiveled on her heels to sit down near the window, propping her crutches against the chair beside her, and made eye contact with the short-haired pixie at the end of the bar. Carter was incognito in a blue smocked sundress and espadrilles that she had borrowed from somewhere for the occasion, and the corner of her mouth turned up slightly, a tell that only Aleta would notice.

"I'll have the Green Hungarian," Aleta told the hostess, and looked expectantly at her companion.

"Hitachino Red Rice Ale," came the quick reply.

"Dr. Madison," the woman nodded and smiled as though she had a secret. Aleta wasn't mad at her, she had secrets of her own.

When the hostess had withdrawn to leave their drink orders with the bartender and alert their server, Aleta spoke, as directly as she could.

"Let's cut to the chase, shall we? I'm not an idiot, and I *am* a woman of color. I *know* we don't all look alike. Nor do I buy that all Asian women are interchangeable. Dr. Himura is a known quantum, and you're not her." She crossed her arms to punctuate her statement and telegraph her displeasure with this deception.

"Just a security measure, I assure you we were not trying to demean your intelligence," came another voice at Aleta's elbow, and she turned toward it, seeing a second woman, impossibly stunning in a cream dress, who seated herself gracefully in the chair next to Aleta. She was unusually tall, and her black hair was drawn back severely from her face, which betrayed only good humor without a trace of guile. "I am Azuma Himura. I am pleased to finally make your acquaintance."

"Finally?" Aleta asked, puzzled by the woman's word choice, but she never got an answer because their drinks arrived. She accepted her wine with her right hand, a subtle message for her sister, and noticed that when the beer was set down before Azuma's companion, the woman pushed it gently across and positioned it in front of her employer.

"Thank you, *Ni*," Azuma murmured, turning back to Aleta. "Now, Dr. Madison, I wanted to speak to you about that specimen evaluation that you requested."

"Is that so?" Aleta inquired calmly, smiling sweetly as Alaina appeared and without ceremony draped herself in the chair across from Azuma.

"Oh, I see," Azuma said, looking at Aleta with genuine respect. She looked from one to the other of them carefully. "Lovely, really. Your sister?" she inquired.

"Yes, brilliant deduction." Alaina replied, putting on her no-nonsense tough girl face, and Aleta struggled to maintain her own serious expression.

"I cannot speak to what standards may exist elsewhere," Aleta began, sparing her sister a raised eyebrow as she returned her attention to Azuma. "Here in the United States, we maintain strict patient confidentiality. I understand that you processed the specimen, but it was under a strictly anonymous request for evaluation, so unfortunately there is nothing I am authorized to discuss.

"Furthermore, I do not take kindly to misdirection of any kind. The results I received bordered on insulting."

"A necessary exercise on our part, and ultimately I endorsed it," Azuma said calmly. "I knew you must have information which would make you suspicious of the reported outcome. It appears I owe you an explanation."

As she spoke, she leaned in close, dropping her voice to a whisper, and this startled Aleta sufficiently that she put up her hand as a barrier, and it encountered Azuma's ribcage on the left, just lateral to her breast. The jumping juddering rhythm that translated through her chest wall could only have been her heartbeat, and Aleta jumped, pulling her hand back as though she'd been electrocuted.

Wide-eyed with disbelief, she studied Azuma with no small amount of distress. "But…you…that's impossible…" she whispered.

Azuma, in turn, retrieved Aleta's hand gently, and placed it against her chest, holding it in place with her own, watching as Aleta measured the odd syncopation by feel, the clinician narrowing her eyes as she mapped out the rhythm.

"Your…arrhythmia, it should be fatal," Aleta marveled. "But how?" She had forgotten herself, leaving her hand against Azuma's chest a few moments longer. Alaina had started to stand up, but Aleta shook her head, signaling that she was ok. Realization came a moment later, and she turned back to Azuma. "You're - another one, you're like him!"

"As brilliant as you are gorgeous," Azuma said with genuine admiration, and Aleta blushed. "But not exactly like him. I tried to pay you a visit at your home recently, but your lycanthropic friend was having none of it."

"What? I don't know about this," Aleta said skeptically.

"You were asleep," Azuma told her. "Regrettable that he did not tell you about it, but I suspect he was trying to protect you."

Alaina was on her feet now, and rightly angry. "A, what's going on?" Her own eyes were dawning with some realization of her own, and she was shaking her head slowly. She took a step away from the table, jerking away, and in her haste, knocked over her chair. Its clattering noise garnered the attention of several patrons nearby, and *Ni* stood to retrieve the chair, holding it for Alaina to resume her seat.

But Alaina was having none of it. Her eyes were wide and afraid as she focused on Azuma, whispering, "It was you. I-I saw you. *I saw you.*" Her hands shook violently, and Azuma stood up, understanding that whatever was happening should not happen here. She helped Aleta to her feet, in the hope that she could calm her sister before there was a full-blown scene.

Into that tense moment, out of nowhere, a murmur arose near the bar. The four of them turned to see another tall woman, like something out of a dream, gliding toward them purposefully. Like the women at the table by the window, she was an exceptional beauty. Unlike them, she radiated some wondrous pull, like the moon on the sea, coaxing the tide from its lofty seat in the heavens.

But her looks were more sun than moon, radiant creamy skin, platinum afro like one of the enormous halos that encircled the heads of the saints of old Renaissance paintings. Her eyes were wideset, golden, and knowing, and her lips were lush and plump, the epitome of black female beauty, a standard bearer.

She moved with the grace of one of the great cats, unselfconscious, confident, powerful. She wore a gauzy dress with a loose, flowing collar, and her sandals laced up to her knees. Her bare arms looked strong, the muscles well defined and balletic. She paused at the end of the bar to gesture to Carter to follow her, and the two of them approached the table.

Alaina sat down in her chair as if her strings had been cut, but *Ni* kept her feet, her eyes wary, her posture tense.

"*Ni, tsukamatte iru,*" Azuma warned, and her young guard relaxed, and sat down finally, although it was clear she didn't want to do so.

Aleta watched all of this with fascination. She wasn't sure that *Ni* had a choice. Sheer energy washed over the table, and every hair on her body stood on end. The newcomer was clearly responsible for this, whatever it was radiated off her in waves, and it was ultimately calming. She glanced at Azuma, and even she seemed chastened, turning her eyes downward, avoiding a challenge.

And Carter was overcome, although she made no noise whatsoever, her tears flowed silently from her eyes as she looked in wonder at their new guest from her vantage point at the woman's right shoulder. She looked more beatific than usual, and even more diminutive next to their visitor's extravagant height.

"This is ill-advised," the woman spoke sternly, and it was clear she directed her words at Azuma.

"My apologies, Sorceress. I can explain," Azuma said quietly and carefully, knowing well the power this being commanded.

The Sorceress turned concerned and kind eyes on Alaina, who was still in significant distress. "Alaina."

Alaina returned her gaze as though she were compelled to do so by the soft words of the other woman, and whatever she saw in the Sorceress' bright eyes appeared to calm her perceptibly.

"Alaina, you are safe. I promise it," the Sorceress told her, her lovely accent thick and sweet, the lullaby of faraway Africa. "Perhaps you are willing to allow us to move this discussion to a more private place? May we reconvene at your flower shop?" Kusini knew that surrounded by so many natural and living things, she could continue to draw upon her power and keep the spirit energies as positive as possible. She couldn't predict whether the Dragon and her priestess were going to behave, but she knew why Alaina was so terrified. How she knew, she was unsure, but felt as though the information had come to her in one of her unbidden dreams.

Alaina blinked slowly, as if processing this cost her some effort. Aleta began to be alarmed for her sister. She didn't understand what was happening, but this Sorceress knew what was frightening her. Aleta felt terrible that she did not.

Alaina finally managed a single nod, and got to her feet slowly. "Of course."

The women walked out of the restaurant single file, Carter in the lead, Aleta coming at the end of the queue. The frat boys at the bar stopped drinking to ogle them as they went past, unable to resist the veritable catalogue of beautiful women walking by, even though they were, save for Carter, certainly too old and intimidating to be approached. Aleta would have found it amusing, but she was too distracted by these other events, and too worried for her sister.

9

OUTSIDE THE DOOR, THE SORCERESS pulled on the material at the neck of her dress, bringing it over her head in one practiced movement. Azuma started in surprise on seeing those golden eyes peering out from the folds, recalling the journey on the road to Tokugawa, returning from Ryukyu those long centuries ago, and the female rider who had accompanied her, the eyes of the hawk, the sand-colored robes. The answer to an old question.

They gathered at the cars, Kusini hesitating briefly, before asking Alaina how to reach the shop on foot. "Carter and I will walk," she explained.

It was only a few blocks away, so Alaina gave simple turn-by-turn instructions for Ni, who was holding the passenger door of an Audi R8 coupe for Azuma.

"Aleta, I can bring you back to your car. Ride with me, please?" she asked, and Aleta heard the plea in her voice.

"Of course I will," she nodded, handing her sister her crutches while she lifted herself into the passenger seat of Alaina's old Jeep Apache. Alaina stepped up onto the running board to help Aleta with the harness and stowed her crutches in the footwell behind her.

Alaina climbed into the driver's seat but didn't start the vehicle. She sat quietly, and Aleta reached across for her hand. "Tell me. Just tell me. I missed it, whatever it was."

"It's her. The woman I saw on that balcony in Japan. I'm sure of it," she said with a strange sort of emphasis, which Aleta thought was an aftereffect of being disbelieved for so long.

Alaina's pulse pounded away in her wrist where Aleta's fingertips had come to rest, and Aleta knew her sister was afraid. "I believe you. I do."

Alaina was visibly relieved, and she pulled out of Aleta's grasp to start the truck and get them going.

"But how did she find you?" Alaina asked, still not making a connection, because Aleta had kept the details of the past several months from her.

"I think it is just a really odd coincidence," Aleta said, honest but skirting the bigger picture. She didn't think the time was right to explain all that she knew, or suspected, and there was still so much she felt she didn't know. "Let's go and get some answers."

When they arrived at the shop, Azuma, *Ni*, and Aleta waited on the sidewalk while Alaina unlocked the doors and let them inside. The moon was up in the east, and Aleta could see the Sorceress and Carter approaching from the corner. Looking at Azuma and the Sorceress side by side, she had the same jarring thought she'd had when looking at Weston and Amaoke together. The two women were exactly the same height, towering over Carter and Aleta, and making Alaina, who was nearly six feet tall, look short. It was uncanny. She had a moment where she wondered whether all four individuals were the same height; calling upon memory and applying her clinical observation, she suspected it was so.

Once inside, the Sorceress looked around in admiration. She glanced back at Alaina, who was locking the door behind them.

"Let's go through to my studio," Alaina suggested, as they all stood awkwardly together, waiting for something that none of them could name. She led the way through to the back of the shop, to a wide room styled with greenhouse glass along the entire back wall, with transom windows that could be opened to allow fresh air to circulate.

The moonlight filtered in, and for a moment there was a glimpse of a lovely, manicured English-style garden beyond the windows. Then Alaina turned on the track lights, and everyone blinked in the brightness, now seeing only their own reflections in those windowpanes.

The Sorceress turned away from the windows and seemed to take the measure of each of them in turn, before reaching long arms toward Azuma and Alaina. It made Aleta think of the arms on a clock face, or someone showing the points of a compass.

"Alaina. I promised you your safety, but I understand that we all need assurances to feel utterly secure," she said. "I am Kusini. They do call me the Sorceress, but I prefer my own name, both because it was a gift of my parents, but also because it ties me to humanity more meaningfully. You and Azuma have a strange history, incidental, it's true, but significant. Azuma, you must provide the assurance that Alaina requires to recover from an old fear that time has failed to extinguish."

Without touching either woman, Kusini shepherded them close together, and said something that Aleta and Carter did not understand, but Azuma and *Ni* seemed to make sense of it.

"Azuma," Kusini commanded in that same calm lilting voice, "Look upon this child and see her. Declare for once and all what you see."

Azuma stepped in close to Alaina, and Aleta started to protest, but Kusini held up one long silencing finger, turning kind eyes upon her to let her know that all was well. When they were close enough to kiss, Azuma gently cradled Alaina's chin in one hand, tilting her face upward. Brown eye to brown eye, a moment only, though it felt much longer. Then Azuma smiled slowly, nodding, beginning to understand Kusini's purpose.

"*Tekide wanai*," she declared. "No enemy of me or mine."

"The Dragon Goddess is gifted to know her enemies on sight," Kusini said by way of explanation, although she had to know that her statement raised more questions than it answered.

"You are safe from me and mine," Azuma clarified this more directly to Alaina, who seemed genuinely relieved, if not even more confused. "I apologize for frightening a child not able to understand. You could not have known that you were never in danger. I live by an extremely strict code. You were never meant to see us."

"How did you-?" Alaina whispered. "You knew?"

"The moment I saw you. I lack the ability to forget, much to my regret. An unfortunate coincidence my meeting with your sister, and only that. I was not coming for you," Azuma explained.

"And now, dear Alaina, I must ask you to leave us alone," Kusini said gently. "What is to be said here is not for you. I say this without malice, rather that you understand your life has a path separate from these events, and I send you to live it in peace. I assure you your sister will be safe with me."

Alaina withdrew through the door to the shop, looking concerned, but Aleta gave her a reassuring nod. Carter pulled a stool from beneath a nearby workbench, and brought it to Aleta, who sat down, grateful for the kindness.

"Let's agree there shall be no more mischief regarding Dr. Madison," Kusini warned Azuma.

"Why wouldn't he tell me you'd visited the house?" Aleta asked the question she had been worrying over since the subject had been presented at the restaurant.

"To spare you unpleasantness," Kusini answered, before Azuma could say anything. "Censoring information is not always about deception," she continued, thinking of 'Kisye's admission about rolling the Jeep, and his accident on the post road, understanding Aleta's disquiet. "Perhaps just as often it is done out of love."

Kusini gave Azuma a significant look, wanting to make sure that her own presence, and Weston's, were not mentioned. She had reasons of her own for withholding information from Aleta, reasons that Aleta herself would likely find patronizing, reasons that were nonetheless merciful and had a purpose that would only come to fruition long after she and the others were gone.

"Do you know where he is?" Aleta asked, aware that Azuma and *Ni* appeared equally curious about the answer.

Kusini got a faraway look in her eyes, and said, "By now, the priest and the wolf should be with Ambakisye." Then she seemed to ground herself once more, remembering something, recalling that the name meant nothing to those assembled here. "Ambakisye is my husband. Everyone is exactly where they are supposed to be."

"Is he safe?" Aleta asked, desperately concerned that she was not to get answers to her many questions, but most concerned that she had seen the last of Amaoke, that the prophecy in his last words was developing, all of it beyond control or even rationality.

"How he would answer that question, I cannot know," Kusini said wisely, and her eyes were both sad and kind. "But you know him first and best. Think on how he might respond to you if he were here. Take comfort from what you know. And Aleta, you must never lose hope in life. You must look ahead, to a future you cannot see or imagine, and live as fully as you can. I imagine it is what he would wish for one he loves. I imagine it is what you would wish for him."

Aleta could not stay her tears, and she felt Carter's soft touch on her shoulders, and finally, her arms encircled Aleta's shaking form. She took a deep shuddering breath, reestablishing her own control, wanting to honor the request of this strange woman who brought both a kind of peace and this strange brief chaos into her life.

"And now, Aleta, I must ask you, too, to leave us," Kusini looked directly into Aleta's eyes, and Aleta felt so light inside, unburdened, as if Kusini could take all these frightful encumbrances from her. "When you leave this room, you must not look back, you must look forward. One step at a time, back into your life. Hold on to your faith, and keep your heart open to every possibility, until the end of your many days."

Carter gently handed Aleta her crutches and helped her to her feet. They embraced warmly, and Carter started to accompany her out, but Kusini spoke out.

"Carter Thomas, stay, if you will." The command was softened into a request, but Carter knew better. Nevertheless, she saw Aleta to the door that separated them from the flower shop, and Alaina. When Aleta had disappeared through it, she pushed it closed with both hands and leaned against it, briefly putting her cheek against the cool wood, closing her eyes, and saying a prayer for all of them.

Then she stood up straight, and turned to face the remarkable woman who radiated such power, love, and serenity. Carter wanted to embrace Kusini, but she understood somehow that touch and the Sorceress were complicated opponents, and she stayed the instinct as best she was able.

She stood expectantly, knowing that what she was about to hear would change everything she knew. She didn't know that it would change her as well.

"Carter, a decision comes for you, and you alone can decide the course of your own history," Kusini's words were a riddle of sorts. "Instructions you have aplenty, but there is no higher authority than your own heart, for that is the seat of your God."

Although Carter had not consciously noticed it, during this short speech Kusini had walked with her the length of the room, and they found themselves standing together at the door to the garden. Kusini opened it for her, and Carter stepped through to the night beyond, already seeking a place to pray.

Kusini turned back to the Dragon and her priestess. "And then there was one," she said softly, not as an insult to *Ni*, rather acknowledging that she who served was motivated by the will of the Goddess.

"The daughter of Israel must join us in the desert, in that Place of the Fallen, where we shall face our enemy and meet our end. Here our paths diverge, but we will all be together again sooner than you know." Kusini paused thoughtfully, and added, "Although I cannot predict when next we meet, the events we anticipate are unfolding, carrying us onward to our collective fate. Old friends and new will be needed, and we cannot prevail without love. Have you found yours?"

Before Azuma could reply, the lights flickered and dimmed, and she and *Ni* found themselves alone. They, too, let themselves out through the garden and disappeared into the night.

Aleta and Alaina waited together in the shop for an awfully long time, expecting the others to reappear. When it became clear that the others had gone, they stayed on, trimming roses together in preparation for the next day's demand, talking about childhood memories, and surprising to both, soon laughing together. It was the laughter that triggered the forgetting, which was the blessing that Kusini's magic had granted them.

10

NI DISCOVERED THE COLLECTOR'S SWORD shortly after her return to Japan but said nothing to her mistress. Instead, she went to *Ichi* with her request, knowing that if she were truly acting in defiance, *Ichi* would chastise her and report her insolence to the Dragon Goddess.

"How did the weapon come to be returned to her?" *Ichi* asked, but *Ni*, in her typical fashion, said nothing, which was her way of communicating both that she did not know the answer, and unlike some of the others, she refused to waste time on speculation. *Ichi* respected this, and asked another question, this one truly rhetorical.

"Are you so certain that she would deny your request?" *Ichi* already suspected that Azuma would have consented to *Ni's* involvement in any attempt to learn more about the fate of the Collector, but her fellow priestess refused to answer. For all that the two of them usually achieved an impressive level of inscrutability, it was an open secret among the *Akai* that *Ni* and the Collector were intimates. *Ichi* raised her eyebrows like the schoolteacher she had once been, and it was as effective as ever at eliciting a response.

"She certainly wouldn't discourage me, but you know she would want to be involved. It's too dangerous. Akenomyosei would welcome her walking into the Death Bringer's trap. It isn't certain any of us would return."

"Or all of us, if it came to it," *Ichi* replied, and *Ni* could see that she agreed with her own assessment. "And what of the Collector?"

"If he is alive," *Ni* observed with a trace of bitterness, "He would order me not to attempt it. Even if he has survived, and we somehow manage to get him out…" She let her voice trail off, leaving the rest unsaid.

But *Ichi* picked up the thread immediately and said aloud what *Ni* had not given voice to. "He might send us all to the Butterfly Garden for endangering the Dragon."

"We are all of us already on borrowed time, *Ichi*," was *Ni's* answer.

"And can you say that you are dispassionate enough about either eventuality?" *Ichi* wisely asked.

"He freed me from more than one prison," *Ni* answered, not caring whether her response made sense to *Ichi* in all the ways it did to her, knowing that *Ichi* might ignore the subtle insult. She continued, "I would gladly give my life *for* him, and if he were ever to require such, surrender it *to* him."

"Ah. At the expense of our mistress' life, turning from the vow you made to put her before all else, before the Collector, before yourself?" *Ichi* saw something dangerous in her friend's eyes and waved her hand in a gesture of peace. "Stop. I am merely contemplating aloud what we both know. I know that you are not suggesting any betrayal, are not turning away from your promise, that you will willingly submit to my direction."

"*Hai*," was the automatic response, as *Ni* knelt before her High Priestess to show that she would be ever obedient.

"Very good," *Ichi* approved, and in a rare display of gentleness, she placed a hand on *Ni's* head, exposing her fondness for her faithful lieutenant. "Because I, too, must be obedient. I can speak to her on your behalf, or-"

"No. I will do so myself," *Ni* replied, smiling slightly down at the floor. *Ichi's* response was as she had expected, for if *Ichi* had disapproved, she would not have given *Ni* the option to advocate for herself, although *Ni* had been ready to accept whatever punishment was merited in the event *Ichi* failed to understand.

11

"YOU SOUND JUST LIKE HIM," Azuma told *Ni*, not bothering to hide her annoyance or her amusement when her priestess asserted that Azuma should not, under any circumstances, be involved in any attempted rescue of the Collector.

"A fine compliment, *Aijin*," *Ni* replied with no little irony of her own. Smiling, she continued, "Every time he has left us, he tasked me with ensuring that no risks were taken with your security. It was no different upon his leaving us this last time."

"So what would *he* advise me to do in this situation?" Azuma asked, humoring her. She turned to the kitchen, moving a few feet away to warm sake on the stove.

"He would forbid any of us to attempt it," *Ni* answered honestly. "And enforce his will to the letter, as well you know."

"Well, it is said that it is easier to beg forgiveness than to ask permission," Azuma mused softly.

"If it comes to that my life is forfeit for my arrogance and my defiance," *Ni* countered, in a tone equally quiet. The necessity of forgiveness was a liability that she knew the Collector did not countenance. If you needed to be forgiven, it was just as likely that you needed to be dead. It was a sentiment that each of the *Akui* readily embraced.

"And why you?" Azuma asked, without looking up from her task.

"Why not me?" *Ni* asked, managing to do so without a hint of challenge or defiance. "I was never a samurai. But I have been one of the Crimson Guard long enough to know that I am willing to face death before asking another to take that risk in my stead.

"That said, neither can I leave you exposed while I am gone. I have a suggestion regarding your ongoing security," she said, accepting the drink Azuma handed her.

"Let me guess," Azuma smiled, and they toasted warmly before downing their sake. *Ni* understood the ritual. It was Azuma's way of letting her know she had permission to proceed, and she relaxed somewhat. "The Soldier."

"I will ask her, of course. I did not think it proper to make the request without your permission," *Ni* said, setting down her cup.

Azuma filled it and her own once more, and said nothing about Michael Israel, preferring to put off that discussion for the moment, wondering if it was even remotely appropriate that they ask at all. She was certain that Michael Israel would welcome the challenge, but she was emotionally compromised, and still had a career to consider. She had human choices that Azuma feared she was purposefully avoiding. Assimilating her among the *Akai* would be less than ideal, for while Michael Israel did reach for death, Azuma would never allow her to undertake the initiation ritual. The young woman had been hunting a monster all her life, under no circumstances would the decision to embrace that kind of power be without risk, and Azuma had too much leverage in that relationship already.

"You haven't fed," Azuma looked closely at her priestess, reading the strain and exhaustion of the last several weeks in *Ni's* face.

"I will make arrangements to do so, *Aijin*," *Ni* assured her, sipping her sake this time.

"I am here now," Azuma said, placing a casual arm about *Ni's* waist. "My feedings do not seem to affect your judgement like the others, and during the ritual for your initiation to the *Akai* you were less affected by my blood."

Ni did not have to say anything; when the Dragon fed, it knew the thoughts and motivations of anyone from whom it received a blood meal.

"It is because you were exposed to his venom before mine," Azuma said, watching *Ni* struggle with some distress over this reminder of her intimacy with the Collector. Azuma wanted to reassure her that she harbored no jealousy about their relationship, but wisely felt that further discussion of the matter would increase her priestess' discomfort rather than lessen it. "And my blood will prepare you best for what you are about to face, will it not? If you refuse to allow me to accompany you, surely you will allow me to assist in this way? I am not so repugnant, am I?"

This last statement made *Ni* smile. It was the same question the Collector had asked her, long, long ago, in another life, before he had made good on his promise to help her build a new one. So when her beautiful mistress opened her arms in invitation, *Ni* stepped forward into that embrace without further hesitation.

12

NI FOLLOWED MICHAEL ISRAEL THROUGH her flight check as the sun slipped away beyond the western horizon of Tikrit. The two women glanced at each other across the private helipad while the rockets were loaded, and *Ni* nodded her appreciation for the machine. It was a Sikorsky, a prototype she was unfamiliar with, but its controls were like that of a Comanche. It was built for stealth, which was exactly what was needed.

She doubted they had permission to use the firepower, but then, she doubted they had permission to be here.

Michael Israel had refused to shore up Azuma's security detail, and judging by the Dragon Goddess' reaction, *Ni* knew that Azuma had predicted this outcome early on. *Ni* should not have been surprised that the soldier had unequivocally refused to stay behind; she suspected her mistress had allowed her to introduce the idea because she knew that Michael Israel was better positioned to accompany *Ni* on this particular errand, and she was not proven incorrect by the exchange that followed.

"What? You, the very high-profile CEO of a global biotechnology company, are... what?" Michael Israel had not bothered to hide her disdain from Azuma. "You're planning some black ops incursion into Iraq?"

"The blackest," Azuma had told her, explaining the premise, and from that moment, Michael Israel had attached herself to the rescue. She refused to hear any argument about preserving her career and her government service, despite Azuma's considerable doubt that the operation would, or could, be successful.

Azuma had her own qualms about sending anyone to the Place of the Fallen, and wondered that she should even allow it. Selfishly, she had already planned an attempt to rescue her Collector. Privately, she knew, as she was sure he did, that the potential sacrifices necessary to accomplish it were too great. In many ways, *Ni* was the ideal candidate to dispatch, some of them only best understood by Azuma. And like the samurai she was, Azuma accepted that death was a daily possibility, and that the *bushido* called for any action that would right a moral code. The *Akai* held such as their religion in the affairs of their Goddess.

"And how do you propose to execute this scheme?" Michael Israel had inquired, with all the swagger she had earned.

"I have powerful friends," Azuma had replied. "And bottomless resources."

"My friends have better toys," the soldier had informed her. "And with all due respect, the tactical expertise you will need is well beyond your wheelhouse."

"I'm glad we see eye to eye," Azuma had laughed. "I'm sending *Ni*. My resources remain at your disposal, for I think that your 'friends' also speak the universal language of currency?"

Michael Israel had then given *Ni* the once-over visually, and she did not look convinced there was anything there to write home about. "And? Who else?"

"I think you'll find you have more help than you need," Azuma had offered this cryptic reassurance. "It's my only condition for the advantage of using my resources."

Ni had taken no insult whatsoever from Michael Israel's doubt. She wanted people to underestimate her, encouraged it where necessary. But they did so at their peril.

Now they found themselves here, on a windswept evening that hinted of spring, ready to climb into a vehicle that didn't exist, to take an unrecorded flight into the interior of a hostile country. *Ni* was patient with the safety process, during which she picked up a few things that she could not have learned otherwise. The contents of the bag she stowed in the hold she did not share with anyone, and the mechanics knew better than to question the staff of a VIP client.

Michael Israel's black pilot's jumpsuit bore no identifying markings, and she sealed her military identification tags into an envelope that she handed to the ground crew chief with a nod.

If the other contractors were curious about the black *yoroi* that *Ni* wore, they kept it to themselves, probably assuming it an eccentricity. She flexed her toes in her *jika-tabi*, anxious to be underway.

As soon as the mechanic signaled they were 'go,' they boarded and secured their harnesses. Michael Israel waited until full dark before strapping on her night vision goggles and lifting off. She flew dark out over the expanse of desert, with *Ni* on watch for unlikely obstacles. They had to avoid other sanctioned surveillance missions that would be occurring this night like every other.

They did not talk, each woman appreciating the silence. *Ni* noticed when Michael Israel began to climb steadily for a short distance, and then she was explaining, "I want to minimize the dust we stir up on landing," before executing a near-perfect modified drop spiral and setting them down. *Ni* was impressed. It was a tricky maneuver to master for pilots who had decades on the controls; she suspected that much of the soldier's talent was unnaturally augmented by her fearlessness.

Despite the precaution, it took several minutes for the dust to clear, and according to their navigation they would still have nearly two kilometers to cover on foot before they reached the site. *Ni* pulled on her hood, adjusting it in seconds, leaving only her eyes exposed. She climbed out of her seat and zipped open the bag in the hold.

"I have spare weapons," Michael Israel offered, but her voice died away when she saw the two swords that *Ni* was liberating from the military duffel, watching her stow them crosswise on her back.

"I thank you, but we have a saying about guns. 'If your opponent has a firearm, you run toward them, a blade, you run away.'" *Ni* punctuated this by turning away from the helicopter and initiating a rapid jog in the direction of their objective. Michael Israel smiled to herself and sprinted to catch up to her.

13

THE NIGHT WAS QUIET, AND the winds had not picked up much, which was helpful. There was no moon, and if Michael Israel wondered how *Ni* was managing without NVGs she kept it to herself. She was surprised to find that even with *Ni*'s slighter build, her stride length was long and powerful. Not the liability that Michael Israel had thought she might be.

And without the navigational capacities of the soldier's watch, *Ni* was charting the proper course somehow. About half a *klick* out from the site, *Ni* slowed to a walk, then stopped.

"Anything we should say to each other ought to be said here," *Ni* observed, although she feared that nothing was out of the evil reach of Akenomyosei and its familiars, even at this distance.

"I assume you've read the file, seen the maps?" Michael Israel asked.

"Yes." *Ni* did not tell her that Azuma had paid for some additional surface ultrasonic evaluation and telemetry. "When we arrive, you cover the stairway – just keep going down. If you reach the wall at the bottom, turn around and get out. It might be a fight just to do that. If I have not reconnected with you by the time you reach the surface, return to the helicopter and go back home."

"I cannot agree to that," Michael Israel protested.

"You do not have a choice. If in the time specified you cannot escape this place, you may not escape it at all. Someone must report back to Azuma if at all possible. If you see me coming up the stairs, turn back immediately. Time will be even more critical if

I manage to succeed. They will know we are there, and it will be a sprint to the top, so no unnecessary wasted energy."

"I won't leave you behind," Michael Israel nearly growled with frustration, not liking an operation that she could not control.

"Leave whom behind?" *Ni*'s voice came from somewhere in the darkness ahead. The soldier looked around, but even the NVGs told her nothing. She sighed, consulted her watch, and resumed their earlier pace, headed for the site.

Ni easily increased the distance between herself and Michael Israel, and slowed when she neared the pit. She could feel it there, as if alive, waiting to swallow anything that came near, a black hole of nothingness that would suffocate light, air, and life. She ignored the stairs, coming to a stop at the rim of the oubliette, and leaped, turning back toward the edge as she pointed her feet downward, windwalking into the depths.

Ninety meters from the surface she glided onto the wall and found a foothold perch. She slid sideways, suspecting she would discover an opening, and she was not disappointed. A crumbling stone with a slippery curved face that was brighter than the material around it, the convex frontal bone of a human skull. And what had looked like stone and sand on the way down was now a wall of skulls and their fragments, a catacomb, a vision supplied by the forces at work in this place.

She pulled it away, and a whole section collapsed, not quite a doorway arch, but large enough for her to enter a larger interior space where she could stand. It was colder here, deep in the earth, and an eerie scream brought her to attention, tilting her head as she stood still, part of the shadowy gloom. She reached for her sword involuntarily, but the hilt in her fingers gave her little comfort.

Ni feared that even her augmented senses might not serve her; the darkness was like a blanket around her, and she was having difficulty locating the source of the sound. Another scream cleaved the blackness and she realized it was the result of the air moving from the hole she had created through the structure, and she smiled. A giant echo chamber, built for terror, but also a reassurance to the warrior because it signaled that air was escaping out the other side. She recalled that there were numerous passageways off the stairway documented by the excavation team.

And she was picking up something else, just a sense of it. The Blood Tie between herself and the Collector was attenuated compared to the connection that existed between him and their mistress, but *Ni* could still use their bond to find him, so she focused on that energy that was uniquely his, relieved that she had found it, for it meant he still clung to life.

But they were not alone. The whole place was alive with something unlike anything she had ever experienced before, like a consciousness, an organism, and she had its sleepy attention. A hive, of one mind and many voices. If she concentrated, she could separate the babble from the movement of the wind through the labyrinth. Perhaps if she were not a supernatural herself, corrupted by the Blood Ritual, that interest would take another form, but she had a sense that she disrupted the order here less because of what she was.

It also meant that she had to work quickly to take advantage of the head start she had over Michael Israel. When the human arrived, the motivators of this place would awaken in a new way.

She tried to conduct her search methodically, logically, but still found enough blind turns and dead ends to feel her frustration mounting. She fought to remain calm, especially when she realized that the structure was changing, an endless shifting maze that was responding to her movements, perhaps anticipating her. She could spend a hundred years here and never find him, never get out.

So she did something else, she thought about those first days with him in Yoshiwara, the sweetness of feeling that another could finally see her, and listened to what her instincts were telling her. With this approach, she felt the walls were opening up to her, curious about this wraith that used emotion and faith to navigate.

And then something even more extraordinary happened, as if in response to this exercise, new images flooded her brain, and she was seeing herself as she had been long ago, the mortally ill girl in a deep blue kimono. But it was not the mental image she had of herself, this was what *he* had seen, how he had viewed her, through a lens of admiration and desire and she gasped aloud in relief, realizing that he was feeding her these visions through their bond.

She kept moving, not trusting her eyes, rather her soul, and she knew she was close because the visions flooded her, the two of them, all the memories he could send her, and if she had known fear and uncertainty before, this swept it away. She felt, rather than saw, a slight movement to her left, something subtle, disturbing the air current, and as she approached she realized that the quality of the light had changed slightly, and she was in a small chamber.

Ni could faintly make out a shape along the far wall, low down. A deep crimson mark marred the stone above it, arcing downward to the form that was not quite still. Now, she could smell his blood and sickness, and she knew she had found him.

She knelt slowly in front of him and reached out to touch his shoulder. His hair was longer than usual, his beard grown out, his robust form much wasted. She saw his eyes move weakly before he spoke.

"*Anata wa kurubekide wa nakatta watashi no ai,*" he whispered weakly, and *Ni* smiled. It was useless for him to tell her she should not have come now that she was here, but he had softened it with a term of endearment, which gave her some hope.

"*Hai, Sensei,*" she agreed with him respectfully. "*Mada watashi wa koko ni imasu.*"

She reached out to take an account of him. His shirt and pants were clotted with blood and filth, and she could smell his injury, but could not make out its location. She gently moved him to a sitting position, using the wall of the chamber to support him, but he was far too weak to sit up without assistance.

While *Ni* was certain she could carry him, she knew their escape would be complicated enough without such a hardship. Worst of all, she would be unable to defend them if it became necessary.

"The Dragon Goddess, she must not be here," the Collector protested, his voice a cracked ruin.

"I would not be so foolish as to ignore *all* your teachings," *Ni* reassured him, gesturing for him not to waste his breath. "She is far from here, as safe as any of us can keep her."

This observation amused him in its truthfulness, but even his smile was short-lived, becoming a grimace of pain whenever he breathed.

"You came alone?" His tone incredulous.

"No. The soldier was here as well. But I have wandered in this place for hours. Surely, she has gone."

"Time…" The Collector wheezed in the effort it took to say that one word. His hands waved ineffectually from his lap. "Here, it is not what it seems. It does not flow like water; it is not of the world."

"Don't talk," *Ni* admonished him, seeing how terribly it taxed him. She did not understand his statement but filed it away to consider at another time.

She pulled gently at her hood, stretching it down from the neckline of her clothing, loosening it, her creamy skin bright in the gloom. She cradled his head and leaned forward, ignoring his efforts to push her away, realizing that Azuma's gift of blood had been something more than a pragmatic attempt to strengthen her. It meant that *Ni* had greater reserve, something she could pass on to the Collector to begin his restoration.

But still he refused to feed, so she stretched out next to him, pulling him into her embrace, as inexorable in her will as she would be with any other. She implored him, "As you love me, you must, *Okurimono.*"

Her use of his given name surprised him, so unique and so intimate, as it had only ever been used by his father, who bestowed it despite his mother refusing to give him even this, a name. To his knowledge, it only survived memory because Azuma happened to know it. Yet his Mistress had never used it. But he understood how *Ni* had come to know it as soon as he tasted her blood, augmented by that of the Dragon, so he accepted *Ni*'s gift, for that was what she had forever been to him.

14

AFTER THE COLLECTOR FED, HE was able, with *Ni's* assistance, to get to his feet. In his weakened state, he was susceptible to the traces of venom from Azuma's blood, and it impaired him more than he cared for, but it meant that he was restored enough to participate meaningfully in this escape.

Ni kept a physical point of contact with him, a hand on his flank, and though it felt reassuring to him, he knew she was using their bond as a kind of key to unlock the mysteries of this labyrinthine prison. She said nothing of the distress she was feeling to find him so debilitated. And he participated, as he had when he realized that she was near, searching for him.

It felt like many hours had passed when they came through an archway onto the steps. The darkness here was less dense, and their preternatural night vision served them as expected, because the stairway was open to the stars.

Ni turned in a circle, considering, and the Collector saw that she carried *Hōfuku* on her back, next to her own sword. He smiled at her foresight and her confidence that she could find him, that he might need it. She did not sense any activity from lower down the stairwell, so she turned toward the top, securing his weight with an arm firmly about his waist, and began climbing at as brisk a pace as she dared, unsure that he could sustain it for very long.

It seemed they climbed longer than expected, but then she saw a bobbing cone of light painting the outer wall of the structure, the dancing spectres that accompanied it identified it as the glow of a flashlight.

Ni held still, hand on her sword, taking the opportunity to let the Collector rest for a moment against the wall. She nodded at him as she let go, pushing herself into the shadows at the inner face of the curve.

In a few moments, she could hear brisk, efficient footsteps making their way closer and closer, in an unmistakably disciplined rhythm. It could only be the soldier. *Ni* stepped out into the cone of light as Michael Israel appeared and whispered the other woman's name to identify herself.

Michael Israel stopped smartly but said nothing, considerately pointing the flashlight at *Ni*'s feet before swinging it toward the Collector. She nodded, and when *Ni* reached for him once more, securing a supporting arm about his waist, Michael Israel took up station on his other side, and the two of them began climbing, assisting him, and sharing the burden.

And then the screams began again, as they started to rise higher and higher, and the voices, when they came, chilled the three of them to their bones. In sibilant voices that spoke an unknown tongue, their words were understandable over the cacophony from the echo chamber.

"Curse, Priestess, Soldier." They were named without naming, and the air temperature dropped despite their proximity to the surface, and a foul stench assaulted them, followed by an increase in the air currents coming from the catacombs.

Ni glanced across the Collector at Michael Israel. "Can you run?"

"Yes," she nodded, and both women adjusted their grip, shifting their burden upward by firmly grasping his belt so as not to drag him. *Ni* let Michael Israel set the pace as they took the stairs upward at a jog, and it immediately felt as though there were thousands of hands reaching out from the shadows and trying to pull them back down, the wind pressing down on them so violently as to steal their breath.

The Collector helped as he could, using their support he pushed off each step to lighten their load as they ran toward the surface. *Ni* was pleased; the Mistress' blood was restoring his strength more quickly than her own ever could. The stairs seemed endless, the early morning stars getting no closer, but just as they were able to make out the stones at the top, the barrage of physical insults ceased, and the silence was absolute.

This served to heighten the tension rather than relieve it, it was too convenient, *Ni* observed to herself. She felt the rigidity coiling in the muscles of the Collector's broad back, and knew he was suspicious as well, preparing for the worst. He gave her shoulder a squeeze and moved out from under her arm, nodding at Michael Israel who also released her hold on him.

The Collector's hand stole to the hilt of his sword, and he gently freed it from its *saya*, lifting it from where it had ridden upon *Ni*'s back. He did so without taking his attention from the landing at the top, and *Ni* looked more closely. There appeared to be a man standing there, a man that the Collector seemed to recognize.

The three of them resumed their climb, but now the Collector led them, slowly, demonstrating as he put his back to the outer face of the stairwell, with Michael Israel following his lead. *Ni* came last, her torso half-turned to protect against any attacker coming up from below.

The wind had settled down at the surface as well, only a few swirling eddies of sand remained of the earlier stronger gusts. The sky was lightening rapidly.

As they emerged from the stairwell, the man turned toward them with an expression of amusement and something else. At first, *Ni* had difficulty identifying it, but then she knew it to be malice when his smile turned to a subtle grimace, and she heard Michael Israel gasp, as if she were in pain.

Ni did not recognize the man, he was young, perhaps not yet out of his third decade, with a shock of brown hair a shade redder than that of the soldier, hazel eyes, and a handsome, full mouth. But it was clear by the Collector's stance that he knew the man, and even more obvious that Michael Israel recognized him, as her gun hand dropped to her side and a sob of what sounded like grief came from her mouth. She took a step toward the man, but the Collector said, quietly, "Michael Israel, you must not."

Ni was still in the dark, but apparently the Collector had made some connection she could not.

"*Michael?*" The soldier spoke in a soft, questioning voice, taking a step closer to the man.

"It isn't him," the Collector spoke into the silence, adding, "It just wants you to believe so. That is not, and never has been, your brother. What you see is an illusion, the essence of who he might have become had he lived. That, instead, is the beast that stole him from you. He wears your brother's skin." What he suspected, he was now confirming, that Tatsuo Tomo's changed appearance was explained by his theft of another shell, one that had once belonged to the soldier's twin brother.

"Bithiah," the man spoke in a reasonable, pleading tone. "May you live a long life. How I have missed you." Forcas reached for her with the guileless smile of a young man greeting the sister he had not seen for nearly the whole of her existence. He knew how badly she wanted her brother back, knew it was even more important to her than retribution. He opened his arms to her, inviting her to come to him.

Michael Israel took another step, and her gun hand wavered, but it was still pointed at the ground. *Ni* saw the reflected shine of her tears when she pushed her NVG up onto her head.

The Collector stepped toward the soldier and applied a short sharp blow to her shoulder where it met her neck, and she folded sideways. He caught her expertly and leapt away so abruptly that he disappeared from *Ni's* view. Forcas' face changed, betraying its inhumanity, and hissed a scream of frustration, turning on *Ni*.

"*Move quickly, my love, stolen flesh is yet flesh.*" *Ni* heard the voice of her mentor although she could no longer see him, so she drew her katana, and slashed at the man in front of her, and he fell apart, clearly not the human he appeared to be. This disintegration brought back the voices and the wind picked up, seemingly lifting each grain of sand to torment her, like the stinging of a thousand hornets, and as she turned to make her escape, she was suddenly grasped by a thousand hands and pushed, pulled, dragged downward, deeper into the stairwell. Blinded by the stinging sand and suffocated by the attentions of the many spirits that attacked at random, she was disoriented and confused.

She thought she heard the cries of the Collector over the din, but any fragment of an understandable communication was torn from her ears by the cacophony and she was rendered deaf, marooned without even a sense of touch. The sensational flurry of activity had confounded her such that she was not even able to confirm she still held the sword she had carried only moments before.

The gift of Azuma's blood saved her, as it held open the bond she had with the Collector, and she remembered that the laws of physics could be disguised but not changed for these beings, fleshless wraiths or no. She swung her sword with all her might, hoping to connect with something solid, and was rewarded with the sound of steel connecting with stone. She opened her eyes briefly, concentrating at a point between her feet, trying to use proprioception to feel the solid ground beneath them. She struck again and saw the sparks of contact on the steps.

She gnashed her teeth in frustration and tasted blood in her mouth, which gave her an idea. Keeping her eyes closed tightly, she trusted her training and took a slow, deep breath. Time slowed down, and she allowed the blood to flow for a few moments. She was still, seemingly unmoved by the horde, and then she spit a mouthful of her blood on the stones, recalling all she could about her nursemaid's stories of the *yokai*. Like all demons, they thirsted for the blood and flesh of the living.

She felt the exodus as they screeched and screamed and slid over and around her, off her flesh, fighting for this new prize. They were unable to recognize that even this was a decoy, as the *Akai* could no longer be counted among the living, and even if by the tiniest technicality they did live, the blood would poorly satisfy these beings as it was not of pureflesh. But *Ni* did not wait for these creatures to learn of her deception, and she shot upward, launching off the landing near the opening of the oubliette, and windwalking out of the sand cloud before settling again to the ground, sprinting in the direction of freedom.

She easily caught up with the Collector and relieved him of the burden of the soldier's weight, pulling him along in the maelstrom, fighting blindly to reach the helicopter, hoping against hope that by the time the demons could follow them they had enough of a head start. There were still too many sand particles carried on the dawn breeze, and she was painfully aware that she had not enough knowledge of the Death-Bringer to predict whether it could yet reclaim its form in time to take up the chase, or alternately, whether it had trapped them in some spiritual realm that would set them to wander aimlessly for an eternity, or simply hold them to be picked off at its leisure.

But soon enough, *Ni* sensed a void in the swirling sand, and saw the insect-like silhouette of the helicopter where it still perched on the sand. She adjusted course, and they ran to it, *Ni* leaving the Collector to ensure that Michael Israel was secured in the jump seat in back while she climbed up front. He joined her directly, and by the time he had his own harness in place, she was lifting them off the earth, thankful that her attention to the preflight check would now serve in their escape. She had learned enough to familiarize herself with the schematic of the controls. The sand dropped away, the rotors screaming as she turned east, just as the sun broke the distant horizon.

15

THE COLLECTOR HAD BEEN BACK a week. Still, Azuma stayed in Tokyo, not sure where this reluctance to face him had come from. More than once *Roku* had offered to bring the Range Rover around, knowing she would prefer to drive herself into the mountains, but she had refused, feigning work, sleep, or any other convenient excuse.

She knew it was disgraceful, knew she was avoiding something, but could not admit that it was her own guilt and likely nothing untoward she expected from him. She was gripped with remorse over the way they – she – had spoken the last time she had seen him, and somehow it was worse now that he was back, alive, relatively safe. She tried to tell herself he needed time to recover from his hurts, reacclimate to being home, but she ran out of excuses long before she was able to overcome the inertia she had created.

So the next time her private vehicle was offered, she accepted it. Changing into jeans, boots, and a dark oversized sweater, she set out into the chilly afternoon. Snow flurries were forecast, and if it were cold in the city, at elevation it would be frigid. The drive was distracting and oddly comforting, a simple mechanical task to counterpoint her feelings.

The staff were not surprised when she came through the front door, because *Ichi* and *Hachi* had come ahead, and they offered food and other comforts, but she reassured them that those things could happen in time, and made a rare apology that she had not forewarned them herself of her arrival.

She dawdled in her private rooms, and sat at her desk for a time, finding odd tasks to complete that did not really need her immediate attention. A stray glance at the ordered rows of Post-It notes revealed a break in the pattern that she did not recognize. A small pink note had been deliberately placed among a group of yellows, and it was not only discordant for its color; the strong, decisive strokes of the *kanji* were not written in her handwriting.

The Collector had placed it there, lovingly, precisely, its borders equidistant from each of the notes around it. On it, he had written four words, spare and direct. *The centre cannot hold.* Yeats. It made her smile, this apocalyptic reference. He was allowing her to save face, deflecting the indignity he knew she would feel from an apology, but she didn't want easy, not this time. It was the indignity she was supposed to feel, supposed to face. She was aware that it was dangerous to try to hold monsters accountable, but it was the accountability he had required from her all her life that had kept her from becoming more monstrous.

Barefoot, her hair loose, she wandered through the house and down the rear stairs to the garden. She crossed through the ornamental plantings to reach the back entrance to the Collector's residence. It was unlocked, and she let herself in carefully, trying to avoid letting in too much of the frigid air behind her. She wiped her feet on the mat inside the door, and stepped into the hallway.

Where she preferred more spartan decorating, the Collector chose his appointments with careful consideration for the senses. The floors were heated, but laid over with deep carpets of the softest fibers, as it was his habit to go barefoot at home as well. This thoughtfulness now made her sigh aloud, curling her toes into this sensual comfort, welcoming in its smallest detail.

The walls were textured, the paintings bold or muted depending on a particular room's design, and every window framed an aspect of the garden to its greatest advantage. The hallway turned at an angle before it ended in the great room, where the ceiling soared away, and one was confronted with a wall of windows that overlooked the grounds stretching off to the precipice in the distance, with a view of the valley beyond.

The open plan was inviting, a fire blazed in the fireplace that was the focus of the seating area, the kitchen stainless steel and white, the countertops pale wood. The Collector was preparing a meal, and the aromas coming from the kitchen were enticing. He stood with his back to her, chopping vegetables, and did not turn around when she entered.

Indeed, he did not speak, but she was not naïve enough to believe that he did not know she was there. Azuma came up behind him, and turning around, pressed her spine to his and leaned against him, smiling as she felt the broad muscles of his back accept her weight, confirming his knowledge of her presence. She was ever so slightly taller than he, and she arched slightly, placing her head against his shoulder and closed her eyes, aneled by this contact. He did not stop his task, and she felt the small knot in his apron against her lower spine, felt the effort of his movements in his right shoulder and torso, felt pushed and pulled by his even calm breathing like the waves on the sea.

And because it was home, and relief, and love, and everything she had known, she should have been prepared for the sheer overwhelming emotion that overcame her. But her habit of holding herself at such a firm remove was ingrained by centuries, her refusal to reveal, much less show, any perceived weakness.

He felt the subtle change in the tension of her posture and put down his knife, flattening his hands carefully on the countertop. He anticipated the tremor that passed through her, more like a shudder, like the first rushed raindrops ahead of a squall, and then the extraordinary sounds of her weeping, her spine curving slightly away from him as her grief bowed her.

He turned, balancing carefully so as not to break contact with her, capturing her shoulders in his strong hands, turning her around to face him, though she resisted, her apology coming out in sobs and gasps as he pulled her close against his chest.

"Some things," he told her, seeing the look in her eyes, "a very few, you cannot control. And you are not meant to."

He held her tightly, and soon enough, she stopped her futile resistance of this comfort, and leaned into him, now crying freely, but silently, her own feet against his, until he could feel the erratic rhythm of her stubborn heart, the only true fragility of the Dragon. He whispered against her hair, "Oh my little girl, the heart has to be let out sometimes."

After a time, as he knew she would, she extricated herself, and took a step away, and restored all the distance she needed to place between them. The corner of his mouth betrayed his amusement at this maneuver, and he nodded, turning back to his cooking.

In a few moments, she moved up beside him once more, disguising whatever it was that she truly wanted to discuss behind her real curiosity about what he was preparing.

"Those are beautiful prawns," she remarked, admiring the ones he had already peeled that were soaking in ice water.

"Here, try this," he offered, taking a clean spoon and dipping it into the saucier, bringing it to her lips. He smiled as he watched an expression of pleasure move across her face upon tasting it.

"Heavenly," she complimented him. He wiped his hands on a towel and flipped it onto his shoulder expertly. He quartered blood oranges and added their juice to a cocktail shaker, pouring out drinks for the two of them.

"I didn't mean to intrude on your hospitality," she protested, but he gave her a look that would not brook refusal, so she accepted the glass he passed to her.

"I think you'll like this," the Collector said. "It's something I made up just now," he admitted. "What shall we toast to?"

Azuma shrugged, suddenly unsure again.

"To an extraordinary life," he said, lifting his glass and not taking his eyes from hers.

"Indeed, and to extraordinary companions," she agreed, taking a sip of his concoction.

He watched her reaction again, and was pleased.

"That's – seductive," she concluded.

"Then I have succeeded," he nodded, returning to his knifework. "I have many things to discuss with you about my confinement," he told her. "I hope to be able to have a full and frank conversation with you about all that happened and what we should plan for regarding Akenomyosei. But I regret that our discussion will have to take place another time. Tomorrow, perhaps?"

Azuma paused, concerned that perhaps he was tired, or still not feeling well, for all that he appeared as vigorous as ever. His expression was polite, and she realized that he was dropping a hint that she should leave. And then she made the connection, the fire, the amazing dinner, the powerful cocktail.

"So you have a date," she said, gently teasing him, falling easily into the rhythm of their friendship once more.

"I wish it were so simple. I'm calling it an atonement and hoping for-" Here he stopped, at a rare loss for words.

"Understanding?" Azuma supplied.

"Just so," he agreed. "I have much to explain regarding the way I was ensnared."

"Seeking sustenance is a different thing than chasing desire," Azuma was already trying to make his argument for him.

"Perhaps. But perhaps it was more complicated than that. And are the two ever completely separate? The largest lie is the one we tell ourselves," he observed wisely, and she knew he was not looking for excuses.

"Ah, that's why you are trying so hard," she teased, making sure he heard it in her tone. Privately, she suspected that he spoiled *Ni* at every opportunity, and wondered again at how easily he had always kept his personal life secreted from her in spite of their Blood Bond.

"Whatever I am *hoping* for," he replied archly, "it is much less likely to happen if you continue this Blessing of Your Gracious Presence." He punctuated his statement with an ironic bow.

"I'm glad to see that your sense of humor is intact," Azuma said, just as there came a soft knock at the front door. The Collector tensed slightly, and Azuma found this an endearing reminder of his humanity. He gave her a significant look, half pleading and half admonishing.

She gave him an inscrutable smile, just to see what he would do.

"*Aijin*, don't be a Blocker, as the kids say these days," he suggested, pushing past her and snapping the towel at her behind as he headed for the door. "Tomorrow we shall resume combat exercises, since I am certain that in my absence you have been lax in your regimen. Let yourself out the back, if you would."

16

THE FOLLOWING DAY DAWNED SNOWY and dark, and wet ragged flakes tumbled from low forbidding clouds although the temperature was less bitter than it had been the day before. It was the Collector's suggestion to meet in the dojo, and Azuma thought nothing of it. A workout with a challenging adversary was welcome. She wondered if he were up to their usual level of competition and decided she would assess whether she needed to go easy on him the first few rounds.

"What discipline?" the Collector faced her, squared his body, and bowed.

"Do you have a preference?" she asked.

"Dragon's choice," he told her, so she smiled.

"Krav Maga," she replied, feeling as though practical application of their shared aikido, judo, and karate disciplines was going to be most useful. He hated hybrids, but respected their utility. Additionally, her sparring with Michael Israel had reminded her of the ways in which the Israelis had perfected these martial maneuvers, and she was ever looking for ways to improve. That battle had motivated her not to become complacent in her training.

She bowed, maintaining eye contact, and he waved her in, signaling his readiness. They traded blows, deflected, parried, and sparred for several minutes, then he spoke again.

"You've been practicing," he said in an admiring tone. "Again."

This time, when she engaged, he put her on the ground before she had time to realize what he had done. He backed away, saying quietly, "Let's talk about what else we have learned." His demeanor was as stern with her as it could be, which told her she had missed something. Since she was a child she had learned to loathe his disappointment when she missed a critical lesson.

When he reached for her hand to help her up, she took it, and immediately regretted it, as he used it unmercifully, twisting her wrist, forcing her onto her belly. He knelt down, putting a knee into her sciatic nerve, not bothering to let up on the pressure on her wrist, even when the pain forced a gasp through her teeth.

"I am susceptible to the same weaknesses as our adversaries," she sighed, admitting to her own limitations. "I allowed myself to believe that I could prevail, that I could save you. I went in blindly, not knowing the layout. I put myself in the trap. I was arrogant and reckless." Azuma bowed her head, looking at the mat through tears of shame and pain. "I failed you, failed to heed your best teachings."

"Perhaps it is I who failed you as a teacher," he replied tersely, refusing to let her off the hook. "Did you think that by staying away yourself you could defend such a decision? That 'begging forgiveness' is preferable to obtaining permission? Oh yes, perhaps you should have thought about what I would learn when I fed from *Ni*. That your blood would help her but also contains all the magic any evil would need to utterly destroy us all.

"I seem to recall in one of my earliest lessons trying to get you to understand that your power, without restraint, is equivalent to chaos, and that such a thing would not be countenanced by me?!" he thundered at her.

"*Sensei*, I-" Azuma began, but he increased the pressure on her wrist and twisted his knee further into the back of her leg. She let out a small scream through clenched teeth.

"No! It is too late for excuses. Your apology is worthless. I have explained this to you, but it appears I must again do so. A friend needs no explanation, and an enemy will not believe the one you supply. I ask you again whether there is anything you have to add," the Collector's voice was softening now, he knew that she was chastened. Knew she would consider more carefully her actions in future, especially where her heart was concerned.

"*Bangō*, esteemed Teacher," Azuma replied. They both knew that she could let the Dragon out, turn on him, defeat him, but it would be the ultimate sign of dishonor. He was her source of accountability, and the only family she would ever know. He let up on her somewhat, and when he stepped away, she thought he was done. She glanced up, and his hand was on *Hōfuku*. Although it was still sheathed, she was shaking. Though he would never attempt the deed himself, it was a reminder that even gods could be dispatched from this world.

No matter the emotional cost, he wanted her to lead with her head and not her heart. It used to be so easy for her in those early days when she had let Akenomyosei and Tatsuo Tomo manipulate her. When she had blindly followed the traditions of her father and his father before him. It was much harder to do these days, as she had learned to allow herself to feel.

He waited. Watched her shoulders slump forward, defeated. Waited her out, knowing that she did indeed have more to say. They both knew that if he unsheathed his sword he would have to use it; both also knew he understood that it was not his place to discipline her, nor had it ever been his right to take her life. He wanted her to have the reminder, that her survival was critical, the only true aim of his efforts, until such time as they came to an end, to the battle against a god even greater than the one he served. Wanted her to see his sacrifice for what it was, not merely the convenience she pretended it to be.

"I *love* you," she said, making her excuse anyway, not getting up from the mat, her hair obscuring her face. He had to relent. She was infuriating, but she was his.

"And that was never a reason to act. In fact, emotion is the most unstable foundation from which to make such a decision. I remind you under no circumstances do you risk your life for mine.

It is a debt to you which *I* must be allowed to pay, and you cannot engineer an outcome for me other than the one I am predestined to have. You do not have the authority to interfere with the fates, Goddess or no," he told her, although his tone now was more kind. Gently, and ever so quietly, touching her shoulder to signal she could get up, he added, "Do not think that such a sacrifice means I disdain your love in any way."

17

THAT AFTERNOON, THE COLLECTOR BEAT Azuma at chess three times before he said a word to her, incredulous at her inattention.

"Are you letting me win? Or simply enjoying my company?" he asked, trying to draw a distracted answer. He was successful.

"Yes, *Sensei*," she said to him, setting up the board once more.

"No, you're just barely tolerating me today," he admonished her. "It's good this wasn't a lesson in swordplay; I'd have died of neglect." The irony in his tone passed by her as well.

Azuma finally looked at him as if she were surprised to find him there.

"Something is bothering you, and it is not my lecture of this morning." He looked at her appraisingly, but she shook her head, not wanting to waste time on anything that didn't seem entirely credulous.

"I'm just tired. It's as if I feel the centuries in my bones. And the end that is coming, although I believe I could use the rest," she told him, but they both knew it wasn't the whole truth.

"What does Master *Go* have to say of late about your heart?" the Collector asked kindly, separating what he could divine from the deeper concern that she was actively trying to conceal from him.

"The rhythm continues to decay, at an apparently accelerating rate," she gave him a wry smile. "Such a relief to have my private physician among the *Akai*. He's brilliant, and loyal. But he is a child of modern science, and he has been stubbornly trying to figure out how to pace me. Lately, I know I have confounded and terrified him, because he is talking transplants and reminding me that I am rich enough to engineer and print a new heart."

"He ignores the magic inherent in the makeup of the gods," the Collector wisely observed. "But he cannot be blamed entirely for being purposefully naïve. He cares for you."

"He offered me his own heart," Azuma said, her voice dropping to a whisper. "Do you think they see me as so pragmatic as to keep my priests for spare parts?"

"I think their tradition and their religion demands that they make whatever sacrifice they must to protect and further the life of the Dragon. The Dragon is their God. That god is you," he told her, unnecessarily. "I think you have given the *Akai* a better existence than the one Akenomyosei intended for them. They are no longer just mindless sacrifices. They have lives, indulge appetites, are trained and respected for their varying strengths."

"Perhaps I am fortunate that the hole in my heart isn't any bigger," she replied wryly.

"Perhaps. But it's certainly smaller than Ietsune intended," the Collector said, needing to remind her of something else. "All the forgotten gods be thanked," he added, almost as an afterthought.

She looked up, surprised.

"I, for one, am glad of you," he told her more directly what he was feeling, and more warmly.

"I changed the rules for you," Azuma murmured, knowing that point was the one at which she had truly broken with Akenomyosei.

"And then broke them again for me when I most needed you to," he added, referring to *Ni*.

"Why did you toast to an extraordinary life?" she asked. "Really, is that what you think this has been?"

"Most extraordinary," he nodded. Without hesitation, he said, "I wouldn't change a day of it, or trade you for any other family. I count my blessings every night before I close my eyes and every morning that I open them. I will be counting them in the next life and beyond."

18

"NOW THAT I HAVE BROKEN down your defenses," he transitioned deftly, all but trapping her with his gaze, "Tell me what is really troubling you. Your heart isn't even half the story, it's merely a diversion. I doubt you spare a moment's real worry on that, while poor *Go* spends many a sleepless night fretting over it."

She smiled, knowing better than to challenge his observations. That razor-sharp acuity of his was both blessing and curse.

"Just something I saw in Buenos Aires," she told him. The Collector wasn't sure if she were aware that she was shaking her head, ever so subtly. "I just wish I could trust what I saw, or that one of the others had seen it as well."

"You don't trust it?" he prompted, concerned both about her tone and her posture.

"Akenomyosei. It was there, sitting like a damn spider in the center of the web. I saw it, sipping a Nespresso, of all things, not a hair out of place. The Monster knew what was happening, and it wanted to be seen."

"It wanted you to know that it could take everything out of your hands. That's what it does. It feeds on the chaos it causes."

"But what did Kedron know that needed to be kept from me?" she asked.

"Perhaps nothing at all. It was diverted by robbing you of your vengeance," he suggested.

"I suspect it wasn't even there for me at all. Something in those eyes, something…it was almost surprised to see *me*. And this time it had a *twin*. That doesn't seem possible, but I had it in my line of sight, and all the while I am watching its double enter another door in the building.

"This being was its mirror duplicate, hair, posture, mannerisms. The only difference was the color of their suits," she told him.

"What about Tatsuo Tomo?" the Collector asked, his tone even and soothing in counterpoint to the tension in hers.

"I agree. They are two sides of the same coin, and even though I have never seen the two of them wear the same face, I could believe it, except for the impossibility of it. Just after my sighting, most of the *Akai* and myself were watching helplessly as Tatsuo Tomo murdered Iago." She sighed in frustration and fury at the wastefulness of the boy's death.

"Let it go," he suggested. "It sounds as though you could no more save him than Iara."

"He was a child," she protested, detesting inadequacies, even those constructed erroneously by her ego.

"A child with a demon on his back, trapped between monsters, it would seem," the Collector observed. "Please." He put a hand on her arm. "I need you to tell me again about Kedron."

"I've gone over and over it. So many times I don't know what to believe. The Death-Bringer, confronting us, ripping a child to shreds and for what? If Kedron betrayed Akenomyosei somehow, he got off easily. I'm just thankful that *Hachi* wasn't in the room. If she had been there…" Azuma trailed off, staring into space, thinking about the fear and surprise trapped in Kedron's death stare.

"His neck was broken?" the Collector prompted her.

"Yes. Spectacularly. The force necessary to do that, to pop his skull off his spine...*Go* said it had to be extremely violent, had to require some sort of preternatural strength. And the finesse, to do it leaving the skin intact and unblemished. It would have made very little noise, because the bleeding into the brainstem may have precluded any outward signs or sounds of distress. Yet there were no handprints, no bruising, no other marks on the neck. The smallest nosebleed was the only obvious sign of violence. It simply defied logic."

"That this surprises you or *Go* is unfathomable to me," the Collector said, and still was not understanding it, no matter how many versions of the story he heard. Supernatural happenings were nothing new to any of them.

"There was no sign of struggle, no evidence that any effort was spent. Of course it was supernatural, but it isn't Akenomyosei's signature. You taught me well. Every killer has a tell that will eventually betray them. This was almost not obvious enough for it, too dispassionate. It likes things a bit more outré."

"So you surmise that this...twin...this double...somehow wears the Monster's face but has a different mode of retribution?" he asked her, genuinely struck by her concern, trying to comprehend what she was trying to communicate.

"It was cold, but not dispassionate. This was personal. Whoever or *whatever* did it took great satisfaction from doing it in that particular way. Ritualistic. Almost religious. Cultish," Azuma said. "All things that could be attributed to Akenomyosei, or be undertaken in its name. And whatever – whomever – it was, it evaded *Hachi* and *Ku* afterward, escaping the hotel without being seen. So I have no confirmation regarding what I think I saw. None at all."

"But why are you so concerned about what you saw?" the Collector asked.

"I'm not certain. Just a feeling. That I saw something I shouldn't have, or perhaps was manipulated in such a way that it means me to be conflicted about it. It means something, I just don't know what. It's as if the answer is dangling just beyond my grasp, and I probably shouldn't try to solve it, rather remember it, and not question it beyond the fact that there is something here that may be important later," she reasoned. "Like a monster we're missing."

19

"TELL ME ABOUT THE SPECIMEN retrieval in New Orleans," Azuma finally asked him, as much to indulge her curiosity about what had actually happened as to hear his assessment of the Wolf, since all of her information about the encounter had been secondhand.

"Ah. A miscalculation on my part, and perhaps a perfect storm, with the clinic's miscommunication contributing to a situation that could have been avoided," the Collector told her. "They notified me of the pickup window for the specimen when the subject *arrived*, not when he departed. He was still there, flirting with the lab tech when I came to collect the sample, which with any other subject would have caused me no difficulty.

"I am accustomed to the phenomenon of disappearing in plain sight when in the States," his tone betrayed some amusement. "At first, I wasn't sure how he spotted me, but having had time to consider it, it had to be my scent. And he didn't immediately react, but I think he had some buyer's remorse when he realized I wasn't strictly a human courier. He's smart, avoided a scene inside. He confronted me on the street."

"Confronted?" Azuma leaned forward, looking concerned. This was the part of the story that most worried her.

"Nothing physical, I assure you. He let the beast out enough for me to see it, a challenge across four lanes of moving traffic. I showed him my teeth, created a traffic disturbance, and windwalked my escape."

"So we have no specific measure of his capabilities?" Azuma asked.

"Even under another set of circumstances," the Collector reasoned, "it wouldn't be wise to engage him. There was no way for me to reliably gauge the strength of this opponent, and the public exchange of aggression was not warranted. I was on an errand on your behalf, the objective was the specimen, and it would not have been prudent to jeopardize the information we could gain from it."

"But I know you too well. You have an opinion about his talents," Azuma pressed.

"Ah. Of course I do. But not based solely on one emotionally charged interaction," he said. "Instinct can only inform so much. My suspicion alone assures me that he could be very dangerous, more dangerous than I can possibly confirm by our traditional approaches.

"Unlike the Sorceress, there is very little mythology surrounding him, indeed he has managed to fly under the radar, it would seem. I started a file on him; I welcome your opinion on what I have discovered," he informed her, flipping open the file on the conference table between them, but speaking from memory rather than reading.

"Amaoke-none-Severnoj. The name itself is interesting, Indigenous given, Russian surname, possibly an alias. Primary bank accounts at Royal Bank of Canada, but secondary accounts at HSBC and Bank of Montreal. His bank accounts would suggest that he is the beneficiary of some complex intergenerational wealth, but he lives at the poverty line.

"Interrogation of social security records reveals spotty employment over the past twenty years; this period in New Orleans seems to be one of the longest and most stable stretches. Employment history reveals a pattern of blue-collar hard labor: lumberjacking, arctic oil rigging, whaling, construction. He worked a season smoke-jumping in California.

"Withdrawal patterns from the bank suggest he pays his rent in cash; he has almost daily debit charges at RBC from the grocery, so he buys only the food he needs for the day in question. No evidence he owns, or has ever owned, a cellular phone. His only extravagance, if I can call it that, is a number of purchases of branded work boots. They seem to be of the same make, but he may need to replace them often. The nature of his work may contribute to significant turnover in his footwear. He eats out rarely, appears to frequent a restaurant called *Delachaise* over any other."

"If he is a transformative monster, that may explain the need for frequent footwear replacement," Azuma interjected.

"*Transformative monster?*" the Collector was politely incredulous. "Is that the scientific term?"

"It is a categorization. He and I take on other forms. I don't suspect it of the Sorceress, but cannot rule it out," Azuma replied.

"In that case, I wonder if he regularly forgets to put on underwear. Perhaps *that* is a feature of the transformative monster," he teased. It was his right, she supposed, he had run around retrieving random items of clothing and doing numerous other things for herself and Tatsuo Tomo for centuries.

"A gentleman would pretend he hadn't noticed. Perhaps an eccentricity of the affliction. You'll have to ask him," Azuma suggested.

"First chance I get," he assured her, turning back to the file and continuing his report. He needed to make no comment about his state as a gentleman.

"He owns extensive acreage in the central wilderness of Alaska, and a tract of land in the Northern Maine woods. He allows sustenance hunting and fishing on the Alaska property but restricts access to Alaskan Natives. The tract of land in Maine is titled to a Nathan Guinness, which may be some sort of misdirection, it has been so titled for over two hundred years; the property taxes and insurance are paid from the BMO account in Quebec, and Severnoj's signature appears on a recent farming lease to a local farmer for the arable portion of the land.

"The name first appeared on a register in Bethel, Alaska Territory, in 1951, accompanying a request to record an estimated date of birth, which was listed at that time as December 24, 1928. One could argue that was perhaps a father with the same name, but I have my doubts. He is currently a registered member of the *Kuskokwagmiut* Group of the Central Alaskan Yup'Ik, and carries a U.S. Passport in the same name, date of birth listed as December 24, 1978. He has tribal nation identification, and an Alaska State Identification card, no operator's license."

"He doesn't drive?" Azuma spoke as if she couldn't imagine such a thing.

"It appears not. No evidence of registered ownership of any vehicles, either. Perhaps, if he is the type of *transformative monster* we suspect, he avoids it out of an abundance of caution," the Collector replied.

"Not a mindless beast, then," Azuma commented thoughtfully, ignoring the jab.

"We would be foolish to make such an assumption," the Collector admonished. "The man I observed was well-groomed, well-dressed, apparently of sound health…and mind."

"I wondered about that," Azuma admitted. "Considering that the requesting physician is a psychiatrist. Is there a connection?"

"Unclear. But there is something interesting that the financial interrogation uncovered, especially in conjunction with your discovery of him in the doctor's residence."

"Indeed. In the middle of the night, although he appeared to be standing guard more than anything else," Azuma said.

"Why do you think so?" the Collector asked, not understanding her meaning.

"When you entertain a lover, do you sleep with *all* of your clothes on? On top of the covers? With your shoes on? No part of it felt like an assignation to me," she related the particulars of the encounter for him again.

"Interesting. Well. Look at this," he instructed her, searching through one of the tabulated dividers and separating a page from the sheaf of financial documents. He turned it slightly and slid it over. She sat hunched over it, reading for a few moments, her lips moving slightly. She raised her eyes to him in surprise.

"That, too, was of interest to me," he told her, nodding.

"Could they be lovers?" Azuma asked aloud, but it was rhetorical. "What do we know about her? Dr. Madison. She doesn't strike me as someone who would blur that boundary. In my specialty, which is non-clinical, it's frowned upon. In Psych, I imagine it borders on criminal. Still, it happens."

20

THE COLLECTOR PULLED THE SECOND dossier toward them and flipped it open. Azuma leaned her upper body toward him until their heads were nearly touching so she could take a look.

"Aleta Abigail Madison, age 38, born June 5, 1982, Metairie, Louisiana. Graduated Archbishop Chapelle High School Valedictorian, William and Mary College *summa cum laude* with dual degrees in Psychology and Biochemistry, then Howard University Medical School where she was *Alpha Omega Alpha,* earned her medical degree and Doctor of Philosophy. Post-graduate work and forensic psychiatry residency at Georgetown. Laughlin Fellow to the APA in 2004, further postdoctoral work at Bellevue, returned to New Orleans for private practice. Board Certified in Psychiatry, widely published. Member of National Association of Doctors, Fellow of both the American College of Psychiatry and the American Psychiatric Association. Involved with a number of Catholic charities, has outpatient, inpatient, and forensic prison practices. Consulting profiler to the Federal Bureau of Investigation of the United States. She has been an expert witness in several capital criminal cases, her testimony has been balanced between use by both prosecutors and defense attorneys. No evidence ever married or in a significant relationship, no records indicate ever having had a domestic partner of either sex."

"Married to her work?"

"I don't know," the Collector said. "This reads a lot like *your* CV."

"A sexual indiscretion with a patient seems unlikely, on balance," Azuma rubbed at her temples, thinking it through. "She seems too religious and conservative."

"You like her," the Collector observed something congratulatory and defensive in her tone.

"I do," Azuma admitted. "She's a sharp, tough lady."

The Collector looked again at the photos appended to the file. "It doesn't hurt that she's hot."

"I'm supposed to apologize for finding her attractive?" Azuma scoffed at him. "As if *you* don't." She gestured at the headshot on top of the pile. "She gives *Hachi* a run for her money. I don't know. Dr. Madison seemed…worried about Amaoke in response to what the Sorceress was telling us. I couldn't really read more from just her behavior, but I think she keeps her cards close to the vest. I just didn't get the sense that they had been intimates. Her reaction was mostly one of concern, without any of the tells like flushing or subtle awkward discomfort that she would have discussing him with strangers if he were her lover. There were some tears, so there is some kind of emotional connection."

She was quiet for a few moments more, almost frowning down at the two files on the table. "What if he isn't her patient? Why does a psychiatrist need a genetic profile? None of her scholarly work suggests she is tracking or trying to find familial connections to mental health or any of the psychotic disorders. Of course they exist, but this is so outside her area of expertise. Perhaps there is a non-professional connection, a personal friendship. Maybe she ordered it to maintain his privacy. Something she said to me confirmed she knew about him, really knew that he is *other*, because she made a connection between him and myself."

The Collector gave her a look, not understanding how that was possible. Azuma waved it away. "She noticed my heart rhythm," she clarified. "Any clinician would know it to be incompatible with life."

"Noticed?"

"We were in close quarters for a few moments, that's all," she told him.

"Sounds like a hardship," he murmured, teasing her in earnest.

"Is it just me or are you a royal pain in the ass since you got back?" she pushed back at him, smiling.

"It appears my death may be approaching, and if I'm going to turn over a new leaf, I need to get on with it," he offered, with a look of mock innocence.

"I want the old you back, at least provisionally, so we can speak – what was it you said? – frankly and fully," she ordered.

"*Hai, Aijin.*" He bowed his head, but she could see he was still smiling. "How may I be of service?"

"That's even worse," she groaned, unable to keep from laughing, and he joined her. It must have been so startling in itself as to cause a minor skirmish from the outer offices, and both *Ku* and *Ni* put their heads into the room to confirm what they were hearing, the Dragon and the Curse sharing a rare moment of mirth.

21

"SO WHAT HAPPENED?" she finally asked him about his capture. "How did Tatsuo get his hands on you?"

"Exploited my hunger," he said. "At least, that's what I recall."

"The courier told me that when he left you, you were with a woman at the bar in the hotel," she told him, as much as for clarification as to prompt him to tell her more.

"True. I was tired, needed to feed. Wasn't sure where I was going to satisfy my thirst, but she – Lilith – came in while I was having a nightcap. Sat down next to me. Sexy as hell," he said, sounding a bit guilty, and a lot remorseful.

Azuma said nothing, she knew the feeling well. Abject hunger for a blood meal blurred the line between appetites, was akin to desire, and it could engender misplaced instinctual cravings. There was a reason it was referred to as bloodlust. Still, she recalled that some of what she felt for the Jade Princess centuries ago had given her pangs of guilt she could still almost feel. The unfulfilled desire for Megumi, transfixed with a ravenous need to feed had confused her feelings about Bi Xiaohui in the moment. And the same impulses had perhaps fueled something unhealthy in her mutual obsession with Iara. Some things aren't good for you under any circumstance; it doesn't mean you can always resist temptation.

She knew he didn't want her to make excuses for him; she wouldn't want him to make them for her. If it feels like an infidelity, it probably is. Neither did she want to point out that *Ni* had probably faced the same dilemma; that fact was something she was certain he did not want to contemplate. Azuma knew that he was aware *Ni* had fed from her prior to his rescue, and decided she would be surprised if that didn't bother him on some level, not that he would ever share his feelings on the subject.

"Lilith had this purple hair, which struck me as a sign she might be a risk taker," the Collector explained. "She was well-dressed, a progressive thinker. She seemed receptive to a good time, didn't bat an eye when I told her I was leaving the next morning.

"As soon as I bit her, I knew exactly what she was," he said, uttering an oath behind it, and Azuma recognized that his tone was purposeful in telegraphing the level of anger and frustration he still felt about it, since she could count on one hand the number of times she had heard him utter a profanity in any language. "All that I know about night demons, and the *yokai*, I should have known better."

"Why?" This time Azuma didn't hesitate to let him off the hook. "They have never attempted to interfere with us. They recognize us as being night creatures ourselves."

"I think they avoid us because you are a god," he corrected her. "She, *it*, was a handmaiden of Akenomyosei. And looking back, although I couldn't have known it at the time, Tatsuo Tomo watched the whole encounter unfold. He escorted her, basically, was sitting at the bar with us the whole time, right under my nose, and I had no idea."

"He has a new face," Azuma told him. She lamented the fact that she hadn't thought to mention it to him when she had learned of it.

"Yes. A stolen face. A face that belongs to the Soldier's dead brother," he told her. "We almost didn't make it out of the *makom* with Michael Israel; it tried to lure her in."

Azuma's expression betrayed her surprise on learning of this development.

"Tatsuo Tomo spoke to her as if he were her brother, delighted about their reunion," the Collector added. "Michael Israel was conflicted about it, and wary enough, but she wanted it to be true more than she wanted to preserve her own safety."

"As she would," Azuma whispered, stunned at this revelation. It had to mean something very significant, but her mind could not begin to unravel this mystery now.

"I woke up in their dungeon; they stood me against the stones and had somehow driven *Hōfuku* right through me. I was impaled and upright for a very long time."

"But you were gone for weeks," Azuma protested.

"Perhaps. Time isn't the same in that place. It's manipulated. It felt like an eternity," he told her. "For a while I think I forgot that I cannot be so easily killed. It was worse than the bamboo forest."

"My fault," Azuma was shaking her head slowly.

"Not possible," the Collector disagreed. "If anything, it was the magic in your blood that saved me."

"I'm amazed you can find any positive to this," she said sadly, and her tone told him she would never let go of her belief that she was somehow responsible.

"There's no end to the positives, as I see it," he reassured her. "First, I don't think they understand their own power, much less that of others.

"I didn't die when they impaled me. They truly seemed to misunderstand the reason for that. Then they assumed that I would die if they *removed* the sword. Perhaps that was something Akenomyosei suggested."

"It spoke to you? I always assumed it was avoiding you," Azuma was fascinated.

"I think my praying was finally enough of an irritant. It offered to teach me new prayers, ones that it suggested were edited out of the sacred texts. Possibly things that would serve some dark purpose. But it was after the Monster came that Tatsuo Tomo tried to remove *Hōfuku*. He was entirely unsuccessful.

"I realized that so much of the mythology has survived because some of it is true. That sword is powerful, it has dispatched many souls, which gives the steel a magic of sorts, a magic tied to me. I didn't realize it was a talisman as well.

"I offered it to him, but he was enraged. He refused to ask me to give it to him. This tells us that we are dealing with prideful beings. Petty. Impulses poorly controlled, which is destructive but useful.

"Eventually, he sent the other demon, Lilith, in the same guise she had appeared to me before. Assuming that their prey does not learn. You cannot set the trap in the same way and expect the same outcome. She was sent to do the asking. I let them have the sword. I assumed it would accomplish two very important things.

"First, if they believed that the removal of the sword would guarantee my death, they would leave me to die. That gave me the advantage that I wish I had for every enemy. Akenomyosei somehow believed me dead. It is dangerous to assume an adversary is dead before they actually are."

"But you would have died, eventually," Azuma insisted.

"What have I taught you?" the Collector asked her sharply, always teaching, expecting her to remember her lessons.

"Ensure your enemy's death with your own eyes," she nodded.

"And while I lived, retribution and retaliation were possible, because there was a possibility that the Blood Tie could lead you to me, even though I was on the other side, in the Land of the Dead. By allowing them to have the sword, I knew their martial strategy consisted only of the limits of their petty machinations. They would want to taunt you; specifically, Tatsuo Tomo would want to taunt you, since you stole his place in the world, the most reliable way in which he was allowed to pass over and do mischief.

"I knew they would deliver the sword as a message, and that you, the deity, would then use it to follow the Blood Bond, and there would be no way to hide me, even in the beyond. They are only capable of satisfying their immediate desires, they have no ability to strategize even one step ahead, nor can they see their own weaknesses, for they are blind to such insights."

"But if they were unable to wield the sword, how did they impale you? How did they ultimately deliver it to me?" Azuma asked. She had not yet told him of the way in which the weapon had been returned to her, of Akiko's demise.

"We must assume that possession of the flesh can be meaningful and directed, though it yet destroys the possessed. These demons manipulate the dead, and can manipulate the living, where one is damned or simply willing to trade a soul for power, for pleasure, even for release. I am certain, just as we do, they can find those who reach for death and use them as messengers," he reasoned. "That extends their ability to wreak havoc where they cannot hold to flesh or where they cannot control a fleshly form. Possession is their way through, and they covet flesh for all that they disdain humanity."

Azuma knew the truth of it. Akiko had been their messenger, and as soon as she had taken possession of his steel, her fate was sealed. Tatsuo Tomo used her to deliver the physical item and then had no difficulty exacting her death. That explained why the sword was in her hand. It hadn't been placed there, she had accepted it, carried it, delivered it. Had she known that she would become part of the message? Azuma closed her eyes. Beautiful, tragic Akiko. Perhaps she had.

22

"AKENOMYOSEI DID SPEAK OF YOU as though you were lost to me forever," Azuma said. She was still recalling the ugly scene in her office.

"I think they must have discovered their miscalculation by now," the Collector smiled, and there was no warmth in it. There was no indication he found any humor in it.

"But if one of the *Akai* made such a mistake?"

"I would retire them," he assured her.

"So is there no division among them when such a blunder occurs?" Azuma wondered.

"Perhaps among the lesser demons, but those three seem to be a unit of sorts," the Collector observed. "I assume that they kept any knowledge of Lilith from us as a sort of evil surprise. We thought we knew our major adversaries."

"Possibly. I could see that. But perhaps it was never necessary. We – or more properly, I – was following the path set for me, so no reason to believe I was ever going to be a problem. Perhaps Akenomyosei thought I would see her as a rival? Or that since Tatsuo Tomo was intimately involved there was no need for another actor?"

"No matter. We know about her now. We should expect there are others," he told her.

"You said they were three. That's a sacred number in most religions," Azuma pointed out.

"Indeed," the Collector agreed, but like the teacher he was, he couldn't resist pointing out the holes in any conclusion. It was an infuriating and valuable asset. "So are four, seven, and twelve. It doesn't hurt us to be prepared for more."

"And something else," Azuma continued, nodding to acknowledge her agreement with his statement while returning to an earlier observation. "You said 'the three of them' as if they were some sort of unit. I still believe there is some separation in power between Akenomyosei and these two. I have never felt that Tatsuo Tomo was anything but a lieutenant, or a general, to it."

"It is likely," he agreed. "But they remain together for a reason, and that may be important."

"It certainly bears careful consideration," Azuma knew that there would need to be further discussion on this point, and mentally filed it away for later. She knew her restless mind would work on it subconsciously, perhaps all that he had learned would be of help in defeating the Monster.

"What we must now face," he said somberly, "is the fact that I am compromised."

"I wondered about that myself," Azuma told him. "You haven't said much about your time there, in the shrine."

"I don't recall enough of it to trust the parts I do remember," the Collector was quiet for several moments. "We must move forward, and operate with an abundance of caution. You must leave me out of the finer details of any tactical plan to reengage at the Place of the Fallen. We must assume that I was allowed to escape, there is no other prudent explanation. The place eats the souls of the living and the dead, and under no circumstance that I can fathom should it be a place that one can leave readily. Especially not an enemy. Especially not two beings fueled by your blood."

"Michael Israel has now been in and out twice," Azuma pointed out.

"I have considered this. It is all part of an elaborate plan, the particulars of which we cannot see and should try to understand, and it relates somehow to Tatsuo Tomo's stolen identity. It has a plan for her, and it is patient. Perhaps we frustrated its aims this time, and it must only inevitably delay setting whatever outcome in motion.

"Irrespective of all of this, while I will give you every assistance in providing the details of what I learned, what I know, and even what I think," he began, needing to caution her, "under no circumstances should I directly participate in any tactical decision-making about our approach to the Place of the Fallen."

It is doubtful that the extent of the Sorceress' power can be measured without invoking devastation.

23

AS SOON AS THEY STEPPED out into the night air, Amaoke put his nose to work. Without the distracting scents of the crush of humanity inside, there was more information to be had. He sneezed out the remnant smells of cologne, smoke, and musk and inhaled the fresh air. After a few moments, he caught the barest whiff of something familiar, though he didn't immediately know why.

It was part of the complex and puzzling scent of the stranger's clothing, and he thought hard about it, needing to remember where he'd smelled it before. Then it came to him, and he smiled to himself. It was the Sorceress' scent signature.

But he was wary of revealing what he knew, because outside the club, his hearing was also augmented, and what it told him was even more surprising. The man had no heartbeat, he took no breaths to fill his lungs, Amaoke could scent no blood from him.

Yet he was, or had been, human, because Amaoke had learned that the monsters he had catalogued, Weston, the Dragon, the Sorceress, had traces of the Morningstar's scent layered beneath their human scent signatures. He surmised he did as well. This creature had no such taint, indeed there was something about the scent he *didn't* carry that suggested he had once been pureflesh. That reassured Amaoke, but did nothing to assuage his concern.

Predators need to categorize other living things, and until this moment, Amaoke had successfully done so with every natural and even the non-natural beings he had encountered. He knew that witches sometimes had familiars to do their bidding, some of them were even rumored to raise the dead; having experienced the Sorceress' power firsthand, however, he doubted she needed any such help.

Then the newcomer turned back toward them when he reached the corner ahead, allowing Weston and Amaoke to catch up, and the final piece of the puzzle fell into place. Because as he got closer to the man, the Sorceress' scent sharpened specifically, and it was both stronger and more personal. Amaoke would have loved to know less about certain things sometimes, but not much could be concealed from his nose. This man was her lover, was mated to the Sorceress, and while it explained a lot, it raised even more questions.

Weston stepped past him to turn the corner and stopped so abruptly that Amaoke nearly ran into him. He saw, over his friend's shoulder, six or seven youths, similar in complexion to the messenger, lined up in a loose semicircle. And then he saw what had given Weston pause: they all held machetes.

He sighed, and gambled, speaking to the messenger, who was now behind him. "We need to speak to the Sorceress. We mean your wife no harm."

The man moved much faster than Amaoke anticipated, and he was pushed up against the side of the building, the man's own machete magically produced. The blade was pressed firmly against Amaoke's neck and he snarled, "Ask me how I feel about hearing my wife's name from your mouth." His red eyes were impressive, and would've been frightening were his captive anyone else.

"Brother," Amaoke said quietly, signaling to Weston while behaving as though his words were directed at this man, "It would be a bad idea, a *very* bad idea, to have this situation deteriorate." Amaoke was caught between the proverbial rock and hard place, because the Wolf would defend its existence in deadly fashion, but he dreaded his fate when the Sorceress discovered he had rent the flesh of her husband.

The shadows were already moving, and then Amaoke felt Weston's demons, crawling over him like an infestation, the wind swirling around the group of men as they danced and shrieked, trying to shed whatever unseen beings were attacking them. It was effective, as they were susceptible to suspicion and had been persecuted for magic they didn't possess. They backed away, one or two of them dropping their blades in the street.

This enraged the messenger, who was obviously feeling the demons moving over his own flesh, but he pressed harder with his blade against Amaoke, the keen edge breaking the skin, and the smell of his aggression triggered the Beast.

Amaoke did his best to limit the changes, but made sure that the man felt his flesh rippling and changing under his clothes, and reached up to grasp the man's wrist, wrapping human fingers around it. Amaoke concentrated on focusing the change, so that as his grip tightened unmercifully, forcing the man to let go of the weapon, it was the triangular claws that now held on, and those red eyes widened in the first signs of fear, realizing that what he had in his trap he could not handle.

"You good, Brother?" Weston asked, and Amaoke could feel the priest's familiars sliding off his skin.

"*Unh.*" The Beast grunted a response, and Weston turned to look at him, worried. But his concern was misplaced, Amaoke had control of himself, if not his voice, and he pulled back the change, pushing the Wolf away, opening his hand to let the messenger go. He bent down and picked up the man's machete and returned it to him, handle first, a peace offering, and the man made it disappear again inside that voluminous jacket.

Weston nodded to the others, and they came forward cautiously, retrieving their own weapons. They looked to their leader, who had no answers.

Then all the hairs on Amaoke's body stood on end, and he held very still. Power and emotion, and the night was silent and close, a vacuum, each moment stretched out upon the next.

"Make peace," a familiar voice came from the shadows of the alleyway, and she sounded not quite angry. Stern perhaps.

The men in the street were unnaturally still, their eyes betrayed their concern.

The messenger turned to the darkened mouth of the alley. "'Sini-ma, do not."

"These men are not the enemy, 'Kisye," she said softly, neither Amaoke nor Weston understood that she was saying the man's name. "Their women wait for them, as I wait for you when you are away. They are much like you, gifted, loving, dangerous. We are allied in our hatred of the Monster."

"But-" the man started to protest, glancing directly at Weston. Something unspoken passed between them.

"Never mind that he wears the face of the *Mjusi*," Kusini spoke firmly, and finally stepped out into the light. "That is not his fault. Who are we, of all people, to make assumptions based on appearance alone. Step closer to him, my husband, and you will see what is truly there. The eyes cannot lie.

"That the demons attend him is a legacy unasked for," she added, coming closer. Her lovely features were hidden in the folds of her hooded garment, but she pulled the cloth from her head gracefully. She had braided her hair down against her scalp, the intricate plaits accented her lovely face, almost like a platinum crown. Her golden eyes burned into Amaoke, and then she smiled. She turned to Weston.

"I am the Sorceress you seek," she said, unnecessarily. "My name is Kusini; I prefer to be addressed by it, if you would. My husband is Ambakisye."

Amaoke nodded at both of them, and introduced himself, adding, "This is Father Weston."

"Weston is sufficient," the priest said, smiling, although Amaoke sensed the familiars were more excited than ever. Despite Weston's smile, and his calm appearance, Amaoke scented a new distress coming from him. It was sudden and unmistakably related to Kusini's arrival.

Kusini looked around at the men in the road. "Andwale, it's all right. All of you, please, introduce yourselves to these men. They are our friends, both because they are good, but also because they share our enemies, and work against the evil of the Ghost and the Darkness.

"Please take them to their hotel and have them gather their things. It will be better to stay at the safehouse for a few days." She pulled her hood back up and placed a gentle hand on Ambakisye's shoulder. "Husband, you need to feed, and these men must be hungry. I will tell Henri to expect you shortly."

And then she was gone from sight, just like that, there one moment, gone the next. Amaoke was certain he would never get used to it. He heard her amused laughter in his ear. *We have much to discuss, my friend.*

W

Sometimes the shadows do move, when I am passing from light into darkness. A form awaits me in the upper hallway at St. Constantine's; confronting it rationally, it simply becomes another empty corner, turning into another room, where mundane familiars make spooky sentinels that have followed me into every place I have lived. Since childhood, I have combatted these haunts with the knowledge that my own familiars are even more powerful.

It is better to believe in possibilities than be unprepared by swallowing a reality.

The Sorceress is powerful, a power that causes a discomfort I cannot explain. Her energy repels me, more evidence that what I am is not in balance.

I have never presupposed that what the light holds cannot be less than what the darkness conceals.

24

ANDWALE ACCOMPANIED THEM BACK TO the hotel, where Amaoke retrieved his knapsack, and Weston gathered his own things. There was a sense that in leaving behind the hotel, they were leaving behind much more, as if departing from society to join a smaller cohort, a symbolic act. Amaoke felt as if he were at a crossroads, although there seemed only one way forward, whatever choice had been made was behind him now.

They took a circuitous route through the city, traversing a night market to reach a second busy thoroughfare, food vendors still open for late night customers, and then a mosque, closed up and dark. Weston seemed unperturbed, but he was too quiet, and since they had left the Vatican, not quite himself.

Amaoke also wondered how carefully his friend had studied the small map of the city he had gotten from the hotel, as he seemed content to tolerate the obvious subterfuge. The street they eventually turned down was paved with cobblestones, one side dominated by a stucco wall that bounded a private garden. At the end of it there was a Judas door next to an ornate metal grate that had been constructed to enclose a paved driveway.

A banded iron window had been cut into the door, and there was an electronic security panel installed to the right of it. Andwale punched in the code, and they were admitted to the garden. Several paths curved away from them, a few on into the flowering yard under the trees, and one that doubled back to a side entrance of a residence adorned with elaborate Middle Eastern architecture, with graceful expansive arches and enormous shuttered windows.

Halfway to the house, a giant of a man stepped out of the shadows, not as menacing as his size would suggest him to be, because his face was open and friendly. It was the face of a man who laughed often. His voice was a smooth baritone. "Welcome. Please remove your shoes in the salon."

"Thank you, Henri," Andwale nodded and led the way into the house. The three men were quiet as they removed their footwear, and Weston admired the hummingbird mosaic in the pool.

"Feel free to soak your weary feet," Andwale whispered, indicating the pool. He saw Amaoke's confusion upon noticing the numerous pairs of small shoes lining the walls of the salon. "And speak softly, there are many children here, and they are sleeping."

Kusini appeared from one of the doorways about halfway down the length of the room. She carried towels and a soft rug. "Please." She indicated the shallow pool, again inviting them to step into it. "It is one of my favorite things about this house."

Amaoke and Weston complied, rolling up their trousers and stepping into the water. It felt better than Amaoke had imagined it would, and he wondered how badly he had been neglecting his feet all these years if a bit of cool water felt this good.

She knelt to put down the rug for them to step out upon, and this bothered Weston. "Kusini, we can manage."

Amaoke was uncomfortable as well, as much from her gesture as from the change in Weston that he sensed was caused by their being here, in this house. His distress was cresting, and Amaoke felt it keenly, sympathetic to it as much as it confused him.

"Nonsense. This was the very first home I ever had," she told them. Her own eyes seemed to rest on Weston with some concern. "It is my pleasure to welcome you and extend our hospitality. Come. Ambakisye has prepared food for us. He is a marvelous cook; you are in for a treat." She handed each of them soft towels for their feet. "If your feet are cold, we have slippers."

Weston accepted the offer of slippers, but Amaoke shook his head, preferring to go barefoot. The floors were lovely Spanish tiles, perhaps original, probably restored, and surprisingly warm.

They followed Kusini into the most interesting room that Amaoke had ever seen. It was a kitchen and a garden and a conservatory and a museum all at once. At one end, what appeared to be an enormous stainless-steel walk-in freezer was flanked by industrial stainless-steel Miele appliances, incongruous next to a stone fireplace big enough to walk into. The fireplace was empty and cold now at the end of the summer, but skylights and the windows to the garden let in the night breeze, their wooden shutters propped wide open. Plants grew abundantly both inside and outside, flowering varietals mixed with tiered, organized vegetables. There were a number of peppers, tomatoes, and squash. Cucumbers flourished next to fragrant gardenias.

The curved adobe ceiling soared above them, with several niches carved for a variety of sculptures, small succulents, and what appeared to be occupied birds' nests. Hundreds of hurricane lamps provided a soft natural glow to the space. There were items of interest aplenty; enough to look at for a very long time.

Ambakisye was at the huge butcher block, expertly taking apart the hindquarters of a goat. He appeared to be preparing a dish anchored by roast eggplant and peppers, and Amaoke could identify only a handful of the spices he'd put in it. Its smell was mouthwatering.

Ambakisye cubed the meat, putting half of it into the dish and setting half of it aside. He didn't look up when they came in, so Amaoke took a seat at the extensive wooden table that was the centerpiece of the room.

He sat facing outward, and Weston faced inward, nodding gently when Kusini offered water from the silver pitcher that had been set out. Amaoke saw sliced fruit and nuts set out, with a soft raisin bread and a block of something that was probably cheese.

Weston, normally ravenous, was not his usual enthusiastic self at the prospect of getting a meal, and this was concerning to Amaoke. Since the Vatican, at times he seemed distracted and odd. His sense of humor was blunted, some days nonexistent. He still had bandages on one of his hands from an impromptu boxing match with the mirror in their suite at the priest's residence. Try as he might, Amaoke had not been able to get him to discuss what had occurred, and he remembered the fear in his friend's eyes that suggested he could not remember what had happened.

Strangest and most ominous to Amaoke, his scent had changed sharply two days prior to their departure. Sadness, and a bit of something that was reminiscent of sickness. Most troubling of all was the way the new scent called to his Wolf; there was something appetizing about it, which further disturbed him.

The fact that Weston was ignoring this bounty after several days of catch-as-catch-can meals was so unlike him. He had such an enthusiasm for food, life, fellowship. Amaoke had no knowledge that this behavior was something of a regression, and those who had known the priest as a child would have thought this reserved version normal for him.

Kusini was aware of Weston's distress also, although she did not know him well. She made eye contact with Amaoke, and said, "You must be tired from your travels." This observation was directed at both of them, but Amaoke knew she was referring to Weston.

He didn't answer at first, just looked up at her slowly, distracted, and Amaoke thought his eyes did look tired behind his spectacles. As if on cue, he yawned. "I apologize. I think I must be more exhausted than I realized."

"Perhaps sleep is needed more than food," she observed wisely. She had never been anyone's mother, Amaoke thought, but he appreciated a hostess that would let you off the hook now and then. She would take no offense if Weston did not partake of their hospitality in favor of rest. It was a kind gesture.

"I'd like that," Weston nodded, although it was less a surrender than an agreement.

"I can show them where they'll be sleeping, *mpenzi*," Ambakisye offered, his tone almost friendly. Amaoke suspected it was more for his wife's benefit than out of any real sense of acceptance of their presence here. "The food is ready. If you'll watch the rice?"

"I will take them," Kusini ignored his expression of concern. "Henri and I can take down the linens."

She led the way out of a side door to the garden, and Amaoke accompanied them, wanting to be sure Weston was settled, and thinking it was more considerate not to have to ask her to repeat herself or make another trip just to show him the same thing.

A nightingale called out when they were under the trees, off somewhere in the garden, a plaintive but beautiful sound.

She led the way to a building that had once been stables, a long low building at the bottom of the yard. Amaoke recognized the distinctive shape of the structure, as enough time had elapsed since animals had been housed there that their scent was no longer detectable. There were high windows inset just under the eaves of the roof, and lights were on behind some of them.

"We converted the old stables into small studios for visitors, or sometimes there are families who need temporary housing," Kusini explained. She didn't seem to expect a conversation, seemed content with their respective silences.

They entered the third door from the end of the building, and Kusini stopped in the entrance hallway to open a high cabinet built into the wall, from which she pulled very inviting linens. Amaoke took them from her immediately, and shepherded Weston into a chair under one of the lamps in the main living space. The priest looked worn out, demoralized even.

Amaoke helped Kusini make the larger bed on the main floor after tossing the remaining linens up to the floor of the loft, where he planned to sleep. She showed them the bathroom and said that the kitchen was always open, if Weston should decide he wanted something later.

"I hope you know you are welcome to return with me and eat now," she said to Amaoke, and he nodded.

"I'll be along in a moment or two," he assured her, turning back to Weston.

"Are you getting sick?" Amaoke asked him, glad to see that the young priest was already removing his collar and stripping off his shirt. Weston pulled his belt, stepped out of the slippers, and lay down across the bed. Amaoke turned on the ceiling fan and cracked the window transom on the garden side.

Weston only shook his head. "Don't know. Tired. Worse than I thought," he said.

Amaoke flipped the coverlet over him, frowning at the heat Weston was radiating. "Sleep, man," he said. "Don't worry about me. I've got your back."

But if Weston heard it, it was a miracle, because he was asleep before Amaoke finished the sentence.

25

"HE'S BURNING UP," Kusini observed when he returned to the kitchen. Ambakisye had gone, but the food was still on the table.

"I know, but I don't really know what is wrong with him," Amaoke admitted, nodding his thanks as she invited him to sit once more. She sat on the bench opposite, watching him keenly.

"Dark magic, it feels like," she told him. "He's not fighting off anything physical. His battle is spiritual, within him, part of him. Do you think he would let me try to help?"

"I don't know. Ask him," Amaoke recommended after a few moments of consideration. "He's pretty open to new ideas."

"His faith is not one I think of as accepting of new ideas, as you say," she murmured. "His Church has been spying on me for a long time."

Amaoke found this both interesting and startling. "You might be surprised. Ask him about it. He's a proponent of the truth and probably knows why they do it. I get the sense that he is important to their Church, and its leader. He would tell you what he knows. It's who he is."

Kusini thought carefully on this, but said nothing other than, "Let's eat." She gestured to the food. "I apologize, but Ambakisye will not be joining us. Please, enjoy yourself. There will be time for talk later."

Amaoke ate, enjoying a home-cooked meal, knowing how rare such kindnesses would probably become in the days ahead. "Your husband is unhappy about us being here," he remarked when he had finished the food, pushing his empty plate aside, not coloring this observation with any particular emotion.

"Ambakisye is one who has paid dearly for loving me. Because of this, he does not accept change easily, especially when he recognizes its potential danger to his wife." Kusini stood up, then, and began clearing away the remaining food and dinnerware, so Amaoke joined her, ignoring her gesture that he should relax.

He hoped she would have more to say, but she was quiet a long time, as they packed up the leftovers and washed the dishes. He noticed that whenever she got close enough, the hair on his body stood on end, as if she were magnetized. She was certainly lovely, and he took a few moments to just look at her, something he'd studiously avoided in the presence of her husband. She was smart, strong, interesting. She checked every box he had.

"You lied to him," Amaoke observed, and smiled at her raised eyebrow, less a challenge than a congratulations.

"About Henri? And the linens?" she smiled. "I am quite sure that my husband knew it to be a dissemblance; it was my way of telling him that I took no danger accompanying the two of you alone."

"If you were my wife, no matter how powerful, the instinct to protect you from strange men would still be strong," Amaoke observed insightfully. "I can hardly fault him for that; he is a good man."

"You understand." She nodded. "He is one of the best. As are you," she added softly, and Amaoke was surprised to find himself completely off-balance, holding a handful of wet flatware and blushing like a youth.

She reached for the items, skillfully avoiding direct contact, accepting them from him using the towel in her hands, but he still felt a jolt of her power in the transfer.

"I notice you do not deny that danger," she said.

"I expect that we have all faced it alone," he nodded. "Now that we are together, I should think it even greater than before."

They were quiet for a time, and he helped organize her efforts to replace items to the pantry and to the refrigerator and freezer.

"Please do not hesitate to help yourself to anything you need here," Kusini repeated, sincerely wanting Amaoke to know it was in earnest. "This is a place of safety, and peacefulness."

"Andwale said there were children sleeping upstairs?" Amaoke asked, and Kusini's gaze drifted upward. She smiled.

"Those with our shared affliction have long been persecuted. It can be a death sentence to be born with albinism," she told him.

Amaoke was surprised, and saddened by this. "Many living things display these characteristics in nature. In my tradition, they are sacred, spirit animals reminding us of the higher path. It means that you are touched by the gods."

"In some twisted way, we are similarly coveted for a magic that we simply do not possess," she told him, pleased to hear that he was naturally disposed to see things as they should be, although she was not surprised at his reverence for anything that occurred as part of the circle of life. His expression betrayed something; she responded to it. "My magic only worsens the superstition, only allows those who would kill and maim us for power to point to it as proof that such things are necessary evils.

"In many ways, I am indirectly responsible for the suffering of the people who come here. Most of them are children who have been abandoned by their parents, which is actually a kindness, since they could turn them over to our witch doctors to be sacrificed, and bow to the tenets of a religion that has not changed for millennia. They take our body parts or our lives to create potions, potions believed to confer power. More than a few have already been attacked, or some of their mothers have, and they were brought here as a caution, to prevent further loss. One of the boys here was betrayed by his father, who gave away the secret location where he and his brother lived with their mother. The man did it for money, suspicion, spite.

"They represent a small percentage of the survivors. Most children cannot survive the loss of a limb," she told him, and he could hear the deep well from which her sadness flowed. Amaoke could see that she carried a burden as terrible as his, as terrible as Weston's.

26

AMAOKE SLEPT FITFULLY IN THE loft, and after a couple hours, when it was nearing dawn, he gave up the approach. He knew he needed to rest, but Weston's own restlessness was affecting him, his friend's thrashing and occasional moans betrayed his suffering from feverish dreams.

Amaoke sighed, took a deep breath, and let the wolf come forward, immediately feeling better. He padded down the steps to the main floor, sniffing Weston carefully, not liking what he scented. Too much Morningstar, and more sickness than before.

He turned around twice at the foot of the bed and lay down facing the glass doors to the garden. He'd guessed right, he felt more secure in this form, and he promptly fell asleep.

Yet it seemed only moments later that a whispered scurrying of Weston's familiars ruffling through his fur awakened him, and he came right to his feet. He was wide awake, and something moved in the darkness beyond the glass, coalescing, and he heard the deep, rich laughter of the demon he had tussled with outside the trailer in Iowa.

And she was there, although he could not make out her features well, and when she came to the glass, she pressed herself against it suggestively, scratching her nails along the trim. Behind him, Weston spoke from the bed, but it was her voice that Amaoke heard.

"Oh Beastie, beautiful Beastie, when this is over I'll take you for long walks," the demon taunted him. At the door, she got down on all fours, putting her face on a level with the wolf, and licked the glass.

Amaoke planted his feet and snarled a warning, then stepped forward, and her face changed, and she turned her gaze toward the main house and speculatively studied the upper floors, making sure he understood the threat. Then she put her middle finger into her mouth and sucked on it, punctuating her intent.

His growling alerted Weston, who was on his feet and out of the bed unnaturally quickly, holding the Redeemer aloft, saying, "*Out Beel-ze-bul, you make of yourself a harlot, stolen daughter of Eve. Lilith, I name you, you who were and were not, you shall not feed in this place which is sealed from your plagues, and all those who live here reside beyond your reach, in the embrace of the Lord our God. And He shall protect them with fiery swords, and his Angels shall be on their guard.*"

Weston's skin was covered in a sheen of sweat, but he strode right up to the doorway, and the demon writhed unnaturally there at his feet, before crawling away, crablike, scuttling sideways with her arms and legs bent opposite normal, disappearing on the lawn. As she receded into darkness, Weston seemed to lose his balance, and he reached out a strong hand and grabbed at the thick ruff of fur around Amaoke's neck as he fell, causing the wolf to yelp in surprise and pain.

Amaoke shifted back as quickly as he could, looking around for something to wear. Weston's bag was closest, so he grabbed the jeans he saw at the top and pulled on the shirt he'd discarded on the chair.

"Brother, are you doing okay?" Amaoke asked, and Weston nodded weakly, waving a hand at him, trying to catch his breath. Amaoke could see that whatever he had done to ward her off, it had drained the last of his friend's tenuous reserve.

"She tried to manipulate me," Weston didn't sound all that surprised by it, but he did sound disturbed. "We have to-"

"I know. I'll do it. You stay here. I need to make sure she didn't get to Henri, and go up to the house. I'll be back," Amaoke said, checking briefly to make sure Weston still held the cross, stopping to make sure his hand was closed firmly around it. "Can I help you back to the bed?"

"No time, make sure…" Weston's exhaustion worried him, so Amaoke propped him gently against the foot of the bed, pressing against him to indicate he should stay put, and dashed out the door.

27

HE FOUND HENRI, UNCONSCIOUS BUT breathing, in the grass under the trees, bespelled perhaps. His scent did not betray any major injury, so Amaoke shook him gently, which seemed to bring him around. At first, his eyes were focused indeterminately, off to one side, looking at nothing, and his head turned toward Amaoke before his eyes did.

That delay, indeed that movement, made Amaoke recall the three ghastly women in Iowa. And when Henri's eyes caught up with the movement of his head, he did not appear to recognize Amaoke, suddenly surging up from the ground with surprising energy and strength, aggressively trying to defend himself. Amaoke held him off, and said his name sharply a few times, finally shaking him roughly to discourage any further violence.

This seemed to clear whatever ill magic the demon had used on the man, and Amaoke was glad to see the light of reason return to Henri's eyes.

"Please, sit down, rest a bit. You were attacked. I will bring Ambakisye," Amaoke told him, helping him move to a place under a sycamore with a broad canopy, where Henri could lean against the wide, smooth trunk. Amaoke did not linger, merely left him in the dark garden, thinking he would be safe a few minutes more.

He went up to the house and let himself in through the kitchen door. He followed his nose, tracking Kusini's scent up the back stairs to the dormitory level, but could not locate her behind any of the doors, relieved that there were no signs of mischief here. He went back downstairs to the rear rooms of the house, and found her scent was strongest near the back salon, a room that smelled of textiles, paint, and fragrant wood.

He raised a hand to knock softly at the door, but it opened before he could touch it. Ambakisye stood in the shadows there, and he beckoned Amaoke inside. Amaoke could see Kusini asleep on the bed near the windows, and he felt awkward, not wanting to intrude on their intimate space.

"I don't sleep well," Ambakisye told him, considerately disrupting the discomfort of the situation. He sounded kinder, and in the moonlight, Amaoke could see that his eyes were a soft amber color now. "She rarely gets the rest she should," he indicated his wife, and then turned back to Amaoke with real concern.

"Is Weston ill? Did something happen?" he asked astutely.

Amaoke shook his head, not addressing that now. "We had a visitor. One of the Morningstar's minions. I think Henri was attacked, but he's okay. I wanted to make sure the children were safe."

Ambakisye scrambled through the door, but Amaoke put a hand on his arm, and whispered, "I was up there already. All is well."

"Thank you, Amaoke," Kusini's voice came from inside the room, and a moment later, she emerged, wrapping her abaya around her shoulders and blinking herself awake. She turned and gently kissed her husband on the shoulder to dispel the distress she saw in his eyes. "'Kisye, would you start the tea? Amaoke, could you bring Henri inside? I want to check on Weston." She spoke calmly, as though she were commenting on the weather, or what to pick up from the market, and Amaoke felt surprisingly compelled to move.

Ambakisye knocked once, softly, on a door across the hallway, and Andwale emerged momentarily, pulling on a shirt and closing the door again, very gently, behind himself. Amaoke scented a woman and two infants sleeping inside. He shuddered, thinking that perhaps it was a bad idea that they were here, given the type of attention they could garner, and the many pureflesh housed in this sanctuary.

He didn't wait for the other men, merely turned toward the door to the outside and went out to the garden to assist Henri. He saw the brightness of Kusini's abaya rippling in the dawn breeze as she turned down the path toward the stables, and hoped that Weston would be all right.

28

KUSINI COULD SEE WESTON THROUGH the doorway as she approached, lying on the floor at the foot of the bed, curled up into a ball, shivering violently. Walking through the door was like wading into a crowded party; she could feel the temperature drop as his familiars tried to jostle against her, sliding away from the noxious stimulus of her touch.

She was certain that this was the cause of the priest's illness, these beings, whatever they were, seemed bloated and overblown, like psychic ticks. She had noticed this same type of energy during her last brief encounter with the other three, at Aleta's residence, but had not recalled it such a forward presence.

Kusini realized that the collective energy of the other three beings had drawn her into that room in Aleta's house, felt that somehow the four of them were connected, and she suspected that whatever drove her power, whatever animated the beast, was working in concert with these demons, augmenting them. It was as if the Morningstar meant for them to somehow feed off each other and simultaneously drive one another to fuel its plans. If her instincts were correct, this phenomenon had the most immediate and devastating effect on Weston. He was very young, and since he had been traveling with Amaoke without apparent ill effects, she could only conclude that these familiars were responding to her power, perhaps even protectively, and she was making him ill.

She finally reached his side, feeling the heat he radiated from a few feet away. The energy these creatures were generating was eating him up. Without help, he would be lost to them, and, she worried, become some sort of devastating extension of the Morningstar. She did not have to expend much imagination to understand why he wore the monster's face, although she knew in her bones that Weston was essentially good, mostly a product of his humanity, and she could see it was making him even more vulnerable to the effects of her presence.

He sensed her there, and opened his eyes, weakly turning his head to her. His hair was soaked with sweat, and she reached down gently, using a fold of her abaya, and sponged some of the profuse perspiration from his face and neck.

"Weston, these beings here with you have grown too strong. They are drawing something from my presence, something that is endangering your life. I know that your beliefs may be very different from my beliefs, but I think I can help you find peace."

Weston retched violently and turned desperate eyes on Kusini. He was hyperventilating now, close to shock. "My familiars...have been...here...always..." he concluded. "Can't...I pray...they don't go..."

Kusini nodded. He had never lived with the possibility that there could be an alternative. How like the Morningstar, to saddle this youth with such a plague, and never leave him with the slightest belief that he could rid himself of it. Perhaps he had tried.

"May I try?" she asked softly, searching his gaze for something she needed, something like a sign of his acceptance, since he didn't know her well enough to trust.

"But I...am....an exorcist..." he protested, and she could see that he was losing the fight. He felt that if his own gifts were not enough to dispel these haunts, nothing else would, or could.

"I think you need a dose of your own medicine," she suggested. "My methods are certainly going to be different than yours, and I could fail, but I fear I must do something to help."

He nodded weakly, too spent to speak any more. She looked at the cross in his hand and gently removed it from his fingers; the energy she sensed from it was not entirely clean. He looked distressed, until she slipped her fingers into his pocket, finding his rosary, somehow knowing it was there. This, a simple expression of his faith, imbued with his belief, she pressed into his palm, pushing the silver one aside, and felt his sigh of relief.

"Pray," she told him, feeling the room get smaller and smaller, concentrating her efforts, hoping the balance would be enough but not too much, the Bantu massacre always haunting her, and letting out such energy here would be disastrous.

She let the demons come, close and curious, although her power kept them off her form, feeling them swarm him as he weakened, collapsing inward. She listened to the slow, stubborn beats of his heart, slowing further as she waited, until the seconds stretched out unnaturally long, the latent silence between beats expanding. She held her breath, then, placing her hands over his chest and whispering, saying it in hardly more than a breath as she exhaled, revoking the invitation, "*Nje, mapepo yasiyokubalika.*"

And in that space, between heartbeats, she let her thumbs cross, a fleeting touch and letting go. And the pressure was immense, pressing down on both of them, before it rushed away, pushing everything out, the demons ahead of that crackling arc of electric fire. The same power he had used to punish them she used to banish them, send them back scurrying, to the *Mjusi*, knowing it would know that she had done it. Then there was a sensation like a sonic boom, but coming from inside his body. And Weston saw the eternity stretching and stretching, and Kusini's eyes were closed, concentrating, praying in her own right, listening for it, opening her eyes with the next beat of Weston's heart, and in that moment, the demons were no more.

She gathered him close then, looking him over, relieved at what she saw in his eyes, surprise and freedom, and then, mercifully, the shock of it overwhelmed him, and he shut down, losing consciousness in the safety of her embrace. She dabbed gently at the blood that trickled from his nose, delayed a moment, and she saw that it had already stopped, nodding, knowing he was okay.

Ambakisye and Amaoke found the two of them there still, twenty minutes later, on the floor, a *Pieta* at the foot of the bed, Weston sleeping safely in Kusini's arms as her tears fell for all of them, knowing it was merely a beginning. One battle won to start the war with the Darkness.

29

BY THE TIME THE MEN had settled Henri in his quarters to sleep off the effects of the demon, the sun's rays were beginning to pierce the shadows near the outbuildings. Henri was afraid, speaking rapidly in his own language with Andwale and Ambakisye, but Amaoke was unsurprised that he did not remember what had happened, only recalled something he could not describe, and the sense he had been attacked. Andwale translated for Amaoke, saying that Henri was apologizing, worried that he had fallen asleep on duty, and had some sort of nightmare.

"No," Amaoke shook his head. "This was something else. Not his fault."

Andwale nodded and looked speculatively at Amaoke. "The priest? Or you?" he asked, not making it an accusation, merely curious.

"Possibly the fact that we are all here together, Weston, me, and Kusini."

"You two are like the Sorceress?" Andwale was less surprised than interested in such a thing. He had thought her unique.

"I don't think there is anyone like Kusini," Amaoke told him. "We have our own gifts."

Andwale said no more, merely pressed his lips together somberly, digesting the information. Perhaps too polite to ask more, since he did not seem particularly afraid. Amaoke wondered if Andwale knew the whole truth about Ambakisye.

And he was right about the numbers of pureflesh here that were vulnerable to any evil attack. The place was transformed in daylight, the noise and activity of many children on the move gave it life and dimension.

The housemother was begrudgingly welcoming, which he felt was more out of a sense of respect for her employers and ingrained good manners. Amaoke could see that their presence made her nervous, or suspicious, or perhaps both. He observed with interest her more comfortable interactions with Ambakisye, and could smell her nervousness when in the presence of Kusini. She was positioned here because of her real care for her charges, so Amaoke could hardly blame her for any reluctance to accept the presence of outsiders.

The children were another story entirely. They were used to being deferred to here, and the adults that resided here encouraged their freedom, knowing it was unlikely to be found for them outside these walls. They fully expected the newcomers to understand that they were welcome diversions from the routine, and those of schooling age were largely disappointed that they would still have to attend to their classes and miss what was happening at the house.

Those that were left behind were amply prepared to find adventures for their new adult playmates, as Amaoke and Weston quickly learned.

They were fascinated by Weston's cassock skirts, and even more bemused to find he had pants on underneath them. It was discovered very early on that beneath the folds of the garment was a useful and clever place to hide during hide-and-seek, and that the young priest was very good at keeping secrets and a straight face. This utility was only betrayed by the giggles that appeared to be coming from somewhere near Weston's legs. That and the fact that there was a finite amount of room, limiting the number of souls that could be contained there, although its capacity was certainly tested.

And Weston himself seemed to be clearer, recovered from exhaustion. The debilitating weight of worry that had attended him in recent days was apparently lessened, if not gone.

With Amaoke, his hair was the draw, and no matter the fierceness of his visage, he was shepherded away under the trees to be combed and styled. They seemed not to tire of this game, and he patiently endured these attentions, finding it supremely amusing and not the least bit annoying. The housemother worried, fussing at the children and apologizing, trying to shoo them away, but he just laughed and tried to reassure her that he wasn't bothered by them. He knew they were merely curious. Their happiness was good medicine after the long trip and the events of the night before. It was a welcome peace before the storm he was sure was coming.

30

"AREN'T YOU AFRAID AT BEDTIME?" the children inquired of Amaoke, gathering near him where he sat on the dormitory floor. Kusini watched from the shadows of the upper hallway.

"Of course not, and no one would dare bother you while I'm sleeping here," he explained, half smiling at their earnestness.

"Why not?"

"Because I'm the Big Bad Wolf," he told them, showing off his teeth, watching their eyes grow round as saucers. "I EAT monsters who scare children like you."

They shrieked with delight, collapsing onto him, all demanding he sleep in their room.

This was indeed a place where everyone was in the service of the many children who lived there. The better part of the day had been spent responding to their whims, a day in which he had been mobbed, jostled, leaned on, questioned endlessly, and scrutinized over nearly every inch of his body.

It was a blessing, as his life had been mostly devoid of children. They owned this place, which was what he suspected they needed, given what Kusini had shared with him. He was pleased to see that they were secure in the knowledge that the house was a safe place as well.

They were well-behaved generally, and had completed their small chores and schoolwork without complaint, and then had spent a great deal of time swarming the gardens and enjoying the outdoors. After dinner, they played a version of dead man's bluff (with Ambakisye ironically cast in the role of the dead man) in the salon, screaming with laughter as he splashed theatrically and chased them, while the other adults tried unsuccessfully to remind everyone that the goal was to have more water inside the pool than without.

Even Weston had been recruited, and he was at that moment reading bedtime stories to the older children in another room. Amaoke was grateful when Kusini came in, and helped him get everyone into their beds. Then she sat next to him where he leaned against the wall, the two of them quiet, listening to Weston's expressive voice from down the hall, not speaking until the children were asleep.

"I think we should consider curtailing our time here," he said to her finally, whispering in her direction, not wanting to disturb their sleeping charges, but not wanting to give up the opportunity for a few private words with her.

She sighed, softly. "I agree. Weston is better, but I don't know him well enough to understand what he feels about what I did. I had planned to give the two of you some time to rest, but it seems we must press on, get somewhere where we are less a risk to innocents."

"I'm sure he is relieved and grateful," Amaoke told her.

"A part of him surely isn't," she replied, and he searched her face in the shadows to help him better understand what she was thinking, but her golden eyes did not betray any secrets. She motioned with her fingers as if brushing something away, and he understood she had more to discuss with him later.

He must have dozed off, because it seemed only moments later she was whispering to him to come downstairs. Some time had passed, and the house was quiet.

"That was rude of me," he chuckled, when they reached the kitchen, slightly embarrassed. Ambakisye was in the adjacent room, moving a load of towels from the washer to the dryer. He nodded at them as they went by. "I didn't mean to fall asleep on you."

"You needed rest," she said kindly, inviting him to sit with her at the table. Ambakisye reappeared, joining them, and started cutting up peaches and apples that he set out for them as they talked.

"Is Weston asleep?" Amaoke asked, worried that he was neglecting his friend, fascinated at how facilely Ambakisye functioned with just one arm. Amaoke was in awe of the precision of his knifework.

"Father Weston," Ambakisye drawled, not looking up from his task, "is in the garage, interrogating the suspension of my car."

Amaoke almost laughed. "He's a trained mechanic. After school job in high school. Some sort of mechanical wunderkind. Definitely a car freak."

"He's some kind of car whisperer," Ambakisye agreed. "I tinker, but the man put me to shame. So I am exploiting his expertise so we can make the most of this road trip out to the countryside. When I am done here, I'll go give him a hand, not that he needs one."

"Ask him about his everyday car," Amaoke suggested. "But only if you are free for the next hour or two."

"I heard that," Weston, on cue, strolled into the kitchen. Aside from some tiredness about the eyes, he looked to be back to normal. "Kisye, I could use a hand if you have a moment."

"I happen to have a hand," Ambakisye told him getting to his feet and rinsing the knife in the sink. "Besides, I think these two are about to get melancholy."

Weston put a hand on Amaoke's shoulder and raised an eyebrow at Kusini. She shook her head and smiled, so Weston and Ambakisye took their leave.

Once they were out of range of hearing, Amaoke looked at Kusini, and they both said, simultaneously, "*Kisye?!*"

"I'm jealous," Amaoke teased. "Fastest bromance on record."

"Bromance?" Kusini looked confused.

"Never mind. A word I shouldn't be using. Something Weston taught me. It's a joke," he explained it poorly, but she didn't seem to mind, catching on in a moment.

"It is unusual. Although Ambakisye is definitely the 'people person' in our relationship," she said.

"Well, Weston is the 'people person' in ours," he said, and they laughed together.

31

"YOU WANT TO TELL ME what is bothering you?" Amaoke asked.

"I worry about everything," she admitted. "Right now, I am not worried about what I took away from Weston, rather I am concerned about what is left behind. I think the three of us being in proximity was potentiating the effect of his demons, but by sending them away, what effect?" She shrugged meaningfully, but said nothing more.

"You think freeing him from that burden was a mistake," Amaoke observed, and watched her carefully. Her eyes looked lost.

"I think that at times when my magic could do the most good, it is subverted by what the Morningstar intends," Kusini's tone was one of lament.

"Is that what happened with Ambakisye?" Amaoke asked, noticing that Kusini was not at all surprised by his observation.

"Perhaps, but the example I think of involves something much more sinister," she told him. "Many years ago, centuries really, I unleashed my power in anger. I was protecting something precious, but in a situation where I directed my retribution to the wrongdoer I inadvertently unleashed death upon thousands. I destroyed my enemies as well as my friends. Ridding Weston of his demons involved calling upon that kind of magic, and the Morningstar often twists my intent. My control is much better now, but it is still within me, that destruction." Amaoke listened as she relayed the story of the tragedy on the Bantu nation.

"It exists in all of us, good and bad. I have spent many years trying to be better than the beast inside me, to leave behind the ugly reality that I have been a murderer, an eater of pureflesh, the basest, simplest evil that the Morningstar could unleash upon the world. But to deny that darkness is as much a part of me as light is to fight two battles, neither is winnable. I must accept both sides of myself, beast and man together, and by doing so, I am thwarting the chaos that the Monster bred into me.

"Your power is a gift, and because it can be as destructive as it is protective, your fear of that will control you in such a way that you will perhaps hesitate to use it when it is needed most. That is what the Morningstar wants. It wants to breed that doubt within you." Amaoke observed Kusini's body language as he spoke to her, watched her surprise at his understanding, her relief at his forgiveness, her astonishment that he recognized the way in which she had for so long allowed the *Mjusi* to control her by manipulating her fear of ever fully expressing that power again.

"Whatever you did for Weston was a kindness, because I suspect his battle is the worst," Amaoke continued. "To uphold everything that is righteous, knowing that in every fiber of your being lives a wretched evil and to fight it off every day of your life must be nearly unbearable. I cannot imagine what he has suffered in a few short decades, but it may approximate what you and I have faced over long centuries.

"He is changing, constantly, something integral to him is breaking down. It started before we left home I think. Did you see him eat today? He had not one bite of food, and this is a guy who doesn't miss any meals."

"He is turning away from life," Kusini observed. "There is in him a sort of martyrdom. I fear that without those familiars to battle, he becomes more of a shell, more malleable to the Morningstar's plans."

It was Amaoke's turn to be surprised. She had voiced the concerns he had felt for weeks, but still he disagreed with her. "I think you freed him from the struggle with the demons, allowing him some space, some peace to prepare for the greater fight of his life. The Morningstar made Weston in its image, so whatever it has planned for him is worse than any of us can imagine; I think it needs him to complete whatever diabolical end it contemplates. Any reserve you bought him might make the difference. I think the fate of all of us hangs in the balance."

32

AMAOKE AND KUSINI BOTH GLANCED out the window when the quiet of the night was suddenly disturbed by a soft but determined muttering, and then two people came through the garden door in quick succession. Azuma, barefoot, dressed in a sharply tailored sleeveless grey dress with an asymmetric neckline, her expression an interesting mixture of confusion and annoyance, followed by Henri, who simply looked confused, gesturing to Kusini in apology.

"I should have known," Azuma said, with as much irritation in her tone as it also held a dawning understanding when she saw the two of them sitting there at the table. "I assume our other friend is nearby?"

Kusini stood up gracefully and smiled in welcome, but her words were not for Azuma. "It's alright, Henri. We were expecting Dr. Himura. Sooner or later."

This statement surprised Amaoke as much as it did the night guard. Henri paused, still doubtful, and looked pointedly at Azuma's bare feet, but Amaoke could see that he was too polite to protest. Without saying a word, he gave one last suspicious look at the three of them and stepped back outside. Amaoke was impressed with his fortitude; it was possible that he had already experienced many unusual happenings here and took them in stride.

Azuma stayed where she was, but gave in and began examining her surroundings with real interest, as if forgetting the shock that she was suddenly in a place she had not been minutes before. Amaoke watched her reactions of surprise and pleasure as she took in the remarkable details of the space, and suspected that he must have looked much the same the first time he had seen this room.

Seeing her in the light only confirmed his initial impressions of her from the encounter in New Orleans. She was beautiful, with a face that could belong to a teenager or a forty-year-old, depending on the intensity of her expression. At the moment, caught up in wonder at Ambakisye's magical kitchen space, she looked young and vulnerable, and her bare feet helped the illusion along nicely. Until one considered the understated power of that dress, the studied careful posture of capability, strength, and an almost regal power. Of all of them, by appearance alone, she was most obviously a god. And her eyes, at turns dangerous and knowing.

Kusini, for her part, saw something else. There was an uncanny resemblance between Azuma and Amaoke that she was seeing for the first time. The straight black hair, the striking beauty of their bone structure, the arresting eyes, one pair brown, the other blue. She doubted either of them could appreciate it as she did. But there was no more time to consider this, because at that moment, Ambakisye and Weston returned to the house, summoned, she suspected, by Henri, who would of course be under instructions from her husband to report such an irregularity.

And Weston's arrival had yet another effect on Azuma. She gasped in surprise and shied away from him, involuntarily, before she could master her reaction. This startled everyone but Weston, who understood that anyone who had been in regular contact with the Morningstar would react in this way to his appearance. Amaoke had ample time to get used to it, and Kusini had somehow expected or anticipated or known of it. Azuma's reaction was similar to Ambakisye's initial response, if more intense, which told him quite a bit. She had a relationship with the Morningstar, a complex and developed relationship.

Weston stood very still, his expression open and questioning, allowing her to process what she was seeing, although not for the first time. Their initial encounter had been very brief, it had been dark, and he had not been the greatest threat in that room requiring her focus.

But her discomfort didn't seem to subside. She was able to ignore Ambakisye entirely as she considered what she saw. Weston's reaction was one of polite deference to the situation, the way one would react when meeting a stranger, properly, for the first time, perhaps a child who is shy and unsure. Azuma could see that it was nothing like the smug, self-satisfaction that was the hallmark of her every encounter with Akenomyosei over the centuries.

Azuma opened her mouth as though she were about to speak, but then closed it again, perhaps deciding against whatever it was she had intended to say. She stepped close to him, unmindful of the soiled t-shirt, the motor oil and grime that streaked the rag he held in his dirty hands, uncaring whether her dress would be ruined.

She looked carefully at his hair, the way it curled lazily over his ears and brushed his shoulders. She considered his eyeglasses for a long time, and when she reached for them Weston remained very still, allowing her to remove them, seeming to understand what she was searching for in her examination. She set them aside, pushing them onto the nearby countertop, and took the liberty of placing her hands on his shoulders, running them over the broad muscles there, down over firm deltoids and onto his upper arms, surprised by the strength he possessed, even more surprised he allowed this.

Azuma gazed into his eyes. Brown eye to brown eye. His were human, warm, deep, perhaps amused.

"*Watashi no teki wa inai,*" he whispered softly, in a voice, that voice, so like Akenomyosei, speaking to her in her own language, and the truth of it was profound. His Japanese was comfortable and confident, some magic in this, surely, but it confirmed what she saw for herself. Not an enemy. Not the Monster, although Akenomyosei's influence was obviously at work here. It was seductive, and convincing, although it did not put to rest her questions about the assassin priest the *Akai* had described in South America, did not allay her suspicions about the Monster's double, the one most implicated in Kedron's death.

Again, as Kusini observed this half embrace, she was struck by the resemblances between Azuma and Weston as well, making it seem as if they were not strangers meeting formally for the first time, rather relatives who had not seen one another for many years.

Ambakisye took this odd happenstance in stride, as if it were commonplace to have strange half-dressed women suddenly appear in his home in the depths of the night. His offer of hospitality set them all in motion again.

"Would you like some tea?" he inquired of Azuma, not really waiting for her response. He went to the sink, and washed up carefully before setting the kettle to boil.

Azuma let go of Weston, it seemed reluctantly, and she kept glancing at him as though she were looking for something she expected to appear. He joined Ambakisye at the sink, and turned his attention to washing his own hands.

Azuma looked lost for a moment, then she approached the table, almost shyly now. Amaoke shifted a bit to make room for her on the bench next to him. "Please," he said politely, gesturing for her to join them.

She sat down, murmuring her thanks, and looked at Kusini. "Did you do this? I had just gotten settled in my office, and slipped off my heels. I didn't even get to my email. A full schedule today, as always." She did not sound angry or annoyed, merely curious, and perhaps a bit amused. Azuma appreciated the mischief of it; the *Akai* would certainly be puzzled to find her shoes, phone, and suit jacket, but not her. She suspected after what had happened in New Orleans that only *Ni* might deduce what had occurred. Her retinue would find her soon enough.

"It wasn't me," Kusini told her, noting that both Azuma and Amaoke were surprised to hear it. She unwound her headscarf and handed it across the table to Azuma, who accepted it gratefully, wrapping the cloth around her shoulders and arms like a shawl. "I think it is the result of two of us being in proximity to Weston," Kusini explained. "When that happens, I think there is a power shift that requires we are all present, like some sort of quorum. But it is centered on Weston, directly tied to his presence.

"In New Orleans, I was drawn to the three of you, and I found myself in that room, ready to fight. Such a thing had never before occurred to me."

"But you sent us away," Azuma protested, and she didn't have to say that the sensation of being in her office one moment, and finding herself here, in the garden of this house, was similar to that event, which had sent her back to her mountain home.

"That was a directed spell," Kusini replied calmly. "Active and intentioned. When I joined the three of you in New Orleans, initially I was feeling much as I assume you do now. With the exception that I was reading some distress and apprehension that I was unable to pinpoint."

Azuma nodded. "I had a sense of something, like the feeling you get when you know there is something you should be remembering but you cannot, and then I stepped out of my shoes and sat down to get some work done before the office filled up. Just as suddenly I was here." She shivered, involuntarily, and even she recognized it as her own frustration at the complete lack of control. None of them spoke. Not even Weston seemed to want to ask the obvious questions, just leaned against the counter facing the other three.

They all knew how much comfort they would have drawn just from knowing this was Kusini's magic at work. To understand that it came from elsewhere, from the darkest source, the Morningstar, made it all the more terrifying, a dangerous font of power that none of them could fully understand. And the one that it was meant for, Weston, the dark heir, had no desire to understand how to control it. To do so would be casting himself further into the abyss.

33

THE FIVE OF THEM SPENT the next several hours trying to make the most of an admittedly awkward situation, strangers feeling their way forward out of a shared necessity. Ambakisye's tea was strong, smelling of star anise and nutmeg, and Amaoke wondered if it was that or the excitement that powered their alertness. Azuma, of course, had slept through the night in another part of the world, so she probably didn't need much help staying awake.

They spoke in hushed whispers, not wanting to wake anyone above stairs, and did not deal with anything of great seriousness, knowing that this peaceful haven was not a place to bring such a discussion. They did begin to standardize the way in which they referred to the Monster, such that ongoing communication would be simplified, since it was identified to each of them in different ways. Morningstar, Mjusi, the Darkness, Akenomyosci, Satan.

And the Ungalek, which was called other names as well – Ghost, Tatsuo Tomo, Forcas, Asmodeus, Death-Bringer.

"The Monster goes by many names, as do its most powerful familiars," Weston said. "Evil must hide, and confuse, and build intricate intrigues. If there is no consensus about what it is to be called, then there is a chance that there can be no agreement about how to combat it."

"And are we really fighting one thing?" Azuma asked. "In my tradition, it is said to be a Dragon, like myself, although I have never seen it take that form."

"We are fighting everything, and nothing," Weston said wisely, and followed this profound observation with an explanation. "Evil is a part of the human condition, a legacy of sin. The confusion the Morningstar creates is meant to make it easier to believe that there is no larger entity that drives such a thing, to make it simpler for the deniers. All great evil leaves few witnesses to its actuality. Its real power lies in this division, this simplified deceit.

"Whatever they were before, what my tradition calls angels, they had names. But those names were taken from them so they could no longer impersonate the divine. Those names had power. Islamists still use some of them in their sacred texts and in their mythology, they call it Azazel, because the Morningstar was 'God's dear one.' But after the fall, the Monster was called something else, Iblis, to denote that it was now cast out, no longer holy, no longer able to call itself Azazel.

"But even within the churches of the Judeo-Christian-Islamic tradition, there is no canonical agreement about these names, which contributes to the confusion, and furthers the Morningstar's mischief. The power and truth of this knowledge has been largely ignored, changed by oral tradition, or lost entirely. There is a purpose to it."

"I was always taught that all beings are both good and evil, and the choices that are made are what balance us. Choose to do that which honors others, and nature, and you defeat the Spirit of disease, suffering, disaster. That if the balance was not maintained, it opened the world for malign spirits, such as the Ungalek, to cross over and do mischief." Amaoke nodded to Weston, who smiled. They had spent many hours noting the similarities in their worldviews.

"Our tradition knows evil as interference, an interference as old as creation. When Ngai created the world he intended immortality for the people he populated upon the earth, because he loved them, because they were created in his glorious image. But the *Mjusi* gave the people a different message, told them of their certain deaths, created doubts, cemented a belief that they would die, and this belief was so strong that they lost the message of the gift that Ngai wanted for them. The Ghost and the Darkness are the purveyors of bad dreams, omens of destruction and death, responsible for the evil that influences and lives in men and women to this day, encouraging suspicion and superstition to drive them, to rule them over reason." Kusini explained the prevailing religion of her tradition, and unsurprisingly, there were commonalities aplenty.

Only Azuma appeared uncomfortable with all of this, although she listened no less carefully than the others. When she spoke, what she said betrayed more than she might have wanted, loneliness, despair, frustration, and anger. "You all speak of gods as if you know of some promise of redemption. I only know of the monsters that begat me. And the others abandoned the world so long ago that they have forgotten their own names."

"Redemption only requires leaving the mind open to possibility," Ambakisye's soft voice surprised everyone but his wife, who smiled. "That possibility is called by many names, be it faith, or hope, even love. In our Muslim tradition, we have a saying. *Insha'Allah.* As God wills it.

"This is not merely a wish, as those with more secular interests might see it, or those outside of the faith. This is a reminder that when speaking of the future, we must recognize that many things are outside of our control, and possibility is a miracle that belongs only to God. This is one of the most common phrases in our faith, because the recognition of this tenet of belief is no mere suggestion. Instead, the *Quran* commands us to use it, as a way of signaling our obedience to faith. All is in God's hands and will proceed as God wills." Ambakisye concluded this short speech, and Kusini squeezed his hand gently where she held it in her lap. She had never heard him recognize the legacy of his father's religion in this way, and most of his expressions of faith were not so directed, adopting her habit of referring to Ngai, a syncretism of his own. It was a practical concession that he had made long ago, and she suspected it helped him deflect some of the shame that had complicated his early years in this house.

Into the silence that followed, Ambakisye spoke once more. "Come, my friends, it is time for rest and reflection. Sleep well, the first leg of our journey begins at sunset."

Azuma shrugged off the offer to equip separate sleeping quarters for her, suggesting instead that she stay with Weston and Amaoke. "I think we will all feel more secure that way," she said, acknowledging that she was unknown to them, and that trust would have to be earned. She didn't want them to have to maneuver unnecessarily with any endeavor to monitor her actions. She suspected Kusini knew she was a blood-drinker, and Azuma was aware of the many people asleep elsewhere in the house, guessing this was some sort of refuge.

So she accompanied Weston and Amaoke out to the guest accommodations they shared, immediately stretching out on the bed when they arrived, not bothering to have a discussion about sleeping arrangements. She pulled Kusini's voluminous scarf up around her head and shoulders and promptly fell asleep, calling on the soldier she had been, pragmatic enough to sleep whenever she could.

Weston and Amaoke exchanged looks of amusement, and Amaoke whispered, "Take the loft." He knew Weston's vows did not countenance having a woman next to him in the bed, but Amaoke was under no such constraint. He stretched out atop the coverlet on the other side of the bed and was asleep before Weston finished scaling the ladder to seek his own rest.

34

IT WAS LATE AFTERNOON WHEN Amaoke awoke, startled for a moment by the young woman reclining next to him on the coverlet, watching him intently. Azuma smiled at him indulgently, and at first he suspected it was sympathy for the process of awakening, or not recalling where he was in those initial moments of consciousness. Then he realized that she was awaiting his reaction to the fact that she was wearing his pants.

Apparently she had raided his bag, finding a spare pair of canvas cargo pants and requisitioning them as her own. She'd removed her dress, and had worn some sort of camisole underneath it that was perfectly serviceable as a top in this warm climate. Kusini's scarf was still draped loosely around her neck and shoulders. She looked lovely and well-rested.

"I hope you don't mind," she said, seeing that he'd noticed what she was wearing. Clearly, boundaries were thin to nonexistent with her, but Amaoke wasn't bothered. The wolf had a similar spare practical nature, so he couldn't really criticize.

"They look good on you," he pronounced, sitting up and turning away from her, putting his feet on the floor. "You find anything else of interest in there?"

"Should I have?" Azuma asked with mock innocence. "Lucky for you, your secrets are safe, since you keep your pants near the top."

"Thank goodness. A lazy thief," he laughed, and she did too.

"I prefer the term economical," she protested with good humor.

"Children, don't fight," Weston's voice floated down from the loft, still thick with sleep. His face appeared above them, and he blinked, strangely owl-like without his spectacles. He stumbled down the ladder, his hair in spectacular disarray.

"That hair. I am jealous," Azuma teased.

Weston merely made the sign of the cross in her direction and continued on to the bathroom.

They shared a simple meal of flatbread and boiled eggs with tea and fruit up at the house, and Amaoke was pleased to see that Weston was eating better than he had been. Ambakisye shared his goat meat with Amaoke, not terribly surprised to find that its rawness was part of the appeal to his new friend.

Ambakisye scared up a pair of sunglasses for Azuma, and Kusini brought sandals that fit her perfectly. When Azuma attempted to return her scarf, Kusini pressed it back into her hands. "You'll need some cover for the sun out there on the road, and after dark it can be chilly, especially in the open car."

"You're not coming with us?" Azuma asked her.

"In my way," Kusini reassured her. "I don't travel by motorcar. It…complicates things. I will see you all in a couple days." She turned to Ambakisye. "You'll make it to Eyasi tonight?"

"That's my goal. The roads should be dry enough. We can get water at the wash and continue on to the plantation tomorrow. Andwale should reach our hut by noon." The others had turned their attention to completing the loading of the Scout, so Ambakisye pulled his wife into the alcove off the kitchen and kissed her thoroughly. "Have a care, *mpenzi*." His fingers lingered at the nape of her neck, and his amber eyes were expressive of his love.

She traced his mouth with her fingers. "And you, my love. Thank Mwana'jua for her hospitality."

"I will do," he promised, kissing her again, making her serious expression more mirthful.

"Go," she whispered. "Go, before I decide I cannot let you go."

He turned away then, without saying more, and took his leave of her. She stood there in the alcove for a long time, not turning to other tasks until long after she heard the vehicle turn out of the drive, long after she could no longer hear the cacophony of the gears and the motor, long after the sun was gone.

35

AMAOKE WAS RELIEVED WHEN THEY finally turned in at an inconspicuous gap in the vegetation, hoping they were closing in on their destination; he was suffering from some serious fanny fatigue, between the Scout's dubious suspension and the rugged terrain they called a road. He had thought on more than one occasion during this trip that he would have gladly endured more of the Charger's jet-fueled life-threatening mode of transport if this was the alternative.

He would have preferred to stay with Kusini, who refused to get into a motorized vehicle, but he knew that the thought of Amaoke alone with his wife would probably have pushed Ambakisye over the edge. So he had reluctantly agreed to travel this way. Ambakisye's driving was marginally less suicidal than Weston's, not that it made the trip any less uncomfortable. He shuddered to think what the man could accomplish on a four-lane highway.

The initial part of the trip had been shorter, and the roads had been better maintained. The first night they had stopped off at a bend in the road, followed an old path that Amaoke had seen was a runoff of some sort, an old wash from an ancient creek bed. Hidden between two hills was a small clearing that contained a large round hut next to a long shed that housed chickens, goats, and a makeshift workshop.

Amaoke had helped Ambakisye by gathering water from the freshwater reservoir further down the hill, since he knew the animals would be unsettled by his presence. They weren't happy about Azuma either, so she followed Ambakisye's instructions to get the cooking fire going while he and Weston tended to the livestock. Then she swapped out their empty petrol cans for fresh fuel cans she found in the workshop and strapped these onto the back of the Scout for the next leg of their journey.

None of them had had much to say to one another, they were all tired and lost in their own thoughts, until a small blue bird had arrived, perching on Ambakisye's shoulder and chattering jealously at the other three.

So he had introduced them to little Yabluu, explaining how she was a bit of a mascot, or a spoiled child, depending on your perspective. It was the first insight that any of the others had into the depth of Ambakisye's kind nature. Amaoke knew that birds were smart and ruthless; for one to trust a human being was extraordinary and took a great deal of time and attention. For a bird to knowingly perch on the shoulder of any unnatural creature said quite a lot about the man Ambakisye had been.

They all slept well, and woke to warmth and sunshine. Around midday, Andwale had arrived in an ancient Toyota pickup with his wife, Amivi, and their infant twins. He and Ambakisye took a short walk away from the group for a few minutes of privacy, and Azuma conveniently disappeared over the hill, so Weston and Amaoke each took charge of a baby and helped the young mother get herself and her children settled inside the hut.

Then it was time to climb back into the Scout and head onward.

Ambakisye, Weston, and Azuma all took turns at the wheel on that second day, and if Amaoke hadn't known better he might have assumed that a prerequisite to a driving license was some sort of reckless abandon. He could not decide which of the three was least dangerous.

It wasn't that he didn't have some idea what traveling through wilderness was like; it was that the dry heat and vast expanses were so different from what he knew in his faraway home. He did love seeing all kinds of wildlife, strange and beautiful and fantastic. Amaoke could appreciate these things, knew that for many, himself included, it was a once in a lifetime experience. But the repeated jarring of his person was a real test, for the wolf's patience, if not his own.

"Just up the road here," Ambakisye gestured, as if they were close, as if he could read Amaoke's thoughts.

"Where? In Kenya?" Amaoke growled, and felt Weston's hands on his shoulders, squeezing in reassurance, sensing his friend's impatience and his distress. He passed Amaoke some beef jerky from his backpack.

"Ignore him," Weston told Ambakisye. "He's not a fan of car travel."

"It's only another forty minutes or so," Ambakisye promised, trying not to laugh at the expression this bit of information caused Amaoke to make. He indicated the hills in the distance.

"Those are all coffee plants, there, beyond the trees. It just takes us a bit to get to the house as it is on the other side of the farm, you see."

"I thought coffee was grown best at altitude," Amaoke said, truly curious and desperate for any distraction.

"Well, there are many different places it can be grown," Ambakisye explained. "There are coffee farms outside Arusha, near Kilimanjaro, but in general, equatorial coffee plants can grow in plains areas, and if they get enough water during the rainy season, these low-altitude plants produce even more fruit and can be harvested year-round.

"Did you know that coffee is made from the bean, or the seed of the fruits, which are called cherries?" Ambakisye just kept on, entirely serious, warming to the subject, which fascinated Amaoke and the others, making at least one of them forget, for a time, how sore his backside was getting.

36

A fierce-looking, albeit tiny woman awaited them when they pulled into the clearing near the house. She was seated in a chair on the veranda, but stood up when the Scout came to a stop.
She reminded Amaoke of some of the elders of his own nation, her face kissed by sun, wind, and time.

He was first out of the vehicle, and she met him at the steps, her fierceness disappearing with her eyes among the many folds of her face when she smiled. That smile was a welcoming thing, like sunshine. From her perch at the top, she was almost eye to eye with Amaoke where he stood at the bottom, and she examined him carefully.

"This one comes with friendship," she remarked, perhaps to him, perhaps to Ambakisye, perhaps to no one at all. "I can see it."

Ambakisye was behind him then, and Amaoke sidestepped to let him go up first. The woman's smile came again, and this time it stayed. She reached up and up to embrace him, taking his measure, patting his sides when he let go. "And how is my favorite today?"

Ambakisye shook his head in resignation, knowing it would do little good to try to disagree with her. "Good day to you, Miss Mwana'jua," he greeted her warmly. "Surely there is one better than I in your heart?"

"Occasionally," she admitted. "And when they are, I tell them so," she assured him with a mischievous smile.

Ambakisye turned to introduce the others, and they were waved inside, where it was cooler. She gave them cold drinks with lemon and fermented ginger that were quite refreshing, and looked at each of them in turn with curiosity. She took to Weston immediately, and perhaps sensed that Azuma was far from home, because she teased her, saying, "Try to be less pretty while you're here. Everyone is used to me being the best-looking woman on this farm."

This must have caught Azuma off her guard, because she flushed deeply, but understood it to be said in jest.

"Thank you for always extending your hospitality so graciously." Ambakisye gave voice to his gratitude. They could all see it was sincere.

"Ridiculous," she retorted, getting up and making her way to the back door, where she grasped a machete that was leaning near the screen. "I know you'll earn your keep." Then she gave them a wink and went out to the back.

"That's our cue," Ambakisye told them, standing up and stretching carefully. "If she's working, everyone else should be, too. One hundred years old and she does more in a morning than I do in a week." He looked critically at Azuma, noting her exhaustion. "Not you, though. Traveler's disease is only cured by sleep."

He showed each of them where they would be staying, and the men left Azuma to rest. Weston carefully folded his cassock and put it away, trading his black clothes for jeans and a t-shirt, and then the three of them went out the back door. The roastery was beyond the clearing, and they could hear Mwana'jua talking with the men and women inside the open structure. It was already hot, but the entire yard shimmered with the heat from the endless fire, and the aroma of roasting coffee was enticing. Amaoke had always liked the sharp, strong smell of coffee, finding it generally pleasant, although it was not a beverage he drank.

He gathered his hair over one shoulder, braiding it quickly in a single plait as they crossed the courtyard. Ambakisye walked straight down the center of the building and passed out on the other side, Weston following, but before Amaoke could catch up he got distracted by the workings of the coffee roasting process, stopping to watch for several minutes. Mwana'jua noticed his fascination, and ambled up next to him, pressing several small warm beans into his palm. He looked at her questioningly, so she plucked one of them back and popped it into her mouth, chewing enthusiastically. She gestured to him to try it.

He must have hesitated a moment too long, which earned him a look of displeasure, as if she were saying, *was I wrong about you?* So he put the remaining beans in his mouth and ate them.

He was pleasantly surprised at the taste. It was smoky, and rich, the beans disintegrating in his mouth, nutlike and strong. He nodded, smiling down at her, so she dropped another handful into his pocket, then patted his arm, sending him along after the others.

Amaoke found Ambakisye and Weston by following a familiar sound, that of axes rhythmically splitting wood. He discovered them momentarily, watching Ambakisye wielding the axe one-handed, not an easy task, as Amaoke knew, having done it once himself. Weston was making a go of it as well, but Amaoke could see that he had never done it before, and he was struggling a bit. Part of his difficulty was the natural learning curve of the task, and part of it was his inexpert stance and poor grip on the implement.

Amaoke stepped in behind him, out of harm's way, and tapped him on the shoulder. Weston stopped, and turned to look at him, adjusting his eyeglasses on his nose. Without a word, Amaoke demonstrated grip on the handle, and adjusted the position of Weston's hands. "Choke up on it a bit; your arms are long, and you have to get used to the weight when you swing it. Stand like this." He took the axe and showed Weston how to set his feet and angle his torso to make things easier. "And it doesn't require a great deal of force. I know you are strong, just get the axe head in the air and let its weight and gravity do the work. You know what? Just watch me for a few strokes so you can see what I mean."

Amaoke went to the wall of the shed and scrutinized the available tools that hung neatly under the eaves. He selected one of the axes, the most old-fashioned he could see, and set up station, positioning his first log economically and then gripping the axe carefully. He stepped forward, demonstrating stance once more for Weston's benefit, and swung, gracefully, emphasizing the moment of inertia at the top of the swing, before the axe head came down with a soft *whump*, splitting the wood. He set his next log, repeating the action, and then once more, seeing Weston nod and turn to his own task, doing better immediately.

Amaoke lost himself in the work, glad to be moving, happy to be useful. He was tired of all the waiting, still not entirely clear about why Weston's church had sent him to find Kusini, wanting better answers himself, as she did. Did the church have some use for her power? These concerns bothered him.

He could certainly see that the ways in which she used her power and her feelings about the Morningstar aligned with theirs, and Amaoke hoped that his friend's major motivation in coming to her was to further their work toward thwarting the Monster's evil. And as much as he was growing to like Ambakisye, his knowledge of what he was created another mystery that worried Amaoke. And Azuma was yet another riddle, another piece of the puzzle. He knew that she took another form, as he did, but he did not understand the significance of it, and had spent less time considering that event in Aleta's bedroom than he should have. If Kusini was right, something about Weston forced the four of them together, some sort of new magic that even Weston had been ignorant about, and the Morningstar definitely had a hand in it.

37

THEY WORKED NEARLY CONTINUOUSLY FOR the next few hours, and Amaoke was unsurprised that so much wood was needed to keep the roastery running. There seemed to be plenty of hands willing to help, and it was probably a nice change of pace to have extra workers around.

The fires inside were banked as sundown approached, the farmers headed home to their families, and by the time Amaoke, Weston, and Ambakisye had refilled and stacked the split wood in the attached shed and put their axes away, the sun was a red ball sliding over the edge of the world and out of sight. They retraced their steps back up to the main house, where lights were already burning in the kitchen.

Kusini had arrived, and she was chopping potatoes and turnips at the butcher block while Azuma and Mwana'jua shelled peas at the table.

"For goodness sake, 'Sini-ma, you don't have to cook." Ambakisye left his shoes on the porch outside the door and Weston and Amaoke did the same. He embraced his wife, smiling when she didn't let go right away, ignoring, as always, his current state of filthiness from the heat and the work.

"You mean you don't want me to," Kusini replied with a smile of amusement, indicating that she didn't mind the slight.

"Why not?" Azuma asked, sensing there was a story to be told. "Is there something wrong with her cooking?" She sounded ready to defend the other woman, just on principle.

"Not necessarily. It will keep you alive," Ambakisye allowed.

"Isn't that the purpose of food?" Amaoke asked, not entirely following.

Ambakisye rolled his eyes. "Another philistine. Yes, staying alive is a good thing. But *living* suggests you are allowed to get some enjoyment from the experience, not just the meanest survival."

Weston laughed at Ambakisye's word choice and explained it to Azuma and Amaoke.

"I have this stew that I make from root vegetables and meat," Kusini told them. "It was something easy for me to make in the bush, while traveling. What I ate with my father out on the Maasai mara when I was growing up. I made it for 'Kisye a long time ago. He didn't complain about it, but essentially took over the cooking in the relationship."

"He ate it though," Azuma observed, something inexplicable and mischievous in her expression.

"He did," Kusini admitted. "But I think he was too polite to do otherwise."

"Politeness probably had little to do with it," Azuma shook her head.

Kusini looked slightly lost, and glanced at Ambakisye but could glean no clarity from his expression either.

"Was this *before* the two of you got together, formally?" Azuma linked her fingers together, and Amaoke wasn't sure who blushed the most, himself, Kusini, or Weston.

Mwana'jua came to Kusini's rescue. "She means he ate it because he didn't want to ruin his chance at getting your *special favors*." She didn't even look up from her bowl of peas, simply said it in the same tone of voice she might use to ask someone to pass her the salt. The collective blushing worsened, poor Kusini's cheeks were on fire.

"Sometimes I *am* polite," Ambakisye argued. "I need a shower, and then *I* will cook. Don't listen to them, *mpenzi*."

Weston and Amaoke joined in to help with food preparation, then took turns getting cleaned up before supper once Ambakisye returned to start the meal. Afterward, Mwana'jua excused herself, perhaps understanding that the others were waiting to begin any serious discussion until she left.

"Well, since your arrival cut into my afternoon nap, I'll just be off to bed early," she pronounced, although by Amaoke's reckoning, it was nearing midnight. He could hear the songs of the night insects through the screen door, a sound that he considered one of nature's most beautiful symphonies.

The heat was still oppressive, it hadn't cooled off during the night as it had previously, and the breeze only pushed the hot air around. From the smell of it, it was moving ahead of a storm.

Weston and Azuma cleared the table and started on the dishes, so the other three joined them. They created a sort of assembly line of wash, rinse, dry, and put away that made short work of the task. No one spoke. It was understandably awkward.

"Can *you* cook?" Azuma suddenly asked Amaoke, trying to break the ice.

"I do cook," he replied, "but I am sure what I am capable of falls squarely in the category of survival. I've kept myself alive."

She laughed. "I can't cook at all. I might be able to keep myself alive, I have never tried. I can warm up a mean sake."

Weston frowned. "I *am* better at eating than cooking. I *do* know how, but even though I had some great teachers, I never improved much. I can do fajitas, but the woman who taught me how to make them would probably be mortified with the results."

"I don't understand," Ambakisye spoke up. "What's the point?"

"Besides the obvious defense of your lovely wife and her shortcomings in this area, as you see it?" Azuma asked, smiling to show she meant no harm. "Does it strike any of you that the four of us have some uncanny similarities, down to the smallest particulars of our lives? The cooking detail is interesting, but in my case doesn't tell the whole story, because whether I can cook or not is irrelevant, because the mainstay of my diet does not require me to do so. And I would guess Amaoke could also survive very well without cooking."

"I'm confused, and perhaps I should ask more questions," Amaoke replied. "How is it that you know anything about me?"

"I don't, not really, not the details of who you are. I am, however, privy to the details of what you are, and that is where it gets complicated. My company was hired by you, through the offices of your delightful Dr. Madison, to evaluate your DNA." She held very still, watching him react to this news, knowing he was processing the entire encounter once again, sure he was considering all that he had experienced, and all that he knew.

"But that process should have been random," Amaoke shook his head, thinking about the way that Aleta had discovered the best laboratory to use for the assay, and ignoring for the moment Azuma's comment about Aleta.

"You voluntarily submitted your DNA for evaluation?!" Weston turned to Amaoke with an incredulous expression.

"A calculated risk, my friend. After much discussion and very good advice from Aleta." Amaoke put his hand on Weston's arm, in a gesture for calm. Even Kusini was surprised.

"I have worked diligently to make sure that such requests, when made, particularly those flagged for privacy, or those in which the physician has a special concern regarding results, are referred to us. I have contacts in many countries, and we have government contracts as well. I have used my influence in the field to position my company to find any anomalies. But for all the millions of similar requests we have received, only yours had an extranormal finding."

"But you sent someone to personally carry the specimen," Amaoke protested. "I assume the gentleman who collected it works for you?"

"Yes. We came up with an algorithm to try to anticipate those requests that had the highest likelihood of an extraordinary result, and for those few specimens, I sent the Collector to take possession of them. High priority specimens, with certain criteria. There were only a handful of them over the years, and only yours, as I said, had an unexpected finding," she explained.

"The Collector?" Amaoke repeated, thinking she was being purposely vague.

"His name has nothing to do with the service he provided for me in your instance," she replied with a small smile. "He is called other things, of course, but that is the name we use when referring to him. You will meet him again. He is regretful that the animosity shown in your encounter could not be avoided."

"What guided you in creating the algorithm, Azuma?" Kusini asked, knowing the answer but prompting the other woman as to how she could help Amaoke understand.

"The results of my own genetic assay," Azuma replied, looking gratefully at Kusini for leading her there.

"I'm lost," Weston spoke up suddenly. "I know about Amaoke, but I don't know what I should about you. And you mentioned that something is special about your diet? We've all been eating the same food for two days."

"Blood," Kusini told them, needing Azuma to know that she was aware of the particulars of the Dragon's condition. "She must have human blood to survive. So perhaps we could argue about whom the Monster burdened the most, but we are all afflicted in devastating ways."

"Human blood?" Weston's hand went involuntarily to the cross around his neck.

"I could drink yours," Azuma admitted, "but it would poorly sustain me. I need the blood of the pureflesh, specifically. I have survived on the blood of my priests, those of a sect dedicated to Akenomyosei, created to worship the Dragon, but even this is not entirely ideal. I must have the blood of the pureflesh, whether that of the evildoer, or from a mortal lover who consents to trade blood for pleasure. My feeding need not be unpleasant, nor does it kill them."

"What happens if you do not get it?" Weston asked wisely, although they could all guess the answer.

"Without a blood meal, I succumb to my basest appetites, and return to a state of being that I prefer to avoid, the Dragon without control. It was best that we left the house in Dodoma, and you may have noticed that I avoided contact with Andwale and Amivi's family at the hut. No matter how well-fed I may be, the blood of children is irresistible, and I avoid them at all costs. Their blood calls to me, and it creates an unnaturally strong temptation, one to which I am proud to say I have never succumbed, if I can be proud of anything." Azuma seemed to understand the enormity of what she was admitting to them.

"That's why you chose to sleep in our quarters," Weston whispered, horrified at the implication but admiring of the precaution she had taken. "Avoid temptation…"

"…and ensure restraint." Azuma finished the thought.

38

"YOU DON'T SEE IT, DO you? You are all obliquely referenced by your own mythology," Azuma looked pointedly at Weston. "Word made flesh, right? That would be you."

She turned her attention to Kusini and then to Ambakisye in turn. "Both of you, in the image of your god, the Great Ngai, Possessor of Whiteness, and Olapa, the holy couple, a literal manifestation.

"And I, the Dragon, representative of the marriage of male and female, as in all the old gods of Japan. Amaoke, the Guardian, the Beast, in touch with nature and humanity alike in the best traditions of his people. Constructs all of us. Engineered to represent the magic of each of our beliefs, so that we would buy in to the lie.

"The Morningstar thought he'd failed with you two," Azuma nodded at Amaoke and Kusini. "He created me and bound me in duality with the Death-Bringer to ensure a lasting power."

"How do you know this?" Kusini inquired softly.

"The Monster was bold enough to complain of it. After the ascendance of Weston, the Dragon was to intervene if the two of you didn't fall in line with its plans. Because whatever else it has in store for us, it needs all four of us in order to come through."

The room was silent as this revelation was absorbed, but Azuma did not wait to see if the others were keeping up.

"But I broke faith with the Morningstar when I cracked the code to free myself from that forced duality," she continued.

"Wait a minute," Amaoke held up a hand, and Azuma found it particularly endearing. It was simply a gesture, but it reminded her of the politesse of her graduate students. "So are you saying that now the Morningstar cannot control you?"

"No." Azuma's smile was both sad and beautiful, resigned, vulnerable in a way that none of them had witnessed about her before. "Akenomyosei put a failsafe in me that he didn't think to put into the two of you that came before me.

"My heart is not a normal heart. At least not for a human. It has a decaying rhythm, one that your Dr. Madison recognized, much to her distress," Azuma told them, looking at Amaoke. "The Morningstar promised to make me whole once the ascendance was achieved."

"But what if there was a miscalculation?" Weston protested. "And you died, or were vulnerable to assault?"

"That's just it. I *am* vulnerable to assault. There are a multitude of martial arts maneuvers – really, something as simple as a precordial blow could interrupt the rhythm and kill me outright.

"Which explains the *Akai* and why their loyalty is so important. There are twelve of them, spies but protectors alike, who hate having anyone between myself and them. They are like a living phalanx, a shield of bodies between me and the world," Azuma revealed, breaking one of her cardinal rules of alerting another to a weakness, in the interest of generating trust, because of the four, she knew she was a target of their collective suspicion, and she understood the reasons for it.

"It is also why my dear Akenomyosei hates the Collector so much. I had a vision, in the temple, as a child, during a time of torture with Tatsuo Tomo. More like a recurring dream, if you will. A man, pierced by the rays of the sun, who spoke wisdom to me, who saw what I saw, shared the same heart.

"When I found the Collector, he was impaled on bamboo which was one kind of piercing, and when you consider his forced birth at the hands of my grandfather and my father. . . well…"

"Meaning that his life was badly affected by their actions or injured, and because piercing can also be a proxy for phallic intrusions, his birth was the insult of the Rising Sun," Weston mused.

Azuma nodded. "Yes. You understand. At any rate, I knew him to be my own salvation, so I did not sacrifice him as the Morningstar would have preferred because I had seen him take a needed role in my future life.

"I had no living parent, no invested caregiver during my childhood. While he is only five human years older than I, he has yet been a mentor of inestimable value to me. If I am honest, he has been the only real family I have ever known.

"And the three of you are all stronger and more powerful than I was led to believe. This is because the Morningstar wanted me to think I could defeat all of you, that I was somehow *special.*

"And you are all poor," Azuma observed, and then amended herself, looking directly at Amaoke. "Well, not you, not exactly. But your money has accumulated over centuries, and you live very humbly."

"So perhaps I should hit him up for a donation to the Church." Weston's tone was surprisingly bitter and sarcastic, and Azuma recoiled slightly. "And you are exceedingly wealthy," he observed, not bothering to hide his impatience with the superficial, not grasping where the conversation was headed. "Why is that, I wonder?"

"I suspect it is because I conformed to its desires for so long," she replied, saying aloud what each of them had already privately guessed. "I built my corporate empire long before I first actively defied the Morningstar. My rebellion started very recently."

"But I still want to know the significance of having us all together," Amaoke said suddenly.

"While it is very possible that our alliance conforms to something the Morningstar wants, I would like to believe that each of us, in our own way, has reasons to attempt to oppose it," Azuma said frankly. "Whatever mythology you ascribe to, there is a place, in the deserts of Iraq, that the Israelis discovered based on information inadvertently provided by an American intelligence officer."

"Inadvertently?" Amaoke asked, thinking it was unusual for a government official to accidentally reveal something clandestine.

"The Americans did not understand the significance of what they were sharing, but it was a place that the Israelis suspected was something else, a marker, for a place of legend in their faith. They call it *makom galut*," Azuma replied.

"The Place of the Fallen," Weston said. "It's importance lies in the aftermath of the creation story, in that there were a group of angels who rebelled against God, angry that He put mankind before them in importance. You remember what I told you about Azazel? There was a war, in Heaven, and the rebel angels and their leader were cast out, and fell to Earth, lighting the dawn in their descent, and their impact created a burning pit. There has been argument among many faiths about the event, and whether it was associated with a physical location. Finding such a place could prove significant on many fronts, canonical, archeological, and historical.

"It's why the Monster is referred to as the Morningstar. Lucifer means the Lightbearer, and some ancients believed that it was this event that brought unholy fire to humankind."

"The Israelis sent a crew to investigate the site, and what they found was a large central pit, surrounded by a spiral staircase, that narrowed in diameter the deeper they excavated, like an inverted shrine. Between the oubliette at the center and the outer stairwell are complicated catacombs, like something out of M.C. Escher." Azuma's voice wavered slightly, and it served to punctuate the information she was giving them.

Amaoke shivered, remembering his time of torture in the pit at the hands of the *Ungalek* and the Morningstar. He wondered if it could be the same place.

"What else did they find?" Weston was curious, and of two minds about it. He was sincerely interested in the answer for personal reasons, but also wondered if the Vatican knew of the discovery and had not told him about it.

"I have the complete files on the dig, but what they found was less important than the outcome of their intrusion. The excavation was pretty extensive, and they uncovered a great deal of interest. The team never got the chance to report any findings or complete the excavation, because they were slaughtered at the site, both the scientists and the special forces detail that the Israeli Defense Force provided them for security. It was Forcas' handiwork. The Death-Bringer leaving a message, but I don't think the message was for the Israelis. Partly, the message was for the four of us," Azuma told them. "I think the Morningstar is tied to that place, and that it wants to get us there, for whatever it has planned for us. What if we could work together to trap it there, and destroy it?"

"And how are we to know that we can trust you?" Ambakisye barely reined in his contempt. "That you are not just a clever decoy, here to lead us where the Monster wants you to take us?"

"You must not make any hasty decisions," Azuma told him. "One way or the other. I only suggest that we share what we know, and once you have all of the information, you will decide. I do not ask for your trust; it is not a gift to be bestowed like a courtesy. It is something that must be earned, not as an isolated event, but in an ongoing fashion, cultivated like the rarest of blooms.

"Just as you must look upon that fair face," she nodded at Weston and continued, "knowing that it has been the face of the Other but understanding that Weston is a singular being. If we judge him on his appearance, and mistrust him, when his actions prove him faithful, we do him, and ourselves, a grave disservice."

"And how do we know that isn't exactly what the Morningstar wants?!" Ambakisye rejoined. Amaoke did not envy this man his position here. While not one of them, he was exceptional, and Amaoke could see he still wanted to protect his wife from all of this. Amaoke doubted she was one who needed protection, but in many unsubtle ways Kusini deferred to her husband. He admired their bond, and suspected that Ambakisye involved himself in the world in ways that his wife did not, perhaps could not, given her extraordinary abilities.

"You want us to go blindly into an underground maze, knowing there are *two* of them?!" Ambakisye continued, gesturing at Weston. "I like the guy fine, but what if I come upon him, and it is the other one? Then what? And not just me, we will all have to guard against meeting a supposed friend and trusting that we are not exposing our backs to the Devil himself."

"I have a suggestion," Amaoke's quiet voice carried among them because he said so little. He glanced at Weston with a roguish smile, wanting to break up the mounting tension. "If you are in doubt, go for the groin first."

Weston shook his head, amused, and pushed his hands through his curls with a resigned sigh.

"I thought you were his friend," Ambakisye protested, confused about the unspoken agreement that had passed between the other two men.

"He is right. The Morningstar has no gender," Kusini looked at Amaoke with admiration and a hint of mischievous humor in her golden eyes.

"It's the safest option," Weston grumbled, but good-naturedly. "I'm willing to take one for the team if I have to. It's not just a good cause, Ambakisye. It's the ultimate cause. Whatever it takes to prevail."

"I guess I should be thankful that *I* don't have a doppelganger." And for the first time since they had met him, Ambakisye genuinely smiled. That smile showed who he really was, fun-loving, open, kind, and vulnerable, and Amaoke suspected that was why it had taken so long for him to share it. It was a smile that brought people together, movie-star and politician wattage, without any of the superficiality or insincerity of either. The smile of a man who is capable of great love. His wife certainly did not seem to be able to take her eyes from it.

39

"PERHAPS I CAN MAKE IT easier," Azuma suggested, and even she looked amused. "At the very least, less painful. But to do that, to give you all of the information I have collected, I ask that you accompany me to my home. I think that there you will be able to see the big picture, and I am well-equipped to keep us safe and ensure that everyone's needs are met."

"Why can't you bring the information to us?" Weston asked, as wary of Azuma as she remained of him.

"I could, but I suspect that the four of us together will attract the Morningstar's mischief. Do you want to put others at risk?" she asked, gesturing toward the hallway and Mwana'jua asleep in one of the rooms beyond. "The *Akai* are my guards, and they are trained to defend me against supernatural threats. You should also meet the woman who found the *makom,* because her story is inextricably linked to that place. And there is the matter of my dietary needs. I have arrangements in place at home that are inadvisable to try to recreate abroad."

"Let's let everyone get some rest," Amaoke suggested reasonably. "Sleep on it. I don't have objections to arming ourselves with as much information as we can gather, and staying together may be unavoidable now anyway."

"The room I am in has two beds," Azuma said, now sounding almost timid, perhaps chastened by the fact that for the first time in her life she was not resoundingly in charge. "Weston, would you stay with me?"

"Of course," Weston smiled, understanding that some of his behavior earlier may have made her feel like a monster, something he should confess as uncharitable, and hypocritical. He decided he would ask for her forgiveness once they were alone.

Ambakisye stretched and yawned, and reached for Kusini's hand, but she only squeezed his gently and let go. "Get some rest," she advised. "I will join you shortly. I need a walk, and want to speak with Amaoke, who I can see is wide awake."

Ambakisye appeared disappointed for a moment, but then looked carefully at Amaoke. He said, "Mwana'jua gave you coffee beans."

"Oh, dear," Kusini lamented, and started to laugh. "Have you ever had caffeine before?"

"Not really," Amaoke allowed. "Is *that* why I'm so wired?" He'd thought it was because of all the travel disrupting his schedule, and the moon waxing full.

"Essentially it's a drug, man," Ambakisye clapped Amaoke on the shoulder. "You have to get used to it, and it can keep you awake. Goodnight, you two." He took his leave of them then, after brushing his fingers down his wife's cheek.

Amaoke held the screen door for Kusini, following her out into the yard, and she walked with him some short distance beyond the buildings, out under the trees. She perched on a tree stump at the edge of the garden, and he leaned against the trunk of a young acacia a few feet away.

"This is an amazing place, and Mwana'jua is quite the character," Amaoke observed, seeing that something was bothering her, hoping she would be comfortable enough to share it with him.

"She's one hundred years old, and she has run this place since she was a very young girl," Kusini told him.

"She seems quite fond of Ambakisye," he said, hoping it might prompt her to say something about his observation that Mwana'jua seemed indifferent, if not outright cool, in her dealings with Kusini.

"Who isn't?" she laughed. "He is quite the charmer. Her relationship with me is more complicated, I suppose.

"I delivered her, right here, in this house. Her grandmother was waiting for me out on the post road, because her daughter, Mwana'jua's mother, had sent her to find me there. She had some sort of sight, could see what was coming. She knew her child was going to be born with albinism, knew that she would die from complications of the delivery. She did not tell anyone this, just sent Zalika out to find me.

"Mwana'jua knows I attended her birth; she blames me for her mother's death, and I have never explained to her that it was foretold and unavoidable, the will of the gods. We could have lost her as well, had I not come by on that day. Oh, I don't take credit for her life, by any means, but I think it was always a possibility that both mother and child were in peril. She also resents the fact that my gifts put those of us with albinism at greater risk, for the reasons I explained to you before.

"Mwana'jua has always done a great deal to help those with our condition, and my very existence is a significant source of our continued endangerment." Kusini sounded sad, a deeper sadness than could be borne of this story alone, and Amaoke wondered if she would ever be able to see that she was a greater blessing to her community than a curse. He stayed quiet, saying nothing, hoping she would share with him whatever it was she had wanted to tell him, as he guessed that her original intent in taking this walk had nothing to do with the current subject of discussion.

Eventually, she obliged him, relating the story of the events of her encounter with Azuma and Aleta in New Orleans, wanting him to have further perspective on Azuma's quest to interact with him directly. It confirmed that she had been looking for him all along, confirmed what she had told them this evening about looking for others that were like her, others that could perhaps join her in a campaign against the Morningstar.

"But why interfere with Aleta?" he asked.

"I think because she could more easily find Aleta, assumed Aleta was shielding you," Kusini replied.

"I understand that, but it is manipulative," he said. "It makes me angry."

"It made me angry as well," Kusini admitted. "But it serves no purpose, being angry with her. I made it clear that her mischief was not going to be tolerated, and at the time I told them that you and Weston were with my husband. Remember, she is a creature of impulse and the Monster has gratified her. She was never shielded from its cruelty, never had a human parent to protect her interests or teach her how to be better. In that regard, you and I and Weston were fortunate."

"Can we trust her?" Amaoke asked, though he didn't really expect an answer.

"She behaves this way because she doesn't trust herself." Kusini's answer surprised him, almost as much as the questions that followed it. "Do you blame her? Do you trust yourself? Can any of us, really? Not knowing what the Morningstar has planned?"

40

MWANA'JUA SLEPT POORLY, BUT SHRUGGED off her bedclothes along with her stiffness, knowing it to be the singular reality of the elderly. The others remained abed, and this she didn't mind, knowing that rest was what they needed more than anything else, and she suspected it was a difficult thing for them to achieve as well, despite their apparent youth.

She went out into the dark yard and stretched, thanking Ngai for blessings of a good harvest and a long life, thanking Olapa for never burdening her with a husband, prayers she repeated daily. She caught the fresh scent of rain; the storm that had threatened the night before had come, but the dust at her feet was dry, so it had fallen off to the east, sparing the farm. She wasn't particularly superstitious; she understood the harsh realities of life better than most. She had been lucky in many ways, and when luck would not serve, hard work had.

And she saw things. Mostly things that were to come, very few that she did not understand. Her grandmother had told her that her mother had the sight, had explained what that meant to Mwana'jua. Yet she herself had never told Zalika about the things she dreamt about. The things she just knew, about the people who came to work on the farm, about the others who came to take refuge there, about how her appearance made them feel. What years the coffee yield would suffer from poor rains. How she knew when Grandmother was going to die.

So the things she could not see frightened her a bit, but angered her more. She paid attention to what the Sorceress did, never denying her refuge, because Mwana'jua knew it was necessary. But the sight never showed her anything about her mother, never gave her any clues about Kusini, and on balance this was frightening, because what she did feel about the Sorceress was dread, and sadness. Ambakisye was equally a mystery, but he was easier to love, his life intersected with hers in a way not associated with any tragedy, or raw feelings. She had loved him secretly since she was a little girl, although she could sense he could be dangerous.

It was a simple thing to blame the Sorceress for the loss of a mother, even if Mwana'jua was wise enough to understand that Kusini was not at fault. It had always been a way to shield her from other feelings she might have had if she were not so confounded about this blind spot in her own intuition.

After making the rounds of the outbuildings, she gathered eggs from the sleepy hens, carrying them cradled in the folds of her skirt as she had since she was a girl. She climbed the steps to the back door, turning to push the screen with her shoulder and enter the kitchen.

When she saw the man sitting calmly at the kitchen table, she nearly dropped the eggs, nearly lost control of her bodily functions. She hadn't seen him coming, not the first time, not this time.

He stood up, quickly moving to her side, placing surprisingly gentle hands under hers, ensuring the safety of her burden, and she was as grateful as she was afraid. He stood very still, not moving away until she had deposited the eggs into the basket on the sideboard and nodded to signal she was alright.

"Have you come to steal more of my skin?" she managed to ask, with the bravery of one who has nothing to lose.

He bowed, his handsome face betraying some amusement perhaps, and no small amount of respect. "You knew I was here.

Yet you didn't try to stop me, didn't call for help." The Collector helped her into a chair.

"Do I look like a fool?" she asked him, impatiently waving him away, letting him know she was fine. Or at least as fine as she could be. If he knew that she was aware of what he had done, perhaps he was here to ensure the information died with her. Her sight had told her nothing about him, but her instincts showed her that death followed him, and she would not have protested, then or now, if it meant he left her with her life. She was wise enough to sense the generalities of his vocation.

"I made coffee," he said, stepping away to bring her a cup of the steaming brew. It smelled divine, strong, as she liked it, and she accepted it in hands that shook terribly, hoping he would think her trembling an affliction of her advanced age and not her fear.

He sat down, and she noticed that he had been drinking it while he waited for her, which made it less likely it was tainted.

"I drink it only rarely, but yours is extraordinary," he complimented her sincerely, and saluted her with the cup before taking another drink. Then his own attention was drawn by something behind her, and he stilled too.

Mwana'jua felt the strong head under her hand as the wolf came to stand beside her, its thick white fur surprisingly silky against her arm as it leaned into her thigh. It was enormous, and she knew instinctively that it was not a dog even given its obvious similarities. This creature was as unlike a dog as a lion is a housecat.

She could feel and hear its loud and rhythmic breathing, like a bellows in the silence, and then it laid back its ears and growled softly, an obvious warning to the stranger at the table. It was protecting her, and she knew it to be another surprise, not so much because she couldn't read the wolf either, but because the wolf seemed to have sensed that something was off, and it had awakened. Mwana'jua was startled, because she got one brief vision of the one she had known was a friend on his arrival the day before, a natural guardian. A protector.

The Collector knew immediately what, and who, he was looking at. Yet even he, after all his years with Azuma, was not prepared for the reality of the beast before him. He relaxed as much as he could, trying to master his fear, recognizing a more dominant predator, not wanting to provoke Amaoke. Amaoke, for his part, was wondering what magic had kept the man's scent from him so long, until he realized that the coffee aroma had flooded his nose, and perhaps this was purposeful.

"Easy, my friend. I am here at Azuma's beckoning. I mean no one under this roof harm," the Collector murmured the words softly, keeping his hands relaxed on the table, both of them remained in the wolf's line of sight. He was sure the animal could scent *Hōfuku* where he had placed it near the entry door down the hall.

The wolf stopped growling, but its ears remained flattened against its head, a deadly sentry intent on protecting Mwana'jua. Then one ear flicked up, momentarily, and back down, a silent acknowledgement signaling Azuma's arrival in the kitchen.

Azuma murmured something softly to the Collector in Japanese, something Amaoke did not understand, although her tone was that of one calmly greeting a friend. She turned to Mwana'jua and looked with as much curiosity and fear at Amaoke as the Collector had, but marshalled her emotions with a sigh.

"I apologize for any difficulty my friend's arrival may have caused," she said contritely, giving her own bow to Mwana'jua. "I asked him here to escort me home. We meant to cause no offense."

Mwana'jua grunted in disbelief but said nothing about knocking on doors and arriving at a reasonable hour. There were things happening here that she was not meant to understand. She couldn't police everyone's ill manners and was uninterested in such a task anyway.

"Everyone out of my kitchen before I lose all patience," she said instead, nodding as Azuma and the Collector retreated obediently.

"And you." she said sharply, bringing her face down close to Amaoke's and ruffling the fur on his neck. "No matter how useful, I don't allow animals in this house." With that, she tapped him gently on the nose, banishing him as well, turning away to start breakfast for everyone.

41

ANY DISCUSSION AS TO WHETHER or not to accede to Azuma's request was bound to be brief, in Amaoke's estimation. There was the enticement of the information she had to share, the very real need to decide how to proceed, the unavoidable obligation of their larger task. Her dietary needs were both the most stringent and the most dangerous. While it was possible, likely even, that there were details she was privy to that she had not yet shared with the larger group, he was confident that she did need their help. Just as they needed hers.

As uncomfortable as it was, the four of them needed time together, needed a cohesion they had yet to find. It was likely that without some sort of mutual understanding and trust they would have no possible chance to thwart the evil they faced.

Breakfast was a heavier affair than such a meal should be; the arrival of the Collector had been a signal of the inevitability of their shared future. It made Azuma's ask more urgent. Amaoke would have preferred another few days of chopping wood, and the illusion of normalcy, but even he knew that it was his need for such a peace that would drive him on, as there was no peace for any of them without pushing through to the ultimate truths of their collective existence.

"I will go with you," Weston finally spoke, sitting back in his chair and looking at each of the others in turn. "I think, if

Kusini is correct about what is happening among us, that my decision may give Amaoke and Kusini no other choice."

Kusini was leaning against Ambakisye, who had not eaten with them. He sat quietly, his shoulder easily supporting his wife. She sipped her tea thoughtfully. "'Kisye and I will accompany the group as well." She said nothing about her concerns regarding travel; she was comforting herself by considering what Amaoke had told her about embracing those aspects of her power that created difficulty and unpredictability as well as those that she could best control. She assumed there was a need for flight to traverse such a distance reasonably, and she merely hoped that her presence wasn't going to threaten the function of the plane.

"It isn't a prison," Azuma said, and this was an oddly reassuring reminder that they were staying together physically, but that did not mean they had to agree on everything. "If we get there and anyone wants to leave, it is simple to make such arrangements. I must return, for pragmatic reasons if any of you accompanies me it must be voluntary and uncoerced. Anything else is unthinkable to me."

"If we are to be successful in overcoming these curses that plague each of us, if we are to face the Monster on its terms, terms which we do not completely understand and likely cannot fully know, we need time," Amaoke reasoned. "Perhaps that time will be short, but it is necessary for us to reach some sort of accord. We have to be able to work together or we are defeated before we begin. I don't know what the Morningstar intends, but I doubt it serves its purpose for us to stay together, to learn about each other, and to *trust* each other. If we don't go, if we don't try, we are simply surrendering to the worst. And even that," he looked at each of them in turn, "will be even more devastating than we can imagine."

The decision made; they took their leave of Mwana'jua. It was like stepping out of one reality into another. Back down the steps of the farmhouse, not to the aging Scout, rather they climbed into the air-conditioned luxury of a supercharged Range Rover with every amenity that one could imagine, and some that even surprised Weston and Ambakisye.

Instead of being jostled unmercifully, Amaoke was treated to advanced suspension and a relatively smooth ride out to the post road, where they turned north and east at the junction, toward Arusha this time, the great Kilimanjaro dominating the view out the left side of the vehicle. Then, arriving at the airport, waved through like dignitaries, barely even having to stop at the checkpoint, never mind that neither Kusini nor Ambakisye had passports. Not bothering to park on the tarmac because the Collector drove the vehicle right up the loading ramp into the back of the Airbus A320 Phoenix that was parked on the apron, looking like something out of another world.

Weston's mouth was hanging open, and he whispered to Amaoke as the massive SUV disappeared into the belly of the plane, "Dude, remind me not to complain about her wealth ever again." Amaoke chuckled; Weston was a kid in a candy store with all this shiny machinery.

They climbed out, crew members at the ready bowed to Azuma and the Collector, and then at their guests, then tried not to appear confounded about who to put on the small elevator that would take them up to the cabin, and in what order. Each of the group was dispossessed of their belongings, stewards appearing to stow their personal items, and Amaoke reluctantly surrendered his knapsack, not wanting to give any offense to this abundance of courtesy.

Azuma nodded to Ambakisye and Kusini, sending them up first, and then said to Weston and Amaoke, "We can wait for the elevator to return, or take the stairs, if you prefer."

So the four of them went up the staircase through a door adjacent to the hold, Azuma leading and the Collector bringing up the rear, emerging at the top in a luxurious cabin tastefully appointed in red and gold silk, with cream leather seats, and ebony wood tables and trim accented with painted lacquers, uniquely Asian. There was a full bar, and a large round table that looked as though it would seat twelve people, as well as several doors leading to private spaces both at the front and rear of the cabin. The place resembled more a small luxury apartment than the cabin of an airplane.

A trim man awaited them expectantly, and a very attractive hostess was already serving Kusini a cup of tea.

Azuma addressed the man who awaited them warmly, bowing as he did, and introduced him as Konoye Ko, her pilot. Ko gave them a brief introduction to the plane, taking them up to see the cockpit. "After takeoff, you may join me here to get a different perspective if you like, or move about the cabin, get something to eat or drink, or take your rest. We should have smooth air all the way into Narita," he told them, the last part of his statement directed at Azuma.

"*Origato, Konoye-san.* The plane is yours." Azuma bowed once more, and Ko took his leave of them, returning to the cockpit.

There was a woman seated near the front of the plane, waiting quietly, saying nothing, and toward the rear of the plane, beyond the bar, were a sharply dressed pair whose posture and stance belied their vocations. These had to be members of Azuma's security detail. Each wore a samurai sword across their back. Azuma turned to introduce them with a smile.

"This is *Ni*," she gestured to the woman first, and the others could see that she had warm feelings for her guards. Azuma was unsurprised that *Ni* had come; although she had been aware that the Collector was coming for her because of their blood bond, she had not known who had accompanied him on this errand. She should have guessed it would be *Ni*, who she suspected was not likely to let the Collector out of her sight anytime soon.

Ni nodded and bowed, maintaining eye contact, more successful in mastering her curiosity about the newcomers than her partner, who was introduced as *Roku*. He, too, bowed to the collective group in greeting.

"Please feel free to sit wherever you are comfortable. We will be taking off soon. Our hosts are Miyahira and Kuno," Azuma indicated the women who were waiting expectantly near the cockpit, one of whom had delivered Kusini's tea, "and our stewards are Keiji and Fukumoto. Do not hesitate to ask them to attend your every need; they are most efficient." She bowed to them as well.

Finally, she turned toward the young woman who sat patiently at the front of the plane, and Azuma beckoned to her to join them. The woman looked somewhat surprised, but rose gracefully, and made her way to the larger group. She was stunning; her skin the color of café au lait and covered in a fine sprinkling of chocolate freckles, her dark hair shaved to her scalp, large gold hoops hung from her ears, and her peach-colored jumpsuit was sharply tailored. She wore some sort of complicated strappy sandals, and multiple gold bangles on each wrist; they made a pleasing music as she moved. She came to stand very close beside Azuma, and turned large calm brown eyes on them, her lips curving slightly.

"This is Selene," Azuma introduced her. "She is my..." she trailed off, but it wasn't at all awkward, even though it seemed she hadn't decided how to complete the introduction.

"Current obsession, I hope," Selene concluded without guile or embarrassment, apparently content with whatever arrangement they had.

Amaoke understood immediately, and he glanced at Kusini and Weston, seeing that they did as well. This was Azuma's consenting companion, a source of her food, and she wanted them all to understand that she was neither ashamed of the woman nor her particular appetite. Selene looked healthy and happy, so the arrangement had not been to her detriment.

"It is a pleasure to meet you, Selene," Kusini said, stepping forward to greet her. Weston shook the young woman's hand warmly, ignoring Selene's slightly surprised expression that a priest would be so readily accepting of what he had just learned of them. Azuma made eye contact with Amaoke and he nodded, seeing how much relief their understanding brought her, both regarding her needs and Selene's gender. She had feared to be judged anew a monster, or judged for other things that were nobody else's business. She was showing them everything, showing them who she was, being as transparent as possible.

But Amaoke sensed something else here, as well. The two women were comfortable with one another, but this was not love. At least, Azuma did not love this woman, but Selene seemed not to mind. He guessed that they were both benefiting in some way from their agreement, even though he could see that it wasn't simply a financial transaction for either of them. He recognized the blessing this represented for Azuma, the order it allowed her in her daily life.

Amaoke declined the offer of a preflight beverage, and each passenger found a seat. Almost magically, their personal belongings were deposited near them by efficient stewards and Amaoke could not help but marvel at what Azuma had built for herself. He wondered what other magic they all had to look forward to together.

He'd slept fitfully the night before, likely the result of his unnaturally caffeinated state, but the effects were ebbing. He ignored the odd surge and sudden weightless feeling that accompanied takeoff, pleased with the degree to which his seat reclined, and was asleep within minutes.

42

THEY FLEW NORTHEAST, AWAY FROM the sun, and through the night, touching down at Narita about fifteen hours after takeoff. It was already nine in the morning on a busy day in Japan, three a.m. for those who had acclimated to the Tanzanian time zone, chilly spring at their destination, scorching fall left behind.

A second Range Rover awaited them on the tarmac, this time the Collector, Azuma, and Selene climbed into it, leaving her guests in the capable hands of *Roku* and *Ni*. The two vehicles sped quickly around the airport perimeter, and Amaoke quickly learned new ways to be terrified in an enclosed vehicle, almost longing for the road trip to Iowa in the minivan, even the land speed time trials in the Charger to get to Louis Armstrong Airport would have been preferable. *Roku's* driving style seemed to consider the enormous number of cars speeding around them inconveniences to be ignored. It appeared he expected them to yield, just on general principle.

The others seemed to have no difficulty falling asleep; Ambakisye watched the landscape from the middle row of seats, his wife leaning against him with her eyes already closed. Weston pushed his glasses up into his hair, slouched down, and tipped his head back against the headrest, ignoring imminent death and destruction. Amaoke shook his head, hoping to keep his claws out of Azuma's upholstery. Their escorts remained silent up front.

They did not follow the signs pointing to Tokyo, instead headed north and east toward Mito, and exited the highway not long after merging onto it. *Roku* veered to the right, onto a well-maintained but much quieter motorway that meandered further north through hillsides dotted with bamboo forest which alternated with more open farmland the farther they traveled. After the better part of half an hour, they slowed, entering a quaint village populated by less than a dozen wooden buildings, and turned east, both vehicles topping a steep hill before turning onto a private road carefully marked by a sign that Amaoke could not read.

He suspected it warned against trespassing, as such signs seemed to look the same everywhere he'd been. The vehicle's tires pattered over cobbled stones, and they passed beneath a series of Shinto arches and into a forest, the bamboo spires close to the road on either side and seeming to reach to the heavens. The cars bounded over rounded hills and followed a few curves, and Amaoke could smell the sea. He kept expecting to see it emerge ahead of them, but it never did.

About two miles in, they arrived at a motorized gate set into an ornamental arch built into a stone wall. The wall looked ancient, it was mossy and marked with signs of water exposure. The gate itself appeared to be made of wood, and opened automatically, likely triggered by Azuma's vehicle ahead of them. Amaoke looked back once their car was through, and as he had expected, the gate was also closing automatically, but on this side he could see it was reinforced with steel.

Ahead, in the near distance, he could see a group of ornate buildings, with elaborate gardens, and he saw sunlight glimmering off water through the bamboo, but this was only a pond some way beyond the main house. The place in total was larger than the village they'd recently passed through. They pulled up in the center of the compound, in a large rectangular clearing, with the main house to their right. Amaoke saw at least four other buildings arranged with precision around the courtyard, which was excessively wide for such a thing.

The buildings were made of wood, and all had ornate roofs with clay tiles and ornamental carvings at the corners. Each had a veranda that appeared to run all the way around the structure, and there were modern sliding doors interspersed with large screens. An open-air staircase ran up the center of the massive home, protected by the roof, leading to an upper floor.

Amaoke could see that there were even more buildings beyond the central group, probably stables, from what his nose was telling him. There were several people standing expectantly at the entryway of the main house, and at least five others scattered at interval about the courtyard, dressed similarly to *Ni* and *Roku.*

They all disembarked from the vehicles, and Azuma greeted her house staff in response to their bows. They had a brief conversation in Japanese, and then switched to English, which was the language that everyone had in common. Amaoke suspected she had given such an instruction.

"*Himura-san,* all is in readiness for your guests," one of the staff said to Azuma, but it was clearly intended for the entire group.

"Thank you, Naito." Azuma turned back to address them. "Naito and his staff are here to attend your every need. Please do not hesitate to employ their good services. Everyone in residence here speaks more than one language, alas not Swahili," she said in an apologetic tone, looking at Kusini and Ambakisye. "English is our common language, and I have given instruction that out of the utmost courtesy we will speak it while you are our guests.

"You will be shown to your living quarters here, in the main house," she explained. "The bathhouse is across the parade ground, which is where we are standing now." She pointed to one of the buildings adjacent to the main house, divided only by an ornamental garden. "It may seem unusual to you, but please ask for help with preparing for bathing. You do not have to suffer the cold, all will be attended to, and we have every modern convenience in place to see to your comfort.

"There are stables behind the outbuilding directly across from the house. The second residence is for the *Akai*, although they spend a great deal of time here, in the main house, and we all take our meals together, although food will be prepared to order at any hour of the day or night. Tomoko, my chef, will meet with each of you privately to learn of your dietary preferences, and he can source anything that we do not currently hold in the pantry here to suit you.

"The beach is east of us, a short walk, but there is an excellent view of the ocean from the bluffs, which you can reach on foot by cutting through the bamboo here," Azuma told them, using her arm to point the way. "The property is surrounded by gardens, there is a pond here, and a shrine through the trees that way. My home is yours, please avail yourself of nature, relax, and be welcome. I hope you will be happy during your time here."

43

FROM THEIR VANTAGE POINT AT the southwest corner of the parade grounds, *Hachi* and *Ku* watched the arrival of the newcomers. The others were scattered about, waiting for Azuma's signal to come down to the house to be introduced.

"Hmmm," *Hachi* murmured, and *Ku* recognized her tone. Her golden eyes had found her prey.

"See something you like?" he asked, teasing her, able to guess what it was she had noticed.

"Oh, yes. But why is the gorgeous one wearing a dress?"

"He's a priest," *Ku* said with a sigh, as though he were dealing with a younger sister, or perhaps was praying for patience. "That might affect whatever you are planning."

"It's a technicality. They don't always follow the rules," *Hachi* waved at him impatiently, which *Ku* always found amusing, since she was so small, and he was so big. She behaved as though she were seven feet tall.

"Yeah. He took a vow of celibacy. And you took a vow of – remind me again? Kick-ass?" *Ku's* deep laughter rumbled in his chest.

"But oh, that hair! That's boy-band hair," she breathed, actually fawning over it.

"I don't know," *Ku* argued, stroking his bald head for her benefit. "Bald is beautiful." Not that he had a choice, congenital alopecia had robbed him of ever having any hair of his own, and he had never let it bother him. It certainly had never seemed to diminish his romantic prospects among either sex. He'd been told plenty that he was handsome in his own right. There was really only one opinion that mattered anyway.

"Yes, but no one makes it look as good as you do," *Hachi* winked at him, and gently pinched a fold of his forearm to let him know she meant it. Then she changed the subject. "Is the mistress going to regret bringing them here?"

"I gather from the Collector that there really was not a choice. They could be enemies, and keep secrets from one another, or work together against Akenomyosei," he replied, and there was something in his tone that *Hachi* didn't understand.

"Something is bothering you," she said. "What is it?" She knew *Ku* to be the most philosophical of all of them, and often, the most priestlike.

"Are we violating our vows to Akenomyosei in this?" he asked, sounding more like he needed reassurance than anything else. He didn't sound as conflicted as his question suggested.

"When has that monster ever paid us any mind, other than in our training and our torture up on that mountain?" *Hachi* nearly spat her words out. "When we ascended to the *Akai*, we ceased being priests of its sect. Our directive is the well-being of the Dragon, that is why the Crimson Guard exists. I have no conflict; my loyalty is to our mistress alone. The Dragon has declared Akenomyosei her enemy."

Ku sighed. "Easy, little one," he said to her, and she understood it was with endearment and no belittling. He was the only one who could get away with it, the only one who would dare. "I agree with you."

"If any one of us does not, and you know of it, you must warn them," *Hachi* said, her tone serious and somber now. "Such sentiment will earn them a trip to the Butterfly Garden." She shivered involuntarily, prompting *Ku* to place a warm hand on her shoulder.

"The whole situation is Kafka-esque." He said it calmly, then quoted for her, *"'From a certain point onward there is no longer any turning back. That is the point that must be reached.'"*

"Quoting philosophy," *Hachi* said, and he could hear the smile in her voice. "Just for that, I think you might get lucky later."

"A wise man gladly accepts the blessings life brings," *Ku* replied, and turned his attention back to the group at the house.

44

While the others rested during the afternoon, Amaoke explored the grounds a bit, making his way down to the beach and watching the waves. He was on his way back up to the house when he heard a helicopter, and emerged from the bamboo just in time to watch it set itself down, a mechanical dragonfly perched in the center of the courtyard.

Shortly after touchdown, its rotors remained spinning, and Amaoke saw Azuma and Selene emerge from the house together, ducking down and walking toward it. He watched as Azuma helped her into the passenger compartment before securing the door behind her, and he realized he was witnessing their farewell. Azuma had no sooner stepped away from the aircraft than it lifted aloft once more, straight up for several meters before turning south and disappearing. Azuma stood alone in the courtyard, watching it go.

Amaoke did not want to appear to be intruding, so he backtracked over the bridge and sat in the sun for a time near the pond. When he got too chilled to remain any longer, he went back inside and stretched out on the *shikibuton* in his room, contemplating the events of the last five days, which felt more like they had taken weeks.

After dinner, Azuma took them across the courtyard to the large building directly opposite the house. "This compound was the stronghold of my family in feudal times. I grew up on these grounds. This particular building was my office and library, when I was Shogun here. The courtyard used to be a parade ground for my samurai. I have modernized the structure; there is a laboratory and medical facility at one end, but I kept the library for sentimental reasons, for tradition. It is a good place for us to speak together, and I can share with you the information I promised to provide," she explained as they walked together from the house.

Once inside, she gave them a small tour, proudly showing them the lab and clinic first. There appeared to be rooms for recovering from injury, and these were appointed more like bedrooms than any hospital room Amaoke had known about in his lifetime.

There was a large central space, enclosed on all sides but with large windows from waist level to the ceiling to allow for observation. "We do have a need for the occasional procedure, and this facility was built for evaluation and treatment of myself and the *Akai,* as we have special requirements that call for discretion, to say the very least." Kusini saw a great deal of specialized equipment and monitors, at least as advanced and some far more advanced than the equipment she had seen when assisting World Health Organization medical personnel in some of their field hospitals.

There were bathrooms between rooms, and they passed a curtained alcove in a recess in the hallway between the recovery area and the treatment room. It contained a daybed and a reading light.

"Master *Go* and I are both physicians," Azuma explained, gesturing to the alcove. "I do very little clinical work, but it is the focus of his practice, though myself and his fellow *Akai* comprise the totality of his patients. If we need to monitor an injury or illness, which is rare, one of us can sleep here in this space. It is mostly for convenience."

She led them to the opposite end of the building, where a glass wall separated a well-appointed office space from the library, which was lined with a diverse collection of books, some ancient and some new. Weston was enthralled. He noticed that along one wall, there were several small pigeonholes containing scrolls. Azuma noticed his interest.

"Help yourself to any of my books," she offered, genuinely delighted to see that Weston loved to learn as much as she did. "I can sit with you and translate some of the scrolls, if they are of interest to you. Some of them are accounts written by my father and my grandfather."

"I would like that very much," Weston said, accepting the offer, though he suspected he would need little assistance with translation, given the Morningstar's sinister legacy that allowed him to understand much of even those languages he had never formally studied. He would need her help to provide historical context, so he was very grateful she had offered it.

Azuma gestured vaguely to the seats around the room, a silent invitation for the others to be comfortable. Amaoke chose one of the stylish upholstered club chairs near the door, and Weston stationed himself by the windows nearby, while Kusini and Ambakisye sat next to one of the large trestle tables in the center of the room.

"I have assessed the DNA of each one of you," Azuma confessed, without preamble, grimacing slightly because she knew that admission might derail their collective journey toward trust. Amaoke noticed that night was falling, darkness deepening out there beyond the glass.

Kusini's head came up and she stood up in one dangerous fluid motion. It was like watching a cheetah prepare for the kill. She had yet to connect the dots, yet to see that Azuma had engineered all the biopsies she had so worried over. And the energy she was radiating was unpleasant. A ribbon of blood trickled from Azuma's nose, and patches of iridescent sky-blue scales surfaced on her cheeks and the back of the hand she lifted in surprise to her face. The Dragon turned wide eyes on the Sorceress that telegraphed her distress.

Without moving, Ambakisye said softly, "'*Sini-ma*, relax. What's done is done. We need to hear what she has to tell us." When he was certain he had Kusini's attention, he slipped his hand gently around hers, and just like that, a connection was broken, and the surge of her energy was gone. Amaoke was relieved, because whatever Kusini was sending out into the world, it had started to hurt.

"Forgive me my intrusion, Sorceress," Azuma appeared cowed but also sincerely remorseful. She gratefully accepted a handkerchief from Weston, and dabbed carefully at her nose, regaining her composure and beginning again.

"Amaoke provided his sample voluntarily, although it was regrettable that he had an encounter with the Collector that put him in doubt." She had no trouble making eye contact with Amaoke, and he respected her for it. She made her decisions and lived with the consequences; if she harbored regrets, they were for her private reflection alone.

"And mine? Iowa, I assume," Weston said without hesitation.

"Indeed. Iowa Bureau of Investigation. We do some reciprocal research on unusual samples, and they thought their result was an error. It got buried in our protocol and I didn't know about it until very recently. Your DNA is…rather extraordinary, and it raised more questions than it answered, although it supports our theories about Akenomyosei – my apologies, old habits are difficult to break – *the Morningstar*, interfering in our existence.

"The simplest example I will draw to your attention without the aid of any visuals," she said, tapping the tablet she had retrieved from the desk in her office and now held in her hands. "Let's talk about our height, for instance. We are all, to the centimeter if I am not mistaken, the same height. If you will permit me to do so later, I would like to take basic measurements from each of you to confirm my hypothesis. My height is one-point-nine-five meters, or by standard measurement, six feet and five inches. Height is a variably expressed physical trait.

"What that means is that two people, with the same parents and the same genes for height expression, will not necessarily be the same height because of the way their development reads the code built into their DNA. Even intervention into an embryo to control such a thing would not yield this result. It is one of the strong indicators of our engineering as individuals, that we were manipulated to a specified outcome by exploiting our genetic material. I have spent several human lifetimes trying to understand my origins, the last several decades with the means and the tools to read the secrets of our creation, and the coincidence is too great. But it isn't even the most extraordinary thing I found."

The others waited while Azuma clicked and scrolled on the tablet she held, frowning down at it when it was apparently not responding as she expected it to. "I wanted to show this to you, sometimes the technical stuff is easier to absorb when you have a visual, but...I don't know why it isn't loading properly."

Kusini was watching her carefully, and graceful as a gazelle, she moved to the opposite end of the room, hoping some distance would lessen the interference of her magic. It seemed to work, Azuma smiled finally, getting whatever response she had been seeking from the device.

Azuma made eye contact with Kusini, who gestured that she should continue, before sitting down in the far corner of the room near the windows. The Sorceress looked out on the dark vista, lit by dozens of paper lanterns that illuminated the gardens, but Azuma could see she was still listening as intently as ever.

"Here it is. Superhuman chimera specimen alpha is myself, obviously, because I thought at one time that I was the only one. The Morningstar did not tell me about Amaoke and Kusini until relatively recently, when my own investigations into supernatural reports revealed your existence, or, in Amaoke's case, a physician's inquiry was initiated and the results were *unexpected*, to say the least. Kusini is superhuman chimera beta, Amaoke gamma, and-"

"I am delta?" Weston concluded, but Azuma shook her head.

"You are something else. Not a chimera."

"Chimera. A creature made up of many different parts, a mythological being," Weston said.

"You know your Greek mythology, Father Weston, how unsurprising," Azuma softened this statement with a smile.

"Hindquarters of the Dragon," Weston gestured at her and went on, looking at Amaoke, "Head of a carnivorous beast, usually a lion, but a wolf could serve, and a second head, that of a goat." Here he put his hands on his cassock. "Classic symbol of the Devil, demonology, et cetera."

"Okay, so I have a well-developed sense of irony," Azuma admitted. "But it has a genetic meaning as well. It refers to an organism that has some kind of mixed gene expression, either globally, where the simplest example is a mule which has mixed parentage from two compatible species, or at the level of an individual gene, expressing two possibilities at once, which is slightly more complicated a discussion. Suffice it to say, among us, I used the term to refer to the foreign genetic material that we all carry which is *not* human DNA. And due to each of us expressing extranormal traits, I added the descriptor superhuman."

"So, if there is no superhuman chimera delta, what is Weston?" Amaoke asked, confident in his question because Azuma, and Aleta before her, was a particularly good teacher. "Also, no part of the chimera refers to Kusini."

"In one way or another, I can exclude each of us from any grouping of the others," Azuma admitted. "Weston is not a chimera. He only has one kind of genetic material. None of it human, or at least not demonstrably so, since it has not been seen in humans before. His genetic code is the same as the foreign material in the genetic code of the rest of us, but we have preserved human DNA. Hence, we are chimeric, but he is not. I designated him metahuman alpha."

"But alpha suggests first," Weston protested. "So, shouldn't Amaoke be superhuman chimera alpha, Kusini remains beta, and you would be gamma?"

"Chronologically, yes," Azuma agreed. "Scientifically, not really. I am alpha because my own genetic proteins were the first specimens I had to evaluate. I knew Amaoke's results prior to finishing the assay on Kusini's, but because I knew what she was when I evaluated her, and subsequently confirmed my findings prior to confirming his, she is beta.

"We did not know what we had with Amaoke, because he was an outside request that came to us. Was it a contamination? I doubted it, but needed confirmation, which I only got secondhand because I got the specimen *before* I received the report of the interaction between Amaoke and my staff.

"At any rate, Amaoke is the only true beast," Azuma continued, but Amaoke protested.

"But what about you?" he asked.

"You were all live births, I assume? None of your mothers told you otherwise, correct? There is evidence of your infancy one way or the other," Azuma replied, looking at the other three in turn, and at Ambakisye, who was listening with interest.

"To the best of my knowledge, I came into the world as dragon. I grew in my mother's womb, but according to Tatsuo Tomo – so sorry, Forcas – was expelled in an egg sac at birth. I did not take this human form until I had spent twelve years in the temple, a juvenile dragon under the protection of the priests of Akenomyosei. Under the cruel tutelage of Forcas.

"And there is something else you should know. In the image of my own gods, and the tradition of Japanese mythology, I was bound in duality. When I reached sexual maturity, not only was I Dragon Goddess, I was also Dragon God, and on occasion transformed, not into the dragon, rather into my male form."

This was received with shock and incredulity.

"Wait, you can become a man?" Ambakisye was the one who spoke aloud what the others wondered about.

"Not anymore," Kusini's voice was nearly a whisper from the far side of the room, but none there had any difficulty hearing her. "Azuma has prevailed against herself and bound her twin in a cellular prison."

"She's right," Azuma admitted, and Amaoke thought she seemed ashamed of this. After several moments of silence, she explained. "I can control the Dragon, but not *him*. He cannot control the Dragon. Neither of us had control over the other, but I was generally in ascendancy. I am ashamed that I have taken my knowledge and diminished my own capabilities, but to be bound in duality with a shadow of the Death Bringer was ultimately too dangerous. There are other, selfish reasons that I did it, but that was the beginning of the end between myself and the Morningstar."

"Tatsuo Tomo was your twin?!" Weston shook his head.

"Well, a corrupted version of myself, really," Azuma told him. "The Death Bringer had long since departed. It was just the reality of my existence. Think of it as yin and yang, to borrow from Chinese philosophy. Our gods are balanced. I was control, as it were, and he was chaos. I devised a way to prevent his genetic expression, making my life more ordered while constricting my genetic possibility. Both unavoidable sins."

45

"AND MY WIFE, HOW IS she different?" Ambakisye asked the question softly, but Azuma was too pragmatic to believe that he did not already know the answer. Perhaps he just needed to hear the clinical summary, have another put into words what he had until now only articulated in emotion.

"Are you not the best proof of her gifts?" Azuma answered with the obvious, because it needed to be acknowledged.

"You mean longevity?" Ambakisye dissembled, unused to revealing too much. Understandable for their community, and habit, but he also did it to protect Kusini, which Azuma found endearing.

"Well, I can do that. The *Akai* are unnaturally long-lived," Azuma shook her head.

"And longevity suggests *life*," Amaoke spoke softly, but his words carried. He kept his eyes on his hands, which were clasped between his knees, not needing to make this a challenge. "And you're no longer *alive*."

Ambakisye did not answer, but stood up before he could control even this response.

Azuma and Weston could not hide their collective shock, either. They stared at Amaoke.

Only Kusini did not; her eyes were on Ambakisye.

"Husband," she spoke softly, and rejoined the group, seating herself beside him, and he reluctantly sat down.

"What are you saying?" Weston was confused, but he was getting no help from Amaoke.

"Not my story to tell," Amaoke said quietly, looking at the others. Azuma sat down across the table from Kusini and Ambakisye, and Weston gave up leaning against the windows and took the chair next to Amaoke.

"You knew?" Ambakisye looked at Amaoke in wonder.

"Yes. Immediately," Amaoke admitted. "In the nightclub, the moment we met."

"But how?" Ambakisye spoke the demand, but his demeanor was curious, and a little sad, Amaoke thought.

"Because unlike the rest of us, Amaoke experiences the world with all of his senses, and pays attention to a simple thing like instinct. He trusts his eyes only so far, and he knows that what we see can deceive us," Kusini answered.

"You have no human scent." Amaoke tapped his nose by way of explanation. "If I had to track you I would do so by the spices you use in your cooking, and the smell of your wife on your clothing and your skin. I hear no heartbeat from your chest, and you fill your lungs occasionally, but probably only as a bellows, in anticipation of needing breath to speak. It is habit, not necessity. Yet you do not smell of death, nor do I scent any decay. This is Kusini's magic, but it is hardly the extent of it."

"I understand much of my magic," Kusini said sadly. "Mostly, it is under control. But this I cannot fathom. I have no idea how it was done. The Morningstar suggests that this gift of necromancy was its intended legacy." She told them about Ambakisye's attack, how she had found him, dead, cold on the stones. Her grief and his subsequent resurrection.

"But it lies with the truth," Weston shook his head. "If it is giving you an explanation, it is either trying to hide the essential facts of the event, or obfuscate something it cannot comprehend."

"Or control." Amaoke nodded in agreement, then said to Kusini. "You are ignoring the obvious, this is not necromancy.

Ambakisye is not an animated corpse. He is the man you married, led by reason and passion."

"But my control was hard won, and if I do not feed properly, I return to a state that is far more dangerous," Ambakisye replied.

"I understand about controlling the beast inside, perhaps better even than you," Amaoke told him, seeing that perhaps only Azuma could fully understand his point. "I know about the choice that must be made, a choice to control what is inside, refuse to accept the monster. That choice requires a deliberateness that the wildness does not require. It would be easier to succumb to the whims of the ravening hunger inside, easier than fighting it over years, decades, centuries. It was love that restored you, don't disdain the magic in it. It is love that guides the decision to live on, and maintain ascendance over our baser forms, be it ghoul, dragon, demon, wolf…" Here he paused, looking at each of them in turn, his eyes finally settling on Kusini. What passed between them, the others could not name. "…or even Destroyer."

Kusini thought back to the time of the Bantu massacre. She would never forget it, but she had tried to forgive herself, and had much more control over the destructive aspects of her power. She was still discovering some of its limits, which had more to do with how she directed her will, and her abilities were far more nuanced than ever before.

"Love, yes," Kusini agreed. "But I did not direct it as such; the gift of 'Kisye's return was…unexpected."

She was surprised to hear Amaoke's rich laughter in response. "Let me know when you figure out how to control love." His respect and growing affection for her was evident in his tone, and when he put it just that way, she had to smile.

Weston leaned into Amaoke, pressing his shoulder against his friend briefly before straightening up again.

"Well," Azuma began, and seeing their expressions, said hastily, "I'll be of no help on the subject of controlling love, but I may have a bit of information to share on the subject of our dear

Sorceress. We didn't really unpack how she differs from the rest of us."

"I'd thought it was obvious," said Weston.

"Most certainly," Azuma agreed with him. "But there is also a scientific answer. I admit I don't completely understand it, but the implications are enormous. She is the carrier of an incredibly special gene, perhaps the first person, the only being, to express it. I call it the Okori gene."

"Okori?" Kusini asked.

"*Okori* means genesis," Azuma explained. "Not to be biblical, really, but it was the best term to use."

"But you cannot avoid that reference entirely," Weston gestured emphatically. "That word only has a common meaning because of its association with creation, in the divine context. Whether or not one accepts the doctrine, the word persists in our language, I think, because 'beginning' is insufficient to encompass such a thing."

"I agree. It has an eloquence and deeper meaning that is not otherwise expressed with the use of any other word. It is why I chose it," Azuma agreed, and if it was with less passion than Weston, it was of no less feeling.

"But you did not know at the time you characterized my genetic code what had happened to Ambakisye," Kusini protested.

"True. But I didn't have to. This gene produces a chemical byproduct, and one of my investigations into a novel biochemical is to assess its effect on cells. I ask of it, interrogate, if you will, its properties. Is it involved in cellular repair, destruction, growth? Is it a messenger, does it signal the cell to perform some essential task?

"What I discovered was extraordinary," Azuma said, even her voice hushed in a kind of reverence. "Although many of the PWA we sampled carried the gene and its byproduct, in those individuals that had the gene, the protein was latent, meaning it had no effect primarily or secondarily on any cellular mechanism. And in the case of Ambakisye, while he is a carrier of Okori, the protein product was missing entirely. What you have revealed explains that finding in him, I suppose, to some degree of satisfaction.

"But you, Kusini, produce a potent Okori protein. It does something that no other described compound can do. It behaves like a growth hormone in that it stimulates dormant cells to divide, but in rapidly dividing cells, which are at risk of cancerous transformation, the protein repairs DNA. Even in the presence of the worst human carcinogens, malignant transformation is arrested. The protein seems to expand the potential for a certain type of cell to differentiate, to become something else, if such is what the organism needs, encouraging the cell or cells to start to behave like stem cells, irrespective of what they were to begin with. And most significantly, it stimulates injury repair, even *mortal* injury."

"Can you say all of that again in English?" Amaoke asked.

"Of course," Azuma smiled kindly. "Basically, Kusini naturally produces a compound that fixes broken cells, cures paralysis, disease, cancer, and brings dead cells back to life. If it feels like she is all-powerful to us, this is the best evidence that she might not just be *a* god, she might, in fact, be *the* God.

46

"I CAN SHOW YOU," Azuma offered. "I have film archives of my observations on my private server."

"Who have you told about this?" Ambakisye spoke softly, but his distress and anger were unmistakable and unsurprising.

"No one, my friend, no one," Azuma told him. "We are the only five people in the world who know of this. And I think you understand why I would like to keep it that way."

"But your lab, your company, surely-" Weston shook his head. "How can it be that no one else is privy to this information?"

"It was always a necessity that I hide what I am. It started with that. From the beginning, I have had my own separate lab, a private lab. It has always had state-of-the-art security, and is now protected by my own biometrics, including telemetry. Someone cannot just cut off my hand and use it to gain entry. It cannot be hacked, the server is isolated, and all specimens and data are kept there at all times.

"If I assign a broader project to my scientists, I give them a small piece, a specific task, never enough to see the whole picture. Under no circumstances can any of the work be accessed outside the system. There is no offsite transfer," Azuma explained. "If I fail to access the system for a certain interval, the server autodestructs."

"But the implications for human health?" Weston said.

"Indeed. But I lacked her consent to publish. And if I had it, or bowed to the greed of selling it on the pharmaceutical market, further research and development would be needed to gain a more comprehensive understanding of its capabilities. In its raw form, it confers a sort of immortality, and as Ambakisye has shared with us, some of what comes with the life he has regained has not been entirely desirable. Further, how to do it without exposing the source?

"That last part has implications for all of us," Azuma said reasonably. "All of these findings are extraordinary. Each an index event, which means there are evolutionary considerations. Normally, I would be looking for the source of the environmental pressure that caused such an event. Such changes are usually species protective, and herald traits that are intended to be passed on, inherited by the next generation of the species. But based on certain things I have observed in myself; I fear that these changes are rather end-evolutionary. They are unlikely to be passed on."

"Because you are headed to your death?" Ambakisye asked, and there was nothing cynical nor fearful in his tone.

"Possibly. Or perhaps related to our longevity, or some burgeoning immortality. Perhaps the beings who possessed this genetic code had no need to procreate," Azuma told him.

"It certainly fits with the mythology of many religious traditions," she continued, looking at Weston.

"Indeed. Angels were created, not born, but there is conflict as to whether they were fleshly beings or not." Weston could have said more, but did not, wanting to be respectful of the beliefs of the others.

"Perhaps they did not possess it originally, but eventually required it as part of their own evolution, whatever these beings that commune with the Morningstar actually are," Azuma pointed out. "And I think it relates to Amaoke's advice regarding how to craft an attack that will expose the Morningstar's identity in the event of any confusion." She looked expectantly at the others, wondering if anyone else had figured it out. She suspected Amaoke and Weston had, and had no difficulty believing that Kusini must understand as well.

"What am I missing?" Ambakisye looked to each of them in turn, his gaze finally settling on his wife, who looked tired, and very sad. He was frustrated that he did not understand what was causing her pain, she who suffered enough.

"We were married more than five years, before..." Kusini gestured at Ambakisye and favored him with a gentle smile, but it was clear she was speaking to the others. She said nothing more, merely shook her head with no little distress.

"My wife, Nanatha, thought something was wrong with *her*," Amaoke said quietly. "I knew all along that I was the one who couldn't give her children, but I couldn't tell her how I knew, could never give her the comfort of the certainty that she needed to feel she hadn't failed me."

They could all hear his anguish at the inability to lift this emotional burden from his wife. Weston's shoulder made contact with Amaoke's again, and this time he stayed close.

"I thought it was me," Ambakisye whispered, his own pain at this imagined failure was as clear in his voice as it had been in Amaoke's. "I never would have blamed you, *mpenzi*," He turned to pull Kusini close, ignoring the discomfort caused by her heightened distress, transmitted to him through this touching.

Kusini smiled, touching her forehead to his. "Nor I you."

Azuma watched this quietly, but Amaoke could see she was struggling with her own feelings. He already knew that she viewed her weaknesses as betrayals, and was thus surprised when she spoke, more personally than she had before.

"I feel as though I would have nothing to contribute to this conversation. I am not – I do not – engage in any sexual habit that could result in childbearing. I know that my *twin* was certainly prolific in his attentions to the opposite sex, but to my knowledge it never resulted in any issue," Azuma managed to speak to her own truth, finally adding, "I have never had any monthly courses that would suggest the potential anyway."

"And I could argue that my celibacy means that I am uncertain about my own procreative potential," Weston joined the conversation with a wry smile and his voice wavered slightly. "But if I am not really human…"

"You are as much a human, if not more of one, than any of us," Azuma corrected him. "Science cannot strip you of something you essentially possess, a concept that transcends what you are on a cellular level. Humanity is an abstract, wholly separate from biology, and you have it in abundance."

47

AMAOKE KNEW HE SHOULD NOT have been surprised at her kindness, knowing that Azuma expected others to conduct their own emotional work independently, and that hers was a carefully cultivated defense. It did not mean she was unfeeling.

But he did feel guilty when he realized just how much learning about all of this had hurt Weston. The revelation that he had no human DNA had hit its mark, feeding every insecurity he had about his birth, the demons, his appearance.

The priest cleared his throat and sniffed quietly, taking off his glasses. Tears fell from his eyes, and this brought Kusini to kneel next to him, as Amaoke leaned in, putting an arm around Weston's shoulders. It was the first time that it occurred to him how young Weston really was compared to the rest of them. He was not hardened by centuries of suffering.

Azuma approached as well, and stood behind them, putting one hand on each man's shoulder. The group collapsed inward, with Weston at the center, and even Ambakisye took Weston's free hand in his. Of all of them assembled, 'Kisye understood the emotions Weston was experiencing at that moment, had processed them himself many times since his own change.

"It doesn't mean that your genetic differences create some absolute exclusion that separates you in isolation, either" Azuma told him. "There is something else, something I felt was as significant as it seems impossible. And it ties you, Weston, to the rest of us in such a way as to ensure your inclusion irrefutably.

"Our genetic makeup is an amalgam of our parents. We inherit some genes from our mothers and some from our fathers. What that means is that siblings have a certain degree of similarity in their genetic makeup. A certain percentage of the same genetic sequence will identify persons who share parentage.

"That percentage of similarity, or sameness, if you will, can predict confraternity, whether someone is a brother or sister of the person being evaluated, or confirm paternity, which is its most common application.

"Well, our DNA, that of Weston, myself, Kusini, and Amaoke, shows a preserved percentage of genes in common. We are, by the strictest genetic definition, brothers and sisters." Azuma dropped this bombshell into the silence and was not bothered one bit that it persisted. She wanted them to absorb what she had just told them, in all its incredulousness, in all its futile impossibility.

"But our parents were eight *different* people!" Weston said wonderingly, breaking the silence.

"Yes, and your genetic profiles confirm this. It was one of the first things I cross-referenced. Amaoke, Kusini, and I all have different mothers; mitochondrial DNA, which you can only inherit from your mother, was unique in each of us. Weston has no mitochondrial DNA to evaluate. I cannot as easily compare paternal DNA, but in the remaining human genome that each of us possesses, there are differences aplenty to suggest we do not have paternity in common. If Weston had a Y chromosome, I could do Y-PCR on his and Amaoke's genetic sample to see if they were a match, as all males in the same family would be, but I can confidently say that such a match would be unlikely.

"Rather, where we show enough similarity to be part of a family structure genetically is in our uncharacterized genetic material, that with bond structures unlike what we expect to see in human DNA. It is this material that makes up the entirety of Weston's genetic profile. Whatever human DNA I would expect him to possess has been entirely replaced with this foreign genetic structure. This is part of our answer to *how* we approach the Morningstar, and I think it helps us with the *what* as well. I believe that this novel genetic code is really its genetic material, a unique signature of its being. Unfortunately, as Weston has pointed out, it tells us nothing about the *why* of our collective existence."

"Does the Morningstar know we contain this material in our genetic code? If not, perhaps we can use the information against it." Weston surmised.

Azuma nodded. "I have considered this. On balance, the more likely position is that it *does* know, and that this is a part of its greater plans.

"I think if I could have one more piece of the genetic puzzle, I might be able to engineer a way to identify it more absolutely than by sight alone," she added.

"That's good news for his nether regions," said Ambakisye, nodding at Weston, and he sounded more serious than someone who was making a joke should.

Azuma could not help but smile. "I suppose it is. But I don't even know if what I propose to try is possible. It seems that I must find a way to crossover to the spirit realm, the *Yomi-no-kuni*, Land of the Dead, and I don't know of any reliable way to do it.

"I have, at times, had visions, but they were delivered upon me by the Morningstar. I surmise from what the old scrolls say that my father found a way to cross the boundary. He spent years making blood sacrifices before the dark kami opened up the way for him." Her tone betrayed her irritation that she had no control in this matter. "Apparently, Akenomyosei gave him a gift of the gods to return to the human realm, a means to father a child of exceptional qualities, capture the power he craved."

Azuma looked at Kusini, who shook her head gently. Kusini said, "Though I have visions, and at times have been able to intervene upon them, I have only experienced that realm within a manipulated reality supplied by the Morningstar at those times when it wished to communicate. I will admit I have never tried to cross over on my own, and I would have no idea where to begin."

"I may be a conduit, somehow, when I am at my worst," 'Kisye reasoned. "But I have no independent recollections of those times, and it would be too dangerous for us to try to make use of that state of my madness to guarantee order or success."

"I need to get to Onigashima, and try to obtain a sample of the sacred koi from which the Dragon was created. This may be the only key to unlocking the mystery of our supernormal code, and it may give us some insight into the Monster that we could not otherwise divine from our collective experiences." Azuma's significant frustration about this limitation was evident in her voice.

"Is this Spirit Realm the place you go when you die?" Ambakisye asked.

Amaoke nodded. "Probably. But you cannot easily find the dead as long as you still are numbered among the living."

"I wish I could help," Ambakisye said, understanding the implication. "But all of my magic comes from Kusini, and I have never had any experience like you are describing, I do not recall ever experiencing any crossover. When I lose control, I am just gone. I have no memory of those terrible instances."

"I'm afraid I don't have any additional ideas," Weston said. "During an exorcism, I might pull back the veil of reality to dispatch demons, and having my own demons suggests that I existed on the boundary, but I have never been able to rend that fabric on my own. Now that they are gone…well, I still see the Morningstar, look at the other side, every day in the mirror, but I don't trust that as a way to get through to another realm. And there is some mythology about being able to trap a demon within a mirror. Honestly, I don't otherwise know anything of use."

Amaoke was incredulous. And his habit of being quiet was not keeping the attentions of the others off of him. Not anymore. Four pairs of eyes turned to him.

"I cross over in my dreams," he admitted. "I've done it with fasting and ritual prayer, but never with a passenger." He shrugged. "It happens when I am high on ceremonial herbs."

Azuma looked at him speculatively.

"Of course," Kusini said warmly. "You are a shaman, a medicine man. It was your power that called to me when you were caught in the trap."

"You?" Amaoke nodded, enjoying the satisfaction of learning the truth behind that old mystery, grateful to her.

But then he wanted to protest the way in which she had characterized him. He stopped to consider it for a moment. He *was* the elder of his people. He had never questioned the ease of his movement among the spirits. Perhaps Kusini was right, although he had never thought of himself in those terms. Medicine, in his tradition, was magic and wisdom, which was why the most senior elder was the one with the most medicine.

"High, you said?" Azuma had an expression on her face that Amaoke wasn't certain he liked.

"Well, just the smoke of wild celery root. It can be unreliable," he told her. "The best way is in prayer and fasting."

"We all pray in different ways," Azuma replied. "Perhaps a blood connection would facilitate my plan."

"Why do I get the feeling that means you're going to bite me?"

"You might enjoy it," Azuma suggested wickedly.

48

AMAOKE WAS SURPRISED WHEN AZUMA stepped into his arms, her torso against his, her deep brown eyes on a level with his own, mesmerizing, and perhaps amused, because he was clearly uncomfortable, behaving as though this were a predicament he might need to escape.

"May I?" she asked, gently placing her arms around his neck.

"Couldn't you just bite my wrist?" he asked uncertainly, looking around to Weston for help. The priest was trying not to laugh, and just shrugged. Amaoke was unsure what to do with his hands, was completely at a loss now that Azuma was so close to him.

"I could, but it would be disconnected, more painful than necessary." Azuma's chuckle was low, and it vibrated against his chest. "I prefer this to be pleasant, and the intimacy will increase the likelihood that we can cross over together."

"But you just told me you're my sister," Amaoke made one last desperate attempt to delay. "Isn't this against the law in some places?"

"Perhaps," Azuma smiled, seductive now. She freed her arms from his shoulders long enough to place his arms about her own waist. "Do I feel like your sister?"

But that was the problem. She didn't. And Amaoke was responding to her magic, but his natural defenses were in place. The Wolf didn't like his discomfort, and a slow growl started up, rumbling through him. Amaoke swallowed it, not wanting to be rude.

"Kusini, could you just put a hand on his back to steady him?" Azuma asked politely. "I do not think it would be wise for the Wolf to come through right now."

Amaoke felt Kusini behind him, then a small jolt of energy when she made contact, but it was not unpleasant, a low vibration on his spine. He found it soothing.

"Amaoke," Azuma spoke again, softly, her face buried in his hair, her mouth against his ear, speaking with the voice of a lover. "I am not sure how my venom may affect you, so do not be alarmed if you feel lightheaded or even weak. If you relax, and focus on the closeness between the two of us, it should be pleasurable, and not distressing."

Amaoke was not sure he would be able to relax, but then her mouth was on his, and he found himself responding, surprisingly participating, which he suspected was the Wolf giving the equivalent of a mental shrug and taking advantage of the situation. Amaoke was not a man who engaged in gratuitous pleasures; he needed meaningful connection in intimacy.

He could still feel Kusini's hand at the base of his spine, warm and reassuring. His eyes rolled toward Weston one last time, and he found his friend still trying unsuccessfully to control his amusement. Then he felt Azuma's tongue probing, exploring the sharpness of his teeth, and he gave in, and kissed back, his hands tightening on her hips, focusing on her, feeling the odd rippling of her flesh beneath his hold, the Dragon under the surface. By the time he felt the sting of her bite on his tongue, and tasted the blood that passed between them, he was already starting to float away into the void.

49

AZUMA FELT THE CHANGE IMMEDIATELY, Amaoke's
form receding from her embrace as the world fell away, and she
blinked in confusion, looking around. She found herself in a new
place, a lush paradise under a mist.

The flowers should have been more fragrant for all their
loveliness, and there was a dreamlike quality to her surroundings
that recalled the road home from Ryukyu all those centuries hence.

She stood on a sort of path through the growth, a steep
valley fell away behind her, and the mountain rose ahead of her,
although she was unable to see to the top through the cloudbank.
She listened, and heard the occasional bird calls, and the constant
drip of the moisture that fell from the canopy onto the broad leaves
of the ferns.

She wore her *kobakama*, and both short and long swords
were at her waist, but no armor. She had no sooner wondered
whether Amaoke had delivered her alone here as he opened the
spirit world, when there was a crashing sound on the path above
her, someone or something coming fast, running along quickly.

What emerged from the undergrowth was a lanky, muscular
adolescent of about twelve years of age, with endless flowing black
hair. He was tall, completely naked, and he came to a stop about
two feet in front of her, wiggling his toes in the soft soil. He gazed
at her like a lovesick puppy, large, blasted pupils in the center of his
blue eyes betrayed his intoxication. Then he shook all over, not
unlike a large dog, his wet hair clinging to his handsome face, and

he smiled proudly at her, with a mouth full of sharp teeth that did nothing to diminish the charm.

Azuma sighed heavily. While she had suspected that her venom might affect Amaoke unpredictably, she had no idea how to respond to this outcome. She had hoped for a spirit guide, not a lovesick teenager.

But before she could waste more time on lament, he gestured up the mountainside and spoke to her in a tongue she had no hope to understand. She had tasted his blood to facilitate the bridge to this place, but either had not had enough of it to read anything of him, or was thwarted by his own supernatural provenance. Her look of confusion did not seem to bother him in the least, as though her inability to make sense of his language were immaterial.

He came close to her, the top of his head near her chin, and leaned up, placing his nose against her neck, scenting her. She could feel the small puffs of air from his nostrils on her skin, and his wet hair brushing against her. He opened his mouth, drawing great breaths between his teeth, as if tasting the air. Then he stepped back again, as if satisfied, showing her an expression she could not decipher, and grasped her wrist firmly and tugged, indicating she should follow the path uphill.

Then he disappeared once again into the growth ahead. She kept to the path as best she could, but the going was slow, and it felt as if she were making no progress upward. The cloud bank around her and above seemed unchanging, and though the tropical forest was beautiful, there was a forced monotony about it that eventually maddened her. She had the strangest sense of *déjà vu*, as if she had somehow been to this place before.

Now and again, her young companion appeared, nearly always here or there off the path. He was exploring among the trees, and at one point, although she could not see him below shoulder height through the ferns, she could tell that he was marking some of them. He caught her eyes and gave her the eyebrows, with all the exaggerated flirtatiousness of a pubescent boy who is overly enamored of his own charms. She managed not to laugh, after all, she had done this to him and brought it upon herself.

Watching him, she realized too that his movements were not the random wanderings she had first thought they were, nor were they the result of venom-induced confusion. Amaoke was tracking something, and her suspicion was confirmed when he drew close to her from time to time and adjusted her course up the mountain.

She recalled from her father's writings that he had spent many days climbing Onigashima, of his recollection of a beard grown long, of his worries he would ever see the top. Would the gods favor her own intrusion?

They continued like this, through endless days, and dark nights where she was thankful for her preternatural vision. The darkness was even more surreal, and she could hear the sounds of the night demons that did not come out during the day. She could feel the interest of these beings, perhaps it was the interest of the island itself. On the occasions that she felt a dawning fear of the furtive sounds she could sometimes hear nearby, Amaoke sensed it, and his low growl of warning from the trees ahead comforted her. It apparently warned off the worst of the *yokai* as well, for she and her companion were not troubled. And Azuma did feel that it was Amaoke they feared, and she felt terrible for underestimating him. She suspected he had known the dangers of this place, had some understanding of the need for balance.

Azuma wondered if she should face the mountain as Dragon, but found, with no little distress, that she could not call it to herself. And when she could no longer name the number of days they had climbed, the waking visions returned.

An interminable epoch of time passed before Azuma noticed a new level of agitation in Amaoke. He bounded through the ferns directly ahead of her, pointing and shouting in his own language, and soon disappeared from sight. Azuma's own long-legged stride was not enough to keep pace with him.

But he soon reappeared, running back down toward her, expertly stopping himself near her, shaking water from his body and hair onto her and laughing. It was as if he were telling her to wake up, exuberant about something, trying to tell her, his language like a song to her ears, rhythmic, lovely suddenly, despite her inability to decipher it.

He departed again, dashing out ahead, pausing only to look back as if to hurry her along, so she obliged him, quickening her pace. The mist was beginning to thin, and she could just make out a curve that marked the summit. A few moments more and they were climbing out of the clouds, and she could see the sky above, the bright blue expanse. Ahead of her on the path, Amaoke stood in sunshine, the first they had seen. She watched him pause, absorbing its warmth, waiting for her.

50

THEY STOOD TOGETHER FOR A few moments before he pulled her along, hurrying her to the crest of the mountain. The path remained mired in tropical forest, but here, at the top, the mountain flattened out into a plateau of sorts. Azuma turned and looked down, where they had come from, for the first time able to see it in perspective. It was a visual paradise, a feast of beauty such as she had not seen before.

The mountain, wreathed in mists, beyond which she could see the sea, sunlight sparkling upon the waves like a million stars, the beach impossibly far below, as if they looked down from the heavens themselves. It was the perch of the gods.

But she could not linger. She turned back to the path, and though the sun was bright on her shoulders, filtering through the ferns, she felt a chill. Amaoke stood on the path ahead and nodded. He felt it too. The mountain knew they were here, and she felt its power, focused on the two of them like a living being, sentient, ancient, waiting.

She stepped onto the mountaintop and entered a silent realm. No birds sang. The wind did not rustle the leaves. She could hear the erratic beating of her own heart, like a beacon. Amaoke slowed ahead of her, waiting until she had come behind him, and he pushed his arms backward as a signal to have a care. It was also a gesture to shield her, she realized, when he slowed further until she was just at his back.

There was a clearing ahead, and she could see water, a lake of indescribable beauty, its color mimicked that of the sky above it, not solely a reflection. This azure lake had also been described in detail in Ietsune's scrolls, and Azuma realized that her father's poetic words had not done it justice.

Amaoke did not immediately enter the clearing, leaning into her to bring her to a halt. She inhaled the clean scent of his hair, fresh air and pine forest despite the flora that surrounded them. And he was warm, in spite of prolonged exposure to the elements, the damp.

He remained quite still, so she did the same, for several moments they were as one being, crouched there, as if on a precipice. She could hear his heart, a slow metronome of control in counterpoint to the chaos of her own aberrant rhythm, the slow bellows of his breathing, the click of his eyelids, the scrape of his lashes on his cheeks. Time seemed to slow as she watched the motes of dust and moisture move on the warm air, reflecting the sunlight in miniature prisms under her focused attention.

Amaoke straightened slowly and stepped out into the clearing, not waiting to see if she would follow. He headed straight for the water, and though he did not give any indication that he was aware of his surroundings, Azuma could tell that he was watching and listening carefully.

Azuma came after, and by the time she reached the water's edge, he was already wading out into it. She frowned, it seemed almost sacrilegious to enter this sacred pool, so she stood breathless, watching the graceful turns of hundreds of koi, their tricolored scales reflecting the light.

And she noticed something else, something endearing to her, comforting in this forced reality. The koi here seemed to be attracted to Amaoke, congregating around his legs as he waded deeper, curious. It reminded her of her friends in the pond at home. For all that she felt uncomfortable here, out of her element, Amaoke seemed to fit, his energy seemed to sync with this place.

For a moment she wondered about something else, but this she kept to herself for the time being, setting a mental reminder to ask him about it later, hoping she would remember. His reverent behavior did not invite conversation, and it seemed wrong to speak aloud here.

There seemed to be a drop-off in depth, as if there were deeper water beyond the shallows, the blue water darker, and her suspicion in this was confirmed when Amaoke stopped walking. The water was nearly to his waist and he did not look back at her, rather looked out toward the depths, and down, concentrating on something.

And it seemed she watched him stand there for hours, unmoving, wondering how he did so. She had never seen such stillness and such patience. But he was entirely focused on a single point in the water, indeterminable to her at this distance. And then, quick as the blink of an eye, he dove under the water, there one moment, gone the next, and just as Azuma was watching the splash, he came back up, blowing sparkling droplets into the air as he broke the surface once more.

He strode confidently through the water, his long legs kicking through it easily, and came to a stop in front of her but did not come all the way onto the shore. It was odd, and Azuma was not sure he knew he did it, but he kept his feet to the lake side of the waterline.

He had a very mischievous look, playful even, and when she leaned in toward him to see what he carried, he shook, sending water flying in all directions, splashing her purposefully, before he tossed back his head and gave a joyful, open-mouthed laugh. His pleasure was infectious, and though she couldn't help but gasp when the water hit her, she also couldn't really be cross with him.

Amaoke brought his hands up level to her eyes, and opened them carefully, like a magician revealing a clever trick. Between his fingers, she glimpsed their prize, a gauzy-finned koi the same color as the lake. It wriggled yet, ready to fight this foe that had dared interrupt its reign over the depths, this latent god, this baby dragon.

But her exaltation was short lived, for Amaoke, after revealing this success, tipped his head back and dropped the fish into his mouth and began chewing it with enthusiasm. His eyes were bright and proud as he nodded at her.

She screamed in horror and disbelief, putting her hands out to try to stop him, but it was too late. She grabbed his upper arms in anger and dragged him out of the water, unsure whether she could control her rage.

But whatever she might have done next was forgotten, for as soon as Amaoke's feet touched the shore, the sky darkened rapidly, and Azuma immediately realized her error. They had stolen from the sacred pool, taken a dragon from its nursery, a being so rare and exalted that surely the powerful dark kami that ruled Onigashima would not swallow such an insult. Whatever sufferance of their presence they had enjoyed in their time here, this violation had ended it.

But it was not some nameless god that came for them, it was Akenomyosei himself, in a manifestation that Azuma had only heard about and never before seen. More accurately, it was both the Monster and the Death Bringer, riding the wind, an enormous two-headed dragon that descended toward them, spiraling out of the sky, and hitting the earth with a terrible force.

Azuma tried to call the Goddess inside her, but her own dragon did not answer. And Akenomyosei stalked them there on the shore of the lake, darting directly to them like a deadly arrow, Azuma watching in horror as it came ever closer, until she could have reached out and touched the fringed feelers around its twin snouts that now twisted sinuously and furiously about one another, poised as a serpent would, ready to strike. Its eyes were dark, depthless pools that swallowed the light.

It raised one great claw and reached for her. Azuma briefly felt the bite of its strike on her shoulder, before strong arms caught her up, and Amaoke pulled her body in toward his own, turning away at the last moment. The dragon's claw continued its damage, but not to her; Amaoke took the brunt of the assault as it raked over his shoulder and down his back while he shielded her, and then Onigashima was sliding away from her, and she was falling, Amaoke's screams of agony echoing inside her, his blood slippery under her fingers.

51

PAIN. It was so big, it was everything. The only thing.

Amaoke tried to open his eyes, but he wasn't sure what he was seeing. He heard a great deal of commotion around himself, but it was hard for him to concentrate, and he could feel the world slipping away again.

He wanted to say something, tried to tell all the people around him to be quiet. He just wanted to rest, but he wasn't sure they heard him. Where had they all come from? He wanted to wave them off, push them away, but nothing seemed to work. His arms were weak, and his legs felt heavy and warm. Useless.

He heard the plaintive whining of the wolf, but it sounded lost and faraway. In another corner of the room. He had to find it. It was hurt, badly from the sounds of its cries.

"We were attacked," he heard Azuma's voice from far away. "No, leave it. We have to stop this bleeding; I think it went through his spine…"

"He's trying to get up!" Ambakisye now, and he felt strong hands on his shoulders and back. Something touched his face.

"Rest easy, Brother," Weston's voice was at his ear, and his weight seemed to be anchoring Amaoke in place. "It will be over soon."

He smiled. Was he dying? But there was no more time for questions, or thoughts, as he was drifting down again, the world rapidly darkening. This wasn't so bad. Finally.

Surgical specimen 7456578 (FB1)

Specimen collected from subject Superhuman chimera gamma (AS), identified during procedure as foreign body (FB) one (1). It was harvested at a depth of 4 cm, embedded in torn paraspinal muscle at the approximate level of the fourth thoracic vertebra. No other foreign material identified during further exploration of the wound.

Assessment of FB1 reveals grossly a keratinoid material, curved, with a sharp protuberant distal surface. Ragged disruption of the tissue is seen proximally. It most closely resembles the integumentary samples taken from Superhuman chimera alpha (AH); specifically, it is morphologically identical in appearance to the Dragon claw, only larger by approximately five percent after extrapolating the extent of the missing piece.

Microscopically, it exhibits senescent change far advanced to that observed within the archived specimen for Superhuman chimera alpha. The proximal surface has a small scrap of cellular material suitable for genetic testing…

Genetically, FB1 cross references most closely with the DNA of Metahuman alpha (WS), although there is a 0.2% difference between the two specimens, suggesting that the organisms are not identical. This is a far greater value than that seen among any two humans (0.1%), while still far smaller than that seen between humans and their nearest phylogenetic relative (Bonobo chimpanzee, **Pan paniscus**, *0.36%). The significance of this finding is unclear, and may be of questionable value scientifically given the vastly different composition of the genetic structure.*

Marker addendum to transcript, added by **Himura, MD, PhD, Dr. Azuma:**
Specimen filed as Metahuman beta (presumed origin Akenomyosei), see attached detail of genetic assay.

Findings as noted confirm possibility that distinguishing the two Metahuman organisms via differential biomarker may be successful.

[End of transcript]

52

AMAOKE AWOKE TO QUIET AND could not immediately recall where he was. He was experiencing vertigo like never before, and was unable to focus, so he closed his eyes to stop the sensation of motion. His head felt like a split melon, and he resisted the urge to reach up with both hands and hold it together.

"What you are feeling is the hangover from my venom," Azuma's calm voice came to him from somewhere to his right. He thought she sounded subdued. "I can give you something to ease it."

"No." He spoke with a conviction that chastened her. "No chemicals. It isn't safe. The Wolf can be unpredictable as it is."

"Okay," she relented. "The best cure is sleep, if you think you can manage it."

"Finally, something I am good at," he told her, settling in to try to relax. Even her soft laughter hurt his head, so he waved his hands at her, shooing her away.

When next he awakened, she was sitting in a chair right next to the bed he was in. He looked around, realizing he was in one of the recovery rooms in her private clinic. She looked like a child in her oversize sweatshirt, with her hair pinned up, and she tapped away on a computer, peering intently at something. She wore tortoiseshell glasses, which he thought odd. He watched her for a bit, she was engrossed and didn't realize he was up.

Finally, she glanced up and saw him watching. He wasn't sure what his expression was telling her, because she smiled a little. "What?"

He motioned to her glasses. He wondered if there was some eyesight issue, which would be incongruous for a predator. Odd the things that captured the attention.

"Oh. I don't need glasses for vision. These are blue filters, because I get way too much screen time, and it gives me eye fatigue." She indicated her laptop. "A thoroughly modern hazard. I could wear contacts, but I'm a coward about putting anything into my eyes. How are *you* feeling?" She seemed embarrassed to be talking about herself, and changed the subject.

"More like myself. Quite a bit of excitement there at the end, but we escaped," Amaoke said. "How bad was I?"

Her eyes telegraphed her concern, and something else. He didn't know her well enough to discern what it was. Regret, perhaps, although he thought there was some annoyance.

"It was the Morningstar. It destroyed your back, opened you down to your spine. Thankfully, we got you stabilized, and your own regeneration seems to be working faster than I thought it could." She still looked a bit crestfallen.

"But-?" he prompted, wanting her to tell him what was bothering her.

"Well, all that trouble, and peril, essentially for nothing," Azuma held her empty hands out toward him, palms up.

"I don't know about that," he answered in a mysterious tone, and she didn't know him well enough to understand. "Do you have any dental floss?"

"Maybe, I-why?" She looked confused.

But he said no more, just looked around briefly for something he didn't find. "And some water?"

Azuma turned away and left the room. After a few minutes, she returned, with a floss pick and a small cup of water.

"Thanks," he said, accepting the floss first. He used it to pick several small pieces of flesh from between his teeth, then took the cup from her. He sipped a mouthful and rinsed it around, spitting it back into the cup and dropping the pick in behind it. "I think it should be enough of a specimen for a world-famous geneticist like you." He smiled, those odd teeth part of his appeal. He'd remembered that she needed the koi's genetic makeup.

"Ama, I could kiss you," she said, sounding sincere.

"Once was probably enough," he chuckled. "Incestuous thing."

She had to laugh. "But why didn't you tell me?"

"I knew trouble was coming when you pulled me from the lake," he explained. "If I thought you'd stop kicking my ass long enough to listen – and who beats up on a kid, anyway?" He softened this question by putting his hand on the side of her face, against her hair, and to his surprise she leaned into his touch, and put her head down on the coverlet against his hip.

"I thought I'd gotten you killed. You knew what you were doing the entire time," she said.

"Pretty hard to do. Many have tried. I knew that the lake was some sort of boundary. You were out and I was in. Safer that way. I couldn't pass the fish to you, and I wasn't sure we could bring it back with us, so I gambled. If I ate it, it became one with me, so to speak, and I was confident we could leave that place with what I had. When you pulled me out of the water, it tripped some sort of silent underworld alarm."

"But you barely know me, and you saved my life," she said, sounding surprised, as though it wasn't something she had ever expected anyone to do.

"You're my kid sister," he said, teasing, but making sure she knew there was a part of him that was serious about what he'd done. "I was your only sure way out. If I had left you there…" He shuddered involuntarily. They had both seen an incarnation of the Morningstar that was novel to them, and convincingly deadly.

She was quiet, and after a time she sat back in her chair and pushed a lock of stray hair out of her eyes. "I'm worried it is looking for us now."

"Nope. We learned something else," he said. "It doesn't want us to study that koi. It wanted to stop us badly enough that it was bent on destroying us to prevent our escape, despite the fact that all other information points to it *needing* us. That can only mean it is afraid. We must have something it doesn't want us to have. And with your expertise, hopefully we can learn what that something is. I'm fine here. You should get started." With that, he gave her a smug look, leaned back, closed his eyes, and was on his way to sleep once more. By the time she had gathered up her possessions and the precious specimen and was leaving the room, he was snoring softly.

Harvested specimen Onigashima (ON), File Project Mokushiroku

*...although phenotypically the tissue recovered has gross and cellular properties that align with **Cyprinus carpio**, genetic analysis reveals no genomic similarity to that organism. Ninety-eight percent of bond structures are unidentified genetic proteins.*

The unidentified genetic material found in the sample exhibits supernumerary unexplained STR segments with unidentified chemical base/bond structure. It most closely resembles similar genetic material found in the metahuman specimens although the sequencing differs by a calculated seven percent...

53

WHEN NEXT HE BEGAN TO awaken, Amaoke thought he was still dreaming, but furtive sounds continued to hammer their way into his consciousness, until he could no longer resist opening his eyes. The hour was indeterminate, but it felt like early morning, predawn light with soft grey shadows.

There was something moving in the room adjacent to his, but he could not identify what he was hearing. He scented the air carefully, picking up only his own scent and Azuma's; any other information he might have garnered was masked by the astringent smells of the clinic surrounding him.

He stood up, surprised to find he felt steadier than he'd expected to, and other than a small twinge of his lower spine, he was pain-free. He approached the sliding door that led to the shared bathroom, and pushed it open on its track.

Azuma was inside, and at first he thought he had walked in on her getting ready, as she wore only black underwear and a black undershirt. She looked up, surprised to see him there, but he could smell her distress, and something else, a kind of sweaty, male-musk scent not normally a part of her signature.

"I'm sorry," he began, ready to withdraw, but then he saw the tourniquet on her arm and the syringe she held in her hand. Blue scales were emerging and disappearing on her flawless skin, and he could see she had a serious case of the shakes.

"It's okay," she said, her voice as shaky as the rest of her. "I was resting in the alcove in case you needed anything, and I realized I had forgotten to-" she blinked slowly, and tried to take a deep breath, but failed. She saw him looking at the needle. "It is my cure...not what you think..." she was trying to smile, but he could see she was in trouble.

"I'll get the Collector," he offered, but she shook her head.

"He'll be on his way already," she gasped, doubling over and almost dropping the syringe.

Amaoke didn't know what to do for her, so he stepped into the room, closing the distance between them. She was shaking so violently that she could barely hold the syringe. He took it gently from her, setting it aside, and then took her weight as she leaned into him, entirely unsure what to do next.

"...need to get that..." her eyes indicated the contents of the syringe and her arm as she sagged, more scales emerging as she struggled to talk.

Amaoke looked at the needle helplessly, at the tourniquet on her arm, and shook his head. "I don't know how to do that, I-"

"...don't have to...thigh...muscle..." she was jerking uncontrollably, and he noticed her eyes were as blue as his, the pupils slit-like.

He reached for the syringe once more, and had no sooner wrapped his fingers around it than her contortions dragged them to the tiles, her body elongating abnormally, wrapping around him and constricting painfully. He looked down at her legs, now covered with thousands of tiny scales, and guessed, correctly, that the needle would never penetrate them.

He twisted with her, not wanting to lose control, turning sideways, which flipped her over. He could feel her arms receding, shortening as she was forced to let go, the transformation taking her. He pushed the leg band of her shorts up, finding skin, and uttering an apology, drove the needle into her exposed buttock, hoping he was in the right place, and depressed the plunger. He

pulled the needle out and tossed it away, into the corner under the
sink, recognizing that the shaking he now felt was her anger, the
Dragon had broken through.

She turned a snakelike head toward him, taking his forearm
into the jaws of that snout briefly, just a nip, before letting go, just
ahead of the sounds of rending fabric, something he was very
familiar with, as her clothing was shredded by the change.

Amaoke sat very still, allowing Azuma to wrap herself
around him in a configuration most comfortable to her, unsurprised
at her size and heaviness, mesmerized by just how beautiful she
was. She turned that glittering gaze on him once more before
settling her heavy head on his lap. Her shakes were lessened
somewhat, and he could both feel and hear the juddering rattle of
her heart against his hip. He stroked the scales of her flank with a
gentle finger, but she hissed and shook briefly, scales clattering, so
he stopped.

"Sorry," he murmured, letting her settle once more, grateful
that the Collector appeared in the doorway at just that moment.

The man had rushed out of bed, for all that he looked as
composed as a person fully awake. The only clues that he had been
abed were the black pajama pants he wore, and his long hair was
loose. He looked his question to Amaoke, kneeling next to the two
of them on the tiles, and the Dragon let him cradle her heavy head
in his hands.

Amaoke tilted his head toward the syringe under the sink,
and the Collector looked both relieved and annoyed. "She hates it,
waits until the last minute. It makes her rather ill for the better part
of a day or two."

"She was fighting hard, couldn't get the needle into her arm.
She was trying not to wake me," Amaoke explained, unnecessarily.
He should have assumed that she and this man had some sort of
connection he didn't understand.

The Collector nodded. "She has a schedule optimized.
This is her *cure*, and she is supposed to take it on time, or there is

288 | LJ FARROW

the chance…but then, she has been very focused these last few days. Not sleeping right, not eating right, worried over your recovery. It's no wonder she didn't prioritize…"

Amaoke didn't need him to finish, and he spoke in the same quiet tone the Collector had affected. "Tatsuo Tomo was upon her; I could scent him. But then she changed, and it was the Dragon instead."

"Smart, very smart," the Collector observed, and Amaoke realized that he was speaking to Azuma. To Amaoke he clarified, "Only Azuma controls the Dragon, by changing she thwarted her brother's emergence."

"I hope I didn't do something wrong, she told me *thigh*, but she didn't have one anymore," Amaoke said, needing to confess it. The Collector put a hand on his forearm, and it was oddly reassuring, and not as incongruous to their relationship as Amaoke might have thought it would be.

"She'll be sore, but thankful." The Collector almost smiled. "I owe you a debt of gratitude. I thank you for helping her; not everyone would. She is supposed to allow the *Akai* to attend her at all times, but as you can imagine, she is impatient with too much fuss, and she doesn't always sleep where she is supposed to."

They both looked up as a few other faces appeared in the doorway. Several pairs of eyes eyed Amaoke with deep suspicion but seemed reassured that the Collector was present. Amaoke suspected weapons were concealed about these various persons.

"*Kanojo wa antei shite imasu.*" The Collector never turned his eyes from Azuma as he addressed the *Akai*. "Master *Go*, if you would, stay please."

54

"I DON'T KNOW WHETHER TO thank you or punch you," Azuma said, finding Amaoke in the breakfast room later that morning. But he was relieved to see that she was smiling. "My ass?!"

"Not my fault that you needed back-alley healthcare," Amaoke said, shrugging. "It was the only part of you that was still human. I don't remember signing up to give injections in random bathrooms."

She lowered herself gingerly into the chair beside him after setting down her tea, making sure he saw her wince. "Payback is a bitch, I guess."

"I didn't know we needed to square up," he laughed.

"I was poorly prepared for Onigashima and could have gotten you killed," she pointed out.

"Are you still holding on to that?" he asked, teasing, but then he remembered the Morningstar bearing down on them in that terrible form, and it made him recall something else.

"What is it?" she asked, seeing his expression, trying to guess what was on his mind.

"Just thinking about something my mother told me," he said, leaning back in the chair and looking off out the window at nothing in particular.

She said nothing, waiting to see if he would share whatever he was holding. She couldn't read his expression, but there was something immoveable in it, and she wasn't going to push him.

He obliged her finally, with a heavy sigh, as though worried about her reaction.

"She taught me the importance of embracing my duality. That ultimately, the control I sought would only come with the acceptance of wolf and man, rather than choosing man over wolf, or thinking that I needed to control the Beast," he told her.

"But I cannot control Tatsuo Tomo," she said.

"And he cannot control the Dragon," he replied, and she could see he was considering this very carefully.

"Where are you going with this?" Azuma asked him, feeling lost.

"I'm saying that fact is very significant, somehow." Amaoke was searching for the words to explain. "Because I battled Forcas, before you were born, and his essential form is a scaly beast. If Tatsuo Tomo is somehow a straw man for the demon, why can't your twin control something so apparently integral to its natural incarnation?"

He could see that he was telling her something she had not known before.

She said, "That's an interesting observation. I have been conflicted about the decision to exert outside control in the form of gene therapy pretty much since the beginning, but still don't see that I have a choice."

"Is it possible that you discovered something inadvertently that the Morningstar would have wanted to prevent? These are important questions; we all have questions. Maybe together, we can start answering them," Amaoke suggested.

Azuma began to feel guilty about the things she was still withholding from him, and the others. She almost told him about the other thing she had discovered after Onigashima, but couldn't overcome her most basic instinct to keep her own counsel.

His expression changed in an interesting way, and there was a moment where she wondered whether he was reading her mind. Amaoke never told anyone he knew, or was close to, that their scents changed from moment to moment as their feelings did, and that these changes signaled many things, from anger to fear to deception to desire. But he didn't press her further about it, because what he scented now was her guilt.

The descent into darkness is short and abrupt; Priest and Prince, he has been Chosen.

55

IN THE MORNINGS, WHILE THE others were asleep, or at least retired in private quarters, Amaoke walked. He loved the bamboo forest, the leaning straight spires beautiful in their own right; so different from the pines that dominated his wilderness. These were no less awesome, reaching skyward, singing a different song in the breeze, and he had been surprised when the Collector had told him that bamboo was not a tree at all, rather a type of grass.

The gardens were immaculately kept, although the lotus pond was dormant now in early spring. He discovered the ancient temple, its stones mossy and weathered, although the arches leading to the entrance had been replaced and repaired, the new wood fragrant. It was dark and cold inside, provisionally clean, but his nose picked up the taint of old blood and fear. It was a place of sacrifice, and the energy there was dark, reminiscent of the Morningstar.

Once, he had encountered *Ku* and *Hachi* returning from the shrine together; they had mastered their surprise and bowed to him. He returned this with one of his own out of courtesy, but did not investigate further what they might have been doing there. He understood this to be their religion, according to what he had gleaned from Azuma, and he wanted to be respectful of their sacred spaces. At any rate, the temple had a dark energy that he didn't like, so after his early investigations, he avoided the clearing altogether.

One rainy morning, he went out through the mudroom, taking his pick of raincoat and boots from the many that were kept there in readiness. The household was surprisingly efficient, surprisingly welcoming for all that it was a stronghold for monsters. This time, he detoured through the stables, visiting the horses, and was surprised to find the Collector already up, returning from an early ride.

"Do you ride, my friend?" he inquired, and Amaoke could see that he was not just being polite. The Collector was a practical being, and he had left any animosity that they had shared from across a New Orleans thoroughfare in the past.

"No. The horses are beautiful," Amaoke replied, stroking the star pattern on the nose of the mount that was tethered on the central cobblestones, waiting to be groomed. The Collector was cleaning tack, and he stopped long enough to bring a small brush to Amaoke. He came close, looping the strap over the back of his hand to demonstrate, mimicking the long strokes down and away in the air, showing Amaoke what to do.

Amaoke took the brush and adjusted the strap to his own hand, and turned his attention to the horse. She nickered softly in his direction, he hoped in appreciation. "I would be concerned that the animal would sense the beast, and be afraid."

"Most certainly." The Collector nodded. "They are extremely intelligent. One of the best weapons the samurai ever had," he said. "The *kisouma* are the breed those warriors used in battle, but nobles and samurai leaders often used animals from the West, because they were taller and cut a more elegant figure. These were first bred for Iemitsu, Azuma's grandfather, one of the early Shoguns of her line, a cross between our sacred *kisouma* and the lovely black Arabians."

"Are they smart enough to realize they don't want a person on their backs?" Amaoke asked, half in jest, thinking of the wild horses of the American plains.

"Indeed they are," the Collector replied. "If you do not establish that you will lead, they will dump you, then kick you, and perhaps step on you. But if you are gentle and firm, and give them work to do, even if that work is dangerous, they make excellent companions. And they love to be let out, love the freedom of running, with or without a passenger. I shall have to take you one of these mornings. The horses seem to like you; I am not surprised, you have the calm, quiet strength they gravitate toward."

"I would like that," Amaoke admitted.

"I assure you that it is likely you will be sad you have lived without the experience until now," the Collector said, his expression inscrutable. Finished with the tack, he turned his attention to the horse's hooves, examining each in turn, using a pick to clean around her shoes. She danced a little when he released the last one, bumping gently against Amaoke as she did so.

"She likes you, likes the attention you give her. Horses thrive when they are cared for; they are affectionate and loyal," the Collector said. "For a long time, my horse was the best girlfriend I had – a wise man requires someone unafraid to speak her mind, someone who can kick his ass when he needs it."

Amaoke smiled. He couldn't agree more. But with this bit of wisdom dispensed, the Collector relieved Amaoke of the brush to finish the work himself. Amaoke read the signal correctly, leaving the man to his solitude, and went back up to the house, looking for Weston.

But he did not find him there, his room was empty. The groundsman pointed out toward the bluffs when asked whether he had seen the priest, so Amaoke went over the hillside, and started to climb up to the heights before changing course and traversing down through the trees to the beach. Weston was there, as he'd guessed, staring out over the grey waves, listening to the water crash against the rocks.

Unlike Amaoke, he had his hood down, letting the mist saturate his hair. He looked like a child, out in the rain, unmindful of it, enjoying the fresh air.

"It's beautiful here," Weston said, when he knew Amaoke was close enough to hear.

"Incredibly so." Amaoke agreed.

"How does it compare to where you grew up?" Weston asked, sounding wistful, as though he wished he could see it.

"Quite different," Amaoke told him. "No less lovely. Nature is a gift unto herself; one just has to appreciate her in all her guises. Now tell me why you aren't sleeping. This is perfect weather for it."

"Nightmares," Weston admitted. "For some reason they are more and more real. I wonder whether they are things that could actually be happening."

"Feel like talking about them?" Amaoke asked, taking a few steps up the beach, gratified when Weston caught up and went along with him, shoulder to shoulder. He liked this closeness, the fact that Weston did not seem to have any minimum personal space when around other people.

"Not really, although I should." Weston ran his hands through his wet hair, leaning sideways and wringing out the water before shivering and flipping up his hood. "Some of it I don't recall, but most of it is stuff I believe the Morningstar has done, or is doing. Things I want no part of but cannot prevent, or stop from happening. I wonder how much of it is me, and whether I am really there, taking part in these repugnant acts. It feels unclean. Empty. Lonely."

"Is that you? Or do you think it is the Morningstar?" Amaoke asked, truly curious, wanting to explore the idea.

"Wow. You mean, is it making me feel what it feels? Probably," Weston nodded. "But if it were just emptiness, or loneliness, that would be preferable to forced anger, cruelty, lust. I feel less human every day."

"I understand. It has manipulated those emotions in me at times, over the centuries," Amaoke shared, and Weston stopped walking. He was surprised. "A while ago, in New Orleans, it had me lusting after some poor prostitute, heroin addicted, unfortunate, but gorgeous. It had me tormented, it twists appetites; I wasn't sure whether I wanted to ravish her or eat her. She was already gone anyway."

"What did you do?" Weston asked, adjusting his spectacles on his face.

"Locked myself indoors, shaking in the corner, hoping I could resist. At times, when I was younger, and had poorer control, it was harder to do. Admittedly, I have been used as a tool for its destruction, long ago. But I don't rule out the possibility of it happening again."

"That scares me," Weston whispered.

"It scares me too, my friend," Amaoke told him. "You aren't alone, no matter how much it would like you to believe it. Perhaps without the distraction of the demons you feel it even more acutely. But the Morningstar wanted each of us to think we were alone; it served its designs. Yet here we are, together."

"But how do you live with the possibility that you could lose control again?" Weston asked.

"I control what I can. I remember not only who I am, but who I want to be. Separate what I really want from what it tries to subvert. I know I can throw anything at an appetite, meat, sex, you name it. Will it satisfy? And for how long? I prefer meaningful gratification, things that will sustain me in the long run. Perhaps there are those who are weak enough to believe that these things are deserved, that gods should have their fill of such empty pleasures. I think Azuma believed it once. I think she got smart fast, and she got lucky. I think the Collector was not in the Morningstar's plans for her; despite what we know of him, he kept her from becoming the monster it intended."

"Sounds like it owned her father," Weston said.

"You must know something I don't," Amaoke said. "I think her father was looking for the kind of power that the Morningstar doesn't share."

"I only know what she shared with me as we examined old scrolls in her library. Perhaps I do know things it is possible I shouldn't." Weston admitted this reluctantly. "How do you manage it? The times of weakness?"

"By holding on to my faith and my humanity," Amaoke told him. "Both things that you are far more skilled at than I have ever been. Isn't that what you holy men teach others?"

"Of course," Weston breathed it, and seemed relieved. "Lead by example."

"In that case, lead me to breakfast, I'm starving," Amaoke laughed, and added, "And this time, find the humanity to eat some of it, too."

56

"I PROPOSE THAT GETTING READY to face the Monster requires preparation, like any other battle," Azuma said, leaning back in her chair and sipping her tea. The four of them were alone, the others had eaten and gone, and Ambakisye still refused to take any meals in company.

"Can we prepare for chaos?" Kusini asked wisely, turning her golden eyes to Amaoke, probably because he was the most long-lived. Increasingly, the other three turned to him for answers he didn't have, ascribing to him a wisdom he didn't think he had.

He sighed heavily and said nothing. Several moments passed, long enough for it to become awkward. Weston took off his spectacles and rubbed the bridge of his nose. Kusini sipped her own tea, some cinnamon and licorice concoction of Ambakisye's making. Its scent was pleasant to Amaoke.

Azuma rescued the moment, saying, "I agree that we cannot prepare for a scenario we cannot predict, but why not use the knowledge we have about our own gifts to consider what might be thrown at us? If not for each of us, because we have learned to respond by instinct, at the very least for the *Akai*, and Ambakisye, to get a bigger picture of what they might be facing down in the depths.

"It is safe to assume that each of our *special conditions-*" here she paused to look at Weston, who had let her in on the joke. Amaoke shook his head good-naturedly and gestured for her to get on with it. "-mimic the ways in which we will be tested, whether by fear, shape-changers, or lesser demons, which in numbers could be distressing enough to distract us from defending ourselves."

"Meaning that perhaps the tricks we bring to the table are the extent of the Morningstar's imagination?" Weston asked, and there was something fatalistic about his tone. He hadn't put his glasses back on, and this made him look even younger and more vulnerable.

"Would you like to share what you're thinking?" Azuma asked, but whatever was distressing Weston, he wasn't amenable to inquiry.

He pushed back from the table. "You three should probably have this discussion without me anyway." Abruptly, he retrieved his spectacles and escaped outdoors. The three of them watched him crossing the parade grounds on his way to the pond, one shoulder hitched like an angry child.

Kusini stood up too. "I'll go. He's angry because he's afraid, and it is my fault that the only defense he has ever known, whether he wanted it or not, has gone. Please, continue talking. You can fill me in later, if need be." Inadvertently, she pulled her abaya more closely about her shoulders, as if engirding herself with invisible armor, and taking her teacup, departed, the spices in her tea mixing with her scent as she went. It was comforting to Amaoke, he hoped, for his friend's sake, that her presence would be comforting to Weston as well.

Amaoke turned his attention back to Azuma. "I suspect you have something planned?" he asked her, anticipating her response.

"Always," she replied, taking another sip of her tea and arching her eyebrows at him over the rim of the cup.

He waited, and momentarily scented the cool outdoor air just ahead of the Collector's arrival. He stood attentively, but did not sit down until Azuma indicated the place next to Amaoke.

"My friend, would you like to share what you know about the catacombs?" Azuma asked, but Amaoke shook his head.

"No need," he interjected, and Azuma looked confused. The Collector understood immediately. He nodded.

"I was imprisoned there for a hundred years many centuries ago," Amaoke told them, so that Azuma would understand. He made eye contact with the Collector. "Or perhaps for five minutes, who can say? It felt like many lifetimes. Time is not what it seems down there in the pit.

"I read the file. I was never made aware of the spiral staircase, or the maze, but I can tell you the physical structure is constantly changing," Amaoke concluded.

"Or it isn't, and our perspectives are being manipulated," came another voice from near the door to the garden.

The woman who leaned against the doorframe was young, about Weston's age or even younger. Her posture was confident, and she was slightly taller than average, though her build was compact and muscular. She wore canvas cargo pants and the boots of a soldier, which were slightly incongruous with her black hoodie. Her short hair was artlessly styled, if she touched it at all, and he couldn't decide if it conferred androgyny as it could just as easily accent her femininity. She reminded Amaoke of the teenagers in the skatepark near the New Orleans carriage house, and for some reason she looked familiar. He could not have immediately said what it was that he recognized in that face.

"This is Michael Israel," Azuma introduced the latecomer. "She's assisting with some of the preparations for the *Akai*. She was the original intelligence officer that located the buried site. It was her government that made the initial excavations as we discussed…well, you saw the file."

"That's Forcas handiwork, no doubt," Amaoke said, and Michael Israel looked surprised. Her lip curled involuntarily, approximating a sneer, and Amaoke felt cold. He made the connection regarding the familiarity of her face. He'd seen that same expression on someone else. Forcas.

"He's very good," Michael Israel said, nodding in Amaoke's direction and looking at Azuma. She knew Amaoke had made the connection, she could see it on his face. She betrayed a smile that was marginally more friendly than her previous look. "I am a twin. The Death Bringer stole my brother from our nursery, stole his essence really, and now the monster I have chased my whole life wears my brother's face."

"I wondered about the change in his appearance. It was relatively sudden," Amaoke allowed.

"Sudden?" Michael Israel asked softly, betraying too much emotion. She had measured the loss in human years, measured the time in the currency of human suffering. Some of those were the interminable endless days of childhood, where time could stretch in frustrating and aggravating ways.

"Amaoke is a being that has lived over a thousand years, child," the Collector's tone was surprisingly gentle. He remembered the depth of her grief when she regained consciousness after their escape in Tikrit. "Twenty years for us is the blink of an eye. It is an observation of relativity."

"It certainly is not meant to diminish your grief," Amaoke said. "He had another face before."

This reminded Azuma of something, and she made a mental note to have a separate discussion with Amaoke on that subject later.

"Michael Israel has been to the site three times in total, once in a helicopter, and twice on the ground, where she managed to enter and escape that place on different occasions. Everyone else associated with the site has died," Azuma said.

"Was murdered by the Death Bringer, you mean," Amaoke corrected her. "That message on the stones was for you, then," he added, looking at Michael Israel.

She nodded but said nothing.

"The second incursion was with one of my priests, a successful attempt to retrieve the Collector," Azuma said.

"Retrieve?" Amaoke asked, interested by her word choice.

"I was *rescued*," the Collector stressed the word with not a little amusement. "I think my dear Azuma is kindly trying to protect my ego. I am perfectly content that two such capable women would risk so much."

Amaoke laughed, and turned to Azuma. "His ego isn't that fragile," he told her, fairly certain he was correct. He doubted the Collector worried much about who had rescued him, and he was adamant in giving credit where it was due. Certain things speak for themselves. His eyes narrowed then for several moments. "Forcas needs something from her," he concluded. "It needs her alive."

"We are all in agreement," Azuma said.

"I need it dead," Michael Israel interjected.

Amaoke sighed. She was a child, and he didn't deny her legitimate complaint. She was not the only one. Whatever the Death Bringer wanted of her, she was not going to get her brother back, and he suspected if she challenged it, it would take her too.

"You cannot go in angry," Amaoke reasoned. "We have to consider that what we bring to that place could just as easily feed it as destroy it."

She said nothing, just turned her face away from him. For all that it seemed obstinate, he gave her the benefit of the doubt, certain that she was listening, certain that she heard.

"Perhaps we can pick this subject up again later," Azuma suggested gently, and Michael Israel nodded, excusing herself and slipping silently out of the room. "*Sensei*, I will not detain you either. I need a private word with Amaoke."

Make sure he understands what we need him to do. I will ready the others. Azuma heard his voice as clearly as if he had spoken aloud, and he bowed to the two of them and departed.

57

AS SOON AS THE COLLECTOR left through the door, one of the house stewards came back through it, with fresh tea for Azuma. There were two cups on his tray, an abundance of hospitality, even though it was clear that Amaoke was not having any.

"While I claim no knowledge of what happens to you when you change-" she began, but he interrupted her.

"No. Weston knows, but not because I voluntarily demonstrated. Ambakisye has an idea, because he provoked something briefly." Amaoke was abrupt, and Azuma thought she detected a bit of regret in his tone and manner.

"Let's keep it that way for now," she said, waving at the air as if dispelling some offense. "I would like you to help me with some readiness exercises. I need the *Akai* to see what it really is to take on a supernatural."

"No," he repeated himself, even more emphatically. "It's too dangerous."

"More dangerous than what we propose to face? Finding a way to prepare them for the unknown?" Azuma asked reasonably, leaning forward and reaching across the table to take his hand. He didn't resist, seeing in her eyes that she was not being reckless, as he had first thought.

"You proposed that we keep trying to learn what we can from one another, keep asking questions. One of mine is, *are we ready?*"

"I'm not sure that we will ever be ready," Amaoke told her, marveling at how cold her fingers were. She was nervous. Her scent betrayed a small amount of fear, but no guile.

"But we can give each other the benefit of added wisdom," she argued. "The *Akai* only know about the Dragon. I want to teach them about the Wolf, and the Sorceress, and the Demon. I was a soldier, the *Akai* are a warrior sect, and preparing for battle is what we do. I need them to be exposed to your unique gift."

"Why start with me?" Amaoke asked, watching as she smiled, not bothering to hide her satisfaction, now that she could see he was going to agree.

"You are the eldest. You have the best control," she told him, and she was sincere; this was not flattery. "They need to be challenged, and surprised. I think you can do those things. I abhor complacency, and I worry that our modern world has made us so. Even myself."

"What do you propose?" He sighed, his capitulation nearly complete.

"You teach us about the Wolf," she told him. "I have given my priests their instructions."

"Are you going to give me any?" Amaoke sat back in his chair, releasing her hands, and crossing his arms in amusement.

"Simple rules of engagement," Azuma said. "Defend your life."

"So helpful," he laughed, and she laughed with him.

"Whatever happens, do what feels natural," Azuma clarified, and then there was nothing more to be said.

58

KUSINI FOUND WESTON SITTING ON the stone bench by the small shrine next to the pond, praying. His rosary was in his fingers, and his lips were moving silently. Rather than interrupt, she took the liberty of sitting down next to him. She settled her hands around the teacup in her lap and waited, but Weston reached out for her with his free hand, so she took it, and held it gently.

Even when he finished his prayers, they sat for a time, quiet, watching the bamboo sway gently in the breeze. Two snowy cranes drifted down from the sky, circling aloft before descending to the water, lovely creatures seeking rest and refuge.

"It is beautiful here." Weston spoke finally, perhaps sensing that was what Kusini was waiting for, an opening, a sign that he would speak.

"Yes. I feel fortunate that I got to see another part of the world," she told him. "The Collector says that soon the cherry blossoms will come, and their beauty will put the bamboo and all the lovely shrines to shame."

"You'd love the rose gardens at the Vatican," he told her, a bit shyly, perhaps anticipating her next line of questioning. "They bloom a new color every month of the year."

"I would like that," she told him honestly. "Although I wonder why I am of such interest to your church," she said, avoiding any hint of accusation in it.

Weston nodded. Perhaps he had been expecting a confrontation, but he needn't have worried. It was not really Kusini's style. If Ambakisye did the asking…well, it might all take a different tone.

"The Church interests itself in anything of a supernatural nature, not just based on suspicion, although there is an entire group of priests trained to deal with such, as I am," he told her.

"You are too modest, young man," Kusini said, turning those golden eyes to his. "There may be a group, as you say, but none are like you, none has the singular status you do. You are important to your church; you could say so."

"No," he said, shaking his head. "*What* I am is important to them."

"Amaoke says that the leader of your church loves you, sincerely cares for you," Kusini pointed out, not letting him escape the truth that he was loved, and that his own capacity for love was recognizable and redeeming. It was the point she wanted to stress.

"Mmm-hmmm." Weston nodded, and smiled to himself. "He is an exception to almost every rule you could observe about the Church. He is an example of what a church man truly ought to be. Without the politics.

"But I only say that we study the supernatural to make another point. For every inquisitor and exorcist, there are twice or three times as many scientists, priests who spend lifetimes trying to reconcile the unexplainable, the magic, the misunderstood, with the sacred texts. Trying to find a way in the modern world to allow a place for our religion. Both groups are tasked with trying to understand phenomena like you."

As soon as he said it, he was sorry, could see that he had wounded her. "Kusini, I don't see you as a phenomenon. I see you as an exceptional woman. I don't deny that our spying and our intrigues are wrong, nor will I try to tell you that some misplaced idea of the greater good will justify such. Whatever the Church has done, it was parallel to my work, only finally intersecting with my personal quest to understand this evil that I am. I had to lobby for permission to interact with you."

"Because you were looking for a way to fight it, fight the Morningstar," Kusini said, almost like a reminder. "Isn't that what you told Amaoke once?"

"He told you that?" Weston asked, surprised. He didn't think Amaoke one to impart confidences.

"No. Just something I envisioned, or dreamed. I'm not sure how I know some things," she told him honestly, and smiled at the surprise she saw on his face. "You thought you were the only one?"

"I did." Weston was still staring at her. Kusini could see that her admission had restored his faith in certain possibilities. "But why share this with me? Why now?"

"To remind you that you, too, are as exceptional as any of us," she said gently.

"But I can't turn into something else, or call on some incredible power...my demons have gone," he protested, and she heard both the relief and the sadness in his voice.

"Have they?" Kusini asked, putting enough skepticism into her tone to make him question what he thought he knew. "Can they be completely gone?"

"Even if they aren't, I never controlled them," he reasoned, unable to read her expression, but thought she was amused. Amused!

"Did you try?" she inquired archly.

He started to argue but found his own excuses wanting. He hadn't. He'd been afraid, content only to punish them if he needed to, but had never taken it any further. He had delicately toed an imaginary line when dealing with his own supernatural gifts, not recognizing that this was another way the Morningstar was using his sense of righteousness to control him.

"I've always been afraid if I really let *it* out, I won't get myself back in the end," Weston admitted finally.

"Where does the Morningstar get its power?" Kusini asked, wanting Weston to connect the dots that she had so many centuries before.

His eyes widened. "From the Creator. From the divine," he whispered, thankful for the reminder.

"So, my dear priest, whatever strengths you possess, these are not solely the work of the Morningstar, correct?" She led him to it, forced him to examine what he had always known, what he had advocated for and taught countless others yet had not believed these considerations applied to him.

Weston shook his head.

"And what about your mother?" Kusini prompted. "What did she teach you about life?"

"Love. She taught me about love." There were tears in his eyes now, and she squeezed his hand, and the emotion they both felt charged their contact, which should have been painful, although it didn't seem to bother him at all.

"I don't know where to find what I need. I cannot use or control any of it," Weston said, although he was just thinking aloud now.

"You will know when you need it. You have always known, you just have to believe," Kusini reminded him.

"But the destruction, a part of me *is* the Morningstar." He had a reminder of his own.

"Most certainly." She agreed, but she added something else. "But at least as much of you is Weston. Use that first."

59

AMAOKE SLEPT DEEPLY AND WAS not bothered by dreams that he could recall. He was awakened by a combination of sound and scent, the furtive subtle movement not unlike the wind outside. If he were any other, he would have dismissed it as such and returned to his slumber.

He concentrated on the scent alone. *Ku*, if he were not mistaken. The sounds were in the corridor to his left. The position of the moon outside his window told him it was past midnight. He called the wolf, holding still until the last pricking hair had emerged, and wiggled out of his nightclothes, shaking his legs free of them and the bedclothes.

He hopped off the futon on the side away from the hallway and trotted to the far corner of the space, away from the light under the window. He sat down and waited.

The screen slid open silently on its track, silhouetting *Ku*, the outline of his form darker and more substantial than the shadows beyond. Amaoke was unsure whether the *Akai*, transformed as they were, could see any better in darkness than a human being, but knew he was at a disadvantage anyway. His white fur was bright against the surrounding gloom.

He counted on the fact that a person will concentrate on what they expect to see, and used that. He was not where he was supposed to be, and not in the form he assumed they expected. Sure enough, he watched *Ku* examine the top of the *shikibuton* in confusion, expecting to find a man lying abed, only finding disordered sheets and empty clothing.

Amaoke remained still as a post, watching as his adversary scanned the room, once, twice, not seeing the break in the pattern until his third pass, when his probing gaze came to rest on the incongruous figure in the corner. Amaoke exploited the man's instincts further, sitting up tall like a domestic dog, wagging his tail and letting his tongue loll out, looking friendly, misdirection.

Ku's posture relaxed involuntarily, responding as one would to a pet, although Azuma had no dogs on the compound. Amaoke saw the short sword at the man's waist, and his hand had gone nowhere near it yet.

The wolf huffed in amusement, and took advantage of this weakness that people have for defenseless creatures. Amaoke leapt forward, jumping up and over the futon, letting his front paws land at the center of *Ku's* chest, taking the man to the ground and landing on him with his full weight. Amaoke listened as the wind was knocked out of him with a sharp gasp, then licked *Ku's* forehead, perhaps in apology, perhaps as a taunt, one message from the man inside, and one from the wolf.

Then he danced away down the hallway, turning the corner at the end a bit too quickly, righting himself with his tail like a rudder, finding his feet, hearing his nails dig into Azuma's polished floors. He reached the door to the porch, and heard soft running footsteps behind him, someone small coming quickly. He scrabbled with his paws, managing to slide it open enough to get his nose through, and then he shouldered himself into the gap and bounded off into the night.

He was halfway across the parade ground and headed for the bluff when he felt a small blast of air near his flank, the path of an arrow narrowly missing him. He caught a whiff of *Hachi's* perfume and something else, the sharp tang of Azuma's venom on the tip. His tongue lolled out in an approximation of a smile, because now the Wolf knew not to go easy on anyone.

So he changed direction, fairly certain that he could guess where the remainder of the *Akai* would not be, and circled back toward the buildings, where he found an open window into their living quarters. He sniffed around, finding the place where they collected their soiled laundry and upset the tatami baskets, spending a minute or two rolling around in their dirty clothing and confusing his own scent with theirs. Better not to assume that blooddrinkers did not have some augmented sense of smell of their own.

Then he exited the way he had come in, trotting slowly, using the outbuildings to block any view of his escape from anyone that might still be keeping watch up at the house. He resumed his trip toward the bluffs, now hearing and smelling many bodies moving through the forest. The night was clear, and he could see movement on the beach below. They had quartered the stronghold, he was certain.

He took a serpentine path up to the outcropping that faced the sea, and gave them something else to think about, letting forth a long, plaintive howl. That sound, like the cough of the lioness, is a signal. No matter how stalwart the creature, it is a fearsome sound, the sound of a hunter. That sound is a warning, saying run, run, and hide for a time, the wolf will find you by and by.

Amaoke imagined it had stopped some of them in their tracks. But it also betrayed his position, so he planned not to be there when they arrived. He crouched low in the grass, slinking off down the hill toward the shrine, leaving the beach behind. He splashed through the pond, giving away his position, and was nearly punished for it when a second arrow passed close to his muzzle.

He sprinted off into the forest, hoping to find a different kind of tree among the bamboo, and had to travel some small distance to do so. There were a few gnarled oak near the road, and between them he discovered deer scat and wild onions sprouting, so he rolled in these, enthusiastically absorbing more scent, before shifting back to his human form, naked as a jaybird.

He jumped up, knowing his pursuers knew these forests much better than he. Grasping a stout branch, he used it to climb up into the tree, as quietly and carefully as possible, mindful of scraping himself on the bark. He didn't want them to discover him just because he had chafed his delicate behind, because they could follow a blood trail, no matter how small.

He wedged himself in a fork about ten meters off the ground, securing his perch carefully. He listened to the disciplined approach of Azuma's guard; they had fanned out, moving slowly, a few feet apart, tracking.

He watched them pass below his hiding place, forgetting, as two-legged hunters often do, that there is a whole world above them. He admired the synchrony of their movement, the way they communicated without speaking, their advance silent, deadly, and graceful. But he was assured that they had lost their quarry as they moved on, away from the road and back toward the shrine.

He waited a quarter of an hour, using the moon's path through the early morning sky as his timepiece, and then added insult to injury, calling out in the dry scream of the berserker. It was even more of a challenge, killer to killer, come get me if you dare. He was certain the *Akai* were up to the task.

When their sweep returned them to the field near the road, he could see that their postures were more defeated, *Hachi* held her bow differently, the arrow tip pointed down, not horizontal as before. Only *Ni* stayed behind, standing at the edge of the meadow, still and contemplative for a long time, and he worried he had been discovered. But when the light began to change in earnest just after moonset, she too gave up, fading slowly into the shadows under the bamboo and returning home.

If it was a false retreat, meant to decoy him and draw him out, it did not matter, for he ignored it, and went back to sleep where he was.

Two hours later, showered and dressed, he sauntered into the breakfast room as if he'd passed a perfectly restful night, making sure his expression remained bland. The scents of frustration and fury that radiated off the *Akai* told him everything. If he had smiled at his eggs they might have assassinated him. He had no doubt they would bring something new for round two.

60

THE NEXT NIGHT, THEY DIDN'T bother to try to sneak up on him. Four of them had showered, then bathed in the smoke of the incense that fragranced the home. It was the only scent Amaoke registered when he stepped into his quarters to go to sleep; if it was a bit forward he assumed only that the household staff had been aggressive with it while they were straightening the linens and restoring order to the space.

No sooner had he closed his eyes than four of the *Akai* emerged from the shadows, their movement alerting him to their presence, but it was too late, they surrounded the bed. For a moment, he saw *Ichi, Shi, Roku,* and *Jūni* standing over him with satisfied smiles before they clubbed him with a blackjack and the world disappeared.

When he awoke, he was in some sort of burlap body bag, and he was outside, the night air still and cold, being carried somewhere. He tried to keep still, wanted them to be unaware he had awakened. The tension in a person's muscles changes with alertness, and they were obviously skilled in this. While that thought was disturbing, he didn't have time to dwell on it, because *Ichi* delivered a vicious blow to his kidney through the bag. She'd done that before; in Amaoke's opinion she was a little too good at it.

"We know you're awake," she said, and he could hear in her tone that they hadn't forgiven him for the night before.

So he changed, knowing that they would sense that, too, as the balance and weight distribution of their burden changed with his transformation.

"He thinks that will help," *Roku* laughed. But the four of them merely paused to reestablish their hold and continued onward.

"Why is he heavier?" *Jūni* complained, grunting softly as she adjusted her grip.

Taken together, it told him something. They were confident that they had him, as it were, in the bag. They were taking him somewhere, so they had a plan. Some of which probably involved physically punishing him for what he'd done to them the evening prior.

Amaoke turned his attention to the lowest part of the bag, deciding exactly which spot was stressed the most supporting his weight, and ran a sharp claw along it. The rent he created in the fabric worked perfectly, gravity coupled with his weight, and it tore open, allowing the wolf to roll out onto the ground and onto his feet in one graceful movement.

It happened fast enough that the *Akai* moved forward several steps before the realization hit that suddenly their burden was very light, indeed too light. There was a moment of indecision and Amaoke used it, jumping right into the center of them, shouldering *Shi* out of the way to get near *Roku*, who was holding a short brutal weapon, some sort of air-powered tranquilizer gun. Whatever was in the darts smelled medicinal, and Amaoke didn't need to identify it to know that it was the greatest threat at the moment.

They all wore technical black jumpsuits with very light footwear, which was to their disadvantage, because the wolf darted forward, closing his jaws on *Roku's* Achilles, bringing him to the ground. When *Jūni* leaned in to help, he snapped his teeth near her face, and she scrambled backwards just in time.

Ichi managed to grab the fur of his ruff with determination, and she tugged fiercely, causing him to yelp, but he lashed out with his claws, raking her across the forehead. Her blood ran down over her eyes, blinding her, but she did not let go, so Amaoke bucked and turned and started to run away anyway. When she still refused to release him, he nipped, not so gently, at her fingers, and that ended her attempt to hold him.

He ran down the trail from them, back toward the house, pausing to give two short barks of reprimand. But he scented other pursuers in the trees and detoured to the pond. He had learned something new tonight. The *Akai* moved with inhuman quickness when they wanted to, and he knew they could fly short distances.

He had no further opportunity to consider this, because ahead of him, on the path, there was a child standing next to the water. A lovely child, a porcelain doll in an elaborate kimono, her fair hair bumped up atop her head, pinned in place with a jeweled comb. Amaoke almost ran into her in his haste, so he scrabbled in the soil with his claws and was able to stop a few feet in front of her.

Almost too late, he recognized *Hachi*, decoyed and distracting, and heard the scrape of metal as she unsheathed the sword that hung from her *obi*. She smiled at him, and that smile was completely incongruous to the princess before him. That smile promised punishment, pain, perhaps death.

So he pulled a trick of his own, as she swung the sword, targeting the wolf before her. Amaoke danced out of reach on four legs and then he changed back, managing to keep his balance on two legs. She did pause, both in surprise that her opponent had changed, the white wolf now a giant of a man, towering over her, his flowing hair not covering his nakedness, and he heard her drawn breath at this unusual distraction. Most warriors, no matter how skilled, do not face nude adversaries.

But *Hachi* recovered gracefully, advancing on him with deadly speed, swinging the sword once more, and he felt the weight of his mother's *ulu* come to his hand unbidden. He brought it up in a sweeping horizontal arc, where it made contact with her weapon there were sparks, deflecting her downward stroke as it went, and to

Amaoke's horror as he continued his follow through, it opened a gash across *Hachi's* beautiful face.

He watched her own expression of surprise as she backed off several steps, still holding her sword at her side, and the line slowly disappeared, costing her only a few drops of blood, closing slightly less quickly than it had appeared. Her rapid regeneration relieved him, but the rage in her eyes told him that he was in even bigger trouble now.

She advanced again, swinging the sword repeatedly, unrelenting. He fended off her blows, knowing she would not tire, knowing that the *ulu* was a poor weapon of defense against the heavy long sword. On her fourth attempt, he managed to deflect her strike yet again, but not before her blade bit into the side of his exposed hand, opening a deep wound.

He knew that she could make it a battle of attrition, keep cutting him here and there, weakening him through blood loss and pain, which would make it more difficult to change, and would only result in his suffering on four legs rather than two.

His advantage was her diminutive stature, and he timed his blow carefully, sure he wouldn't get a second chance. He waited as she stepped into her next strike, and moved *toward* her, putting his body too close for the hit. Yet it was close enough for him to reach out a long arm and punch her in the center of her chest. *Hachi's* forward momentum increased the damage of the strike to her solar plexus, and she toppled over backward, gasping for air. The blow short circuited her, her arms and legs flopped down uselessly, her sword clattering softly onto the stone pavers of the path.

Then he was attacked from behind, the others having arrived, drawn by the sounds of the battle near the pond. He could smell *Ni* as she climbed up his back, *San* right behind her, striking at his legs. Amaoke managed to keep his feet, but *Ni's* arms were around his neck, tightening painfully, and stars popped up, blurring his vision.

He could scent her satisfaction, but he had yet another trick up his sleeve. He shifted again, not to wolf, but into the more brutal form of the Beast, letting this alter ego come forward. Its habitus was both thicker and taller than his human form, like stepping forward into a nightmare. The change popped *Ni's* arms apart, and she gave a little cry, but the Beast didn't care, merely shrugged her off. Amaoke suspected he'd dislocated her shoulder given the abruptness of the transformation.

San and *Ku* advanced on him, with a preternatural quickness that betrayed their inhumanity, but he tossed them aside like toys, prowling back through the gardens, growling, headed for the parade grounds. *Go, Shichi,* and *Jū* were waiting.

They attempted to surround him; *Go* leapt onto his back. He had a small lariat made of a thin strong wire, and this he dropped over the Beast's head and pulled it snug. The other two waded in wielding their own swords, but these he deflected with a vicious backhand blow, sending the weapons tumbling end over end into the night.

Yet try as he might, although *Go's* companions retreated empty-handed, Amaoke was unable to dislodge him, and the noose was tightening. Amaoke managed to get a claw under the wire and pop it, but at that moment, *Go* shouted something he could not understand, but it was short and direct, like an order.

Across the clearing, he saw *Roku*, no longer hobbled, shouldering his weapon. He fired it, and the dart hammered home, coming to rest in the Beast's torso. Amaoke could see their collective relief, as the *Akai* moved in slowly, surrounding him. But he slapped the dart away impatiently and reared up again, roaring at the pain, able to ignore the dose of whatever was in the dart, as it was not titrated for this new creature that they had not yet encountered.

He admired their bravery, for although he could see their disappointment that this had failed as it registered briefly on their faces, that disappointment soon passed as they continued their onslaught. They advanced on him, the circle of warriors collapsing inward, at the last moment throwing themselves upon him, using their collective weight to try to bring him down, and he growled menacingly, trying in vain to shake them off, but there were too many of them.

The Beast was furious, and when *Ni* reached up to take hold of its muzzle, it was the last straw for Amaoke. He was too afraid to bite any of them in this form, knowing the consequences from the long ago encounter during Nanatha's attack. So he flattened his ears and growled again in warning, shaking his snout away from her grip.

He changed back to human, rapidly enough that the entire lot of them went to the ground around and on top of him.

Either the surprise caused them to draw away from him, because it was so abrupt, or it was what they saw in his eyes, because none of them tried to reengage him.

"Enough," he said, bowing to them respectfully. "None of you wants to be bitten by the Beast."

They all looked at one another, confused, but he did not bother to explain himself. He was relieved to see that Azuma and the Collector had joined them. The Collector passed him a kimono discreetly, almost managing not to smile as he did so. It helped, the adrenaline and tension diffused by the man's amusement.

Amaoke tied the sash slowly and carefully, taking several deep breaths, realizing that the effect of the dart was now an unpleasant reality. The drug was still in his bloodstream. He was suddenly drowsy, and he could tell he was going to have a welt on his head from the blow they took to knock him out. He could already feel the throb of a headache behind his eyes.

Azuma, ever observant, noticed these weaknesses and signaled to her priests. "Let's take our rest. We can discuss what we have learned in the morning. Amaoke, are you willing to give us some honest feedback? After breakfast, of course."

"Of course," he told her, nodding once to punctuate his answer. Without saying more, he turned toward the house, and rest. He smelled the soldier nearby, and caught a glimpse of her in the shadow of the bathhouse, her green eyes bright to his night sight, intelligent, knowing. She was observing carefully, and he suspected she had seen most of what had just transpired. She gave him a brief salute, touching two of her fingers to her temple and raising them slightly with an ironic smile.

Kusini stood just inside the doorway, but she didn't speak, merely touched him on the shoulder as he passed, and he felt immediately restored. He turned back to thank her, but she was already gone.

He fell onto the *shikibuton*, not bothering to pull the screen. He smiled slightly as he heard it sliding shut behind him, never positively identifying the doer of this good deed, although it smelled like Weston, because his eyes were already closed, the lids heavy. Sleep pulled him down into its depths and he did not resist.

61

THE COLLECTOR STOOD RESPECTFULLY AT Amaoke's shoulder, waiting to be acknowledged before he sat down. One of the house stewards appeared almost magically to deliver tea, rice cakes, and quail eggs.

It was quiet in the breakfast room, most of the others had already eaten and gone. Amaoke, too, had finished his churashi, thinking what a shame it was that he had not been born here, where raw fish was a staple of the diet. It made him feel oddly at home, and he knew that it simplified life for Ambakisye as well.

The Collector bowed his head briefly, and Amaoke was surprised to see him cross himself, just as Weston always did, before he began eating. The man noticed his surprise, and smiled.

"I am even more an outcast than you might have realized. Perhaps Azuma did not tell you that I am *Kirishitan?*"

"Not directly. She did say your father was a priest. I guess I was slow to make the connection that he was the same kind as Weston, since he had fathered a child," Amaoke replied.

"Oh, yes," the Collector said. "In those times it was a crime to be a foreigner, and the priests were forced into marriages with Japanese women, forced to publicly denounce their religion, forced to deny their vows and father children, under pain of torture and death. Iemitsu, Azuma's grandfather, and Ieyasu before him were determined to cleanse Nihon ethnically and philosophically. This legacy was enthusiastically continued by Ietsune, Azuma's father, and for a time, I think her own samurai propagated it.

"My mother believed herself disgraced, and would have left me to die in the forest if not for my father and his belief in the sanctity of life. Yet neither was he allowed to care for me. Not publicly, although he did try to do so privately when he was able. He was a very old man.

"It was dangerous then, as I see it may be even now, to be different, to be incompletely Japanese. I was considered a half-breed, an abomination. There are still too many purists in Japan today who would argue that I am *not* Japanese, an unfortunate form of racist nationalism that thrives due to the legacy of this shameful history. My appearance alone has damned me; but I need not explain this to you, of all people."

Amaoke was certain his surprise registered on his face. He, too, had been considered less than, solely because his appearance betrayed him to be not enough of one thing and too much of another. This man saw everything, and up to this point, had said almost nothing.

He waited quietly, allowing the Collector to enjoy his meal, the scent of his tea was pleasing, as so many things he had encountered in this place were. He also appreciated the many windows facing out onto the grounds, each providing a stunning view. He watched the cranes on the pond.

"You know they mate for life?" the Collector said, seeing Amaoke observing them. Amaoke said nothing. Wolves did too.

"Why *do* they call you the Collector?" he asked, feeling fairly comfortable asking the man a more personal question now that he had initiated the conversation about himself.

"Because I collect things," the Collector replied, dabbing at his lips with his napkin, but his eyes were smiling. No sooner had he set the napkin aside when the staff arrived to collect the used breakfast items.

"Like what? Heads?" Amaoke inquired, softening the question with a touch of amusement.

"When necessary," the Collector allowed, smiling, but entirely serious. "Although the nickname probably comes from my collections of butterflies. I am sure they call me other things too, behind my back."

Amaoke briefly wondered if the man were joking. He was certainly an object lesson not to judge a book by its cover.

"I know, not what you expected," the Collector said. "When I was younger, I would catch them by the hundreds and hang them from horsehair in the forests yonder. They called it my Butterfly Garden, although the place has had a more pragmatic use over the last several centuries.

"For a time as an adult, I did preserve and box them, but it seemed so cruel. I donated my collections to the natural history museum in Tokyo some years ago. Now I just make sure the gardens have a variety of flowers so that the creatures are attracted to them. I sit still and watch them; it gives me more pleasure than I can say. Perhaps that means I am entering my dotage."

"Or you have simply learned the value of freedom," Amaoke suggested.

"And its cost," the Collector agreed. "Now, if you would, tell me how the *Akai* performed."

"They are formidable. I am not a trained fighter, so I don't consider it my place to critique them," Amaoke began. "I – the wolf and I – we only respond to what is happening in the moment. There is nothing overtly strategic in it, just a very basic impulse to survive. I only noticed two things that may be of some interest to you. Despite what they do, despite having the experience of understanding Azuma's ability to transform, my changes were still a surprise to them."

"They knew what you are," the Collector pointed out, so Amaoke tried to explain it more broadly.

"They don't seem to expect the unexpected," Amaoke said. "I don't think they are complacent necessarily, although that is a concern that Azuma shared with me. I fear they have never faced an opponent that posed a challenge to them in their augmented state."

"Very wise observation," the Collector nodded in encouragement. "And the second thing?"

"Remembering the four cardinal directions is easy, most importantly, whichever one is behind you must be attended to and not forgotten," Amaoke told him. "We encounter threats on level ground, so down is usually not a consideration. I suppose we forget about up because birds don't generally attack us. But I know that you all have the ability to fly, or drift, aloft. They need to increase their awareness of the three dimensions, and not neglect what is above them. I evaded them for hours that first night, frustrated all their plans, simply by climbing into a tree. I was able to watch them from my vantage point. They never looked up. I hid from them in plain sight.

"Had any one of them caught me in that tree, I would have taken a beating."

62

WHILE KUSINI GAVE THE *AKAI* a fundamental challenge in that her touch was repellent, she also presented a technical problem because her combat skill was as ancient as their own tradition, yet unlike anything they had learned.

She stepped out onto the parade ground at dusk, adorned in the stiff feathered short armor that Amaoke remembered from before, her breasts bare. Her spear she held at her side, its point half a foot above her head. Banded gauntlets encircled her upper arms to prevent sweat from reaching her hands.

She looked calmly at the *Akai*, issuing a silent challenge. No one moved. She and Azuma had discussed a few particulars earlier in the afternoon. Azuma watched silently, certain that some of the hesitation was an unfortunate side effect of misplaced chivalry. Now they were attacking a woman, a woman who was larger than they were, a woman who was reminding them of her womanhood rather directly.

"They didn't hesitate to attack *you*," Azuma murmured to Amaoke under her breath.

"Obviously, but I am not half as dangerous as she is," he answered, and was rewarded with her quick amused chuckle.

Ichi said something softly under her breath, and she, *Ni, Hachi,* and *Jūni* stepped forward. They glanced at each other with small smiles, and then *Ni* shed the top of her *gi*, letting it flutter to the ground, the others following. It was a reminder to the male priests of their sect to not let breasts get in the way of an ass-whipping.

Slow emphatic applause came from the other side of the parade ground where Michael Israel had taken up station to observe. It was evident Michael Israel understood the statement the other women made. She stood next to Weston, who struggled to control his blushing. Azuma smiled, expecting nothing less from these priestesses, who demanded to be seen for their talents, not for their sex.

The stick fighting that Azuma's guard was accustomed to involved use of close martial combat to exchange blows. It was entirely a blunt exercise. Kusini's spear was nearly three times longer than the bamboo rods typically used for it, and tipped with a deadly point.

The four women chose their rods carefully, swinging them experimentally, listening to the sound they made traveling through the air, intimidating in and of itself. *Ni* gripped hers in both hands and flexed it. They spread out slowly, and Kusini did not move as they positioned themselves to approach her, did not move even when they had flanked her, covering any retreat.

She gave them nothing, indeed it appeared she was so still as to be holding her breath. They watched her eyes for clues, but these she turned down and away, so as not to telegraph or betray her next move.

Ichi was the first to engage, rushing in from the right and swinging her stick mercilessly. It whistled through the air, but before any of the combatants or the observers saw Kusini move, she brought the end of the spear up, punching out with the shaft end, connecting with *Ichi's* breastbone, sending her flying backward with a sharp scream of pain.

The other three women attacked as a unit, following fast behind *Ichi,* but Kusini merely sidestepped and bent forward at the waist, their target no longer where they had aimed their assault. She swung the shaft of the spear in a circle over her back, taking out the legs of *Ni* and *Jūni,* putting them on the ground. The wind was driven out of them in gasps of surprised pain.

Kusini jumped like a big cat, turning toward *Hachi*, now those golden eyes were trained on her opponent, and *Hachi* hesitated as if trapped in that gaze, but only for a moment. She marshaled her courage and waded in, swinging her stick with a vengeance. Every blow she made, Kusini merely deflected. She employed no offense, merely defended her position. It seemed the two of them traded blows for hours, and then the other women joined back in, but still, Kusini merely turned and turned again, parrying blows, unfazed, watching them tire.

Amaoke watched, mesmerized by the hypnotic quickness of the *Akai*, gaining an even deeper appreciation for it as an observer. They were often ahead of the place where he anticipated they would be next, as if flowing like water through space and time. They had not tired in their efforts against him, but he was not surprised that Kusini was able to leave them winded, because he was hardly a proficient fighter by any standards, certainly not the kind who could stress an opponent's stamina in combat conditions.

Then, Kusini started punishing them, landing stinging blows to their bodies, pushing them away, moving them where she wanted them. She could see their shock at how painful these lashes could be, and remembered her breathless surprise about it when she had first suffered the same at the hands of Suhuba.

Ni finally realized that her male counterparts were still standing around watching, so she snarled through clenched teeth, "*Jūji suru!*"

They moved as if awakening from a dream, and Azuma wondered if perhaps their inertia was a result of Kusini's magic. But when the men joined in, Kusini changed technique yet again, using the middle of the spear shaft to throw them, up and away from the fight, bouncing their heads against the ground, stunning them.

Even *Roku*, who employed his sheathed sword instead of a bamboo rod, which was marginally longer, using a guerrilla style, learned the task was no easier. She punished him, as well.

When Kusini could see that they were no longer fighting with any precision, merely pushing on out of obstinacy, struggling with exhaustion, she stopped, and stood erect, pulling her spear to her side.   She put her hands together briefly, and whispered, "*Kutosha.*" Enough. It was said with sufficient authority and magic to hold them off.

Master *Go* still looked at her with suspicion and resentment, so Kusini nodded to someone at the periphery of the grounds. Ambakisye stepped forward, carrying another spear, a duplicate of Suhuba's in length and construction. This he handed to *Go,* who nodded and bowed to Ambakisye in gratitude. Ambakisye returned the bow, but returned to the circle of spectators shaking his head in amusement.

Go hefted the spear in his hands, spanning it across his wrists, trying to understand its weight and balance. He swung it experimentally; he thrust the spear tip forward. Then he turned to Kusini, met her gaze, and they bowed to each other.

Kusini waited, allowing *Go* to catch his breath.   He acknowledged her in gratitude, and then took off his own top, looking at his fellow priests, then back at Kusini. She joined him in his laughter.   No reason not to have a bit of fun, and she appreciated the gesture. It both broke the tension and let her know he respected her.

Now that he had a similar weapon, if he had thought it would make things easier, he was wrong. In fact, *Go* realized fairly quickly that if anything, Kusini had been holding out on them, making allowances for their shorter rods and their unfamiliarity with her fighting style.

Armed with a similar weapon and having seen what she could do, he learned that she was about to make an example of him. She punished him as unmercifully as Suhuba had punished her, knowing that the only way to become proficient was to be reminded of your weaknesses, and she knew (as she suspected *Go* did) that pain is a powerful motivator.

She wore him down, wore him down, wore him down, putting him on the ground, slapping his limbs and torso with the stick, giving him one blow to the kidney that forced him to his knees. Then she would wait, while he recovered, and he refused to disappoint her, engaging again, each time gaining something he could use.

On their fifth round, the observers exhausted and yawning, bored with watching *Go* take a beating, he found a rhythm. He was starting to match her, starting to mount an effective offense. The moon had set, the midpoint of the night had passed. Finally, he feinted left and then turned, and bringing the shaft of his spear around abruptly he made contact with the large muscle in her thigh.

"Yes!" Kusini cried out, lifting her arms to the sky in congratulatory triumph on *Go*'s behalf, and she stopped fighting immediately.

But she had one more lesson to teach, no matter how bored or tired the onlookers. Bowing to *Go* in dismissal, she turned once more to *Ni*, who was standing next to Michael Israel, watching the developments carefully.

Ambakisye came out again, this time taking back the spear he had delivered to *Go* and handing *Ni* her short rod once more. Something flickered across her features but then she nodded, smiling.

This time, short rod against spear was not so wildly mismatched, as *Ni* fell into a comfortable rhythm, using what she knew from experience with what she had learned from *Go*'s struggles. In a short quarter hour she was dodging the spear shaft and successfully making incursions to strike Kusini with the stinging bamboo.

Kusini, having made her point, after taking a few of *Ni*'s smarting blows, stepped in close to prevent any momentum in the final blow, bouncing the other woman off her torso and effectively ending the contest. Kusini dropped the spear and spread her hands apart at waist height, pushing outward, signaling an end, then reached down to give *Ni* a hand to her feet, ensuring not to give her a shock, wanting to add no insult to injury.

Before anything could be said, Ambakisye walked back into the yard, retrieving both the spear and his wife, ready to retire for the night. That message was well received, and everyone dispersed in the direction of their own rest.

63

AMBAKISYE MOVED HIS MOUTH DOWN Kusini's neck, trailing kisses along her collarbone, smiling at the way in which she was trying to balance her anticipation and her tension. So he mirrored his attentions on the other side, and she sighed, deeply, but was even more tense.

"What's wrong, *mpenzi?*" he asked her, already knowing the answer, still smiling against her skin and not stopping his attentions.

"'Kisye," she began, wanting to respond more fully, but pausing because she was almost trying to hold her breath now against the pleasure he gave her.

He lifted his head to look at her. "Hmmm?"

She gestured about the room. "The walls are *paper*," she protested softly. "People will hear."

"Let them," he said softly, nuzzling her breasts now. "Perhaps they will be inspired."

"Oh," she said, unable to help herself, but he could feel her muscles coiled, unhelpful to his cause.

He traced the outline of her belly button with his finger, feeling her quivering desire, and relented, curling up next to her and putting his head on her hip, moving his face gently against the junction of her thigh before settling, just looking up at her.

"Are you the same woman who does battle topless?" he wondered aloud.

"That's different," she argued, then considered. "Does it bother you?"

"'Sini-ma," he admonished her. "I'm not that man. I don't own your breasts, don't need to hide them away from the world, certainly. Only primitive societies are ashamed of nudity."

"The Japanese are accepting of it," Kusini observed. "That bathhouse, wow."

"It is amazing; thankfully there are private areas, but the large baths, immense. Enough room for twelve people," he marveled, and then thought of something. "You don't think the *Akai*...?"

"Bathe together?" she completed his thought. She giggled, and nodded, her eyes wide. "I think they might!"

"Okay, then," he said, turning his head and kissing the skin there, feeling her shiver again. "Let's get back to making a few things clear. I am not ashamed of what we do, behind walls, or screens, or outside, on my workbench, or that song you sing when you're..." Ambakisye's eyebrows went up, to telegraph his meaning, turning back to her hip. His mouth moved across her lower belly, and she closed her eyes.

"That song I sing?" she whispered, feeling his hand slide beneath her lower spine and lifting her hips up to him.

"Well, perhaps I am not worried about paper walls because I can achieve my pleasures quietly," he teased, biting gently along her flank. "It shouldn't bother you. I have spent over two centuries drowning in that song; I love that song."

He could feel her relaxing but not enough, so he spoke softly, letting his lips move against her skin. "Do you know why? Because it is the only time, the rarest of moments, when you, who are never selfish, are totally, and utterly, thinking of yourself."

"I am also thinking of you," she protested, and he bit her again, this time harder.

"When I'm doing it right, you don't even know who I am," he told her. "And I love it. Perhaps I taught you how to touch yourself, perhaps I introduced you to that fire that can only start between two people becoming one, but when you let go, I can tell. When you sing that song, I doubt you even know your own name. It's a gift to me, one only I am privileged to earn."

He slid up next to her, and stretched out on his back, pulling her atop him, facing away. Her head arched back into the hollow of his shoulder, and he took one of her hands in his, and helped her explore.

He turned his head to speak against her ear. "One other thing. I'm always striving to make you sing even louder than before. Maybe there are even new gods for you to invoke," he whispered. "Let's find out."

64

"BUT I AM TELLING YOU, he had nothing!" *Hachi* protested, arguing with *Roku* and the others who were still teasing her about missing the weapon of a naked man.

"Oh, come now," *Ku* winked at Amaoke. "Don't call it nothing. You'll injure his confidence."

By now, each of them had heard the story of the magically appearing and disappearing *ulu* during his clash with them. *Hachi* herself had searched the ground next to the pond, trying in vain to locate it. The rest of the *Akai* were merciless about it, but she was not deterred.

She placed herself squarely in front of him and glared up at him. "Where *do* you keep that thing?" *Hachi* was furious, hands on her hips, demanding an answer.

"There's only one place he could keep it," *Nana* was standing next to Amaoke, and he leaned back and looked down with a knowing expression on his face.

"*I will kill you all,*" Hachi spared them a murderous backward glance as she stalked from the room, the others' laughter following her departure.

"Get your affairs in order," *Nana* advised. "I think she might be serious."

"Well, you can tell us," *San* spoke conspiratorially to Amaoke. "Where do you keep it?"

"In the same place that Kusini keeps her armor," he answered, smiling at the way her head came up when she heard her name.

"What nonsense are you propagating, mischief-maker?" she asked, tugging gently on the end of his braid as she came to stand beside him.

"I know you don't pack that thing in a suitcase," he said. To the others, somewhat smugly, he added, "It just keeps showing up in the same dark place as and when I need it." Which was no less than the truth, he was referring to the cave in his wilderness, but he didn't tell them that. Of course they laughed.

"So rude," Kusini told him, shaking her head. "What he means to say is that the weapon is a part of his special magic."

"Magic?" *Roku* stepped closer, genuinely desiring to understand. "How does it work?"

Amaoke looked helplessly at Kusini, and said honestly, "I have no idea, actually. Love, maybe? It was my mother's fish filleting tool; since she died it has just shown up in my hand when I have needed it. It is a physical item. I think it is still in the possession of a friend of mine currently, but whenever I have lost it, or had to leave it behind somewhere, it shows up again in a cave near my home."

"Do you still use it to fillet fish?" *Ichi* asked.

"I do," he told her. "It's a tool that I have known all my life."

"I don't pretend to understand it," *Ichi* said, "but that probably contributes to the way it works."

"Very wise," Kusini said. "Our emotions drive magic, and contrary to what many believe, the positive ones are often the stronger."

65

WHEN THE TIME CAME FOR Weston to do battle, he balked, understandably.

"I have no special abilities that an adversary would necessarily need to guard against," he protested, waving off the suggestion that he should allow the *Akai* a chance to assess him as another kind of unique threat. "I am a pacifist by profession, and have never developed any particular fighting skill."

"You battle demons, both those inside of you as well as those without," Kusini argued softly, pointing out the obvious.

"But now my own demons are gone," he replied gently. "Besides, I wouldn't call controlling my own bad behavior a supernatural feat."

Amaoke decided it was time to speak up. "The essence of your special blueprint may explain why you *could* control the demons – a human would simply go mad – perhaps any of us would have as well."

"But the demons were likely a placeholder for something else," Weston argued, wanting to ignore his friend's logic for the moment. "Something much worse."

"*Ku* tells me you can lift an inhuman amount of weight. He's observed some of your workouts in the gym." Azuma sat back and crossed her arms, looking at him carefully, but she wasn't making an accusation of anything.

"Well, Ambakisye is at least my match, irrespective of having one less arm. Or was that not worth reporting?" Weston replied, and Amaoke was worried. His friend was getting lost in some sort of crisis of identity, and it was robbing him of the lightheartedness he had clung to so desperately before. Perhaps it had been an overcompensation for the darkness that lived within him; now that the demons were gone it was possible that he did not need quite so much in the way of levity and good cheer, but Amaoke suspected it was all part of a downward spiral of despair. He worried that Weston did not think he had anything of value to contribute to their endeavors to ready themselves against the Morningstar.

"And do you not call upon the magic of your faith to dispel demons during an exorcism?" Kusini added, her tone still gentle with him.

"Stop it, all of you!" Weston threw his arms up in frustration. "I wouldn't even know where to start, or what to do. I hope you don't expect me to stand still and take a beating from the *Akai*. I hear you all talking about me, amongst yourselves, wondering if you can trust me-"

"I personally am only wondering when this pity party you are having for yourself will end," Azuma interrupted his outburst, challenging him more directly, uncaring whether this would upset the balance of anyone's feelings. "You, most of all, have valuable information, whether you realize it or not. It isn't that we don't trust you. We see you doubting that you can help."

"Isn't it what you asked me for, Brother? To help you discover a way to thwart the Monster? If it goes sideways, you have our promise that we will do everything we can to prevent the worst." Amaoke wanted to deescalate the situation if he could. "Perhaps an exorcist has some power over the *Akai*."

"They *are* unnaturally augmented beings, these priests of Akenomyosei," Azuma reasoned. "Even *Ni*, who was not raised within their sect, is no longer pureflesh, because the ritual that the

Akai undertake comes from my magic. Its source is the being we seek to destroy."

"It's too dangerous," Weston dismissed them, and not desiring further discussion, excused himself and left the room.

The other three were silent, although Amaoke saw a set-in stubbornness in Azuma's expression that worried him, and she got up after a few moments to follow Weston. Kusini saw it, too, and hoped they were all prepared enough for whatever the Dragon was planning.

Azuma found Weston in the library, a dark shadow hunched over a large volume of color plates displaying Japanese artwork from the Edo period. The book was opened to Utagawa Kuniyoshi's triptych, *Takiyasha the Witch and the Skeleton Spectre.* Azuma thought of the artist, and wondered how a man so enamored of his woodblocks would have responded to the knowledge that this had become the most recognized painting among his many works.

"Ah," she said, looking over his shoulder and nodding. "One of my favorites."

Weston turned back a few pages and asked, "What's with all the cats?"

"Cats are important to Japanese society," Azuma explained. "Useful companions, smiling denizens of teahouses. Kuniyoshi owned about twelve of them, as I recall it."

"Twelve?!" Weston was surprised.

"Yes. An entire category of his catalogued works is dedicated to them."

"It is kind of you to make small talk," Weston said cautiously.

"I am not here to try to convince you to do something you do not want to do," Azuma reassured him. "Self-determination is of the utmost importance to me."

"But there *is* something you want." Weston took off his glasses, and rubbed his eyes. When he opened them, the painting's colors had bled together and blurred on the page, as had Azuma's features. So he focused on something in the far ground, beyond the large windows, the willow tree beside the pond, the small ornamental shrine, the symmetry of the bamboo facings on the bridge in the garden.

"Only if you permit it," she assured him.

"You want to examine me. Because my DNA is different from yours, and the others." He stated this matter-of-factly, but she could see what it cost him. He was still agonizing over the differences.

"I don't think of you as a specimen," Azuma said gently. "Despite what my enemies, critics, and detractors might say, I am not that cold. Perhaps I was once, but no more."

"I know that. I don't think that. I also know if it gives us useful information that will help us better understand the Morningstar, we should do it." He leaned back, and Azuma could see that his thoughts were racing, his eyes moving slightly, but whatever calculations he made, he shared none of them with her. "What do you propose?" he asked finally, donning his spectacles and turning to look at her, seeing her properly again.

"Biometrics. I want to take repeat measurements, like the ones I did when we first arrived. But in addition, this time I want to ultrasound your body cavities to assess for gross anatomical differences – although I doubt we will find anything. Bioimpedance, vital signs. I'd like your consent for blood, and ideally a semen sample, to see if I can shed any light on our collective reproductive inabilities, although I would understand if you were not amenable to that, considering your vocation."

To Azuma's surprise, Weston laughed.

"Well, I did take certain vows, seriously contemplated, and I would like to remain faithful to them," he told her, color rising in his face and neck.

"Oh, no," she said, seeing his discomfort. She put a hand on his forearm. "I know I cannot send you into a little room with a cup and an issue of *Cosmopolitan*," Azuma laughed nervously. "The specimen can be obtained non-invasively in the clinic. It involves stimulating your prostate gland with a low voltage electrical current, which initiates an ejaculatory reflex." She felt her own face getting very hot. "I would give you some sedation, because I don't want you to experience any discomfort. The side-effects are minimal, and you would be recovered from the medication within a few minutes."

"How long would the procedure take?" Weston asked.

"Including our measurements and scans the entire process would be less than fifteen minutes," she told him. "*Go* would assist me, and he would help drape you for the procedure. You will not be uncovered or exposed beyond what is necessary. I respect your desire for modesty, as well. We will not save or keep any images of what we find internally, and there will be no photographs."

"This is an easier way to help than combat practice," Weston pointed out with a smile. "I can take a nap for the cause."

"When would you like to do it?" Azuma asked, touched that he was using humor, trying to make her more comfortable, trying to soften the effect of his earlier surly behavior.

"No time like the present," he said, and his sigh made him sound relieved rather than resigned, which settled Azuma's conscience entirely.

Procedural transcript 7456585:

Attempt to sedate subject with propofol/Versed/morphine per protocol failed. Planned examination and interventions aborted...

Procedural transcript 7456589:

Subject sedated with Substrate 1637b, undiluted preparation per AZ Protocol parameters. Vital signs and airway were continuously monitored and recorded; supplemental oxygen provided.

External examination is unremarkable. Subject exhibits no scars or pigmented markings of any kind.

Bioscan reveals height of subject measures 200 cm, weight 113.4 kg, body surface area 2.482 m², bioimpedance reveals lean body mass 102.1 kg with body fat 10% of total composition. Anatomic evaluation confirms humanoid organ type and distribution, with the exception of the apex of the heart which is slightly rotated laterally. Organs appear to be five percent larger than expected for size and age of subject, the significance of this finding is unknown.
Ultrasound confirms gonadal structures which are morphologically male, blood flow follows hypothesized norms. Blood and tissue harvested according to AZ Protocol and marked MH-alpha. Semen sample collected using prostatic stimulation as per subject's consent.

Dr. Himura and Dr. _____ _____ present for entirety of procedure. Subject monitored directly in recovery by physician staff until at baseline level of consciousness and function.

66

"IS HE AWAKE?" Azuma asked, when *Go* came back into the lab. She was peering into the microscope with a deep frown, and paired with the crevasse between her brows, *Go* suspected she had discovered something worrisome.

"Yes. He is getting dressed now," *Go* informed her. He didn't bother to tell her that Weston had regained consciousness unnaturally quickly following the procedure, and that he seemed to exhibit no ill effects whatsoever from his sedation protocol.

"Would you send him in when he is finished? Tell him I have something I'd like to show him."

Go sensed her distress, her tone as concerning as her expression. "*Hai, Aijin.*"

Azuma was making notes, scrawling hurried kanji across a page that would form the basis of the report she would eventually file, when Weston stepped into the lab. He waited politely, not wanting to interrupt.

"Come," she said, looking up with a smile. "I want you to see something." She waved him over to the bench in front of the microscope and offered him the chair.

He looked at her questioningly, but she said nothing, so he assumed she wanted him to see what she was looking at. He settled himself on the edge of the chair and pushed his spectacles up into his hair before leaning in over the scope. It took him only a moment to acquaint himself with it, he glanced in the eyepiece briefly before leaning away, and Azuma indicated the focus.

He fiddled with it for a few moments before the slide details came into view, something moving, and he was reminded of his ninth grade Biology lab, looking at *Planaria* under the scope; watching the parasite squirm was a shared memory for any student of high school science.

But he realized with some small amount of surprise and displeasure that what he was looking at now was not a flatworm. It was his own sperm, millions of pluripotent cells, mobile, vital. He watched, fascinated for a few moments, but also repulsed by the larger implication of this discovery. Azuma's hunch had confirmed something awful. Something they all feared.

"Does this mean-?" Weston curtailed his own question.

"From a scientific standpoint it confirms nothing but potential," Azuma said, watching the emotions play across his face. Concentration, worry, and ultimately horror. "Before we address what we are seeing under the microscope, I want to briefly go over some other items of interest.

She tapped her finger on her notes, and frowned. "I'm not sure of the significance of this, but you are taller than you were when we arrived here, when the three of you consented to allow *Go* and I to collect your basic biometric measurements. Your organs are humanoid, meaning that you have the same organs as a human being, no more, no less, with a similar anatomic distribution. But they are all five percent larger than the expected norms for a man of your size and weight. This uniform enlargement suggests this is not the result of any disease or underlying abnormality; it is possibly a variant driven by your alternative genetic code."

"So what does it mean?" Weston asked, almost numb to this new information, trying to absorb it as objectively as he was able.

"That is unclear. The change in your height is half the percentage difference in organ volume," Azuma replied, calculating briefly for herself. She cocked her head. "Roughly. One hypothesis would be that the organs are expanding ahead of a change in size, a rapid one. I have no reference for the etiology or indeed, the endpoint of such a transformation. And as this is my first assessment of your internal anatomy, I cannot be certain of your baseline. This apparent enlargement may simply be normal for you. I cannot know, and it would be irresponsible to guess."

Weston considered this. Thought about his reflected self, the Other. The Morningstar and those damnable wings. He searched his memory, grasping at something remembered, something just out of reach, and then it came to him, whole and terrible.

"The Book of Enoch speaks of giants," he whispered, pulling it from what he recalled of endless hours spent cataloguing details while completing his own doctoral thesis.

"What did you say?" Azuma had to strain to hear him.

"Just something I read, something I would have to cross-reference…it's there, I just cannot completely make the connection. I apologize," he said, smiling wanly at her.

"Is there a book I could source for you from the central library in Tokyo?" she asked kindly. "They will release special collections for me, and one of RSI's couriers could deliver it to us here."

"No. What I need is at the Vatican, but I fear that it would be too great a risk to go looking for it. It's too late," he said quietly, looking down at his hands. He put on his spectacles and squared his shoulders, making sure to make eye contact with Azuma.

"You must find a way to kill me," he told her, entirely serious. "We need to let the others know about what you found, and what it could mean."

"I do not know yet all that it means," Azuma protested. "I can infer many things, but I would prefer to take a reasoned approach."

"I have to be destroyed. What we found gives a very clear indication that whatever the Morningstar plans to do with this body will make use of the terrible potential to make more of me," he told her, taking hold of her arm a bit too tightly. It was all starting to make terrible sense, and his thoughts went immediately to Carter. They had told her she was the Bride. He shuddered deeply.

Azuma now saw something in his eyes that made her afraid, something the Dragon was responding to, telling her that he was now her enemy. More than his height had changed. The information she had given him had triggered something unpleasant. And his grip on her arm was painful, surprising in its strength. So she spoke slowly and soothingly, and she used his name.

"Weston, let's consider this carefully and calmly," she told him. "I'm not even sure we *could* kill you, but even if there were the remotest possibility that we could somehow be successful, I would never consider it. Without you, we cannot proceed. Whatever is coming, the four of us must face it together, or not at all. I know you know this to be true."

The Collector materialized in the doorway behind Weston, responding silently to her distress, but Azuma signaled discreetly with her free hand, motioning him away. She suspected the *Akai* were also nearby. She feared escalating a delicate situation that could all too quickly get out of hand.

Weston must have sensed something had changed. He suddenly looked down at his hand clamped on her arm, and seemed to recover something of himself. "I'm hurting you. I'm so sorry, Azuma, forgive me, I – I have to go, I have to get away from all of you."

When he turned away, she tried to catch his arm, keep him talking, but he shrugged her off with no effort whatsoever, escaping down the corridor and outdoors. The Collector came to stand beside her, his question loud in her mind, *Shall we detain him?*

She rubbed her wrist and shook her hand gently, feeling the circulation return. She shook her head sadly. "I fear that would be a grave mistake, my friend. We are meant to let him go."

67

WESTON FINISHED HIS PRAYERS FOR strength, taking refuge in the shrine following his discussion with Azuma. He had avoided the others for some hours, planning his travel, wondering if he was strong enough to do what was needed.

When there was no more to consider, and he was ready to leave, a quiet voice next to him said, "You're fortunate Azuma is not human. If she were, her arm would have been broken. And it is a bit late for reflection under the stars."

Weston tried to push past Amaoke to get to the doorway. Their shoulders collided briefly, neither man deferring, and before Weston could excuse himself he was slammed up against the wall of the shrine with enough force to knock his teeth together. His head bounced off the stones painfully.

"What I don't understand is why your scent has changed," Amaoke's voice register had dropped to a menacing growl of accusation. "Perhaps you can explain that to me, *friend*."

"I didn't know it had," Weston spoke quietly and didn't resist. The Wolf was close, perhaps the Beast, too, and he sensed as much hurt as anger in Amaoke. Weston refused to confront him, even now. He should have known his friend would seek him out, track him to this interim hiding place. But he wasn't really hiding, he just didn't know how to say goodbye.

"Perhaps I never told you, but a wolf can smell a lie," Amaoke's tone was deadly now.

"You have to let me go, Brother," Weston said, still passive, still quiet. "I may not be feeling myself, but I am still your friend."

"Not Weston. You left him behind weeks ago. You haven't eaten in three days, haven't slept for longer. Haven't smelled like a friend since Rome." Amaoke put everything on the table, but Weston only shook his head.

"Perhaps I am becoming something else. Something I don't want you to witness," he said.

"I need answers," Amaoke told him.

"I don't have the ones you need," Weston answered, shaking his head slowly. "I cannot even tell you that this isn't a betrayal. I have known all along that I, more than any of us, must answer for something I cannot control. There are things I have seen, man, things I don't want to believe are real. Things I swear I didn't take part in, yet a part of me knows *I was there*. We have to face it. You have to face it. Somehow, I am one with it, the Morningstar. I hear things, remember things, and it all horrifies me, like I am both the victim and the perpetrator of all my life's sorrows. Responsible for the grief of countless others, innocent of nothing."

"No. The Weston I know is a good man who stands for something. You have defended this world against evil. You can fight this, too," Amaoke argued. "I pledged to help you."

"Don't you see? That's why I have to go on alone. That's why it wants me so badly. Its destruction is in sync with my salvation, and to reach that place on the path will require my damnation. You cannot have the one without the other. I am the Sacrifice and must participate in the downfall. But whatever is coming, I know you will be at my side, fighting for what is right. I have seen it; it has been foretold. In Daniel we are told, *know the exact meaning of the beast, which is different from all the others, exceedingly dreadful, with its teeth of iron and its claws of bronze, and which shall devour, crush, and trample down the remainder with its feet.*

"Daniel did not fear the beast, Daniel trusted that God would protect him. I trust that you are here to protect me. We will meet again; I have known since the beginning of my life that our fates are entwined. I can no more tell you what form that vision will take than you can tell me. Please don't let us spill one another's blood over these truths. I love you too much. I need your love now, more than ever before. And something else." Weston stopped, seeing the glittering glow of the Beast's eyes peering out of Amaoke's face from the shadows.

"Which is?" Amaoke was breathing hard, both from the effort of holding back the change and his continued frustration.

"I need your promise that when the time comes, you won't hesitate to destroy the Morningstar, even if that means you must destroy me with it," Weston spoke so softly that even with his augmented hearing, Amaoke had to strain to catch all of his words. There was truth in this, and fear, too, and it was enough to make Amaoke loosen his grip. Yet he still could not manage to uncurl his fingers from Weston's clothing.

The priest gently put his hands over Amaoke's, and bowed his head to pray. When he finished, he tossed his head to clear his hair from his eyes, revealing his tears. Ever so deliberately, he finished loosening Amaoke's fingers, freeing himself. Then Weston put his hands on his friend's shoulders briefly before making the sign of the cross and blessing him, finally turning back to the archway and disappearing into the darkness of a new dawn.

M

I had to teach the others to deal with the despair, what was lost in the fall. It is too much work, this world, for our oversight alone. Many hands make the load light, or so it is written down somewhere. The Legion integral.

I fear I make use of these writings to twist the truth, but twisted it still holds something they can grasp and believe in. A most destructive weapon, those texts, no matter the name of the one you hold to your breast. Use the manuals against the Maker, and it has all been so much simpler for them to understand somehow. Because they want to believe that there is Other, but in the end, they are all the same.

Weak. Meat. Rotten and rotting.

Soon or late — no matter — you and I shall feed upon them all.

W

Each individual has feelings that would resonate with all of humanity. You could do all those things and more — but that is all *you can do. All you can take.*

You shall not take love from me nor can you feel it for yourself, which is why you seek to destroy its influence in the world.

The part of me that you seek to subvert, that you seek to possess, shall be your downfall. I only hope there is enough of me left to witness it.

68

"IN THE INTEREST OF FULL disclosure, I must now share with you the results of the studies that Weston was gracious enough to agree to undertake," Azuma sounded subdued and slightly shell-shocked. They all had been somewhat blunted emotionally since Amaoke had told them of Weston's departure.

"Why now?" Ambakisye asked, not bothering to hide the bitterness in his tone. Every one of them knew that something had changed, and the disappointment that Weston was perhaps to be counted among their enemies now was a pill not easily swallowed.

"Because now our time is short, and we have no way of knowing how short. We cannot rest on what I am about to share with you. Weston and I agreed that we would tell the group together once the additional studies were completed."

Amaoke looked carefully at Azuma. "Weston knows what you are about to tell us?"

"Only some of it," she replied. "If you will allow me to explain."

"Please, continue," Kusini encouraged her, putting her hand gently on Amaoke's arm in a calming gesture before she took a seat with her husband. She could feel that Amaoke, more than any of them, was struggling with emotions of grief and anger, warring with an impulse even more primitive. Rage. She could feel it eating at him, feel him working hard not to let it out, working hard to find his balance.

"Let's start with the obvious," Azuma began, but then she paused for a moment, both warming up to the task and organizing the best way in which to lay out the information she had gathered. "Weston is anatomically identical, at least grossly, to a human. *Go* and I sedated him, and did bioscans, including ultrasound of his internal organs. His organ structure and placement mimic those of a human, but were enlarged for his size by some few percent above normal. His heart was rotated slightly, which may represent a normal variant or may be the result of some evolutionary event that is tied to his unique DNA. Perhaps something the Morningstar requires.

"Weston additionally consented to the harvest of reproductive material, and we obtained a semen sample from him noninvasively, which is the reason we sedated him. The procedure was uncomplicated, and the results of our early findings were shared with him," Azuma ignored the surprised expressions on the other's faces at this admission, and kept on.

"He had motile sperm at sufficient cell counts to predict reproductive capacity and potency," she said, letting that fact sink in. She made eye contact with each of them in turn, and could see that they grasped where this was going. There was a dawning horror in Amaoke's eyes.

"Weston's immediate request when he learned of this finding was that we find a way to destroy him," Azuma continued.

"Great. And now we've let him go," Ambakisye did not bother to hide his animosity. "Is there any good news?"

"My dear Ambakisye, I am sad to inform you that we *must* deal with the bad news first." Azuma's tone was firm but kind. "The information I have given you thus far is just a piece of the larger picture.

"Before, we discussed our individual inability to procreate. The significance of that fact was not further explored. Indeed, I admit I had assumed it was because we were disposable beings, bred for purpose and not meant to propagate. There is a genetic precedent of course, one we have contemplated before and shall do so again. The mule is bred for its physical properties, but cannot reproduce. At first, this was the only connection I could make to our mutual discovery.

"But my assumption was dangerous, as assumptions are wont to be. The evaluation of the genetic material that Amaoke recovered on Onigashima, the flesh of the carp, showed genetic proteins that were the same as those in Weston, if not the same sequence, of course, in much the same way that a carp and a human will not have the same DNA sequence.

"But then something else occurred to me. Perhaps the line between the spirit world and our world is a correlate in another way. We are caught between those worlds, and our DNA reflects this limbo. We will generate no offspring in either place. But we could consider the carp and Weston to be shadow creatures, mirrors of their related beings in this world.

"Our existence suggests that the introduction of the shadow DNA robs the offspring of reproductive capacity. But it appears Weston is not similarly afflicted. So if he is the vehicle for the Morningstar to walk in this world, the way in which the Monster can crossover and establish itself permanently, with flesh it has engineered for our world, the resulting effect on humanity is clear."

"Because he can make others like himself?" Ambakisye asked.

"No, because he can make others like ourselves," Kusini said softly, her voice shaking.

"And if he can cross over successfully in Weston, that will allow him to transform his minions similarly, not just the ones we know. Imagine the Death Bringer loose in this world, invested in flesh that holds, killing on a whim," Amaoke added.

"The Collector warned me to consider that there were more players than Forcas and Beelz," Azuma said, and Amaoke found it oddly amusing to hear her refer to Lilith by shortening the demon's name in that dismissive fashion.

"If the screams I have heard when the Morningstar appears are any indicator," Amaoke continued, "there are millions of them."

"Given the initial apocalyptic insult, whereby they killed to the limits of their pleasure, even if they got bored with that, they could easily integrate and infiltrate the human population, creating offspring with no ability to create more offspring. The human species, wiped out in a single generation," Azuma spelled it out. "Isn't that what the Morningstar wants? To rid itself of the creature that unseated it as the favorite of the Creator?"

"So now we have to hunt Weston down and destroy him before the Morningstar does," Ambakisye sounded ready for the task.

"No," Amaoke said firmly, his tone indicating his conviction that he was correct. "Weston is the key to the Place of the Fallen. He is the only one who can seek out the Monster in its physical location. Kill him, and you'll never get into the *makom*. The Morningstar would simply destroy all of us and start over again. We get one opportunity to get to it, in the flesh, and now we know what happens if we fail."

69

"You said there was good news?" Ambakisye sighed, not trying to be funny, but providing some levity in a tense moment.

"A bit," Azuma's smile was inscrutable, but Amaoke recognized that she was not just optimistic, she was feeling triumphant about something.

"There were a few things I did not share with brother Weston," she said. "He does not know my conclusion about the end result of his virility."

"Or perhaps he does, because he is and is not the Morningstar," Kusini pointed out.

"Yes, very intelligent," Azuma nodded at Kusini warmly, but did not appear any less enthusiastic about what she was about to tell them. "Using the carp, and a little something else I had up my sleeve, something I told none of you, wanting it to remain undiscussed until appropriate conclusions could be made, I came up with something useful. But the time has come to share it, so I will."

Here she paused, ready to absorb their anger and frustration, if it came, but no one had anything to say. They knew who she was by now, and were unsurprised that she still kept secrets.

"When the Morningstar attacked Amaoke and I on Onigashima, it made a mistake, albeit an inadvertent one," Azuma told them. "During the exploration and repair of the wound to Amaoke's spine, we recovered one of the Dragon's claws."

The others blinked in confusion, so Azuma stammered on, clarifying, "It's-it's like a fingernail. And there was tissue present where the claw had torn away that carried its genetic material, its DNA. It's fascinating, the way it cross-references to Weston was amazing, and the bond structure defeated most of our proteases that we required to reverse-engineer-"

"*Azuma!*" Amaoke, Kusini, and Ambakisye all groaned in unison, wanting to stop her, but they were laughing.

"Darling, I am certain it *is* fascinating," Kusini said gently, wanting to redirect their host away from the science and back to the point. "But give it to us in a form we can understand."

"Of course," Azuma laughed. "Let me come back from the weeds. I was able to isolate, or pull out, a protein moiety – excuse me, a piece of DNA – that I successfully attached to a biomarker. That marker will fluoresce, or glow, when it comes in contact with the Morningstar, and we might additionally be able to use it to identify the others, or mark the true passageways through the *makom.*"

"That is good news," Ambakisye allowed.

"Oh, but there is better news," Azuma told them. "I also created one that will react with Weston's DNA. He will fluoresce a different color than the Morningstar," she said proudly.

"Impressive." Amaoke congratulated her, sincerely awed by her ingenuity, but still worried. "And how do we find him to mark him?"

"Already done," she said, only slightly uncomfortable now. "And his marker was modified slightly to carry another protein, one from my blood, which creates a sort of bond with Weston that I can sense when I am in proximity to him."

"Pretty sci-fi," Ambakisye said, starting to understand. "You LoJacked a demigod."

Azuma laughed. "Kind of did, yeah. The blood bond will only work within a certain distance, but it may mean we can use it to follow him to the Morningstar's hiding place at the site. At the very least, the signal will change if we are too late and cannot prevent the Ascendance."

"I'm guessing you didn't obtain his consent for this," Amaoke said, sensing that Azuma's earlier discomfort was tied to this observation.

"The ethics *are* slippery," Azuma admitted. "And there is a chance that if the Morningstar is able to crossover, or merge, with Weston before we can find one or both of them, that the bond will work two ways, and it will know where I am."

"If all of this isn't just a trap to begin with," Kusini pointed out helpfully. "We have to gamble, but we cannot forget that if we all were — what was your word?" She looked at Azuma and then remembered. "Engineered. If we all were engineered by the Monster we seek, we must remember that there is always a chance it can read us.

"I don't know about the rest of you, but the Morningstar interfered with my life at very discrete moments, as though it wanted to remind me it was watching, but without really causing trouble that could not be averted." Kusini stopped talking, and something unspoken passed between her and Ambakisye. "Nuisance and grievance, but I always felt it was holding back."

"I agree. Torture, intrusion, threats, but ultimately the Morningstar left me alone more than it interfered." Amaoke found it curious as well.

"It needs us, needs our gifts, our lifeforce, our energies somehow. It has left us alone to confuse the issue, but it is clear that we are part of the greater equation. Weston may be the key to the *makom*, but the Monster cannot Ascend without all of us present. At the very least, it may be what it believes it needs, and a ritual to take on flesh might require us," Azuma said.

"Even if the four of you are just sacrifices?" Ambakisye was wise.

"Yes, my friend," Amaoke replied. "Either way, I think we all know and accept that this was only ever a one-way ticket. Win or lose, to get close enough to stop it, we have to walk into the trap."

70

"SO WHEN DO WE LEAVE?" Ambakisye asked, confused when his wife shook her head.

"My husband," she said, looking at Azuma and Amaoke, "we will not all be traveling together. We go our separate ways from this place."

Amaoke and Azuma exchanged glances, but Kusini could see that neither was surprised.

"We must make our way forward separately," Kusini said. "How and when we arrive at the Place of the Fallen is not important, but we must find our way independently of one another, under our own power, ensuring our own magic."

"And we cannot bring our anger and our hatred inside," Amaoke said. "Those emotions will be weapons that can be turned against us. We may need to fight, but we do this errand out of love. Love for this world and the pureflesh in it, love for those we have lost, and love for Weston, who never deserved the burden he has carried for so long. Especially love for him, because he is ours. That binds us to him with a promise that we will not let him go. We will not let the Monster have him."

71

THE SHADOW THAT FELL OVER Margaret O'Halloran as she knelt in her flower garden was familiar, but the being that cast it was unwelcome. Her shoulder bruised immediately when it touched her, and she sat back on her heels and sighed.

"You're not him, and there's no mistaking that," she observed wisely.

"Why, Maggie May, we're flattered that you recognize us," it answered her, in a borrowed Irish brogue that she'd heard in her dreams for over sixty years, a voice now layered with uglier, deeper tones, the voices of the damned. Those she had heard, too, once. Long ago. "And you're wrong, dove. We are him, and he is us. He is here, because you are."

"No. I know your lies, now. And I'm no longer the child I was. You took that from me, among other things," she said, still not ready to see that face, the face of the only child she had ever been given to love, the face of the monster that had taken everything from her, on a bright spring day, her sixteenth birthday, when anything seemed possible, and the dark divide she faced was yet unknown to her. "He'd take no part in this."

"And I'm forever grateful," it crooned softly at her, but each word was like a blow, cutting and burning, and she felt her face flush with shame at what she had done with this creature, for it. "He takes part in all that we do. He has no choice; he has never had a choice."

She recalled the first time she had laid eyes on Weston, when Padraig had brought him home. She hadn't been prepared to look on that face, but she mastered herself, and didn't betray her dismay. For that cherubic face told her only one thing, that Weston wore the mark of the beast, that he was demonspawn. The face she had seen in her nightmares, even though he was so clearly not the monster she had known, and she felt a sort of pity for him, akin to the pity she felt for herself, that he should be so afflicted.

Putting that aside, ever so bravely now, she turned her face up to see it, see the face of the handsome boy that had lured her to her ruin, Weston's face, remembering. Remembering that day and the days that came after, unsure of who she was. Succumbing to her lusts repeatedly, wanton with desire each time, and horrified after. Unable to stop, even when she could see what it was, even when she knew the gorgeous illusion was simply a veil over an ugly reality.

She'd snuck away with him, and willingly submitted to her passions, not knowing the monster to be incapable of penetrating her flesh, believing her beautiful lover was giving her this pleasure, this sweetness that overcame her fear of any sin. Not seeing that she was given as a surrogate sacrifice, that the invasion was spiritual, that it was feeding on her desire, swallowing her gifts, damning her utterly, while satisfying the lusts of a mortal man.

She'd never told Padraig, or any of her other brothers, nor dear Mother. How could she? Her dreams of the convent were lost, because she knew she was unclean. She had lost more than her innocence; she had tainted her soul. Her face burned with shame, even now.

"Ah, Maggie, don't be ashamed. You were so lovely, your skin flushed, your back bowed, every part of you begging to be satisfied. Nothing wrong with that. The world wants you to believe it a sin, but you should celebrate the satisfaction of such pleasures."

Margaret straightened suddenly, getting slowly to her feet. She brushed clippings from her apron and considered the demon defiantly. "I don't know what you've come for now. You took all of it. I'm an old woman, nothing here to tempt you anymore."

"But you're wrong, *me girl*." Now her father's voice came forward, and she felt cold to hear it again, coming as it did from the Monster's mouth. "We got only a taste, then, of all that you were. Beauty, passion, fire. And now it is seasoned with your decay. And we have time, nothing but time to devote to these attentions. Let's not waste any more of it on pointless regret. We won't think less of you if you don't protest. You do remember how much you loved it. You can drop the ladylike pretense with us."

And when it reached for her hand, she shed a single tear, but did not hesitate to take it. She knew she was owned completely, and she wanted to surrender. She didn't bother to pray for strength, the strength she had would soon be a liability that prolonged her suffering. She hoped she wouldn't scream. The harvest had begun.

72

IN THE MORNING, AFTER BREAKFAST, Amaoke followed Azuma, Kusini, and Ambakisye out to the courtyard, where two helicopters waited, poised to carry them away from each other for the last time. The mood was somber.

Azuma broke the silence, addressing Kusini and Ambakisye. "I have arranged for your flight to leave from Haneda today, it is more centrally located, and I thought you might like to see more of Tokyo before you departed. The crew are at your service, just as before, and I have ensured you will have transportation out of Arusha should that be your desire."

Kusini smiled, she was far more confident than she had once been that she could successfully travel in an enclosed vehicle, and tried not to worry about the delicate electronics involved. *Faith*, she thought to herself, reassured by Ambakisye's hand in hers.

The two women embraced warmly, and Azuma held on, not wanting to let go yet. When she stepped away from Kusini, her mouth trembled slightly, but she maintained her composure. "It has been my honor to know you." She bowed to both of them.

"We are blessed with your talents, and are most grateful for your hospitality. You have given me an opportunity I never thought to have. I have never been away from home," Kusini told her.

Ambakisye turned to Amaoke, and the two men embraced, Ambakisye pounding on Amaoke's back affectionately.

"See you, Brother," Amaoke said, as Ambakisye let go.

"I think you will," Ambakisye replied, with mischief in his eyes.

Then Kusini stepped into Amaoke's arms, and the two of them stood with forearms linked, looking at each other for a long time. "I dreamed of you for centuries, but I underestimated how much I would love you," she told him. "I don't know if this is the last time we shall meet, my dear friend, but I do know it is not goodbye. Bless our Azuma with some of that good medicine, will you?"

"Yes, ma'am," Amaoke replied, and stepped back from her, feeling a zap of energy as her fingertips slipped off his own.

They boarded the first helicopter, and Azuma came to stand beside him as they watched it go. He put an arm around her shoulders, and to his surprise, she leaned into him, accepting this comfort, perhaps not realizing how much it helped him too. When Kusini and Ambakisye's transport was out of sight, she pulled away.

"Our turn," she said, indicating the other helicopter.

He sighed, and she turned toward him with a look of amusement. Amaoke hitched his knapsack onto his shoulder and said, "Let's do this."

It was a new kind of torture, the harness that kept him in his seat was like bondage, and the smells of the upholstery and machine oil and fuel flooded his nose unpleasantly. *Ni* and *Nana* were up front, so Azuma sat in the passenger compartment with him, which helped, because her scent was pleasant, and he concentrated on separating it out, its familiarity alone helped soothe him.

As he had suspected, helicopter travel combined the worst of vehicle motion and air travel. The odd sensation of going straight up, spiraling, and hovering were terrifying.

"It will be better when we level off," Azuma promised, her voice clear in his headset despite the deafening noise of the rotor, and she wasn't wrong.

The view from the helicopter was so unique, the changing vista below him so interesting, that soon he was distracted fully by it, forgetting to be terrified – almost. They passed over some urban and suburban sprawl, Azuma and *Ni* calling out points of interest, and in less than twenty minutes they were over the forest, climbing up and up, headed for a mountain peak.

They followed the path of the valley below them, and curved around a rocky outcropping before climbing steeply, and Azuma pointed down and to the right, and he could see another estate, built near the top of the mountain, connected to a road that disappeared through the trees, on the other side of a stout suspension bridge built over a chasm.

That bridge actually interested Amaoke, it had taken a feat of engineering to build, and he imagined the fun he would have had, suspended in space over the rocks below, watching it come together. But *Ni* flew on, hovering over the buildings for a few moments more before setting the helicopter down gently on the marked apron that overlooked the valley below.

The residence and grounds here were even more elaborate than those at the stronghold. While the stronghold was more rustic, ancient and traditional, this build married modern architecture to the aesthetic of Japan.

Shinto arches adorned the drive, and the ornamental gardens were spectacular. Crushed gravel paths were set down in graceful patterns, the widest one ahead of them, leading to what he guessed was the back of the house, cedar and glass, facing out to the expansive green vista, the endless sky. The cherry trees along the walkway were trying to believe it was really spring, and one or two of them had blossomed, tentatively committing to the possibility of warmth and new life.

Azuma pulled off her headset and turned to Amaoke. "Welcome to my home. You survived the flight."

"Yes. The views almost made me forget my mortal terror," he replied, laughing at her expression of amusement.

73

THE COLLECTOR WAS WAITING FOR them on the steps of the main dwelling, and he tilted his head to listen to something *Ni* said to him before she and *Nana* continued on into the house. His attention returned to Azuma and Amaoke immediately, and he welcomed them.

"*Aijin*, Konoye Ko would like a word with you. He indicated there was some urgency, said to reassure you that it does not concern the Sorceress and her husband. Their flight took off without delay and they are safely en route home. Michael Israel is in the bathhouse, I believe, and Selene is here. If she will be dining with you, I need to let the staff know there will be one more for lunch," he recited. Amaoke was very interested in the spare efficiency with which the Collector communicated, as if to waste one word might derail the entire operation.

"Ask her," Azuma recommended, responding only to his last comment. "She may not have time to take a formal meal with us."

To which the Collector only nodded, holding the door as they entered the house and withdrawing to see to other tasks. Amaoke set his knapsack down in the entryway and removed his shoes, following Azuma's lead.

The interior of the home was reminiscent of a luxury hotel. They had just come through a back door that was larger than most front doors. The room was adorned with fresh flower arrangements and tasteful furnishings. It smelled good, too. The sort of place where he was almost too afraid to sit down.

Selene was seated at a lacquered desk in an archway off the main space, her fingers flying over the keys of a laptop, the small earpiece in her ear flashing, the little blue light like a tiny strobe. The neckline of her cashmere sweater had slipped, leaving one shoulder alluringly exposed, or perhaps it was purposeful, the fashion of the moment, Amaoke did not know. Her trousers were linen, and he saw that her feet were bare, her toenails painted the same neon orange color of his highway vest, and there were rings on a few of her toes.

She glanced at them with a smile, and Azuma leaned down to brush the woman's forehead with her lips, then left her to her continued industry with the computer. Azuma then led Amaoke onward, down a short hallway and into a more formal office.

"Talented, smart, tough women. One of my favorite things," Azuma said.

"We have that in common," Amaoke agreed. "What does she do?"

"Selene is a forensic accountant with an international reputation. She can speak to numbers," Azuma told him, and then quickly clarified to avoid any misunderstanding. "She does not and has never worked for me. I find it wisest to separate business from pleasure."

"Is she American?" Amaoke asked, fascinated at the ways in which Azuma both maintained strict secrecy while just as comfortably being self-revealing.

"She grew up in the United Kingdom. Her parents were Cape Verdean, I believe. Please, make yourself comfortable," Azuma said, then looked apologetically at the many items piled atop various chairs. She cleared one and indicated he should take it. "Sorry, it all makes sense to me. I had to ban the Collector from this room, because he has a nasty penchant for organization."

"Imagine that," Amaoke laughed.

"Yes, it is monstrous, really." Azuma considered. "My 'public' office at RSI is very spartan, not a Post-It note in sight. They threatened to take them away from me. I can only really think in spaces like this one."

Amaoke looked at the wall of Post-Its next to the window, along the side of one cabinet, covering a quarter of the surface of her desk. Each group a different color, not a single one of them legible, not that he could decipher *kanji*. "Perhaps they were concerned about damaging your reputation," he suggested, smiling.

"By *Fūjin*, yes, keeping up appearances." It was Azuma's turn to laugh.

"Why am I here?" Amaoke asked, understanding that she did nothing without strict consideration. He could see this residence contained her most private spaces; it was truly her home. She had brought the group to the stronghold, and he suspected it was because their business needed to be kept apart from her heart. Yet she had brought him here, where he knew he did not really belong. There had to be a very compelling reason to do so.

She was about to answer when her attention was distracted by something behind him. The Collector, returning to collect them.

"Lunch?" Azuma guessed.

"Yes. Just you and Mr. Severnoj for now. I've prepared a few things for you to carry this afternoon. Your pack is ready."

"Thank you, my friend. If it isn't too much trouble, would you take Amaoke down so that he can get started? I want to reach out to Konoye Ko. Has Michael Israel eaten? If not, she is welcome to join us."

"She is dining in private. She said she had some details to work out regarding your earlier request," the Collector replied, turning to Amaoke with a smile and an abbreviated bow, indicating he should follow.

"She's not going to make it, is she?" Amaoke guessed, as he and the Collector made their way into a generous room surrounded by paper screens off the main kitchen. The short table was accompanied by sumptuous floor cushions and was set for two.

"Unlikely," the Collector agreed. "She does have many things to attend to on any given day. I hope you are not inconvenienced by eating alone."

"I may have done it a time or two," Amaoke reassured him. "What happens after lunch?"

"A hike in the mountains. Azuma thought you might enjoy it, and she has something she wants to discuss with you privately," the Collector told him, inviting him to be comfortable before he stepped back out of the room.

But as it turned out, Amaoke was not alone at all. The young woman who brought his food kneeled demurely at his side, her kimono sleeves folded back smartly, and anticipated his every need, whether it be for more water, fresh tea, or another serving of sashimi. When he was finished, she asked whether there would be anything else, waiting several moments after he demurred, as if giving him a chance to change his mind, before she rose, bowed carefully, and departed.

Someone else came to show him to his room, and Azuma found him there a short time later, listening to an American radio station and attempting to decide whether he liked the seaweed snacks that had been left for him. He remained undecided, thinking that there was something slightly odd about them that he didn't get from fresh seaweed, but the texture and the saltiness were pleasurable.

"I apologize for my absence," she said sincerely.

"I know you are very busy," he said, letting her off the hook. "I cannot imagine what it takes to do what you do."

"I enjoy it," she told him. "But I would have liked sharing a meal with you more. The work takes precedence over pleasure as well, although I try to build some downtime into every day. I knew I'd get you to myself eventually."

"We're going into the mountains?" he asked, sincerely curious about the errand. For his instincts told him it was an errand, no matter how much it might also be an escape.

74

BY AMAOKE'S RECKONING, THEY HAD traveled about five or six kilometers on foot when Azuma stopped at a rocky outcropping between two sturdy evergreens. They had simply walked off her property and into the forest, not gaining elevation, and not losing it, maintaining a level path that curved onward into the wilderness. The valley was off to their left, the twin mountain range beyond it, but its distance was misleading. It looked tantalizingly close, but he guessed it would be a day's walk to climb down, cross the rocky ravine far below, and climb up on the other side.

Azuma stepped up into the gap between the trees and gazed out on the green vista. Unlike Amaoke's mountains at home, here the trees grew clumped together, like with like, sometimes spruce, occasionally oak and other deciduous species, rare aspen, and even wide swaths of bamboo.

"Here," she said, nodding. "Look closely there, across the valley, up and to the left. We got lucky with the weather, even on sunny days this valley is shrouded by mists."

"The breeze and the cold are helping us," Amaoke told her.

She stepped back, allowing him to stand where she had, framed between the trees, gazing off in the direction she had indicated. He was quiet, concentrating on the trees, seeing something and not seeing it, his eyes unable to fully focus on one particular area that looked much like any other stand of trees, but was not strictly what it seemed.

"Extraordinary," he said softly. Azuma smiled to herself, pleased that he'd had no difficulty discovering the incongruity among the trees.

"Take the glasses now," she said, handing him a pair of binoculars. He took them without taking his eyes off their target.

Now, with the aid of magnification, he could see it more clearly. A temple, spectacular in scope, camouflaged nearly as well as things of the natural world could accomplish. Its wall was stone, mossy from many rains and centuries, lending its disappearance into the green ground of the vista, its structure mostly wood and rock, blending with the trunks of the tall trees and the rocky features of the mountain face. Its roof was as delightfully elaborate and as beautiful as any of the temples he had seen in this amazing place, the tiles a deep dark green, seamless among the tops of the pines that grew around it, dappled like the leaves of the other giants in the forest, because it reflected dark and light where their shadows filtered the sunlight onto its multileveled surface.

"What is it?" he asked her, certain that this incredible fortress was the reason for their trek.

"It is the Temple of Akenomyosei. The place that holds the secrets of his sect, where the ritual initiations to his service are undertaken. It is the place where he collected the most powerful witches and conjurers many centuries ago, setting them on a path to collect power. They have removed themselves from humanity, but they continue their deadly industry."

"Which is?" he prompted, seeing something dark and angry in her eyes now, but it was confusing because her scent was only remorseful.

"Many things, not the least of which has been to supply the Dragon Goddess with a special guard. There, the brightest and the best assassin priests are trained, trained for one purpose, trained to kill their own kind out in the world. But they are only released under special conditions, only when there is a need are they presented as candidates, to me, and if chosen, they become members of the *Akai*."

"What happens if they are not chosen?" he asked quietly, but she failed to answer.

Instead, she said, "Because the inhabitants of the shrine are destined for singular purpose, it is the only life that many of them have ever known. They are raised to be ruthless, and deadly, but they are also taught that their lives belong to Akenomyosei, that they are expendable. Those who ascend to my guard were only ever meant to die protecting me."

Amaoke was quiet. "Yet it has never been so with you."

"What?" Azuma was whispering, surprised at his statement.

"You give them back their lives," he said. He saw the regard in which she held each member of her guard.

"Perhaps I am even more cruel than the Morningstar," she said, shaking her head. "I give them a number, which is not the same as a name. Because I exist, for nearly four hundred years, the monsters within those walls have stolen infants for this dark purpose, ensuring that they do not know their own names, securing their fealty to the dark *kami* of this world, torture and punishment ensure obedience and cruel efficiency.

"I transform them during another ritual, which transfers their loyalty to me, confers longevity, and all too often, madness. Those that lose their minds must be retired, and another must ascend in their place. Each of them knowing the singular truths of their existence. How they bear it I cannot know." She seemed defeated.

"It is all they know," Amaoke reasoned. "And I am not surprised that you cannot name the thing you have given back to them, because it is hard for you to discern it in yourself. You have ensured that they are allowed to be individuals, name or not, ultimately bestowing self-respect. This act is called something specific. Love."

Azuma remained quiet, so he took the lead as they made their way further along the ridge to the next vantage point. He repeated his reconnaissance of the temple on the other side of the valley once more, considering its location and size from another point of reference.

"Can you just walk in?" Amaoke asked finally, and she understood that he meant her specifically, considering her business there, and her status as a god.

"No living thing gets in without a sacrifice," she said, and the way she said it made him think that acceptable sacrifices might be unpleasant. "Nor can one get back out without a sacrifice. Akenomyosei demands such. I imagine it will be much the same at the *makom*."

"What happens when you need…" he let his voice trail off, wanting to kick himself for even making her revisit what they had discussed earlier.

"The Collector makes this errand," she explained. "He insisted on it long ago, and I have no idea what arrangements he has made to accomplish his ends."

"I doubt he sits still for any intrusion on his person," Amaoke said, and this elicited a laugh from Azuma.

"I wanted you to know of this place," she said suddenly, changing the subject. "I needed someone else to have the burden of knowledge about its existence. I think this may be another place where the Morningstar could take refuge from the world."

"But why tell me?" he asked her.

"I did something else to Weston when I implanted the marker, not knowing we would need it, but assuming that we failed somehow to stop the Morningstar, prevent Weston's ascendance. In the event that the Morningstar is successful, it will trigger a response in Weston, almost like an allergy, and start a reaction in his tissues, a degenerative process. I cannot say that it will ultimately be destructive, but it should slow him down. If the Morningstar escapes, he may try to take refuge here, in the temple. I need you to know where to look; I do not want him to have any place to hide in this world, because the Ascendance is meant to tie him to it.

"I am taking every precaution to ensure that nothing escapes the Place of the Fallen," Azuma assured him. "In the unlikely event that it does, I want to be sure we did all that we could."

"Belt and suspenders," Amaoke nodded, understanding her reasoning, touched by her naïve faith in him. So he put word to thought, needing them both to face the bitter truth. "Still it may not matter much. After the *makom*, it is likely no one will be alive to stop anything."

M

Evil is not ugly. It can have very silky hair, a Monday's child, facile in its accomplishments. The misbegotten Prince was born on a Monday, you know. You love him, but you cannot see what I see, know what I know.

Though my adornments may seem fashionably mundane, I must present to the world a dignified counterpoint to Forcas, whose choices are sometimes a little too over the top, foppish on occasion. And lovely Lilith, one must admit, purple, the color of royalty, draws the eye, draws the victim into the web, draws the cord from which they shall hang themselves.

I should tell you; did I tell you? Those twins were also coincidentally born on Monday. Or not coincident to anything, because that's how it works with the One at the top.

Try to make sense of anything that happens, lull yourself into believing that something so pedestrian as 'evil' could do no damage. Perhaps it has not harmed you, yet. You are not aware; you lack the capacity to appreciate just how glorious destructiveness can be. Just how subtly it often slithers into your life.

It is this disdain for evil that allows me to make you sacrifice everything of worth until you cannot live without its conveniences, without its excuses, until, alas, it is too late.

For now I live in your own skin and speak to the world with your voice.

75

CARTER WOKE TO THE ECHOES of strange voices and sat up in bed, at first disoriented, shaking off the remnants of a terrifying dream. She couldn't hold on to the particulars, but was chilled through, her nightgown soaked in icy sweat.

The time of night was indeterminate, but dawn was still hours away, and she feared there would be no more sleep for her. Her penitent's cell was cold, she longed to be warm, but Sister Merzede had locked all the novices within their quarters until morning vespers.

She folded back the counterpane and climbed out of bed, settling her feet on the floor carefully, wincing at the temperature of the stones on her bare feet.

"Carter," a soft voice called to her, and it sounded as though it were outside the door to her tiny alcove. She pressed herself against the door, stretching up on tiptoe to try to peek through the grate, but all was shadows and darkness in the hallway beyond, the vigil candle in the sconce on the wall long since burned down.

She pushed up again on her toes, sensing a change in the gloom, and felt the draft ruffle the newly shorn hairs on the nape of her neck. As she leaned against the wood, it gave, her door slipping open, the hinge groaning softly. Strange. It should have been locked.

Carter took a step into the hallway, the cold floor drafts curling around her ankles like spectral fingers grasping for purchase. She leaned forward, shuffling, hands splayed out in front of herself, constructively blind. The darkness was a totality, which was not unusual in this central stone hallway that had no windows.

She navigated without sight (*but not without faith*, Sister Mary Matthew's words came unbidden to mind and she stifled a giggle) to the end of the passageway that led her to the shared dining room. Here, there was some transmitted light from the streetlamps on the corner at the far end of the block. She was thankful for it, as it prevented her from barking her shins on the low benches near the wall.

She realized her hands felt empty, and clutched at her thin cotton nightgown jerkily, until she caught her fingers on the silver links of the Redeemer about her neck. She felt afraid. She was trying to discern whether she was really hearing whispers, or if it was the transmitted noise of the traffic out along Poydras Street. She had forgotten about feeling cold, but knew if she were discovered out of her cell in this state it would be seen as worse than unchaste and immodest. She could feel her erect nipples chafing against her clothing, knew the gown was little more than transparent in her current state.

"*Carter*," the voice (*voices*) came again, and there was something almost seductive about it.

I must be dreaming within my dream, she thought, until the grandmother clock in the Mother Superior's office struck the hour. Three o'clock. The Devil's Hour. She knew she should turn back, put on proper undergarments, her stockings, her habit. She could sleep atop the covers fully dressed; she'd done it before. It worked when she really needed to stay warm.

But something unseen seemed to compel her onward, through the kitchen, where she paused. It was warmer here, the residual heat from the prior days' cooking trapped in the galley-like space. At the door to the yard she hesitated, torn between propriety and curiosity, knowing that she should not go about outside the convent walls in her flimsy nightclothes, unshod, unveiled.

"Carter," it was *his* voice now, more urgent, and more evocative of her haste.

But he's gone, she thought, as she stepped out into the night. A false breeze scurried around her feet, but didn't touch the trees. It pulled and moved her gown, and with it came the whispers, many voices, his on top, *never gone, never gone, never...*

The ground was soft and damp, and although the soil clung to her feet it was very cold, heralding a frost as the dawn advanced. The dark expanse between the convent and the groundsman's cottage stretched out ahead of her, and she was surprised when she saw the lamp burning from the bedroom window.

She shivered, reminded of the cold, and unmindful of her predicament, gathered folds of her gown in her hands and began to run over the lawn, heading for that square of light in the distance, her beacon. How many times had it waited, just like that, on early mornings before a shared departure, when they would set out together into the waning darkness to travel toward some unfortunate soul?

I don't care if I am dreaming, let him be there, her mind begged, knowing that the way she felt for him was forbidden, knowing that in her deepest secret heart she refused to believe it a sin, feeling it real and whole and sacred, the best gift she had ever been given. In spite of the struggles she had watched him suffer through, she knew the love for her in him was not the Church's love for a Christ-bride but the personal love of a man for a woman. She thought often of the blasphemous stories of Jesus and the Magdalene, had wondered many times about them, how a man, holy and pious and strong and loving might pick a woman that everyone thought was wrong, because he might see through to something inside of her that others could not fathom.

I could be your Magdalene, she thought, and it came unbidden to her mind, along with another thought. Weston knew her secret heart. And she already knew what she had to do, knew that it would mean turning away from something she had held so dear, something that had been her only aspiration, until the day she had met him.

Perhaps he had always known it, perhaps that was behind his questioning of her calling all along. He would never turn her from something she desired, even if he knew it was wrong. Perhaps he had encouraged her to keep her safe from the demons, from himself. But because she did not understand, and could never understand, Carter believed that she could save him, that there was a way they could be together. At that very moment, as swiftly as her decision was made, something changed.

She felt it, charged, in the air, like the foreboding sense of a coming storm. She remembered the feeling of being at the bottom of the field when the clouds piled up so fast she could not turn away, and that first deafening crack of rolling thunder, when her three-year-old legs could not make themselves move, how she had felt, crying and calling until Mama came to get her, and run with her, almost beating the rain to the house.

This was even more powerful, and it propelled her toward the storm, the forbidden, the danger. She reached the cottage and felt a moment's despair, knowing the door would be locked. But she was happily surprised to find it opened for her, and she stepped inside, closing the door behind her, leaning against it with a sigh of satisfaction. She closed her eyes, placing her hands against the wood. Here it was warm, as it always was, the scents of memory flooding her senses, incense, paper, the smell of his hair when he'd been outdoors, here, where he had been hers alone.

She was disappointed to find the house empty, the lamp burning in the bedroom unrevealing of anything useful. She switched it off, but turned to the bed, sad, exhausted, and feeling the beginnings of heartbreak. She slid between the covers and sighed in pleasure at the discovery that it was as inviting and comfortable as she had guessed it might be. Well, she could pretend he was here, and she could sleep, perhaps his memory would keep the dreams away. She would deal with the consequences of her rebellion when she woke.

But she tossed, and turned, dozing and waking, unable to find peace. She focused on the sounds of the city around her, and was just settling down when she felt the bedclothes shift, as if to accommodate the movement of another, and she felt a blast of warmth against her body, and then she was turned onto her back, another form moving against her beneath the comforter. It startled her fully awake, and she sat up.

The room was no longer entirely dark, a candle burned on the desk in the corner, and it took her a moment to remember where she was, and now she was remorseful, because she had no idea what she would – or could – say to the Mother Superior about all of this.

She turned to the clock on the far nightstand to check the time, and gasped aloud.

Asleep, only inches from where her outstretched hand supported her weight, was Weston. He was facing away from her, the blanket pulled up to his arm, and she stared at the powerful muscles in his bare shoulder and upper back. His hair curled lazily down his neck, and it looked so soft. She reached out to touch it with a loving hand, and it seemed to move under her fingers. She was startled for a moment, until she realized that it was because he was moving, too, turning toward her and pulling her down to him in one graceful maneuver.

His hands gripped her body expertly, tugging on her hips, moving her with ease, and his power took her breath away. He didn't talk, didn't resist her arms as they twined around his neck, simply buried his face into the softness of her chest, and she gave in to her desire, and didn't care anymore about how she would explain any of it. It didn't matter, only this.

His mouth on her exposed skin seemed to burn, and his hair was as silky as she had imagined it would be where it moved and brushed against her chin and neck. She moaned as she felt his hand on her thigh, sliding up and over her left hip, traveling higher beneath her gown until it came to rest upon her scar, his fingers tracing the outline of it on her skin, as he murmured, "Mine. *My Bride.*"

She barely heard the last two words, but when her muddled mind realized what he had said to her she recoiled in horror, trying to pull away from that inexorable grip. That was when she realized that she hadn't imagined it, his hair *was* moving, independent of the laws of physics, gravity, their shared kinetics, and suddenly it felt like snakes crawling against her skin.

She struggled, pushing at him, needing to see his face, his eyes, certain that this impostor was that Other that he'd warned her about, the one that mothers and priests and nuns ward you from, the Prince for whom she had been marked, and then she knew. The Prince of Darkness and Death was her bridegroom, not her beloved Weston.

Tears sprung to her eyes. "Show your face," she demanded. "If I am your Bride, you cannot refuse." She cradled its head in her hands, almost gently, but insistently, tugging at it, until it stopped nuzzling against her.

"As you wish." Its response was no longer the voice she loved, but a chorus of screams, and it turned those dead, blasted, shiny orbs up at her, and when those eyes met hers she remembered it all.

"The car – in the car – you were there," she whispered the accusation, though she wanted to scream.

"I've always been here," it croaked, "and so has he."

Carter reached for the chain around her neck, and yanked on the Redeemer Cross, exposing its blades, ready to do battle for her soul.

"Oh good, you remembered the cross." The Morningstar chuckled, and she didn't understand what that meant, but soon enough it showed her. And then she screamed, and screamed, until she could scream no more.

They found her shortly after sunrise, lying on the lawn, naked, battered, and confused, her feet and legs plastered with soil and pine needles, still clutching the Redeemer in one bloody hand.

W

'The Demon is a repository of the collective memory of evil, the antithetical echoes of life. It has will and motivation but needs flesh to animate and orchestrate chaos.' This is the essence of our teachings on the subject. Catholicism has not canonized, or acknowledged Enoch's teachings about the Nephilim, but personally I have catalogued enough to confirm the book's fealty to the subject.

Saint Albert the Greater warned that demonology as a scholarly pursuit is as dangerous as it is flawed, as it "can only be taught by demons, which teach about demons, but such teaching leads to the demons." All the teachings are circular, like any other bad argument. It is because chaos cannot be categorized, no matter how one attempts the exercise. My studies confirm it.

Albertus Magnus was not wrong. We learn of evil from those who possess the capacity for it, study evil as a vocation, then chase that evil which can never truly be eradicated. I feel as though I have written such somewhere in these pages. Is it still making sense?

My appetite for food has gone, although I hunger and thirst as before. The food has no taste, no savor. I choke down something every day, and feel myself drifting further away from whatever righteousness I fought to gain. Stupid me. There is no salvation in it. There is no durable way to deny what I am. What I become, closer to its center with every second I continue to exist.

I should destroy this diary, but it may be the only way that those who must intervene can prove it was necessary. I hope there is no need to defend such a position. It is also so that if the Church must examine me, I can expect certain promises I extracted will be honored.

The dream was so real, I could hear her moans of pleasure, screams of pain. I woke with her scent on my hands, her blood on my lips. Its taste so real I went to the mirror.

It mocks me, those velvety wings, my torso bathed in blood. My lips smeared with the evidence I seek. Deliciously guilty. I cannot believe what I see, but I know it to be true. I wash and wash but find no blood in the sink.

I lost my temper, but cannot recall what came next. I awoke on the tiles, apparently my mind is damaged. I had shattered yet another mirror with my fist.

What have I done.

76

THE TIGERTEXT ALETA RECEIVED WAS marked urgent. She scanned the message briefly and hurried off the psychiatric ward, swiping her badge impatiently to exit. She rode the elevator down to the second floor and turned left toward the Emergency Department.

Anas Khan, the neurologist, turned his sleepy lovely eyes to her briefly as she entered the room, before returning his attention to the patient. "Oh hey, Aleta."

At first, she thought the tiny form on the gurney was a child, but as she came closer she could see it was Carter. The young nun was battered and bloody. Her eyes moved slowly, not seeming to track, and she did not respond when Aleta said her name.

"Anas, what's happened here? How can I help?" Aleta asked, unsure why she had been paged to this room for an emergency. Seeing it was Carter, she might have thought the young woman had asked for her; seeing the state the nun was in, she knew that Carter had been unable to ask for anything.

"You know her? Good, I wondered about that," he replied. He motioned to her to step out into the hallway, which Aleta found thoughtful; whatever he had to say he did not want Carter to hear it. "She was found down on the church campus at Our Lady of the Redeemer, nude, bloody, disoriented. I'd say disoriented is an understatement. I can't really get her to respond.

"She apparently self-mutilated. Somehow got out of her chamber at the convent. They brought her in and looked her over,

Praj Gupta said she is essentially stable but was acting concussed. They buzzed her head, of course, and that's what got me involved. Obviously there is clinical evidence for concussion, but no skull fractures or other overt injury on CT. MRI and LP are pending. I just arrived to do her initial examination. I assume they called you for the psych angle. She did a pretty elaborate carve job on herself. Praj has the chart. He can probably give you a better rundown. He paged you. He's down by the central desk. I should be out of your way here in about ten minutes."

"Thank you, Anas," Aleta said, grateful for the information. They stepped back into the room. Aleta stood near the top of the gurney and placed a gentle hand on Carter's head. Her eyes moved slightly but did not turn in Aleta's direction. "Okay, darling, I'm here. I will be back to talk to you in a few minutes. Dr. Khan will take good care of you. He might try to tell you bad jokes, but don't hold that against him."

Anas showed a flash of white teeth in response but did not take his attention from eliciting reflexes as Aleta brushed past him to leave. She passed the nurse on the way in, who said, "Oh, Dr. Madison. I'm glad you're here. Dr. Gupta just asked if we had seen you yet. He's in the darkroom, looking at the CT scan with Dr. Reynolds."

"I'll find him, Janice, thank you."

She pushed through the doors to the Radiology Suite and met Praj Gupta on his way out. They spoke with the hushed voices that everyone seemed to assume in the deep shadows of this department. It was a place of relative calm and peacefulness at the center of the bustling chaos that was often the norm elsewhere in the hospital.

"Aleta," Praj greeted her warmly. They had spent many a night together battling the craziness of the city in all its glory. She appreciated his calm demeanor and the fact that he never disparaged a patient, never reduced them to an adjective. He appreciated her willingness to show up at all hours and take difficult burdens off his hands.

"Praj, what's going on? How can I help?"

"Well, I don't have much of the story. The cops are involved for some reason, probably because of the nature of the case. Or they responded to the 911 call. They might have some details I don't," he admitted. "She was found down, must have been wandering outside during the night, sustained a number of small injuries, some bruising, nothing focal except for the cuts on her side. No evidence of a blow to the head or other discrete injury, but she is obviously not at her baseline, which I assume was normal for a 21-year-old woman up until now. Toxicity is negative, CT scan is non-focal. LP is pending. She was stable so I wanted to get consent."

"I saw Anas Khan in her room, he said something about self-mutilation? Are you concerned this was some sort of psychotic break?" Aleta asked.

"I don't know. As you know, I'd like to rule out medical causes before I get you involved, but it couldn't wait," he said. "Can I proceed with the LP?"

"I agree with your workup approach," she replied. "Do you think it is going to be difficult to get approval from the family?"

Pras looked confused now. "Aleta, the convent had *you* listed as next-of-kin."

77

"Me?! Praj, she is a friend, but I hardly know her well enough for that," Aleta protested in surprise.

"Oh?" Now it was Praj's turn to look confused. "I thought-"

"The priest she works with is a good friend of my-"

Boyfriend, Aleta couldn't stop her brain from supplying the word, neither could she bring herself to say the word aloud. She amended her statement. "I know the priest she works with at Our Lady."

"Well, someone from the convent is in the waiting room," Praj told her. Aleta followed his suggestion that she might be able to clarify things further by speaking to them.

Aleta discovered a middle-aged nun, habited in a long robe, wimple, and veil of a deep grey color seated in Reception, holding her rosary and praying silently. She was even more diminutive than Carter, and opened her eyes slowly when Aleta touched her shoulder gently.

"Sister?" Aleta addressed her, hoping she would forgive the intrusion on her religious observance. "I am Dr. Madison."

"Oh, yes. I am Suor Merzede. I am Carter's sponsor at Our Lady of the Redeemer," the woman stood up and took Aleta's hand, nodding vigorously. Her skin was browned from much sunshine, and her accent was that of a native Spanish speaker, but she had used the French word for *sister* ahead of her name. Aleta knew that French Carmelite nuns had founded convents in

Guatemala and French Guiana, and that many of these women were refugees who had sought asylum in the United States.

"Suor Merzede, I just discovered that I am listed as Carter's next of kin," Aleta immediately presented her predicament to save time. "But I fear that this arrangement is potentially not the best one. Perhaps your Mother Superior, or you, as her sponsor, should be consulted instead?"

"Dr. Madison, Father Weston insisted that she have a locally listed next-of-kin. He insisted on your input in the case of her need for medical care. Even the Mother Superior cannot contravene his order. Carter was orphaned several years ago when her father died, and has no real family to speak of. She suffered a terrible trauma in the weeks following his death, and since then it seems her only family has been the Church," Suor Merzede told her.

"Well, I am willing to act on her behalf as long as it is acceptable to your order, Sister. She is stable for now, and the other physicians are finishing their initial testing. Can you tell me what happened?" Aleta asked gently, seeing the distress that her initial statement had caused the nun. She had introduced uncertainty about whether she would help the girl, and she could see that Suor Merzede was both traumatized by the events of the morning and concerned for Carter. It appeared she genuinely cared for the novice she mentored.

"I don't know," Suor Merzede began. "I locked her into her cell after Vespers, the same as always. All of the nuns are locked in at night except for me and *La Superiora*. I do not know how, or when, she got out. In the morning, Sister Agatha and Sister Margrethe were on their way over to the church when they found her. It was so awful. She couldn't tell us what had happened, and she had, oh - *I can't!*" She put a hand over her mouth and shook her head, eyes brimming with tears. She was nearly hyperventilating.

Aleta gently led Suor Merzede back to a chair and helped her to sit down. She brought her a drink of water in one of the paper cups from the dispenser in the waiting room and promised to keep the nun informed.

Aleta stopped to see the ward clerk who was gathering the paper portions of the chart to scan into the system. She signed the consent for lumbar puncture so that the clerk wouldn't have to chase her down at the last minute, and stepped out into the main hospital corridor once more, planning to make a phone call to her sister.

The cellphone in her lab coat pocket pinged, signaling her return to an area of the hospital where she would have a working signal. Aleta frowned, the sound indicating a message, and she hoped she hadn't missed another page.

A quick glance at the phone showed her she had received a regular text message; when she opened it she saw it was from an unknown international number, which was unusual. *Getting spammed from offshore, now?* she wondered briefly, before scanning the contents. It consisted of just four words, stark in the conversation bubble on the screen.

Protect the White Fairy.

Aleta felt cold. She knew exactly who the White Fairy was; she and Amaoke had both used that exact term to describe Carter. *She reminds me of a white fairy,* she had said to him once, in the days after Weston had rescued her from her office, during the time of Amaoke's convalescence in her home. He had readily agreed that Carter seemed ethereal and magical in appearance, noting that the white novice's habit she wore furthered the impression.

Magical. Whatever had happened to Carter was no random event, and Aleta shivered despite the warm spring sunshine streaming through the windows to her left.

She hit the call icon next to the number, half-excited, hoping someone would answer at the other end, hoping it was Amaoke. But all she got was the odd, intermittent, trans-oceanic buzz of the standard international ringtone, which continued for fully thirty seconds before it fell silent once more, unanswered.

So she called Alaina, and asked her to come up to the hospital, giving her an abbreviated report that did not include the detail about the text she had received. Alaina sounded distressed upon hearing the news and promised to come right away.

Aleta didn't want Carter to be alone, playing on her original hunch, which had only been solidified by the mysterious message from afar. On a hunch, she'd decided that it shouldn't be the nuns attending Carter. Aleta herself had clinical responsibilities to address, and knowing that Alaina was looking out for their young friend would keep the distraction of the events of the morning to a minimum. Her other patients deserved her best care, and that would require she be focused on them, not on the mystery that was unfolding, one she felt had some very personal implications.

78

WHEN SHE RETURNED TO THE Emergency Department, Carter's room was quiet. Janice was sitting at the patient terminal, typing clinical notes. She glanced up as Aleta came in. "She's been premedicated. Her vitals and sats are holding. Praj will be in shortly to do the lumbar puncture."

"Thanks, Janice. Would you be kind enough to pull a gown for me?" Aleta asked. "I'll give him a hand."

The nurse nodded and stepped out. Aleta moved to the sink and retrieved a clean facecloth, running it under warm water and wringing it out. She stepped to the bedside and began cleaning Carter's face, which was streaked with tears and dirt, careful to ensure her nasal oxygen was not disrupted. Her hair had some blood in it on the left side, and Aleta sponged this away carefully, but Praj was right, this was not associated with any underlying injury. She ran gentle fingers over the vault of the cranium, but there were no defects there. She resumed her attentions with the washcloth, cleaning Carter's neck and arms, waiting to do the rest until she had a chaperone.

Janice returned with the sterile pack and looked surprised to see Aleta doing this, but she said nothing, just pulled the curtain across the doorway and joined Aleta at the bedside after opening a warm bathpack. The two women looked at each other across the gurney, and had a moment of understanding.

Carter's diminutive size was emphasized by the voluminous hospital gown that had been draped over her, and they removed this, each woman moving economically, having performed this task dozens of times.

She had a large piece of gauze covering her left flank, and Aleta pulled on a pair of gloves to take this down. She leaned her crutches against the nearby cabinet and snagged the stool with her foot to wheel it into place next to the bed. She sat carefully and rolled herself closer.

Under the bandage, she found a raw, bloody mess. A sharp object, like a razor blade, had been used to make hundreds of tiny jabbing cuts, alongside other swipes that followed the outlines of what appeared to be an old burn scar, but Aleta recognized it as something else. There had been a trend come through with some young people during her time at Howard, where in lieu of tattoos, some young men and women were having designs branded onto their skin. These took a long time to heal, and many of them became infected. She had taken care of her fair share of those that had gone wrong during her medical clerkships.

Someone had branded Carter, and the appearance of the underlying injury suggested it was a fairly old event. It had to have happened when she was a teenager, and Aleta thought about what Suor Merzede had told her. It was large, much larger than the brands she had seen during the craze, extending from Carter's axilla to her iliac crest, anteriorly from her inferior breast fold to the lateral edge of her scapula. The raised wings were detailed, and the scar was far more elaborate and preserved than most of the brands Aleta had cared for as a student.

The crisp appearance of the burn scarring was likely the result of meticulous care and cleaning, for a significant period of time following the insult. Which made it seem as though the girl had chosen to suffer through it on purpose. Even Janice was grimacing; Aleta suspected a mirror would have shown her that she was as well. The initial event had to have been torture.

But now, within the last twenty-four hours, a wickedly sharp implement had been used to cut open the outlines of the brand.

Could she really have done this herself? Aleta wondered. The cuts did show some early signs of hesitance, with deeper jabs and ragged edged strokes, which tended to argue for self-infliction, it was just the incredible scope of the job, its bloodiness, the pain. The determination required to keep at it until the end. She put that thought aside, deferring it for further consideration later.

Janice shook her head, and for the first time since she had known this nurse, Aleta thought Janice looked afraid. It puzzled her; Janice was one of the most seasoned, grizzled nurses in the department. There was still something she wasn't saying, so Aleta said it for her, her tone as soft as possible, not wanting to wake their charge.

"Is there a possibility she didn't do any of this to herself?"

Janice shrugged. She whispered, too. "The cops are around, asking questions and not explaining, which is interesting. Usually they like to tell their stories here. Perhaps they will talk to you."

"Perhaps. If anything, they will want to know what we found." Aleta looked again at Carter's left torso wounds. "She's right-handed, if memory serves. How did she get the proper angle to do this so precisely?" She tilted her head, and thought also that it had taken significant force, and she wasn't sure the diminutive nun had that kind of strength.

"Dr. Hill is coming to take a look, but she will probably have to take Carter to surgery to repair some of those lacerations," Janice informed her.

"And they can clean the wounds under anesthesia," Aleta said, thinking it would be better to do so with Carter unaware. "Did they say they found a knife in her possession?" Aleta changed the subject.

"Not that I am aware of. The cops might have something. The paramedics transported her with this, because they couldn't pry it from her fingers at the scene." Janice turned away for a moment and produced something heavy that was sealed in a large Ziploc bag. Aleta recognized Carter's cross with the heavy links, and she accepted the bag, turning it in her hands. The cross was bloody, covered in dirt and pine needles, but its contour was smooth. Nothing sharp there that Aleta could see.

"What else do we know, Janice?" Aleta's tone was leading.

"No other signs of assault, no sexual penetration, no evidence of insertions, no bodily fluids. Praj sent a rape kit anyway. I assisted him, didn't see anything abnormal. Nothing else overtly sexual, no bites. She *was* nude when they found her. The nun with her said they hadn't located her nightgown or her underwear." Janice gave Aleta a look.

"Mmm-hmm. Still seems like there is a sexual element to this. Her clothing could be a trophy of some sort," Aleta said, and caught Janice's expression of dismay. "Sorry, I'm being too forensic. Just thinking aloud. It will be interesting to hear what the police have to say."

"I don't mind that, Aleta. I just worry there could be others," Janice said. "In the trauma bay, she had some rosiness over her breastbone and along one side of her neck, on her thighs."

"Beard burn?" Aleta asked.

"Looked like," Janice confirmed. "The trauma coordinator took pictures, so they will be in her chart."

"I'll take a look when we are done here."

Then Praj showed up, and she assisted him with the procedure, but the fluid looked clear, and the results were likely to be normal. By the time they were done, Alaina had arrived, so Aleta brought her back to sit with Carter while she went looking for Suor Merzede. But Suor Merzede had gone, leaving a message for Aleta in Reception that she had returned to Our Lady. There was a number provided where she could be reached.

So Aleta turned her attention to her other duties, immersing herself in her routine. She was behind at clinic, which she hated, but she made her apologies to her patients, most of whom were understanding, one of whom was angry, but she was always angry, so it was her baseline whether Aleta was on time or not.

It was close to three in the afternoon when there was a break in her schedule, and she finally had a chance to take out her phone. She intended to try the number that had sent the mysterious text again, but when she checked her messages it was gone. She tried to find it in the archive, but she was unable to locate it anywhere. The words had simply disappeared without a trace.

79

PREDICTABLY, THE NEW ORLEANS POLICE detective was awaiting Aleta's arrival on the medical ward when she returned to check on Carter. He was in the room, talking to Alaina about sports, of all things. When he turned to greet her, Aleta could see why her sister had been so animated. He was handsome, his coloring not unlike theirs, could perhaps be mistaken for their brother under different circumstances, his eyes the same green as Aleta's own.

"I'm Peter Lancaster," he introduced himself, and then shook his head with a shy smile, reaching around in his jacket, fumbling through several pockets while he balanced a leather binder, until he came up with his card. "I am a detective with NOPD. My captain is Miles LaGrange."

Of course he would drop that name. Captain LaGrange had been their father's partner for many years before Marshall Madison's retirement. Aleta caught her sister's expression over the man's shoulder and tried not to crack a smile. The moony face Alaina was making made it clear what she thought of Lieutenant Lancaster, as his card proclaimed him. Aleta tucked the card into her lab coat pocket and warmly took his free hand.

"Aleta Madison," she said, shaking his hand. "How can I assist you?"

"Oh, I know who you are," he said, somewhat apologetically. "At least, I-"

"Of course. You know our father," she said, letting him off the hook. She spared her sister a warning glance and said to him, "Perhaps we can speak in the corridor."

Aleta looked pointedly at Carter, sleeping peacefully in the bed, making it clear that whatever information was to be discussed, it would happen away from the patient's hearing.

"Of course," he said, and Aleta was relieved to see that he understood her perfectly.

"Dr. Madison, what do you know about Father Seraph?" he asked her, as soon as they were out of earshot of the room.

"Lieutenant Lancaster-" Aleta began.

"Call me Peter," he interjected, earning a frown from her.

"Lieutenant," she rejoined with authority, "I am not my sister. Any relationship that we have will remain strictly professional. I have clinical responsibilities that are of the utmost importance in this matter. I will be perfectly content to answer your questions, but I am not going to do so in a vacuum. If you would like me to discuss what I know that may be of use to you, you can do me the courtesy of giving me the information you are authorized to release, as those facts may have a direct bearing on my patient's recovery, indeed on the necessary treatment she will require to get well.

"I understand you feel the need to generate some goodwill, so that I will facilitate your access to her during her convalescence and encourage her to remember all that she can to help you build your case, or close it as it may be. I am not a child, and I have a great deal of experience with victim's rights, and in the State of Louisiana, if I am not mistaken, the victim does not have to participate in your case if she chooses not to do so. While such a thing would be lamentable, it will be her choice entirely." Aleta made her position clear.

"I understand this patient is a friend," he said gently, taking another approach. "I know that makes it personal for you."

"Strike two, Lieutenant. Patronizing me won't help either," she replied. "The care of every patient of mine is personal, as you say. Perhaps you'd like to start again?" Aleta took her weight off her crutches and leaned against the wall. She resisted the urge to cross her arms.

"I apologize," he said, shaking his head. His wry smile was appealing; Aleta understood perfectly what her sister was responding to, and she also knew that he probably got his way most of the time. Which wasn't necessarily good for him. Well, not this time. "Let me start over."

She said nothing, just looked calmly and expectantly at him, ensuring that he understood to keep her on even footing with him. It saddened her that she too often had to remind people that she *was* fully capable, formidable even, but it was difficult for them to see past her disability and some needed decisive reminding.

"You were given the details about how she was found?" Peter asked, carefully now.

"Yes, I think I have that in hand," Aleta replied. "She was found outside, on the church grounds, nude, disoriented, bleeding."

"Exactly," he nodded. "Early in the morning, when two of the other nuns from her cloister were on their way to devotions." He paused to flip open his notebook, and consulted his notes. His use of the word to describe the morning mass told her he was Catholic. "Her feet were dirty, suggesting that she was walking barefoot along the path from the nun's residence, the soil there is soft from the rains we've had.

"The sisters said she had a nightgown on when she went to bed last night, as always, but neither that nor her undergarments have been located. Our officers were on scene, still canvassing, when a housekeeper who cleans the rectory and the old groundskeeper's cottage discovered a mess in the cottage bedroom.

"The sheets were bloody, and soiled with the same dirt and pine needles that were found on Sister Thomas' feet," he told Aleta.

"We took the soiled items into evidence; those sheets looked like someone had been murdered on them."

"Did you see the pictures of the injury?" Aleta asked. "To do such a thing would be a bloody undertaking, and it took a long time."

"I agree," he said. "Any guess as to what was used to make those cuts?" he asked, watching her carefully.

"My best guess is something small, something precise, like a scalpel, or a hobbyist's blade," she replied, having seen more injuries than she cared to think about.

"There was some suspicion that she might have done it herself," Peter said. She forgave him this slip, she understood he wasn't being misleading, merely wanted to hear her opinion.

"I can't make it work under any set of circumstances," Aleta said. "She is right-handed, small, and I would expect to see more hesitancy than is evident. How would she see to do it so precisely without a mirror? And if she had been alone, why leave the cottage? And wouldn't her nightgown and undergarments be to hand?"

"I can't see it either," he agreed. "Did the perpetrator have a use for the nightgown, like a trophy?"

"That would be my theory; it fits a forensic profile," she allowed.

"Do you know Father Seraph?" Peter asked.

"Not well. He is a friend of a friend."

"I understand that he lived in the cottage there, and that he and Sister Thomas worked closely together," Peter said.

"I believe so, yes."

"The housekeeper swears that the cottage was locked up, and says that only she and Father Seraph had keys. His key is presumably still in his possession, and hers she must pick up every day from the church office."

"What are you getting at, Lieutenant?" Aleta asked carefully. "Father Seraph is out of the country."

"Is he?" Peter looked at her just as carefully.

"To my knowledge, although the Church might know more." Aleta was confused. Where was he going with this?

"The Church isn't being very forthcoming about him. Additionally, the Mother Superior, Sister Mary Matthew Greaves, expressed a concern she had that Sister Thomas' relationship with her confessor was perhaps not entirely appropriate," Peter said, still watching her very closely. "That they traveled together for the church, on errands determined by the Vatican. Some sort of special outreach."

Aleta could see how anyone observing Weston and Carter might discern their obvious attraction to one another. She recalled her own strong sense that the two of them were emotionally entangled, even if nothing physical had occurred, and of course there was no way for anyone other than the two in question to know the truth of such a thing.

She thought of Carter's negative toxicity panel, and that could only mean one thing: she had been awake and entirely aware throughout her torture. Aleta did not believe that the young nun's state was related to the effects of drugs anyway. Nor did she believe that her presentation boded some neurologic abnormality or psychotic break. It read as post-traumatic shock, pure and simple. For whom would any of us endure such a terrible thing? And for what? For love? As horrific and unbelievable as it seemed, it was certainly plausible, in keeping with a sort of religious fervor that she had read in Weston from the very beginning. A sacrifice, a proof of misplaced devotion. Aleta shivered involuntarily. Peter saw it.

"Sister Thomas was attacked before," Peter now told Aleta. "As a teenager, in Iowa, after her father died. She was apparently a hostage of some biker gang, some group of radicalized women." Peter saw Aleta's surprise at these words, and she recalled what Suor Merzede had referred to earlier, never guessing that it could be this.

"The detective on that case told me it was eventually closed, but not entirely to her satisfaction. She said there was some cult behavior that was never fully explained, gruesome acts, really, things with a certain religious bent. And she told me that none other than Father Seraph was sent by the Church, on two separate occasions, to investigate, and she felt, to intervene. I found that interesting," Peter said darkly. "So I asked her for more details."

"What did she tell you?" Aleta asked, very curious now to know the answer, although she anticipated what was coming.

"That Father Seraph was at one time her main suspect, but she was never able to find anything that could confirm her suspicions, or his direct involvement. I can put you in touch with her if you'd like," he offered.

Aleta shook her head. "Thank you, Lieutenant. You've been very helpful. I will be in touch if Carter should decide she would like to speak with you."

His expression softened entirely, and she could see he was really looking to help Carter and solve this case. These events bothered him as much as they did Aleta, and she was glad to get this glimpse of his empathy. It made their conversation less forensic, and more human. Made it easier for her to perform her next act of goodwill on his behalf.

He took his leave of her and she returned to Carter's room. She smiled at her sister and handed her Peter's business card. "I think he wrote his cell number on the back," Aleta told her. "But be careful; he's not wearing a ring, but he might be the sort to take it off in certain situations. *And* he's a cop." The last a reminder that they knew the life, had watched their mother worry and fret over the dangers their father had faced, the two girls declaring to one another on multiple occasions that neither wanted to fall in love with a policeman.

"You're too suspicious by half; I already spoke to Dad, who actually had nice things to say about Peter," Alaina replied. "He is *not* married, and Dad's inviting him for family dinner next Sunday."

"That was fast," Aleta had to laugh. Even when the world slid off orbit, Alaina always made her feel better.

Alaina winked. "I knew you wouldn't mind; you like them taller, with longer hair." They had also promised one another, long ago, that they would never let a man come between them. Not that their tastes were remotely similar.

But then Alaina saw Aleta's troubled expression. She stood up, and didn't let the lab coat, crutches, and stethoscope get in her way. "All this armor," she murmured, taking her little sister into her arms. "Amaoke will be back very soon, I'm sure of it."

Aleta did not have the words to explain it all to her sister, and saw Alaina was trying to help. It hurt Aleta's heart to keep these secrets, carry this pain alone. Alaina was right, she did love Amaoke. But it was futile, because he wasn't coming back.

And Carter's love was seemingly just as futile; additionally it seemed to place her in peril. Aleta promised herself she would find a solution to it if she could.

80

ALAINA AWAKENED SUDDENLY, FEELING CARTER'S hand moving weakly in her own. She sat up in the chair and blinked in the darkened room. She had told her sister that she would stay with Carter that first night, seeing that Aleta was exhausted. Her sister had also seemed frazzled, and afraid, although she had waved off Alaina's concerns for her well-being. It wasn't surprising, what had happened to Carter was reason enough for Aleta's odd behavior.

"Carter?" she asked, looking to see if the nun was awake. It appeared she was, although she did not turn her head toward Alaina or otherwise respond to the question.

Alaina heard the soft rustling of her whispers, like a mantra, and she wondered whether Carter was trying to pray. She leaned forward slightly and tried to hear what was being said, but was unable to make anything out.

"Sweetheart, I can't hear you. Let's try some water. You're supposed to be resting your voice."

Alaina stood up and poured a bit of water into the small cup on the tray. She helped Carter sit up, gently supporting her upper back and assisting her in holding the water as she sipped it.

But soon the young nun was trying to talk again, so Alaina leaned her head down to see if she could hear what was being said. Just a rustle of her ruined voice, raw for all the screaming she had done, and though Alaina was still frustrated in her effort to decipher the message, she could tell that it was repetitive.

Over and over, on and on, restlessly appealing to someone, God perhaps?

Alaina watched Carter's eyes, roving about, looking around now, as if searching for something, endlessly. Her eyes did not rest on Alaina, but the nun knew she was not alone, for she gripped Alaina's hand again tightly, almost painfully. Alaina would not have believed such a small woman to possess such strength.

Alaina's eye caught on something, something that shined in the soft glow of the night light near the sink. The cross, of course! Alaina had removed it from the bag while Carter was sleeping, had painstakingly cleaned it, washing the blood and contamination away, polishing it until it gleamed once more.

Alaina stood, gently extricating her fingers from Carter's grip, whispering to her soothingly as she retrieved the cross, feeling its reassuring weight in her hand, dragging the heavy links off the countertop. She turned toward the bed, and nearing it, reached out to hand it to the young woman, but before she could complete the transfer, as her hand extended over the coverlet to pass it off, she felt a sharp pain in her fingers and gasped. It felt as though the cross had bitten her!

She pulled her hand back sharply, letting it drop, watching as Carter caught it in one outstretched hand and brought it close to her bosom. Her whispering was even more fervent now, and loud enough to be heard.

Alaina sucked gently on her injured fingers, tasting the blood on her tongue, finally able to make out Carter's words.

"Someday my Prince will come, someday my Prince will come..."

And the shadows seemed to be moving, seemed to converge on the tiny figure in the bed, dark fingers reaching out, other voices whispering in synchrony with the young nun.

The door to the small bathroom creaked slightly, and Alaina watched in horror as dark fingers curled slowly and determinedly around the jamb, and she had no desire to see what came after them, knew she would lose her mind if she did. Afraid now that all her past sins had come back to haunt her, this, like a flashback she'd had during her days of addiction.

She closed her eyes tightly, unmindful of her bleeding hand she used it to clutch her own crucifix in her fingers, feeling the fluttering pulse there at her neck, and she began to pray. "Yea, though I walk through the valley…of the Shadow…"

And the voices were louder now, angry at this incantation, and she felt their pain as it reached a crescendo. "…of Death, I shall fear no evil, for Thou Art with me, oh Lord…" Alaina's voice shook, as did her whole body, the chain of her necklace rattling, too.

The whispering faded, and the air currents moved about her, insistent now, and she opened her eyes, and by the end of the prayer, she realized she was shouting. "…surely goodness and mercy will follow me all the days of my life, and I shall dwell in the house of the Lord, Forever!"

The ghastly fingers retreated back behind the door, and it swung closed with a soft click, and with that, the room was silent once more. Alaina could hear her own breathing, and then her sobs, but she was not finished, needed one last word to bind the spell, to end the prayer.

"Amen," she sniffled deeply through her tears, kneeling down beside Carter, who now slept peacefully, and crossing them both.

She saw that Carter clutched the Redeemer in her hand, and when Alaina tried to remove it, she found she could not loosen those tiny fingers from it. Try as she would, the sleeping nun's grasp was absolute.

81

"THIS MAY SOUND CRAZY," Aleta began, after hearing Alaina's retelling of the events of the night before, "but this makes me even more certain that I cannot send her back to the nuns."

"I'm glad to hear you say that," Alaina said, shivering. She had her own issues with them, generally. "Very glad."

"But why didn't you call me?" Aleta asked. "Why stay here all alone?"

"I wasn't alone," Alaina replied calmly. "You were probably sleeping, which you need to do more of, dear sister-mine. And I had the Baby Jesus, who I naively assumed could get me through it." Her lips twisted with irony; Alaina acted like a hypocrite, but she loved God; she truly believed. Aleta suspected her faith was the stronger of the two of them, until recently, it had certainly been the more tested. "You forget, I have seen monsters before and lived to tell of it. Not my first rodeo."

"You have a point, as always," Aleta allowed.

"And you have not been completely honest with me," Alaina said, without a hint of accusation in her tone. "You know something. My story didn't surprise you. Even the part about the demon in the bathroom."

"What? Because I knew the Devil was involved in all of this?" Aleta shrugged. She had no intention of telling Alaina about her own encounter with the Morningstar.

"To say the least. Your breakdown, your bloody naked man in the middle of the night, and you, of all people, '*Oh, Alaina, it's fine, perfectly normal. Go on home and don't worry about the escaped mental patient wrapped in that quilt. He's my boyfriend.'"* Her sister spoke in a mincing, precise falsetto with a fake British accent, the voice she had always used to mimic Aleta; when they were children, to mock her. Alaina could make anything hilarious. Anything.

"Okay, okay. I wasn't trying to assume you were going to swallow it whole. I *know* you aren't stupid," Aleta soothed, laughing in spite of herself.

"So now what?" Alaina asked, and Aleta realized how much better she felt having her sister to help her.

"I have no idea," Aleta admitted. "I'm not the expert here. She is," she gestured to Carter, resting peacefully in the room next to them.

"Maybe you don't need to be. Perhaps you should ask her advice when she wakes," Alaina suggested. "I'm going home to take a shower. When do you want me back?"

"Whenever you've rested. No rush," Aleta reassured her. "It's my day off. I'll be right here."

"I'll bring you something good to eat, okay?" Alaina said, leaning down to kiss Aleta atop her curls, gently fingering the Mobius loop at her sister's throat, ensuring it was in place before she took her leave.

Aleta had slept poorly, nighttime phone calls or not, and she dozed in the chair beside the bed, awakening occasionally whenever the aides or nurses came in to take vitals or administer medication. She helped the wound nurses change the dressing on Carter's flank, and by early afternoon was trying to read the book she had brought, and failing miserably.

Her phone pinged, and it was the nurse's station, so she stepped out into the hallway, wondering if someone was trying to reach her about one of her other patients. But the ward clerk flagged her to inform her that a Sister Mary Matthew Greaves was at reception, asking if she could visit Carter.

Aleta nodded. Because she was listed as next of kin, she could deny the request outright. As much as it bothered her, Father Weston's instructions could be helpful to her, and perhaps he trusted her discretion more than the women who were tasked with the responsibility for Carter's day-to-day wellbeing. She just wished Weston had discussed it with her first. She hated surprises, but the fault was likely her own. She *had* refused his request to take part in his discussions with Amaoke.

"They can send her up," Aleta consented, curious herself about the Mother Superior.

Aleta went to the elevators, intending to meet the nun and show her to Carter's room, but when the Mother Superior arrived, she was not alone. Suor Merzede had accompanied her, and smiled warmly when she saw Aleta. Suor Merzede was kind enough to make the introductions, and Sister Mary Matthew was much as Aleta had guessed she would be, given her vocation and her station.

"She is resting at present, so perhaps a short visit is best, perhaps some prayer. I must ask you to understand that I don't want to upset Sister Thomas in any way, and I must insist you refrain from talking about her recent trauma, if she awakens," Aleta cautioned them, pretending to ignore the ignominious expression of the elder nun.

Aleta waited in the hallway, allowing the women to see Carter alone, and she heard only their prayers, and then silence. Carter never woke during the visit, for which Aleta was glad.

When the nuns returned to the hallway, Suor Merzede excused herself, saying she would retrieve the car and wait for Sister Mary Matthew. Aleta thought she couldn't escape quickly enough.

"And is her condition stable?" The Mother Superior turned cold grey eyes upon Aleta, her tone at its most imperious. But Aleta was no longer a Catholic schoolgirl, and was unimpressed with the authority this woman wanted to hold over her. She saw her eyes drift over Aleta's necklace with obvious disdain for a symbol that was not a cross.

"She appears to be suffering some shock, but seems otherwise improving," Aleta allowed.

"Then she needs to be returned to the cloister," Sister Mary Matthew said coldly. "We do have facilities for ailing nuns, facilities that address their physical needs as well as their spiritual ones."

Aleta saw right through her. She cared not one bit for Carter, and Aleta suspected she knew why. She recalled what Peter Lancaster had shared about the Mother Superior's observations about the supposed improprieties of her young novice. This woman was jealous, jealous of a lovely, sweet, pious child. One with charms she had likely never had. Sister Mary Matthew believed it was her place to teach Carter obedience. Aleta feared the abuse and punishment awaiting Carter if she were returned to the handmaidens of the Church.

"I think not," Aleta said carefully, not betraying any particular emotion in her disagreement. "She will remain under my care and supervision for now, and until such time as I determine she is fit either to return to service or to further secular recovery."

"Secular? Who are you to determine the best course for her recovery? Young woman, do you put yourself in the position to determine her spiritual needs?" Sister Mary Matthew drew herself up to her full height but still could not quite match Aleta's stature, despite her desire to exert her authority.

"Of course I do not, but neither should you, Sister," Aleta's calm demeanor was infuriating, she could see, to the Mother Superior. "I have been asked to ensure she is well, but beyond that, I understand that I must act as her next of kin, and look to her best interests in all of this."

"You dare speak to me like this? Do you know to whom you are speaking?" the nun asked, incensed because she was unable to bully Aleta. "That child has pledged herself to the Church, she-" The woman stopped short, almost betraying something ugly, something she actually believed.

"Be that as it may," Aleta interrupted quietly, "She does not belong to the Church, or to you. Father Weston's instructions supersede your authority, I believe. We can certainly take it up with the Bishop if it appears there is any confusion in the way I understand it." Aleta could not help but punctuate her statement with a smile, meeting a threat with a threat. She promised herself she would confess this sin of pride, but needed to keep this damnable woman away from Carter.

The Mother Superior's face betrayed her rage and frustration before she could school her features once more, unable to hide her truest self. Then she gathered the skirts of her habit and turned away without another word.

82

WHEN ALETA RETURNED TO THE room, Carter was awake. Her eyes fixed on Aleta now, and it was clear she had followed the exchange in the hallway. She gave Aleta a small smile, and squeezed gently when Aleta took her hand.

Aleta said nothing, merely set her crutches aside and sat down next to the bed. "How are you feeling?"

"Lost," was the whispered answer, and a single tear tracked down Carter's cheek.

"That is understandable," Aleta nodded with encouragement. "Are you in any pain?"

Carter looked thoughtful for a moment, and then stretched gently, pressing her head into the pillow. She appeared to be taking inventory of herself. "A bit. Nothing too terrible. I should thank you for standing up to her." Her eyes glanced toward the hallway; she was referring to her Mother Superior.

"Someone needed to," Aleta said, surprised at the dark emotions her voice betrayed. She looked at Carter apologetically. "Sorry. That wasn't very charitable. My next confession is going to be very interesting."

Carter said nothing, merely raised her right arm and made the sign of the cross, blessing Aleta. "Peace be with you."

"And also with you," Aleta told her.

Carter tried to push herself up in bed, but was having some difficulty, so Aleta stood carefully, bracing herself against the bed, holding the siderail firmly to keep herself up, and then wrapping her other arm around Carter's small torso, careful of her wound, and pulling her up, adjusting the head of the bed afterward. It was like lifting a child.

"You've been out of it for a couple of days," Aleta told her.

"I feel very sleepy," Carter remarked, as though she noticed something was off.

"Some of your medications can do that," Aleta said. "You have gotten pain relievers. But you gave us quite a scare, and your body is recovering from the shock. That can be exhausting, too."

"I know. I remember, from before," Carter said, and did not explain further. Aleta thought she must assume that what had occurred in her past was known to Aleta, and if not, was not something she wanted to discuss.

"Can you recall what happened to you? This time?" Aleta asked gently, wanting to address it directly, give Carter permission to talk if she wanted to.

"I know what happened. I was marked, again, to remind me," Carter replied, but her words made no sense to Aleta.

"Who made those marks? Did you do that to yourself?" Aleta asked, watching as Carter's eyes narrowed, as she thought about it, remembered, possibly relived it.

"I held the blade, my part of the promise, but he – it – was there to guide me," the nun whispered. "To show me."

"Show you what?" Aleta was confused, and even more afraid, hearing Carter's calm and even tone. Defeat she could have understood, but this was something akin to acceptance. "Was it Weston?"

"It was for the Prince," Carter declared.

"Weston? Weston is your prince, isn't he?" Aleta was trying to lead her to it, still sensing that there was something otherworldly about Carter's answers, as if they were through the looking glass, in a place where she would have to make sense of the senseless.

"Weston is my love. The other, the Dark, Dark Prince of Deceit and Death. He is and they are the same, and they are not the same." Carter's explanation was no explanation at all. "It was for him."

"Someone did this to you for Weston?" Aleta was altogether lost. This was not the rambling dissociative thinking of the psychotic; Carter seemed rational and sane, even if her words were not. Then she made a connection between all of the odd events of the last year of her own life. "Was it the Morningstar?" Her voice dropped to a whisper, subconsciously she did not want to say the name.

"Yes, it found me," Carter whispered, too. Superstition perhaps, but they both knew there was an ill magic in its name. "Like it found you, before. You that it fears."

"Why would the Morningstar fear me?" Aleta asked, utterly surprised at this assertion.

"Because you are the Mother of Grace," Carter said.

"I don't understand what that means," Aleta protested. "Can you explain it?"

"I don't know why I know it," Carter said, shaking her head sadly. "It doesn't mean anything to you?"

"No." It made no sense to Aleta, she could relate it to nothing at all. "I wish I could say that it did. But all of this worries me, and I don't know how to keep you safe. Somewhere you can go from here. I just don't think the Church is the right place. I am hoping you have an idea."

"The beast shall protect me, for it is the guardian of souls," Carter said suddenly, a strange knowledge in those deep blue eyes. Aleta at first thought she was still talking about the Morningstar, but no, Carter did not betray any fear when she said it, instead she seemed convinced of something, certain, comforted.

"The beast?" Aleta repeated it, trying to connect that word to anything other than its common meaning, that of monster, demon, evil...or, perhaps, its disambiguation. And somehow then she knew, the beast, the Wolf, the werewolf. Amaoke was a beast, and despite all she knew of him, he *was* a protector. Was that why they had all come together, she and Weston and Carter and Amaoke? Kusini, Azuma, all of them?

"*First the beast, the beast, the beast*," Carter recited softly, poetically, and Aleta thought it sounded like part of an incantation. "He is oldest and wisest, and his power balances all things. He was first, and shall be last."

"Alpha and Omega," Aleta whispered, the thought coming unbidden to her mind. A message, everything, all, beginning and end, a proxy for the divine. She fingered the Mobius loop at her throat. Fitting. Perhaps nothing was accidental, and Aleta was suddenly so disappointed that she had never really acknowledged the power of her faith, especially now, when she realized what she was being shown. Whatever obstacles they faced, they were all touched by God.

"I have an idea," she said, and Carter just looked at her, perhaps slightly curious but mostly accepting and serene.

She pulled herself up using the side rail of the bed again, using her free hand to fish her cell phone out of her pocket. After scrolling a few moments, she found the number she wanted and dialed it.

"Hello, Aleta," the woman on the other end sounded happy to hear from her. "I have been meaning to call you, because I was certain I would hear from you by now. Amaoke left his keys for you. He said you'd be by to pick them up, and that while he was gone perhaps a guest would be staying in the carriage house? Oh, I do hope my procrastination hasn't caused any difficulty or confusion for you." As usual, Amaoke's landlady had a lot to say, barely taking a breath and not waiting for Aleta to respond.

For her part, Aleta was shocked, but realized she shouldn't let such things surprise her anymore.

"Are you still there, dear?"

"I'm here," Aleta's voice shook slightly. "No difficulty at all; I was just getting around to it myself."

"Are you quite alright? You sound a bit unlike yourself," the older woman said.

"I'm fine, just touched that he never fails to miss the smallest detail," Aleta replied honestly. "He's just so thoughtful."

"We've always said so," came the enthusiastic reply. "We've felt so much better having him around here. Safer."

M

What?

Well, some appetites must be fed, some morsels too delicious, and like children, not quick enough to get away. Monsters must eat too.

You're angry now. No matter. You can follow me home, as they will, those three that will have to come deep inside, down into the dark places where I hide. Inadvertent poetry, divine! Down where I will wrap them up, save one, until another time.

I wouldn't come without a fight, anyway, then or now. Perhaps not without a bite! Demented demon poet, doubly divine!

Unless...you can...but then, you only think *you can defeat me. But you, just you, I'll let* you *in on my little secret, which you already know is our little secret, right?*

Sometimes the Monster wins. You might never have heard of it, but that's only because I left none alive to tell that story...

83

When Amaoke didn't come down to join the group at dinner, Azuma was concerned, knowing he should be famished after their hike in the mountains. The Collector noticed his absence at about the same time she did, and they both felt something was off, somehow.

The Collector stood up without a word, but Azuma motioned for him to stay, thinking of *Ni,* who was watching the two of them with wary curiosity. Selene and Michael Israel were engrossed in conversation, so Azuma felt less compelled to stay, thinking she wouldn't be missed for the few minutes it would take to go herself, rather than send one of the staff.

But he wasn't in his room, nor was his knapsack. She turned around slowly, thinking. Knowing that if he were somewhere in the house, or on the grounds, he would have simply left his possessions here.

She didn't sense anything amiss spiritually, no dark energies or intrigue to draw her attention. Her instincts weren't firing away. Amaoke was simply gone. He had known, somehow, that he didn't belong here, no matter how sincere her welcome.

A bright yellow square in her peripheral vision caught and held her attention. It was stuck to the small desk in the corner of the room. She walked over and looked at it. A Post-It. A rudimentary pen and ink drawing, raised wings, detailed with individual feathers.

She picked it up and turned it over, just to be sure there wasn't something she was missing, but there was nothing written on the underside, either. It took her a moment to decipher the message, recall what she had told him about her organization system.

She carried the small note by its adhesive edge, waving it absentmindedly from the end of her finger like a small flag, back down the darkened upper hallway, listening to the sounds of conversation and laughter floating up over the gallery from the dining area below. She paused, picking out details of the different conversations, the subjects similar to any other family sitting down to a meal. It touched her, this was home, and she knew she had taken too little time to appreciate it. It seemed she could best enjoy it in this voyeuristic fashion, because a part of her always remained guarded against sentiment.

Azuma took the back stairs, turning left away from the alcove, and left again, into her office, switching on the lights, trying to look at it as a whole, with fresh eyes, to identify what, if anything, was changed.

But none of her groupings was disturbed.

Then she noticed an orange square affixed to the back of the chair she had offered him earlier that day. On it was written a series of numbers that did not immediately mean anything to her, but then she had an epiphany, and typed them into her cell phone just as Amaoke had scribbled them down.

The absolute location of the *makom*, latitude and longitude, something he must have memorized from the file, his way of confirming their destinations were the same. Just as it confirmed his departure. She smiled. However he would make his way, it would be on his terms. No planes, cars, or helicopters. And it told her something else, something of immeasurable importance, something strangely comforting.

They would all stand together when the time came to face the Morningstar.

The Wolf holds the wisdom of the natural world and is both an enforcer and a guardian.

84

THE HOMELESS MAN WHO DRIFTED across St. Peter's Square was to be counted among the lost, the tourists cringing away from his blasted expression. Perhaps he was harmless, but his size alone could make him dangerous, so none took any chances.

He was dressed like the penitents of old, enrobed in dark and dusty clothes, perhaps a pilgrim, seeking peace in this place where so many came just to be close to the seat of their Church. His looks were certainly more biblical than more modern vagabonds, his long hair and beard reminiscent of the old Renaissance icons. It was even possible that there was enough beauty in that young face that it would have been loved by those old masters.

But he carried that haunted look, the look of those who speak to the beyond, possessed, not necessarily of evil, but of untreated psychosis, those lacking only decent medication and a supportive social network. Perhaps a bath.

For the better part of a week, he eluded the *Carabinieri* who patrolled the square, and who were militant about maintaining the pristine reputation of the *Plaza di San Pietro*. He had an uncanny way of disappearing when sightings of a suspicious person were reported.

And when he collapsed, from madness, hunger, thirst, whichever of these ills caused him to succumb, luckily he did not do so in the Square. Rather, early one morning, at the Gates of

Vatican City, he found he could go no farther, and down he went, in a heap, on the stones.

Although the Swiss Guard do see plenty of homeless people, they recognized his robes, familiar with such as these in a special way. The *Carabinieri* would be of no help in removing this obstacle from their gates, for he was one of theirs, a priest. The Converse sneakers he wore further betrayed his identity, and he was taken to the infirmary.

85

AMAOKE DRIFTED. Let the Wolf come forward, lead. Tracking Weston, such as he now was, across two continents. Needing to return to a simpler way of doing things. Understanding better with each passing day what he was following. It felt right, somehow, catching the scent. And the scent was enticing, sadly more appealing in an unpleasant way. As time went on, he gave up more and more control, until the beast was once again in ascendance, but better able to exercise the discretions of its human counterpart than ever before.

After a week, he no longer missed walking on two legs, his four-legged form needed to maintain this doggedness of purpose, to avoid sentimental regret.   And the creatures he would have encountered in many strange forests and jungles moved aside for him, he could smell their fear, as if they sensed he were a hellhound bound on an inexorable journey, sensed his descent, if not into madness, then into a singular focus, carrying him ever onward. He was uncertain he could have turned from it had he wanted to do so.

He knew where his quarry would be, and he was patient. Their fates were entwined, and for good or ill they would find their end together.

86

"I KNOW I CANNOT STAY," Weston remarked, ensuring that his friend knew he understood what had changed.

"As I can no longer defend your presence here," came the Pope's measured response. "I see you there, sitting in that chair, and the chair offends you. It offers you no real support, no rest, no comfort. The cassock, beloved uniform, now clings to you like a plague, and you itch and fidget, because it only vexes you. The weight of the Redeemer no longer a reassurance, no longer a symbol of safe haven in the arms of Christ, now it becomes the lodestone that drags you to the depths. You are being slowly undone by the sanctity you so loved, once."

"Then you must give me what I ask for, what you once promised me," Weston said, careful to let the man hear the sincerity, the piety, of this request.

"I can no more interfere in your destiny than you can turn from it. Your salvation lies not in your destruction, rather in your continued service. My promise is tied to my vow to destroy an existence when it is no longer sacred. You have not yet crossed that boundary, my son. You will not find your rest so easily. It was you who told me of that once, long ago. You remain a child of God, lost, surely, perhaps damned, perhaps still with a chance at redemption. Because of that chance, I cannot intervene. I cannot sanction a suicide; I will hear your confession and send you forth in love. But this other, I cannot do. Ask of me anything else."

"Allow me to access the archives. This time I need to see the Scrolls, I must complete my research on the Nephilim. Even Father Nicolò does not have the authority to release them to me," Weston replied without hesitation.

The Holy Father sighed, resigned. Making the sign of the cross over Weston and blessing him, he said, "Confess your sins. I shall make it so."

87

"YOUR CONTACT WAS ABLE TO secure the materials as requested?" Azuma stood on the tarmac next to the plane, and she turned to begin walking toward the lighted hanger as Michael Israel reached her side. The others had gone ahead to the Jaffa Hotel, the mild air on this spring evening in Tel Aviv was welcome after the cold mountain air they had left behind. There was something almost romantic about this place, the perfect location from which to stage an ending.

"Yes. I supervised the loading myself. The cargo is secure; Mr. Ko and I sealed the compartment, so any last-minute inspections would be thwarted, but none were requested. This stop will be left off the logbooks, so there will be no record that the plane was ever here, which puts the whereabouts of everyone who boarded it in doubt indefinitely.

"I also took the liberty of filing documents for a night flight training exercise over the desert to cover our predicted window of operation. I didn't want any issues with airspace operation to interfere with delivery of the package," Michael Israel concluded.

"You thought of everything," Azuma said, and her admiration for the young soldier was evident. "No possibility that this comes back to you?"

"Unlikely," Michael Israel replied. "The documents are American, and might cause some confusion as to their origin when interrogated. Not that it would matter either way." She stopped short of telling Azuma how she had accomplished it, and was sincerely unconcerned about how it might appear if traced back to her, but still had her parents to consider.

"You saw your mother?" Azuma asked, as if she were reading Michael Israel's mind. A small muscle in the young woman's jaw jumped, but that was the only indication the soldier would betray of any emotion.

"I did," she said curtly, not inviting further discussion, continuing to walk on, but Azuma had stopped. Michael Israel turned back, and just when Azuma had decided she would say no more on the subject, she saw something in the other woman's eyes.

Azuma stood still, there on the asphalt, halfway between the plane and the buildings. She knew that once they reached the hangar, it would be like crossing a boundary, and Michael Israel would close the book on everything that had come before, everything she had left behind.

She was all too familiar with this emotional maneuver; it had happened every time she had left the Tokugawa stronghold to undertake any martial errand. At the gates, she had to shed sentimentality, had to take a moment to say goodbye to that life, had to arm herself with the knowledge that it may have been the last time she would see it. That she might not return, that she might never see Megumi again. Every samurai, like every soldier, knew it well. Accept that you may be done with the life you are leaving behind, whether or not it is done with you. Then turn toward your death, accepting the reality of it ahead of its actual occurrence, and let go of everything that came before.

"I felt so guilty this time," Michael Israel said finally. "Even with my father. Seeing Forcas as Michael did something indescribable to me. It was like I could see things in the here and now that I was only feeling with my four-year-old self before, angry, incoherent, all my nonverbal responses. I suddenly relived it as an adult, with the perspective of my career, life and death, loss. I understood my father like I never had, like I'd never tried.

"But it is always harder with *Ima*, because she has tried to understand me all along. Every time I left on campaign or assignment, or had new orders, she and I both knew I might not return. We accepted it. But it was only a possibility, something left unspoken but acknowledged. This time, it felt like a lie. On my part. This time, I know my death to be no longer a possibility, it is a certainty. I accept that, but some small part of me feels like I should have told her, wanting to bear the burden of my mother's grief in that moment, have her turn that rage upon me. Rather that than the slow, painful realization, her long years of suffering when I don't come back, but I couldn't do it, I was a coward."

"I think you lie to yourself if you think she does not know. I met your mother, and she knows her child. She knew you were hiding from her in that hotel. She has likely guessed what you keep from her now, knew it the moment she saw you," Azuma said softly.

"But why wouldn't she say something?" Michael Israel asked, frustrated now, confronted with this new possibility. Her youth had blinded her to it.

"For much the same reason that you didn't," Azuma gently replied. "To spare you the emotional burden. Perhaps she has always seen something in you that pulls you away from such things, that you are driven by something that has taken precedence over every other thing in your life."

"How do you know these things?" Michael Israel asked, sounding small and alone.

Azuma stepped up to her. She pushed at a curl on Michael Israel's forehead, but it stubbornly dropped back into place. "Because I know loss. Because I know love. I could say it is because I know you. I tasted your blood, Michael Israel. For good or ill, my victims cannot hide their secret hearts from me."

"But how do you do it, how do you hold all of that feeling? All of that pain?" It was Michael Israel's turn to be amazed, and she tried to imagine the enormity of such a thing.

"Indeed. Imagine all the blood, that encarmined river flowing through time. And never forgetting," Azuma told her. "Deferring, not referring to guilt or remorse. Rather an accounting then, of every detail found in every precious drop that I did not deny myself. The highs, the joys, the victories of a life. What haunts me ever are the darknesses, an accumulation of same that I cannot dismiss. A curse, then, of centuries, the heaviest burden conceivable, having to remember. Yet I think it not too steep a price for what I have stolen."

A small gust of wind came through, swirling around the two women and spiraling off to the west. Michael Israel nodded.

"For as long as I can remember, there was only one thing I wanted," she said. "Even when I was a child, and my *Sav'ta* would ask what I wished for on my birthday, or Hanukkah, I thought it such a waste of time. I wasn't interested in anything but retribution.

"As an adult, I didn't understand the allure of entanglements, the gratifications of desire other than my own need to avenge my loss. I never sought a lover, never wanted one. Even now, I know I should question it, acknowledge that there may be something I have missed. But all I could ever see was my brother's face when he died, and the look of satisfaction on the Death Bringer's face when it happened, as much for my pain as Michael's death.

"I felt that any step off the path was a betrayal of our bond, a betrayal of our love. Anything I enjoyed was something he would never have; I loathed that more than anything else. I even asked myself whether he would have been the same had our fates been reversed. But even that doesn't matter to me. This is the water I carry, the burden I could never set down. I regret nothing. I rejoice in the thought that I may get exactly what I have always wanted, even if it is solely my own death in the bargain. He paid that price, so can I."

Michael Israel fell silent, and Azuma knew she had spoken her piece. She turned back toward the hangar, and began walking.

After a moment, Michael Israel caught up, and Azuma was surprised to feel the soldier's hand slide across her back, her arm coming to rest on Azuma's waist. Azuma responded by putting her own arm across Michael Israel's shoulders. Then she leaned sideways and briefly rested her cheek against the soldier's hair. They returned to the hangar in this manner, content, satisfied with the words that had been spent.

W

The Christian Bible, as it is canonized, or approved by councils of men, speaks only of the Nephilim in Genesis, accepting that such as these were Giants, of mythical status as proven by their survival of the Great Flood.

Judaism holds these beings to be Fallen Angels. The Scrolls, with the lost books, Enoch among them, give life to this mythology.

Their wings were sacred, powerful, and their earthly bodies had to be larger than humans to accommodate them. But they turned away from God's laws, and were stripped of their favored status, taken up by these appendages and cast out. Those others, who fought beside the Monster, and fell in its wake, its faithful conspirators, were treated alike, deformed thus.

The wings are the key to the emergence, my stature changes to accommodate this gift of Heaven.

It is with this knowledge that I seek it out, the only thing that remains to me. A gift, the last one, the only thing I take as I leave the only house I have ever known.

Only with an acceptable form can the Morningstar step into my place in this world, only with its wings is it intact, made whole, potent once more, restored to its power and glory, the place from which it shall Ascend over all it surveys here on earth.

A place of Destruction and Death, a Golgotha, the End of Days.

88

KUSINI AND AMBAKISYE WAVED OFF their driver at the end of the lane, desiring to preserve the privacy of the plantation. 'Kisye hefted both their bags onto his left shoulder, bouncing in place to ensure they were set, and then turned loving eyes to his wife, and offered his hand.

They walked the mile and a quarter up to the house in companionable silence, and he swung her hand a bit, as he had once, during their walks in various places while they had been courting. It felt good to be on familiar ground, to be home, back in the arms of Mother Africa, needing her succor before they left her once more.

The usual daytime industry was in full swing, but there were several people at the main house, which was not usual. Andwale was sitting on the front porch, and he stood up when he saw them, paused only a moment, and came down to meet them.

Kusini saw his expression and she knew, immediately, why he was waiting. Andwale's eyes flashed sadness and relief when he saw the two of them, and the magic of their walk ended when she released Ambakisye's hand. He said nothing, but they did not need words.

She put one hand out in greeting and moved past Andwale, running for the porch, crossing the boards in one long stride, pulling the screen, hearing the finality as the door slapped closed behind her. It had always been the sound of arriving, now it reminded her what was ending.

And here, she felt it, that inevitability, that darkness that she could not pull back even if she wanted to. Remembering. Remembering the very first time she had come through that door, and felt this same ending, one that was not to be avoided, one that had been tempered somewhat by the arrival of the woman who would now be leaving them.

Into the hallway, into the same room where Mwana'jua had slept every night of her life. The room in which she had been born, in which Kusini's hands had pulled her forth, from the womb.

Mwana'jua looked small, she who was small but never seemed so now was akin to that tiny infant long ago. Tired eyes turned lovingly to Kusini, but she only said, "No. You last. Send Ambakisye so I can say my goodbyes, and then I shall need you back."

Kusini nodded, smiling through her tears, understanding that in this, as in all things, Mwana'jua would take charge, have a plan, direct even this, her final day. She backed away from the bed, and turned to the doorway to find Ambakisye, but he was there, at her shoulder. He touched her hand, acknowledging what he saw, so she turned away, and went back out the way she came, not stopping until she was in the garden, among the gravestones, weeping.

She wept for all that she knew was ending. All that was lost. All that she couldn't control. Hoping there was still peace to be found, for she was suddenly so tired. There was still so much to do.

Ambakisye found her there a quarter of an hour later, and with a gentle finger, swept her tears aside. "It's close. She's asking for you. She's not going to last much longer, and if I know her, she still has a lot to say."

"Where will you be?" she asked.

"Here. In our favorite place, waiting for you," he promised.

Mwana'jua was waiting for her, one hand reaching out toward the door, and she waved it weakly when Kusini came in. Kusini took up a small stool sitting next to the vanity, and set it down by the bedside, and took a seat, taking that tiny hand in both of hers, feeling a thrumming energy that she could not entirely credit as solely her own.

"They brought the animals from your farm," Mwana'jua told her.

"Oh. Yes. Thank you for allowing it," Kusini said, grateful to Andwale and Amivi for doing so.

"That little blue bird yours, too? Quite a character."

"Yes. Well, she's Ambakisye's, really," Kusini laughed a little, thinking of Yabluu. Unsurprised she would follow the others here.

"I'm leaving this place to Andwale. Can't properly raise that family hopping around the countryside in an old truck. I signed the deed last year. It's legal and proper. You'll find it in the sideboard, top drawer, next to the kitchen," Mwana'jua said.

"I'll make sure-"

"Girl, stop wasting words and listen. I don't have any extra time," Mwana'jua interrupted her, and then her tone softened. "I know it wasn't your fault that my mother died, know it in my heart, but I could never find anyone else to blame. When I was small, I swore I would outlive you, but it appears that isn't what your magic needs. I have always known that my fate was tied to something, a circle of life that began and ended with you. It's the sight, the sight that my mother had, that Zalika knew was a gift of the women in this family.

"But I never told my grandmother what your presence meant in our lives. I wasn't supposed to live, my mother saw that her child would die with her, and she dreamed of the Sorceress. It was the only way I could be saved, but only if she forfeit her own life. That is what my visions showed me, and I thought for many years that I would rather not exist if I could not have my mother. I refused to tell Grandmother what I knew.

"For you to prevail, I must close the circle. My death was shown to me, in dreams, many years ago. I am a part of your legacy, a part of those deeds, and that life which you have given to others, freely, asking nothing for yourself, is the miracle that will drive your final act of salvation."

Kusini felt tears begin to blur her vision, but Mwana'jua spoke once more.

"You shall not shed tears over me. You must let me go, as I become part of all that you are."

And she was gone, leaving one place for another, and Kusini felt her depart, felt the slackening of her hand. A sensation not unlike one she had experienced here in another time, a century before, when Mwana'jua's mother had similarly let go of this life, as she let go the Sorceress' hand.

Kusini found Ambakisye where she had left him, and welcomed him into her arms, and turning, turning, turning away, took him with her to another place. A place only they shared.

W

He follows me. I cannot see him, hear him, smell him…I feel him. Part of me.

The one who came first…the beast, the beast…

Inside me, like a conscience, hounding me to my rest…waiting for something. Can I betray the one who was there with me in the womb?

Must I betray us?

…and the other is not other, either. Perhaps, what is inside me, what grows there, is simply what has been beside me every step of my life, the Shadow that I cannot shed, needing no sinew to attach it here. Inside me.

Inseparate. Indistinguishable.

The mirror never lied to me.

We own the evil, We shall lay down, in our arms, our embrace its embrace…

…thy will be done.

…and still it comes, with tooth and claw. It has tasted my flesh; it must want more.

…but what have I to feed it that will fend off its hunger for me…I will give to it the masses in my stead, to stay that dreadful appetite…for it was pureflesh that it ate out of our hands when we made of it our pet…

89

SELENE STRETCHED OUT ATOP THE covers and turned to look at Azuma across the pillows with a smug, satisfied smile.

"You're sleepy," Azuma observed, reaching over to run her fingers over Selene's close-cropped hair, her eyes making no secret of her admiration for the other woman's nude form. "Sleep. You don't have to keep me company."

"Typical," Selene teased, one corner of her mouth turning up to show she was amused. "Just turn over, close your eyes, say no more, is that it?"

Azuma blinked quizzically and raised her brows in response, saying, "Have I failed to please you?" It was not a challenge; it was always her sincere desire that her lovers were satisfied fully. It was the least she could do, considering that she was getting the better part of the bargain.

"Pleasure you've got handled," Selene reassured her. "It's the intimacy thing you need to work on."

Azuma laughed. Such honesty. Such a pity that Selene had come so late to the party. Azuma enjoyed her immensely. No nonsense, no punches pulled, entirely a breath of fresh air.

"Never quite got the hang of that one," Azuma admitted, then shook her head. "Maybe once. After that, I just couldn't really revive it." She placed her fingers on Selene's soft mouth, and closed her eyes when Selene sucked gently on one of them. "Did I miss something? Is that what you were looking for here?"

Selene shook her head, sliding in close and snuggling against Azuma. "Not at all. Too messy. Price tag on that has always been too high for me to pay. When you find it, it endangers your dreams, your identity. High maintenance, too. Requires compromise."

"Really?" Azuma gently caught Selene's earlobe between her teeth. "What's that?"

"I'd have to have sex with you even when I don't really want to," Selene smiled, being purposefully obstinate.

"Is that even a thing?!" Azuma shook with laughter. "Best avoided then."

"Thank God we agree," Selene nodded, settling under Azuma's arm.

"I wonder if I failed so utterly at it when I *wanted* to make that kind of compromise that it changed me forever," Azuma said, surprising even herself.

"Can we fail alone when we fail at love?" Selene wondered aloud. "It's suspect when *you* take something like that on, an overachieving, goal-driven wunderkind like you, especially one who is her own greatest critic."

"I say it with all honesty, and a heavy dose of humility," Azuma replied. "The failure was mine alone. And at the time I was still just a girl."

"I doubt you were ever 'just a girl,'" Selene shook her head.

"It's true. I was really in love. Just the once. And then I went through some odd phases. Was celibate, in my way, for a very long time. When I came out of that period in my life, I did the typical self-loathing thing, slept with women I didn't even like; as long as they looked good, it worked for me. It was so bad at one time that my female bodyguards didn't want to be seen with me at functions to avoid being miscast as trophies," Azuma admitted, thinking of *Hachi* at the Prefect's reception, the night she had first met Iara.

"That's so sad," Selene remarked, and she sounded sincerely sympathetic.

"Don't feel sorry for me," Azuma said. "I probably always had someone in the mix that I liked."

"But given all of this, your admission that you did love once, all this talk of other women, taking me into your confidence… this probably counts as intimacy…" Selene's expression changed very subtly.

"What is it?" Azuma chased that expression, even though she suspected Selene had not meant her to notice it.

"I'm not going to see you again, am I?"

"You miss nothing," Azuma said softly, unsurprised.

"I am grateful you brought me all the way to Tel Aviv for breakup sex, though," Selene's earlier expression disappeared behind a careful façade. "I doubt I would otherwise have gotten an opportunity to visit this place."

Azuma shook her head, and then found Selene's mouth with her own, wanting her actions to speak for her, forcing Selene to kiss her now, eyes wide open, because as common as it seems, kissing is one of the most intimate acts that two people can share. It is hard to hide much, impossible to lie, and lays bare the subtlest of vulnerabilities. "I'm not breaking up with you," Azuma told her when they surfaced for a breath.

"Not a denial." Selene arched one brow as she made her point. "You *are* leaving, though."

"Your arrangements are made, not jeopardized by my leaving, and you can change them if you like, extend your stay. I'll cover your expenses; it's the least I can do," Azuma said, watching Selene carefully now. "And I think you should reconsider my other offer," she added quietly, but Selene was shaking her head.

"Not even to assuage your guilt, I won't," she said. "And there is nothing to discuss. I *know* you are a brilliant physician, and I am sure there are things that can yet be done, and strings that can be pulled only by you. And don't mistake me. I am flattered that you care enough about me to offer. Because you do care."

"I do." Azuma wanted no confusion on that point, and she could see that Selene recognized she was earnest.

"I am dying, and I would die anyway, one way or another, sooner or later. The Good Lord just deems that it shall be sooner. I have known this for some time. I'm not afraid of it."

"I know that," Azuma said. "I wholeheartedly support your autonomy in this, it's just – regret is too weak a word to describe what the world loses without you."

"Now this is why I let you get into my pants in the first place." Selene smiled into her kiss. "You amaze me. But I want to be myself, authentically, experience what I am meant to experience, feel what I should feel. It is a part of the journey. And I know there is more to your story than what is shown to me and the world on the surface. I don't want to end up like one of your creepy bodyguards." Selene punctuated her remark with a look that told Azuma that she knew the blood-drinking was probably not just a fetish.

"Are my bodyguards creepy?" Azuma asked, slightly nonplussed. But knowing that Selene was very bright and clearly empathic, she could see it from that angle. "Okay, some of them are a bit creepy."

"Likely a hazard of the profession," Selene said in a lighter tone, and Azuma knew that whatever depths they had just explored in their relationship, it was time to set them aside, and begin reinforcing safe boundaries.

"Do you think that was enough intimacy for you to consider blessing me with the gift of your body?" Azuma asked, resuming their light-hearted banter of before, letting her eyes betray her fondness for her lover.

Selene sighed, mock-dramatically. "Come over here and have your way with me. I'll just lie back and think of England."

"Have you been waiting to use that line?" Azuma was beyond amused.

"Damn right I have," Selene confirmed with almost a straight face.

"That is truly awful," Azuma laughed, and she was grateful when Selene did, too, needing her happiness to be integral to their ending.

90

HACHI STRETCHED OUT ON *KU'S* back with a satisfied sigh, enjoying the warmth of his skin. Enjoying their closeness generally.

"*Ku?*" she said, wanting to get his attention.

He moved his head, glancing at her over his shoulder, but didn't say anything.

"What are we going to face down there?" she wondered aloud, needing to talk about it, not wanting to need to talk about it. Her emotions were at war, but it was evident one side was winning. He knew she wasn't afraid, not really. It wasn't her style. This was about something else; he just wasn't sure what. He hoped, as he always did, that she would be able to get it out. Sometimes she couldn't.

"Anything. Everything. Nothing. Ourselves." *Ku* was his usual philosophical self, and this was endlessly comforting to her. It was as if he worried about nothing he couldn't control. And recognized that he couldn't control anything.

"Just keep whispering that in my ear when we are down in the catacombs," she advised, and he could hear a hint of amusement in her tone. High praise when one could elicit such a thing from *Hachi*.

"And what happens if I die before you?" he asked, matching her playful tone.

"I step over your corpse and keep walking, of course." No hesitation, but she turned over on her belly, her breasts against his skin, and put her cheek against his upper back. He could feel her face tighten as she smiled.

"Oh. Wow. That's just how I imagined it. Exactly what I would want, too." He nodded.

She rolled off of him and came to rest beside him, that perfect face inches from his. "What about you? What will you do if I die before you?" she asked, narrowing her eyes.

"I would fall down, draping myself over your fallen form, weeping, and gnashing my teeth," he replied, and his eyes narrowed too, in anticipation of her reaction, which if she were displeased might involve physical violence. He understood it now. She wanted to be told she was important to him, without really having to ask.

"I like that, but the teeth gnashing?" *Hachi* made a small circle around her mouth. "That was probably…"

"Too much?" he asked, nodding. "Yeah. Okay. No gnashing of teeth, then. Undignified. Duly noted."

"But there is that other thing…" she said, her eyes warming, the color of cognac in the candlelight.

"What other thing?" *Ku* looked confused.

"You know. That thing you did, before, just now," she whispered, mischief, seduction, even deep affection were all there together in her eyes. "You think you could do it again?"

"Oh?" *Ku* raised his eyebrows. "You liked it?"

She didn't answer, just shook her blonde hair a bit, teasing him. But *Ku* knew her secrets, she was ticklish when aroused, so he nuzzled against her neck, making her shriek with delight. "*Did* you like it?"

She pulled away, and held him off with a gentle hand on his chest. "No." *Hachi* let her eyes show him how she felt, and then she kissed him, slowly, surrendering, which was the greatest gift *Hachi* could give. She whispered against his neck, already wrapping her legs around him again. "I loved it."

91

THROUGH THE OPEN WINDOWS OF their suite at the Jaffa, *Ni* could hear the sea. She concentrated on it; though it was connected to all the other waters of the world, and thus the ocean that lapped against the shore at the Tokugawa stronghold, the sound it made coming to land here was very different, something she might never have noticed under other circumstances.

She listened to it so closely and so carefully because she was unable to sleep, her legs tangled in the sheets, her body pressed close to the Collector, unmoving because she did not want to disturb his rest.

On balance, duty and protocol had found them apart on more than half of the nights she had known him, and although they had shared those nights over nearly a century and a half, she still didn't feel she'd had enough of him to herself. It never failed to sadden her when she thought that much of the lost time was given away to others, because they could never get everything they needed from one another. He'd smiled when she had said as much aloud once, and reminded her that it was likely impossible for any two beings to get everything they needed from each other. She wanted to disagree; absent her blood meals among the pureflesh, every other need she had ever had since that time in Yoshiwara had been satisfied by him.

Even the impossible decorum he had established between them, never speaking to her, looking at her, or treating her any differently than any other member of the *Akai* in their public life only made her admiration for him greater. It was a task she was unsure she could duplicate, but she had followed his lead, understood the need for it. For her part, she knew that the ever-present Damoclesian threat that the other members of the Dragon Guard lived under applied to her in equal part; that her performance and her failures in that role should be judged in the same fashion as the Collector judged her peers.

Privately, however, she held herself to a higher standard, knowing that her behavior and any of her failures would redound to *his* discredit, for that very first and only exception he had made for her, feeling he was responsible for her place here. She would no more call into question that judgement he had made than dishonor him by poorly valuing the gift she had been given.

So she never tired of the precious time when they could be together, in the private spaces he kept that only she was privileged to enter, the sweetness of her feelings for him undiminished although those years had changed her far more than they had changed him. The aching desire he could still evoke, because behind closed doors, with the two of them in, and the world without, he was another man, one who had belonged to her longer than even she realized, even before he had ever touched her for the first time, before he had introduced her to something she had never experienced, that intoxicating power of being truly desired.

Her pleasure still mattered to him, had always mattered to him, and he was seemingly expert at all that he did, and she knew that truth to be tied irrevocably to the care in which he took with everything that he deemed worthy of his time and attention. She, who prided herself on control, would promise herself that she was going to maintain some remove, hold herself apart, make of any seduction a challenge for him, and prolong those moments captured so infrequently, would be reduced within minutes to a breathless ecstasy, the currency by which he was rewarded in his efforts.

And if, in her professional life, she was bereft of touch, in her personal life she was spoiled with it, and this too was a treasure that was hers alone, to know such a singularly private being so intimately felt like getting away with a crime. The best kind of secret to have, and it had always sustained her during times of challenge.

"What keeps you awake, my love?" The Collector's question startled her; she had been so certain he slept.

"Holding on to these moments with you as long as possible," she replied. It was not, entirely, a misdirection. Morning would come, and separate them once more, perhaps for the last time.

"You flatter me. But there is more to your wakefulness than this." He shifted next to her, his mouth opening against her shoulder, biting the muscle there, distracting her, so she offered her mouth, which he accepted just as readily, not bothering to hide his hunger for her, undiminished with the passage of time. But he didn't pursue this stimulating diversion, which told her that he had something on his mind.

"I'm not going to like whatever you're about to tell me," she predicted.

"Perhaps not. But you are the only one I have to share my secrets with," he reminded her, and this time when he kissed her, it was unlike before. It was everything at once, and she recognized it as the beginning of their goodbye.

His statement surprised her, as she had always assumed that any secrets he had were shared with Azuma through their special bond, a blood bond unlike the one the Dragon Goddess shared with the *Akai*, unlike the bond the *Akai* shared amongst themselves, unlike the bond he shared with her as a result of their repeated intimacies.

"From the time you enter the *makom*," the Collector told her, not bothering with any preamble, "your time there will be limited. No matter that while you are inside that place time will seem to stretch out interminably, in reality, Akenomyosei will not linger if it senses defeat. You will all need to make a studied approach to the problem, the goal being to get the Wolf, the Dragon, and the Sorceress close enough to stop Weston, and with him, Akenomyosei."

"You speak as though you will not be among us," *Ni* protested softly.

"I have another task," he said gently. "I have made another bargain with the Monster, a necessary one, to protect our Mistress and ensure that her interests were ever safeguarded."

"I don't understand." The breeze from the window was no longer soothing, and *Ni's* skin felt cold. The Collector sensed it, and disentangled the sheets carefully, pulling them and the coverlet up, pulling her in close against the warmth of his body.

"Akenomyosei demands a sacrifice to enter its sacred spaces, and another to leave them. Knowing this, I made it my responsibility to meet the candidates who were chosen to ascend to the Crimson Guard at the Dawn Gate of the Shrine. To gain entry each time and evaluate those who were worthy required a sacrifice. I made that sacrifice my own, finding something that would be acceptable to the Monster, and to the High Priests of the Temple."

"Not just a sacrifice," *Ni* recalled the legends and the rules of her adopted sect, "but suffering as well."

"Just so," he said, not to be distracted from his narrative. "I found that by commission of self-disemboweling, as in *seppuku*, the requirement for suffering was amply met. That I did it with my own hand made the sacrifice more meaningful."

"But you have made that pilgrimage dozens of times over the centuries," *Ni* protested, shuddering, horrified at what he must have endured. Saddened that he had done so alone, even after such time that he could have had her comfort in this. But she thought she understood him; to speak of it would have diminished the magic in it, to receive succor each time would have negated its purpose. And he had hidden each brutal recovery from her as well. "And why is it more meaningful to injure yourself, rather than let another injure you?" She could not immediately make the connection.

"Because the act of *seppuku* only grants honor on the one performing it if it results in death," he explained. "A faithful second must complete the ceremony, beheading the one who commits to the act. To turn away from the honor of that death is shameful, such that this deliberate misstep was the price I paid to leave, the decay of my honorable standing in the eyes of the gods, my perceived dishonor each time the ritual was left unfinished is what I used to pay for my subsequent departures from that place. And it has a kind of symmetry.

"The writings of the Tokugawa are contained still on the scrolls in Azuma's library. Ietsune, Azuma's father, wrote of the false disgrace of his brother, Tsunayoshi. For Ietsune to ensure his reign and initiate the Time of the Dragon, he had to rid himself of his brother. He found a way to mark Tsunayoshi in shame, encouraging him to commit *seppuku*. Ietsune did act as the second, but he forced Tsunayoshi to suffer the pain and weakness of his disemboweling for two days before he collected his brother's head. I thought it fitting that my actions mirror this act, and my end shall complete the cycle that was set in motion so long ago."

"Surely there is more to be said," *Ni* encouraged him when he fell silent, both dreading and needing to hear the rest of what he had to tell her.

"My promise to remain tainted, in a sort of limbo, was the compact I made with the Devil," he explained. "In return, my martial prowess, my assassin's skill, my ability to protect the Dragon Goddess was left intact by the Dark Gods of the mountain. It is not just the blood of the Dragon that fuels my gifts. Getting into the *makom* will require another such sacrifice, in kind with the ones that came before. Such was the bargain I struck with the Morningstar."

"So you will again perform this act of self-mutilation?" she asked, apprehensive for him, not sure this was knowledge that would not detrimentally affect her own performance in their endeavor.

"No. For this occasion, I will not only begin it, but I will complete the ritual, which will rob Akenomyosei of my soul," he said firmly. "I need you to love me enough to act as my second, to remove my head, and set me free. It is the only way to lose the stain of my dishonor and cross to the next life unburdened. Akenomyosei will have to recognize the sacrifice as valid for entry to the Place of the Fallen, and cannot deny those who present themselves to be admitted there. I will use its conditions against it."

"And it is likely that much will be sacrificed within those catacombs that will satisfy the requirement for escape, if such is even needed," *Ni* said bitterly, and worked hard to avoid tears, not wanting him to have to suffer those as well. But he sensed that thing in her tone that she could not hide from him, he who knew her innermost feelings, and he took her chin in his hand. That gentle gesture was her undoing, releasing all the emotion she had held back, and she wept freely, and said, "What if I cannot do it? I fear my resolve will fail me, that these hands that have held you, loved you, could never turn from their purpose and commit this violence you ask of them. What will happen then?"

"I fear that if you cannot accept this burden, I shall not cross into the next life, where I will have the chance to love you better than I did in this one. Love you as you deserve, not the poor substitute which was all I could offer you here. I shall then wander in the *Yomi-no-kuni*, lost among the dead, lost to what we have and what we are."

"But if you steal even one prize from the Morningstar, will it not void the sacrifice?" she asked, not because she could refuse him, but in an attempt to find a way it could be avoided.

Ah, my dear Obara," the Collector began, using her given name, saying it aloud for the very first time. "This time, it is not I that makes the sacrifice, not I who bears the suffering that shall open the way into the dark temple. This time, my love, it is you."

92

THEY STOOD TOGETHER, THERE IN the shadow of the plane, and the *Akai* knew it had begun. *Ni*, their sister, her face made up, now a dark and dangerous *Kabuki* mask, the ebony stripe across her eyes striking and fierce, the red dot on her lower lip punctuating her grief. This the paint she wore to go to war. She had no hood, her head uncovered, these differences setting her apart from her fellow priests in their black *yoroi*.

The Collector, making a deep bow to Azuma, who did not dishonor him by shedding any of the many tears she held in reserve for his loss. She could no more change his mind than he could ever change hers; neither of them turned away from duty, from the demands of what was right and honorable. The wind on the hillside blew their long hair sideways, twin rivers of darkness, and then he spoke.

"The Door Shall Be Opened." His promise to gain them entry to the *makom*.

Azuma nodded, and the Collector waited as *Ni* accepted something from Michael Israel, tucking part of it away at her waist, holding the other part carefully, almost reverently. The two women also shared a bow, before *Ni* and the Collector melted away into the darkness beyond the limits of preternatural night vision.

The wind brought only whispers, and for a long time the night was much as it had been. And then, the deadly song of *Hōfuku*, as it whistled through the air, and the breeze sputtered and died, as if to mark the moment in respect. Silence, absolute and funereal, and then a flash of brightness, the fire unnaturally white in the distance, the glow of the phosphor used for the immolation, because *Ni* wanted to be sure.

And her precaution was warranted, taking no chances with his ritual burning, his concession to her Buddhism, ensuring that she could find him in the next life. For no sooner had she set the blaze than the rain began to fall, softly, not enough to distinguish the unnatural fire, setting him free from this world.

And when she was sure she could release the burden of what was now, truly, her sacrifice, as he had so wisely predicted, she turned away from that sacred place. Securing *Hōfuku* alongside her own steel, the only other thing she took back with her to the others was her love.

93

KUSINI WATCHED THE SUN DESCENDING over the edge of the world, catalogued the way the soft light of those dying rays bathed Ambakisye's beautiful face, turned his eyes into precious jewels. She knew it was likely the last time she would see him this way.

His hand brushed her cheek, then slid gently down her neck and onto her shoulder. She knew he wanted to kiss her, but she also knew that he wouldn't, even though they were alone. He had allowed his own change to overtake him, needing that restlessness, that ruthlessness now. He never took a chance with this bestial part of himself, did not allow certain intimacies when in this state. She understood it and he had explained it to her once; he was another person when he let the madness in, another man. *You are my wife, and he shall never touch you,* he had promised her long ago.

Neither of them were certain about the others, but Kusini knew that all were in readiness, knew that Azuma and Amaoke were nearby. She was unsure about Weston, but she suspected the changes in her feelings about him were an effect of the Morningstar's influence, and she refused to let these emotions muddy her affection for the young priest. If he were here, all was as it should be, no matter the outcome. He had understood the cost better than any of them, perhaps was shouldering the greatest burden of all.

The pit and all of its mysteries lay at their feet. The wind was remarkably calm, there was only an occasional light breeze to send eddies of sand swirling about their legs. The silence was almost oppressive it was so ominous. When the last sliver of light disappeared, the temperature seemed to dip sharply, the air not quite cold, but biting, but it wasn't just the turning to dusk that made it so.

"The others are here," Kusini breathed, almost reverently, in awe at the power she felt.

"Who?" Ambakisye asked, thinking she was referring to Azuma, Amaoke, and Weston.

"The ancestors, the murdered, the martyred, the strong," she told him, and he looked over her shoulder and saw only the evening star, over a hundred million miles away, knowing even it had changed, and what he saw now was merely what it had been, not what it was now.

"'Kisye, look again," she advised, knowing that his own madness was even now eating away at his reason.

So he did, concentrating carefully, and it might have been just a momentary blinding doubt, or a trick of the light, but suddenly they were *there*, and unlike his dream that had caused so much distress, the moment was not chaos, rather it was calm.

Hundreds of them, surrounding the Place of the Fallen, facing the pit, a ring of bodies four to five deep, a circle of spirits that engirded that place. Most with the pale radiance that their albinism had granted them in life, but some of the unaffected, too. Far too many children, but even these brought him a sense of peace. He did not recognize any of them, but they whispered together, and he could hear it, soft but with the power of the elements. *Mfalme na Malkia*, hailing them as King and Queen.

But Ambakisye knew, if he were a king to such as these, it was only because their true queen was his wife. Indeed, he watched her face, watched her feelings flow over it, and felt such awe when he realized that she recognized, or personally knew, every one of these guardians. The enormity of the sheer emotion she must have been experiencing drove him to his knees.

He had thought he understood her life, and her power. Thought he had known her. Yet here, a reminder, that there was always more to discover, and in that moment his love for her was almost overwhelming, matching his regret that he was out of time to learn more of her in this life.

Kusini looked around. She knew every face, had catalogued every insult, every lost limb. Some she had delivered, some she had served in their time of suffering, some she had held in her arms as they died.

Auntie Kizu was there, and Suhuba, with another woman who was the beautiful counterpoint of Kusini herself. Her very own mother, Tumpe, lovely and content. Mnatoa, Ak'ili, and their baby. Chiumbo, the goatherder, his grandfather's spearhead affixed in its rightful place upon his staff, his sister Jumapi'li. Kusini felt each of them, their energies unique, as they were, what remained of them, essential and important, here for her, because she remembered their names and had never forgotten. Mwana'jua was there, although Kusini did not see her, she felt her energy, the love that had radiated from her during that final visit.

She kneeled in the sand next to 'Kisye, bowing her head in reverence.

"But, what – how ?" Kisye asked, finally recognizing some of the faces, sadly, most were those that he had helped to bury on the safety of the coffee plantation.

Kusini shook her head, signaling that the answer was not in her words. She placed a hand over his heart. "Can you feel it, my husband?"

Ambakisye's eyes widened in surprise. He had assumed his overwhelming emotion the result of Kusini's power, but what it actually represented was much more. Creation, life, birth, death, love. The Circle of Life, the power of Ngai, Kusini's well of magic.

It had grown in her life because her influence and impact on the lives of others had grown. No matter the outcome, where her intent had been only loving and good, even where she had been inadvertently destructive, all of her selflessness and sacrifice had only increased her potential. Had only driven the development of even greater capacity for salvation.

Kusini knew. The white chameleon from the gorge came unbidden to her mind. *Kenge*, speaking the truth of all truths. Slow, unable to travel as quickly as the *Mjusi*, she had never despaired, never given up. *Evil may arrive first, but good must not stop toiling onward. It is far better to arrive later than expected and thwart its designs than not at all.*

"It is time," Kusini said, getting to her feet and making her way to the steps. "Once we enter, I do not know what we shall encounter."

The host of spirits had not moved to join them, and this worried Ambakisye. "Aren't they coming?"

Kusini shook her head. "They shall stand watch and let no evil escape this place. It is the duty they do before they go to their rest. A gift of Ngai."

"Perhaps it is also Olapa's gift," 'Kisye told her, knowing she would understand, acknowledging the balance of the feminine and the masculine.

Kusini nodded. "You see much, my love."

"Will you allow me to go before you?" he asked, almost as if he were too shy to request it.

"I am honored to be your wife," she replied. "Never was there anything in my life I wanted more or was prouder to be. When I met you, I found my place in this world and the next."

94

THE WOLF SLIPPED SILENTLY DOWN the steps, into the dark earth, tracking an evil as old as time, chasing a friend. Down and down, until the scent trail led him through one of many doorways, not needing sight to see what lay ahead of him.

But along the way, what he thought his nose had known changed, and blended with other scents, equally ancient, and time stretched out ahead of him. His senses flooded; the brimstone signature more forward here than he'd remembered. A darkness the beast's vision could not penetrate, the miasma of souls sliding over him, a sound like the song of crickets, but repeated to madness, so slight and faint that he could not decide if the sound were in his imagination or without. Making it impossible to apply his hearing to any other problem.

For among those ancient rooms were cold, dark places that set aside magic, and his fur was stolen from him, and he was once more a man. Disoriented after all this time, a Jonah in the whale, without hope of escape or survival. Fear, at the inconstancy, the fragility of his flesh, doubt about why he'd come.

And there was a child here, one of the pureflesh, he could smell its fear, and the scent sparked the Beast's hunger. All that he'd been unable to deny here before, presented to him without guise, not a kid goat at all, one small, defenseless human who could not escape. A gift, from the Morningstar. A test. One bite, one taste, and he would be set free. Free of the endless struggle, free to walk the earth in an honest form, and to help rule it.

It was here, it was with him, but it no longer had a face. His human frailty married to the berserker's amnesiac state, unsure who he really was. Stripped of any of the usual weapons. The laughter, and the insect noise, mounting to madness when Amaoke discovered there were no exits from this, his old prison. He prayed he could resist his basest tendencies.

95

THE *AKAI* DESCENDED UPON THE pit from above, riding the air currents down, windwalking into the dark, depthless opening below.

Drifting ahead of their mistress, following Michael Israel, who was outfitted for her own base jump in technical clothing and night vision goggles, they chose separate levels of the tower to secure. Finding footholds on the curved face of the oubliette, searching for admission to the catacombs beyond.

Michael Israel descended farthest, out of sight, dragged by gravity more effectively to the depths, seemingly fearless of a landing, waiting to deploy her chute until the last second possible, already out of sight of the others. She steered herself sharply around and connected with the stones, releasing the chute, clinging to the wall precariously, watching the black silk carried aloft and away on thermals rising from the depths, disappearing from her view.

In contrast, Azuma aimed for the stairway, sprinting downward, a guardian covering this escape, buying whatever time there was to be had. Her priests had their instructions, mark the outlay of the catacombs, and take out any threats between the Morningstar and its children of purpose. They no longer protected one god, rather four, understanding that the least of these might already be irrevocably lost. They were buying an opportunity to bring an end to the Destroyer, and looking for sacred hiding places.

Two hundred meters below the surface, Azuma felt them, in her soul she knew that the Sorceress and the Wolf had entered the Shrine of the Fallen. Kusini's energy was strong and true, but Amaoke's was not. She was reading rage and frustration from him, but despaired of locating him, so she committed to the dangerous task she had set for herself alone, and opened up the blood bond with Weston.

And was blinded by madness, the howls of the damned a tsunami that threatened to consume her, and she saw him, just for a moment, those brown eyes uncertain and lost, as yet unchanged. He was reaching for her across the bond, feeding her this babbling insanity, and she knew if she kept the connection open she would be rendered useless by it, through their bond he would destroy her reason and regain his own.

She did not need to maintain it; only needed this confirmation that he was here, as lost and wandering as they; if she fed him her reason it would only serve to get him to the Monster sooner. Was that what the three of them were supposed to do? Serve as a conduit, take on Weston's mental anguish, lead him to the Morningstar? Perhaps, but it would not be her undoing.

The priest's wandering meant he had no easier path to evil than the rest of them. She let go of the thread that connected them, keeping only the awareness of this proximity, and went forward to make her own discoveries.

She crushed the capsule on her left arm, dispersing the chemical as she moved through the catacombs, entry from the steps, through the maze, back out along the gallery to the next door, working upward, knowing her priests worked downward, doing the same. Delivering the biomarker in their wake, mapping the *makom*, hoping against hope that Michael Israel had reached the bottom. Hoping that the soldier's importance to this place would allow her to gain entry to the deepest darkest secrets the Morningstar kept.

On the third level above where Azuma had started, she sensed movement in the stairwell, and turned to see a familiar face, both despised and horrifying, the face of an old enemy. Her father.

But not her father, not really, just Akenomyosei wearing that face, whether to cause her to falter or compound her pain she did not know. Perhaps both outcomes were intended. A reminder of a grim part of her history, the hateful progenitor of her curse.

He wore the Dragon's armor, further mocking her, knowing that this inherited costume that had made her recognizable as samurai and Shogun had first been worn by this monster. A monster she had identified from her earliest days. A monster that had coveted the power that was safeguarded for her; had been allowed first use of the very sword she now carried, had quenched it in her beating heart.

"Tatsuo Tomo may already be gone. There is only you to walk beside me now, Daughter," it said. Lies. She looked closely. She sensed no Weston yet, it had not accomplished its marriage to sacred flesh.

"I presume you have made that same offer to Amaoke," she replied calmly, sword at the ready.

"Yes, but he is too, how do I say it, dichotic in his thinking really," it explained, admitting everything and nothing.

"Never to my sister, Kusini," Azuma observed. "She'd die first. Or better, destroy you."

"Put the sword away, my dear," it crooned, condescension dripping from every word.

"Once this sword is unsheathed, it would be dishonorable to put it away without making use of it, dear Father," she refused to meet its dark emotion with anger.

"As you wish," it said, bowing deeply. She watched, horrified, as the armor it wore split and fell from its changing form, the Great Dragon birthed from its shell, one head, not two. Perhaps Tatsuo Tomo had indeed succumbed. Or perhaps, as she guessed, this was personal, between two beings that had an unsettled score.

Its voice in her mind, inside of her, around her. "You cannot win. Even now your beloved *Akai* face their worst nightmares, they face themselves. Not as you have weakened them with your consideration of their nameless nothingness, but as I intended them to be, ruthless, deadly, remorseless, with no thought or hesitation about death, about each other.

"I know you feel each one as they suffer, each one as they lose, each one as they die. And the sacrifice that *Okurimono* made for all of you only opened the door to the land of the dead."

Hearing the Collector's given name was reason enough to engage. "How dare you speak that name," Azuma said. "That name that shall be honored among the gods. For that, I put down my sword, and take up the scales you cursed me with."

"You cannot destroy me," it hissed, now fully transformed, its head moving back and forth hypnotically.

"Perhaps not," Azuma replied calmly. "But I can punish you, I can weaken you. I can delay you from your rendezvous, perhaps long enough to change the future."

She held her arms to the sky, tiny grains of sand swirling about them, and called the Dragon, her armored form now glorious. Now the sands could not cut or sting, could not penetrate, and she was liberated, free to unleash the beast inside of her.

The clashing of the two Dragons was deafening, as they twisted about one another, cerulean and crimson scales shedding against the stones as they fell down and down, together, trading blows. Curled about one another, yin and yang, coiling and uncoiling, sparks flashing off their scales as tooth and claw connected.

Azuma, exploding upward, drifting, ribbonlike, stopping at the point of inertia and turning downward, slamming into Akenomyosei, clamping her jaws about its serpentine collar, shaking her head, scattering its evil armor like fiery rain. Their battle, endless, the force of their collisions galactic.

It, breaking free, weakened, surprised at the insult she had caused it, bleeding. She could scent its fear from the blood it spilled. Then, in a terrible moment of her hesitation, when she sensed, perhaps, that another of her beloved *Akai* was dying, her adversary clubbed viciously at her with a spiked tail and connected with her flank, and she was torn, her inconstant heart exposed.

Akenomyosei struck again, making another hole in her chest, and she could no longer hold onto the form that made her a god, shrinking back to Azuma, hearing the sputtering rhythm that was left of her heart. She sprawled on the stones, the other Dragon coming in close to finish her, but she stretched out her hand, and her sword, the cause of all her misfortune, came to her call, and struck Akenomyosei a terrible blow.

Punished, crippled, it abandoned further attack, spiraling downward and away, leaving her, knowing she would not ever leave this place.

Azuma adjusted her clothing, and stood on her feet, having no choice but to stay upright, keep moving upward, for as long as possible. Her heart was slowing, skipping worse than before, and trying to fall out on the stones.

She held it in place under her arm, and strapping her *saya* across her body like a sling, the sheath in front where she could still reach her sword, she turned back toward the surface.

96

THE AIR BEGAN MOVING AGAIN, and now Amaoke could see glowing motes twirling on the currents. Where these were pushed against the stones, some stuck, painting the surfaces like tiny stars, outlining walls, boundaries, openings. Clearing one of his senses allowed him to tap into the others, and although his ability to scent his quarry was still thwarted, he knew the place of his corralling to be a false cell, from which there were many exits, simply not located where one might expect to find them. And he was blessedly alone, no wandering morsels to tempt him further.

With the visual guide provided by Azuma's science, he regained directional awareness. And then, another gift from the spirits, delivered through an opening near the top of the wall. Amaoke pulled himself up to listen. A song, a lovely song, a sound he could follow, one that would lead him from a dead end.

His soul told him that this was not the song of the siren, and the dead around him flowed out of the dark spaces to escape the magic in it. He was able to gain purchase to the passageway, his shoulders clearing it, claustrophobic and close, he could feel the air moving ahead of him, the tiny bright floating motes clinging to the walls. They revealed that the rough surfaces that grabbed at his skin were the faces of the dead, sharp edges on broken skulls lined the narrow tunnel.

He did not know the meaning of the words he was hearing, but the tune was simple and repetitive, overcoming the deafening cacophony that had threatened to rob him of his own senses. He recognized it as a lullaby, a simple song, taught to children everywhere to ward off the frightful denizens of the night and allow for restful sleep.

He drew closer and closer to the voice, but the sound seemed ever to be receding. When he exited the tunnel and a chamber opened ahead of him, he realized the reason for this illusion. It was not the shifting reality of these catacombs that had caused it, rather it was the slow ebb of a life, the songstress fading as he discovered her. *Hachi*, nearly cleaved in half by some terrible force, dumped down at the base of the wall like a broken doll.

She reached for Amaoke's hand. "My mother was here. I followed her, she was looking for me, calling my name. But then…it was me. She was me, had my sword. Fought like me. Perhaps I split *her* open, and *she* is here, singing, and *I* am somewhere else." She stopped, breathing shallowly.

"Let me help you," Amaoke said, kneeling down and trying to gather her into his arms. "If I can get you to Azuma, she can-"

"No." Her golden eyes were knowing, and he had seen that expression many times before. She was too near death for any intervention to help her.

"I cannot leave you here," he protested, angry that he was helpless in the face of her suffering.

"You think the Dragon wanted you to show us what you are in order to prepare us to fight in this place? You are wrong." *Hachi* gripped his arm weakly, but insistently. "She did so in order to engender camaraderie among strangers, so that we, the *Akai Hogo-sha*, would not hesitate to die for you, so that we could understand that such a death would carry as much honor as dying for the Dragon. This is a good death, here under the timeless sands."

"I-" Amaoke had not asked for this, would never have asked another to make such a sacrifice in his stead, but she was impatient, and he could see in her eyes that she had little time, and there was more she wanted to say.

"*He* found me. He told me to sing, that it would hold off the others that were here to eat my soul," she explained, her grip faltering. "It was Weston, he was just here, before you, when I broke open the capsule." She indicated the cracked ampoule strapped to her left arm. "He blessed me, so it may not be too late. But I fear the Dragon's magic will show him the way just as it shows all of us. Perhaps he knew my song would bring you, too. Perhaps he knows he needs you to follow."

Her eyes held him there; he could see his reflection in her pupils, the glow of the particles she had released enough for him to discern the outline of his face. Her head tipped back against the stones, but her eyes never left his, and he watched her too. He did not move until he saw that she was gone, giving her the only gift he had to give her, his companionship, so that she was not alone when death came for her. It was a negligible thing beside the gift she had given him, the return of all his senses.

97

AMBAKISYE NOTED THE TEMPERATURE DROPPING steadily as he made his way downward, keeping his hand against the outer face of the stairwell, until the wall fell away, a doorway, away from the central catacombs. An unexpected discovery, clearly another manipulation, for this passageway had not appeared on the any of the diagrams or maps in the files Azuma had shared with them.

He turned to alert Kusini to his discovery, and was both surprised and disappointed to find that she was no longer with him. He'd heard nothing, the wind and echo chambers created a cacophony in this place that swallowed subtler sound, but he could have sworn that she was still just behind him. He did not let it unsettle him, knowing that any hurts to her would be felt by him. If she had departed from him, it could only be because she sensed it was part of the greater plan.

Ambakisye was still for a moment, considering whether it was wiser to turn back or press onward. There were tiny points of light floating on the air, allowing him to see more and more of the rooms opposite; it appeared none of these markers had been taken up on this side of the structure. The motes seemed to attach to the inner face of the stairwell, and appeared to be repelled from the outer face. It was possible that this was separate from and not a part of the structure, even likely just a shifting construct of his imagination.

The opening was shrouded in darkness, but his sight was penetrating it for several feet, so he left the landing and moved forward, certain that at the very least he would identify any obstacles before he walked into a blind end. But the archway became a hallway, stretching out ahead. The air warmer here, fetid, stale, unmoving. It was like a living thing, the mouth of some great beast, waiting.

The diameter of the tunnel was decreasing, and soon he could see stone bearing down overhead, and he put his hand up to confirm what he sensed, and soon the vault was encroaching even further. But just when he had resolved to turn back, he thought he heard footsteps ahead, so he pressed on, and coming back toward him, was…*himself.*

A shadow version, confirmed by appearance alone, and he wondered at the magic of this place, so unlike that of his wife.

"Well, fancy meeting you here," it said, hunching slightly beneath the stone vault. "Tight quarters, this." It carried a machete, identical to Ambakisye's own, in a preserved left hand, identical to the one he had lost.

"Here, we present our best selves," it explained. Then it made a bit of a lewd gesture with its other hand, adding, "All of it. You. Whole and fully functional."

"Parts is parts," Ambakisye said, and made his tone as indifferent as he could, proud that he could turn away the sting of it, after all this time was above such insults. "I don't let an arm, a hand, or anything else define me. You, if you are even a *you*, are not the man I was when I had them, working or otherwise. It's what we lose, what we are forced to adapt to, that makes us our best selves."

This was not the response the demon expected, and now he saw that flash of deadness in its eyes, the eyes of the goatherder, the dark dead gaze of the serpents.

"Perhaps. What a surprise you are," It spoke, and Ambakisye could see it was deciding how to proceed, so he remained wary.

"Why doesn't the nightingale sing any longer?" this creature wondered aloud. "What would happen if your father's demon found your wife? What a profound creature *he* was, possessor of the basest of appetites. She would have been a prize for his menagerie – did you know he used women as he did men? Surprising he could divert himself long enough to father you…" The voice trailed away.

"I'd guess any iteration of that man would have bit off more than he could chew with her," Ambakisye parried, watching the calculations continue, the demon pivoting, trying to find a weakness.

"Oddly you've found me, you, and I don't know how you did it. Vexing," it mused.

And somehow, Ambakisye knew the whole of it. It was Kusini's magic, and Ambakisye knew that his discovery was important. This was the way to the Morningstar. He had found the gate.

And seeing this realization on Ambakisye's face galvanized the demon, and it struck out at him with the machete, connecting, cutting a deep gouge in his flesh. This wound did not bleed, indeed, had little effect, and this, too, made the creature both curious and incredulous.

"I'm already dead, asshole," Ambakisye pointed out reasonably, ducking backward into the passageway, needing to find his connection to Kusini, show her the way through. He held his own weapon at the ready, expecting to be pursued.

"Certainly true, and I should point something out to you," it said, just as calmly now. "This *is* a grave. There are many dead here already, but there is always room for more…" The voice became hiss of satisfaction as it receded from him, and then the weight of the passageway came down on Ambakisye's shoulders, trapping him beneath a crushing force.

Ambakisye staggered under this titanic burden, understanding immediately the implications of his predicament. He was now, like

Atlas, holding up the world. Praying his magic could overcome an elemental force, just for a time. Unable to move, he hoped he could hold the doorway long enough, for if he failed, the way through would be lost forever.

98

MICHAEL ISRAEL CLIMBED DOWN FROM her perch, unable to see anything below her feet, which were at the limit of what her vision could show her, even augmented by her goggles. She was careful and methodical, finding hand and footholds by feel, having to trust what her limbs told her, knowing that she should have reached the bottom, but never seeming to get there.

When she reached a place where her footholds seemed secure, she carefully let go of the wall with her right hand, pushing her NVGs onto her forehead and slapping at the ampoule on her left sleeve to disperse the biomarker that Azuma had prepared. The effect was immediate and impressive, the particles carried on the air currents that crisscrossed through the catacombs, attaching themselves to every solid surface, mapping the structure physically, such that any perceptive shift could not disguise the reality of the passageways.

She watched the bright motes coat the wall of the oubliette, and glanced upward, seeing that much of the entire surface above her was already transformed, as the *Akai* had penetrated the upper reaches and deployed the marker level by level. She looked downward, at those markers that were pulled by gravity, but the currents were impeding their fall, the light particles pushed on the thermals rising from the depths, and the floor of the oubliette was still not revealed to her.

She thought she heard a sound on the other side of the wall, something moving, its passage shaking the stones, so she leaned out from her perch to the limits of her arms, holding on, knowing it would be a complete waste to fall to her death now. She could see that some of the stones were crumbling, and looked more closely at the sharp shards, seeing that the mortar was reinforced with bones, apparently the bones of humans.

A bit of scraping made some of them fall away, clattering against the walls of the pit as they dropped out of sight. She pulled again, worrying away at the opening she had already created, and a larger portion of the wall dropped out, including one of her footholds, and she scrambled to reestablish her balance, choking on the dust from the collapse.

She swung her legs through the opening, once, twice, and then let go of the wall, hoping her momentum would carry her inward rather than just bounce her off the edge and down the hole. She was successful in her bid to gain entry to the space beyond, and she dropped a few feet onto a stone floor, already starting to glow from the particles she had released outside.

"*Soldier.*" Eerie voices whispered around her, announcing her arrival, and then an impossibly strong hand wrapped around her face and jaw, lifting her by her head, slamming her painfully against the wall.

The fingers against her mouth were her easiest target, and she tried to grasp one of them in her teeth, but was unable to unclench her jaw, so great was the pressure.

"No biting, dear sister." That voice. That hateful, beloved voice, both the monster who had stolen her brother and Michael, altogether not quite enough of either for her to trust her feelings.

Michael Israel opened her eyes and looked at it. Renewed in her surprise at its appearance, the face of her twin looking back at her with an expression usually reserved for an insect, or some other annoyance to be crushed utterly underfoot. But the creature before her was inhumanly enlarged, over eight feet tall, which explained its strength, the size of the hand that held her now, like a toy.

Its face came close, the handsome smile somewhat lopsided. She remembered that expression, it had always been a hallmark of Michael's happiness, something endearing to show that he was very pleased with himself. She felt a deep ache in her chest, had to remind herself that this was not him, had never been him.

"Bithiah. I must admit to my disappointment that you couldn't stay with me the last time you visited. I would have welcomed you with open arms. Readied you for this day," It stroked her lips like a lover, then shifted its hand enough to place its mouth over hers; she could feel it savoring her revulsion, so she tried to control her emotional response, not wanting to reward it with this provoked reaction.

"You see, the Prince has arrived. The inevitable will occur; I will keep this body, and you will take another, give Lilith a form with which to walk the earth. You get your brother back, and I discover anew my sister, my new lover. It is promised me. Twins should be lovers, there's a morbid kind of symmetry to it, don't you agree?" Forcas tilted his head, and that sensual mouth curled with a sort of evil glee as it looked down at her. "I understand you've saved yourself."

Michael Israel struggled futilely, trying to kick at it, but it caused her pain, because the weight of her body was putting strain on her neck.

"Don't do that. You'll just separate your head from your spine. And what's the issue, really? You won't be you anymore, Lilith is another mind, another conscience, and when you ascend, we'll be equals. You'll want me as I want you. We shall dine on souls every day until all the little ants are utterly distinguished. We can find diverting uses for them first. They won't be able to resist our charms." Forcas laughed at her predicament.

"I'm going to put you down now," it said. "I've forgiven you for bringing along the *Akai*. Although I suppose they have provided a challenging amusement for my minions, they are really no match for such demons. There's no need to fight. I'm not going to hurt you; we have plans for you. And you can't kill me, you haven't got what it takes. Altogether you're too *human*."

But when it set her on her feet, she pulled the shotgun at her hip up and aimed it. This amused Forcas.

"You cannot hurt me with that primitive weapon," it said, sounding bored.

"More primitive than you think," Michael Israel replied, chambering the rounds and firing, blasting the Death Bringer with the salt loads that she had fashioned herself, using salt from her father's salt cellar, the one that he, the rabbi, repeatedly dipped clean fingers into while cooking. She'd guessed right, it was enough to make the monster before her cringe away and withdraw, shaking in anger, its flesh rent and smoking.

She could tell by its retreat that this would only delay the inevitable, and she despaired of finding a maneuver she could execute on her own that could destroy it. She contemplated the myriad passageways that would lead her deeper into the maze, and set out, hoping the one she had chosen would lead her to a solution she feared did not exist.

W

The way opens before me, where there was no passage, one appears.

The way back, from whence I came, is no longer. I cannot turn back, none may follow. It closes behind me, changing, a living cocoon to enfold me within.

Here, in the deepest part of this temple, a small alcove sustains the divine. The favorite, this place where holy Azazel came to rest. No scent of death here, only self. Humble, this dirt floor, lain over with these velvety wings. Their beauty unmatched, these lovely gifts that I have coveted through the glass.

They rustle as I stretch out upon them, warm, alive, growing into my skin.

Speaking to me. Enfolding me, lifting me, they want to fly.

Here, clarity once more. My thoughts my own again. Not robbed of this flesh, surely not. It will still be-

M

Mine.

99

AMAOKE HAD FOUND AND LOST Weston's scent with each turn within the maze, his frustration wearing him down, despite his knowledge that this place was engineered to divorce any sane creature from its reason. His familiarity with the scents of his friend and the Morningstar complicated his task. They were confoundingly similar now, both scents nearly identical to the scent signature, death, and decay that permeated this shrine. But in his consternation another scent drifted to him, familiar, a friend. Michael Israel, and as Amaoke made his way forward, he finally saw her standing in the corridor ahead of him, outlined by the oddly glowing walls.

"Amaoke," she said, and he could see that she had been crying, which was incongruous with her expression, which was frustrated, and angry. "I need your help."

"Anything," he told her, coming closer, wanting to understand what was making her look so...lost.

Then she punched him, a vicious blow, a surprise, and down in this place, this place that made him raw and stripped bare his aggressions, the violence called the Beast. Despite her modest stature, despite having to extend her reach to connect with his face, she managed to generate significant force. He growled, instinctually, a warning, although he was gratified that he remained in control. He did not understand what she was doing, but before he could puzzle it out further, another blow came, and this time the Beast answered, snapping at her hand, catching it in a bite of quick retaliation, drawing blood.

Again Amaoke resisted further counterattack, reigning in the urge to subdue her. Then he noticed something strange. Although she cradled the hand he had bitten gingerly, shaking the fingers against the pain, her posture was relaxed. She was entirely unconcerned about him and any action he may have been about to undertake. She had abandoned her assault. A small secret smile curved her lips, but did not touch her eyes.

And when she finally looked up at him, the eyes, her eyes, indeed as determined as ever, had changed somehow, and he noted in horror their feral transformation. He could not contain his growl of warning, a reflex summoned in the presence of another predator, and when she answered, with a growl of her own, and he saw her teeth, the new prominence of the canids, his aggression was replaced with misgiving and remorse.

She had manipulated his transformation with her attack, provoked the bite. It was a desperate and dangerous move that he nevertheless had to respect. While a gifted soldier, she was no match for the Death-Bringer, but trained to use every possible advantage in battle. She knew the old myths, and just as Prometheus had stolen fire from the gods, she intended to take his magic and use it. She knew enough of Amaoke's nature to understand that he would never have given it willingly.

His fear for her was immediate, but he saw only satisfaction in those green eyes, which showed no regret or doubt until the change began in earnest, bringing its pain and disorientation, bringing the beginnings of terror, a realization that what she had done might indeed backfire on her, might mean her death. Amaoke had seen such a thing only once before, during his murderous rage when he had simultaneously created and destroyed those dark progeny inadvertently borne of Nanatha's long-ago attack.

This time, the Beast held his ground, and Amaoke promised himself to let her have her chance, and vowed to intervene only in the interest of preserving their larger task. He waited to see if there would be madness in this new creature, for if Michael Israel could not control her beast, he would have to put her down. He knew the cost of a berserker, and it was too great a threat to their existing endeavor; it would too easily succumb to the manipulation of the Morningstar.

What ultimately came forth was a thing of beauty. Her green eyes met his own, and they held nothing more than acknowledgement and gratitude. To Amaoke's surprise, her fur, unlike his own, was dark, almost black. She was heavy, muscular, frightful in her fierce visage – he had weaponized her. He quickly recognized in her the beauty of the timberwolves of the harsh mountain forests of Eastern Europe, likely the origin of her people, and he understood. She was apparently drawing something from his experience and control, because she did not behave as a young wolf might, seemingly confident in this new form, not at all regretful of her shed humanity. And after only a moment's hesitation, she caught the scent of her quarry. With the briefest backward glance, she bade him farewell, and turned to the hunt. Were he in human form, he would have smiled, realizing that she was far too dominant to show the proper deference to him, her Alpha, in her departure. He left her to it, understanding the urgency of her claim, the righteousness of her anger, and her need for retribution.

100

NI DUPLICATED HER EARLIER DESCENT into the *makom*, floating down, coming to rest against the stones in the same place she had before. Her only added motion the activation of the ampoule at her left shoulder, an absentminded act, duty done, her focus turned to a more vital task.

She closed her eyes, duplicating her path of before, in this place that was endlessly changing. It was unable to thwart her now, her movements spare and directed, navigating by memory, faith, love.

An outside observer would have thought it an elaborate dance, her graceful turns, no wasted motion, every ounce of her being leading her, inexorably, back to the place of the Collector's confinement. Following instinct with an intuitive grace that was almost reverent, religious, betraying the fervency of her vocation. A priest, not in name only, but in the singular focus that drove this nameless quest.

When she had moments of doubt, she paused, thinking of his voice, the first time she'd heard it, the last. What he had worn the first time she saw him, and the first time he had seduced her, and in the garden at Yamanote, and every moment in between, until the very last. She played the story of their love, and it led her.

She reached the small room, the chapel of his suffering, and ran gentle fingers over the crimson stain that marked the stones there. Then she turned away, standing where he had stood, so long impaled, suffering. She reached her arms out wide and waited, patient, concentrating, until she felt it, just the slightest change in the air flow.

It was deceptive, this tiny draft, but she knew it came from nearby. She had a sense that Lilith was vindictive, petty, jealous. The demon would have wanted to keep the Collector close, so that she could drink his pain, gloat over her prize, this trophy ensnared.

Ni swayed, moving to one side, and the other, and smiled when she was gratified with another clue. Just behind the wall where they had kept him was a hidden space, the opening illusory, there but not easily discovered. *Ni* found it by moving along the wall until she felt a gap, turning in, folding her fingers around the edge of the opening, letting her body follow.

It wasn't far, this altar, vigil candles burning softly, their light unable to penetrate the bones of the shrine, the limits of the chamber. A recess below a stone shelf, and life. Fluttering, rustling, vigorous, beautiful wings, as long as *Ni*, the velveteen feel of the feathers, their purple hue otherworldly.

Ni perched above them, stretching first one and then the other out, taking her time, removing each feather individually, one by one. Hours passed, days, eternity, eons, the stars changed in their orbits, but she was not to be denied this.

And with each pluck, she spoke, her own little Shakespearian joke, "…he loves me…he loves me not…" On and on, tossing each bit of down aside almost gently, creating something almost beautiful in the dismantling, stripping away every drop of magic they contained.

Sensing, when she had reached the very last one, that she was no longer alone, *Ni* turned her dark gaze upon the other, Lilith, Beelzebul, who had come to a standstill in the space, shaking in rage and horror. And this, too, *Ni* plucked, saying in a satisfied and possessive tone, concluding the ritual. "He. Loves. Me."

The demon, enraged, robbed, at first in doubt that the being that crouched upon the altar with this strange and frightful visage could yet be human.

"You shall never leave this place," it spat its rage at *Ni.* "I will enjoy peeling your skin from your flesh, and I will-"

But it never finished, for *Ni* calmly knocked over one of the candles onto the stripped bones, igniting the phosphor she had placed beneath them, and in the blinding whiteness, the demon saw its nemesis slowly pull something very familiar from its place at her side. Leaping over the unholy fire, *Ni* raised *Hōfuku* over her head, bringing it down and down, as it sang its song of death, cleaving Lilith apart. The demon barely kept its feet, turning, with an expression of disbelief for her attacker.

And *Ni* gathered the creature close, the gesture almost intimate, whispering, "Neither shall you." Her arms tightening with her resolve, she leaned backward, falling, delivering Lilith to the fire, becoming light and heat, the immolation purifying and final.

101

THE SCENT OF THE CREATURE that had stolen her brother sang to her. It was everything. The only thing. And Michael Israel chased it deep, following its call through those passages beneath the ground. But when she arrived at that place where she thought she'd find it, emptiness awaited.

The sputtering flames of the torches hurt her eyes, too bright in the gloom of the rest of this nightmare. But there was a sound here, skittering, furtive, like the scratching of the mouse behind the wall.

No rodent here, a new scent, part of what she had chased, but new. A bird perhaps, but too much for thus. A nest, to be certain. And a discovery there, the lustrous mahogany color of the feathers, dappled with gold and the deepest black at the base of each quill. Mouthwatering.

Of these sacred wings, the bones made a sweet repast for this new wolf, and she crunched down to find there was no marrow, only air, but no disappointment this, in her dismantling frenzy she swallowed their power, her jaws crushing them. Cracking them open one by one, growling and shaking them violently, strewing feathers across the chamber.

The dry scream of the Death Bringer's horror rang in her ears, discovering this righteous destruction, the realization of what it had lost. In two great strides it reached the wolf, lifting her up and up

516 | LJ FARROW

before flinging her against the stones, upsetting one of the torches, which burned the scattered remains, each feather a wispy offering.

Her shriek of pain echoed as she bounced off the wall, coming to rest within the depression in the earth. Bounding up again to answer this attack, even with these injuries that were more than her stolen magic could sustain. And she felt the wolf slide away, returning her to her human form. Forcas, curious, losing stature, losing life along with the magic and the power, wanting to watch the animal die, was surprised to see Michael Israel in its place.

This time, she took the demon's face between her hands, nodding, resting her forehead against the one it had stolen from her brother, finding Michael there, in that other cranium, amongst the ruins. Seeing it understand that it could not keep what it had taken from her, the sacrifice she made perfect, her life for his soul.

Knowing it would never be able to keep this flesh, its immortality lost, she reached for her own weapons that had been shed with her humanity, and felt something firm and true come to rest in her fingers. A strange blade, curved, primitive, almost ceremonial, so old she had no name for it. Begging to be used. So she dispossessed the Death Bringer of the burden of her brother's head, paying in kind for his treatment of Milos.

And they collapsed together onto the stones, Michael Israel's broken body entwining about the fallen angel, freeing her brother from this unwanted prison. The twins, reunited in death, curled about each other as they had in the womb, and it was good.

As the fire came to claim their flesh, she whispered her last words, a prayer to see them to their rest, saying, "*Modeh ani*, I give thanks."

102

KUSINI FOLLOWED AMBAKISYE INTO THE maze, until she was distracted by feelings of dread and distress. She called to Ambakisye to stop, but looked around and realized she was alone. She couldn't be sure it wasn't some trick of the catacombs, so she moved back toward the last place she had thought her husband had been, but even this was hard to find, the landmark she was looking for was gone.

So she led herself by instinct, and came to a turning clearly marked by the bright dust-like marker that Azuma's priests were dispersing. There were screams coming from nearby, of a very different character than those generated by the air moving through the structure, at least it seemed so.

She decided it was best to navigate not by sound alone, but by emotion, and after a few twists and turns, and even one or two blind ends, she came upon *Shi*, his eyes staring, his katana traversing the left side of his neck. Dead.

A battle had occurred here, or near here, because she could see signs of a skirmish in the dust, and dark stains obscured the bioluminescence of the marker in gouts and splatters, presumably the blood of the fallen priest.

The wall directly ahead of her suddenly seemed to fade away, and then Roku and Ku were beside her, both of them surprised and concerned to see her. Roku immediately turned back the way they had come, and said, "They're still coming, and they know how this place will change before we do."

Ku pulled Kusini along with some urgency, with Roku defending them from behind. Kusini looked back and was terrified to see two beings pursuing them, both doppelgangers of Roku and Ku, murderous intent in their eyes.

"Get the Sorceress out!" Roku shouted, and to Kusini's great surprise, Ku picked her up as easily as he would a child. She tried to focus her magic behind them where Roku had just been, but the shifting walls of the *makom* had already closed between them.

Ku ran, following the passageways back, in the direction of the stairwell, turning and turning, not finding the way out. So Kusini held her hands together, saying softly, "*Unravel. Show us the path.*"

Ahead, the turns they needed glowed even brighter and Ku ran on with even more determination. They reached the archway to the stairs, and Ku said, "Forgive me."

He thrust her through the doorway and jumped back from something he saw to his right, and the stones moved again, Ku disappearing from sight, turning already to face another foe, perhaps the incarnation of himself once more. Kusini landed on her feet, but skidded ungracefully out to the landing. She had to put her hands up on the outer wall of the curve to steady herself.

She put her head down, frustrated about the dead and dying Akai, fighting demons who mirrored themselves, angry she had no way to help them. Wondering at how she had gotten so lost in the first place. And where was Ambakisye?

She looked around, trying to get her bearings, and found that Azuma was perched on the steps above, her expression unreadable. Kusini suspected that she knew of the fate of each member of her Crimson Guard. Her sword was sheathed upon her back, and she appeared unconcerned about the odd way that Kusini had appeared there on the landing, but even this may have been an extension of her stoic demeanor.

Then Kusini saw that Azuma was hurting, injured by something terrible, and her stoicism was what she was using to endure, to survive as long as she possibly could, to see their task to its end.

"The Ascendance has begun," Azuma cried, her voice nearly carried away by the gusting winds. "I doubt we can stop it now. I'm going up; I have to make sure this stays contained. I have to employ a more practical solution."

"I have to find Amaoke," Kusini told her. "If anyone could find Weston, it would be him."

"You won't have much time," Azuma replied, leaning forward and shouting to be heard. The many tiny granules of sand swirling up the staircase sliced into their skin, and it was hard to see.

"Don't wait for us; I just know that I must reach him before…" Kusini knew further talk was wasted, so she reached for the other woman, but Azuma took a deliberate step away from her, out of reach.

"I need to block the stairwell," she insisted, fearing Kusini's possible influence on her survival, thinking of Ambakisye. With a slightly more mischievous look, she said, "And if I come back from this death I have earned, I will *haunt* you. There is someone who waits for me in the next life, and I am ready to join her. I was robbed of her love once, and I must keep this promise above all others."

Kusini smiled, and shook her head in amusement. She climbed the stairs anyway, and pulled Azuma into her arms. Her embrace was returned warmly, although she only put one arm about Kusini, the other injured or used to mask an injury. Azuma was not the first to refuse a gift of life. Kusini turned away, but then she hesitated, and looking back over her shoulder she saw the iridescent scales of the Dragon as they rippled across Azuma's form.

The creature hovered a few moments, its movements had a dreadful asymmetry now, acknowledging Kusini, rippling and turning in an irregular, juddering Mobius loop, before spiraling away, up into the unrelenting darkness above.

103

KUSINI TOOK THE STAIRS TWO and three at a time, but they seemed endless, and she was having trouble navigating through the maelstrom. Impatient with her feelings of despair, she kicked her sandals away, allowing her feet contact with the earth, and continued her descent, better able to maneuver over the shifting sand that had drifted unevenly onto the steps.

The catacombs were changing once more, and she reached a wall at the bottom, a wall she knew was still far from the depths of the structure. She sensed something familiar, but could not entirely determine why. She closed her eyes and forced herself to be still, and to think.

Instead of opening her eyes, she kept them tightly closed against the insult of the elements, and climbed back the way she had come, feeling along the inner face of the stairwell for an opening, any opening. But the wall was smooth, curving outward into her palms, betraying no entry.

When again she could distinguish the sighing screams the wind made through the catacombs, it came now from behind her, so she turned to the opposite wall, placing hands on a surface that now curved away, and discovered a doorway. She ignored the disorienting disappointment that came with her knowledge that no passageways had been demonstrated *outside* the stairway in any of the excavation materials.

She sighed, knowing that it was possible the Morningstar wanted her to find this anomaly, and trusting, in her soul, that she was headed in the proper direction. Stepping into the space brought some peace from the storm, and she could open her eyes, but at these depths, or perhaps due to the misdirection, there were no markers, no bioluminescence to show her the path.

"*Reveal*," she whispered, stepping forward, letting her body use the magic to move forward, as blind as before but now able to sense the passageway ahead of her. There were many complicated turns, and dust fell down on her from above, which seemed strange, but she felt the rightness of her passage in her bones. There was an occasional rumbling sound, as though the stones were speaking, as though the *makom* was continuing to shift around her. She was drawn onward for what felt like many hours, until she began to sense she was nearing another opening, because the airflow changed direction, and the arch of the ceiling was getting lower with each step, the passageway constricting. She could feel the coolness of a draft near her feet and it seemed as though the darkness was less impenetrable than before, because she could make out something ahead that was lighter than the shadows around it.

She moved toward this beacon, and before she could make sense of what she was looking at, Ambakisye's voice came to her from somewhere nearby. "I kept it open for you."

But what he said to her made no sense, and he sounded wrong. Weak. Hurt.

"'Kisye! Are you alright?" Kusini rushed forward, wanting only to reach him, and now she could see that the brightness was the outline of his shirt in the gloom.

"Careful, 'Sini-ma," he said. "This doorway is collapsing." He sounded breathless, but repeated what he had said before, "I kept it open for you."

As she came close, and reached the place he had spoken from, she was horrified at what she could make out in the gloom. A small amount of light was coming from beyond a crumbling doorway, and she could see that it had once been a stone archway, the keystone now fallen askew, her husband struggling to hold it up, and a network of cracks was growing around him, particularly several large faults that were reaching dangerously toward the vault of the ceiling above them.

Kisye's eyes glowed red with a dying fire, and she could see he was gasping silently between gritted teeth, clinging to reason by a thread, perhaps only by love, and the determination it was driving in him. His body appeared to have been torn apart, and she could see parts of him were decaying, a ghoulish transformation that her magic had prevented until he had entered this terrible place.

His bones and tendons were showing through his skin, which now hung in tatters from his form like ragged clothing, and his face was scabrous and pockmarked. He looked back at her piteously, and she wondered how long he had been trapped there.

"Let me get you free," she said softly, seeing that he did not have much time left. She was trying to sound calm, but hot tears filled her eyes and choked her voice, betraying her grief. His expression did not change, he knew that she was trying very hard not to betray how terrible he appeared to her, trying to be brave, but he knew what was happening, knew it was time.

"No, love, please don't touch anything. Don't do anything. It is already done, it's coming down. Something told me, a premonition, but I knew I had to keep this doorway open for you, knew you would need to get through, in the end," he told her, struggling as the breath whistled in and out of him.

"So I held on, it seems it has been years I have been here, but now I'm tired, I can't seem to find my strength. You have to get to him, get to it. Help Amaoke. You must," he insisted, but he had no wind to put behind his words.

Kusini was crying openly now, tears streaming down her face. "I don't want to leave you here, I don't want it to be over," she sobbed.

"*Mpenzi*, you must," he repeated. "You taught me to believe in our love. It was all I had to build upon when I thought I had nothing. What we are, what we have, can never end. I *will* see you on the other side…" His voice trailed off a bit, but she could feel he was still with her.

Kusini held his face and kissed him through her tears, squeezing past him gently, going on, turning back just as she made it through to the passageway beyond, but the weight of the structure could no longer hold. Its supports were gone, and Ambakisye gave up the fight, never taking his eyes from hers.

"Go," he whispered once more, and then he was gone, disappearing beneath the shifting stones, and she was more alone than she had ever been. She felt it all sliding away after him, her will, her fear, her animus, but she had one last task to complete if she could make it in time. Kusini did not want Ambakisye's sacrifice to be for naught, so she turned away from the place of his entombment and went in search of her brothers, fearing that she would be the only one who could strike any balance between them.

104

The Dragon flew ever upward, her destination the top of the steps, on and on, endlessly it seemed, until she reached the final landing before the surface. Swirling sand obscured her from seeing the stars, but it was of little importance. The stars need not bear witness to her actions.

She shed her scales impatiently, waiting only until she regained her voice, and opened the commlink to her pilot. "Ko, what's your status?"

"Holding. Two-mile pattern, await instructions for final flight plan. I am currently sixteen kilometers due east of your location. ETA less than two minutes, slightly more to impact."

"Execute *Fujin's Wrath*," Azuma replied. "Authorization code echo-zebra-alpha-kilo-india-mike-alpha-kilo."

"We are confirmed. Switching off comms and going dark. It has been my pleasure to serve you, *Himura-san*." Azuma heard the bark of static as he switched off, not giving her a window to order him to punch out. Ko wanted complete assurance that her instructions, and his mission, were carried out to the letter.

She watched, but the sky remained obscured by the sandstorm above the opening of the oubliette, and finally heard, rather than saw, the plane, engines screaming in the dive, and she knew it was over, that sound the sound of the ending as Azuma had planned it. So she climbed up out of the depression created where the steps met the surface. She floated across the lip of the opening, and dove headfirst into the pit, calling the fading Dragon back to her as she spiraled downward, a sparkling guardian ensuring no escape, ahead of the Armageddon she had called down upon them all.

105

AMAOKE FOLLOWED HIS NOSE, TRYING not to let the sounds that came from the catacombs, nor his revived memories of his time here in the pit, distract him from the scent he had picked up once more, for the hundredth, perhaps the thousandth, or even the hundred-thousandth time. Subtle but clear among the many other fetid odors here, it was like a marked path to his quarry.

Down and down and down he climbed, the bottom seeming to recede further with each step he took. He reached a blind ending, and in his anger pounded the earthen wall to no avail. His senses told him the barrier was false, he could smell the space beyond, but not reach it, and he realized the place was indeed changing, moment by moment, a living tomb. It was what he recalled from his nightmares.

Something enormous was moving beyond the stones, moving with renewed purpose, its footfalls shook the earth. The Morningstar.

"Weston?" Amaoke spoke softly, placing his forehead against the wall.

The thing was silent. It stopped, and he heard stones and dirt falling on the other side of the wall. A tentative scratching. He suddenly got a sense of his friend, a chaotic flurry of thoughts, confusion and fear, and an attempt to communicate, and it was, for the briefest moment, Weston. And then, a voice from the blackest depths of the world, the voice of death, chilling Amaoke to his bones.

"Come, friend, walk at my side. We will be as we have been, with time enough to do the many things we have missed."

No lie in this. And suddenly, Amaoke could see it, a vision, of the two of them, not a bloody scene of destruction, rather a quiet office, steel and glass. Two men in suits. Weston, now free of the burden of spectacles, no awkwardness, all pragmatic power, his hair trimmed and neat, overlooking a world much like the one they had left behind, but now in a seat of great influence.

Amaoke standing nearby, surveying that world through the high windows, his Western style jacket and expensive cowboy boots comfortable, his own hair tamed, braided and beaded. He felt important, felt powerful, felt connected to Weston in his bones. Could feel the knowledge that he was in the right place, doing the right thing, settle over him like a mantle. It didn't have to be a nightmare; it could be a kind of peace.

But the men in the suits were too comfortable, and too self-assured, and those things came at a price. The Wolf inside recognized the collar, recognized the veneer of respectability over the subjugation of humanity. Amaoke looked down at his hand. In the vision, he held a shiny red apple, ripe, round, perfect, begging to be eaten.

He passed it to his other hand, turning it over, seeing the rot that had been hidden, its wormy decay removing the veil, the hairy claws that held it stained with the blood of the pureflesh. He could taste their suffering on his tongue, and he remembered it. He knew he could be manipulated to enjoy it. The beautiful lie that hid an ugly truth, a parable he had discussed with his friend once.

"You made me promise not to let this happen. Face me, and I will remind you about love," he promised, appealing to the lost priest, Weston, the man he knew was still part of the thing on the other side.

Amaoke could feel it considering, delaying for several moments before resuming those ponderous steps away from where he stood, toward the center of the shrine, toward the pit. He heard rustling, too, the fluttering of functional wings, and the sound filled him with terror. It could only mean the Monster was made flesh, was now in occupation of the body it had engineered in Weston, preparing to leave the Place of the Fallen.

106

Amaoke also knew the Morningstar would find a way out, and suspected it needed the sheer space in the oubliette to escape. It would use the pit, and somehow it had access to the central shaft. He could not reach it from here, but he prayed he could find his way through one of the upper galleries of the maze, and he turned, calling the Beast and leaping up in a frenzied rush, clearing a half-dozen steps at a time in this, his most powerful form.

At a landing several hundred meters from the bottom of the stairwell, he crashed through a darkened doorway, following that scent that called to him now, like a bright beacon that led him through the labyrinth, which was crumbling around him as its occupants were trying to escape ahead of their master. There were no glowing motes of science and magic to delineate the pathway here.

He was unmindful of the disembodied forms that reached for him, as if they could hold him. He smelled their fear, felt them withdrawing, sliding over and around him to avoid him, chanting about the *beast*. Their prophecy precluded their interference with him, as he was the master's familiar, and something about their mad scrambling to avoid him gave him a path.

After what felt like several agonizing minutes where he worried he would be trapped down there forever, like a raging minotaur with no corridor for escape, he felt stronger currents flowing over him. These were not spirit disturbances, rather, this was the movement of the air from an opening to the outside.

He reached an archway that opened onto the void of the pit and looked down into darkness. He could see nothing. Above him, a noise, like the angry buzz of the hornet, which crescendoed to a scream, the machine whine of a huge engine, straining, not faltering, and he looked up, hardly able to believe what he was seeing, but the impact was indescribable.

Above him a terrible sound, and a brightness, too bright to be the bloom of sunrise. And into this false dawn, from the depths below, a countercurrent, air pushed ahead of the silence. Amaoke saw, rather than heard, the dark wings opening and closing below him, coming fast.

He leapt from the edge, falling away into nothingness, letting his mass carry him farther and faster, falling, falling, not nearly as fast as if he had begun his descent from the lofty heavens, but with a terrible weighty purpose, unmindful of his own fragility.

He collided with the Morningstar awkwardly, the Beast's claws catching its upper back, and Amaoke heard the horrid thundering crack of the broken wing beneath his weight, like the sound of a tree felled by a storm. His momentum bounced him away, against the wall of the pit, where he ricocheted, stretching out desperately in that moment of inertia before the plunge and shackling the Monster's ankle in one desperate claw.

The Morningstar screamed in rage and pain, trying to shed the Beast's weight as it worked to stay aloft on one wing. It struggled mightily as the pit began to fill with smoke, and fiery globs of flaming jet fuel hammered down on them like falling stars, searing holes in everything it touched, rendering the Monster's wings useless, the Wolf and the Demon burning as they plummeted to the bottom of the pit.

Amaoke arrived first, the impact as terrible as he remembered, everything not broken on landing subsequently destroyed with the Morningstar's arrested descent. The weight of

Weston's titanic body drove them both into the quagmire at the bottom, impaling the Beast on the bones of the unfortunates who had died there, some of them at his hands.

Amaoke could hold on to the Beast no longer, and he felt its departure, the form receding from him, leaving him rent. He could see one of his collarbones jutting up through the skin, smell his own blood. His legs were useless, his lower spine was in pieces. He watched with horror and amazement as the Monster pushed itself up, and Amaoke realized it was even larger than before, perhaps nine feet tall. The broken wing was askew, hanging uselessly at its side. It looked upon Amaoke with a furious, pitying expression, unmindful of the inferno above them. The fire had not yet reached the lowest levels of the pit, might not reach it for some time.

"Be reasonable, my friend. The others cannot survive the outcome of their plans, nor will you unless you accept your place in my service, take up position at my side. Feast at the table of my destruction and you shall have power like you have never known."

The Morningstar reached for Amaoke, bending down and offering its hand. Amaoke closed his eyes, knowing that if he took that hand in friendship, it would become easier and easier to look the other way. Knew that easy was the first step toward damnation.

The uninjured wing dangled, its tip brushing Amaoke's flank. Using whatever strength he could call upon, and paying with his own renewed agony, grunting in anger and frustration, he pulled the Monster down to him by taking hold of that wing, knowing it was somehow the key to the Morningstar's renewal, important to its power. The two of them struggled, Amaoke sure to lose, and when the Morningstar had him pinned beneath its weight, it spoke to him with Weston's voice, a final mockery of their friendship.

"You're dying, Brother. Only I can save you now," it said, bending that handsome face down within inches of Amaoke's, and driving its long sharp fingernails deep into his chest.

Amaoke managed to laugh between gritted teeth, and the blood he coughed up with his defiance spattered the Monster's face. He saw the flames as they broke through the lower levels of the structure, the swirling colors of the fiery cloud were lovely, and thought he glimpsed the Dragon, there and gone, devoured by fire, her iridescent sky-blue scales falling like rain, catching the flames like a million tiny mirrors, and he watched them a few moments while he marshaled the last of his strength.

Reaching up, ever so gently, as though he were to embrace his old friend, he grasped the joint of the unbroken wing and snapped it decisively with his uninjured arm, calling on the Beast's strength if not its form, ignoring the Morningstar's howls of pain and rage.

"Funny thing about nature," Amaoke gasped out, only able to generate a harsh whisper. "Wings are an incredible adaptation, obviously a gift of the great spirits. But delicate. One of the only limbs that cannot heal. And unfortunately, one of the most obvious tells, a gift to any predator looking for weakness. A liability. Weston didn't want them. You needed him to get them back, but I won't let you use them anymore. And now you cannot fly away."

The Morningstar rose up over Amaoke, and lifted one great foot, placing it almost gently against Amaoke's forehead, ready to crush his skull. Just before Amaoke closed his eyes, ready for the end, he saw movement in his peripheral vision, and he tried to focus on it, a bright, swirling beacon in the smoke.

He watched Kusini's bare feet come close, and she said one word, a word he did not understand, and the air expanded uncomfortably. Her toes curled against his upper arm, making contact, and she brought her hands together; he could see her thumbs crossed, the shadow of her fingers outlined by the rain of embers coming down around them, and then he was pushed even deeper into the muck at the bottom of the pit, forced downward by a silent explosion that threw everything outward from the point of her magic.

The Morningstar was flung against the far wall of the oubliette and its body bounced upward and away, into the fiery void, its inhuman howls echoing and receding, and burning feathers dropped down on the Sorceress, where she kneeled over Amaoke. He looked up at her face, streaked with soot, watching the blood as it trickled from her own nose and mouth, knowing she had pushed everything she had out of herself, the entire well of her power, leaving nothing to chance, leaving nothing to survive upon.

Her eyes were kind as her body slumped against his, and he didn't even mind the pain it caused. The fire was upon them; indeed her hair was burning, her abaya flecked with sparks, her shoulders starting to blister from the heat. He could feel his own skin retracting, searing as he died. Kusini's head settled in the hollow of his shoulder, and she whispered her own dying word, a word he recognized, in his ear.

"Live."

All his pain and fear fell away, and he succumbed to the peace of oblivion.

107

AMAOKE AWOKE TO BIRDSONG, AND sunlight, yet these were the only familiar things he recognized. He was on a comfortable bed, and for several long moments he held still, deciding, as he had often had to before, whether he was yet in the grip of a dream.

His faculties returned slowly, and he shed sleep more reluctantly than usual, gingerly sitting up and taking note of his surroundings. The hut. The Sorceress had returned him to the hut.

And he recalled those last moments with her, wondering if she had thought he would forget, and in returning him to this place he would remember. He doubted he would ever forgive her this betrayal. It was a reminder so unnecessary, and so cruel, that for a moment he considered finishing the work of ending his life on his own.

For he remembered all of it, the Fallen, the catacombs, the battle, the end, and the memories drove him back down onto the bed. His anguish like a weight on his chest, the grief like a wall of pain, and he succumbed to raw emotion. His sobs were physical insults, and they did not release him gently, indeed, his body spasmed involuntarily for some while after the tears were spent.

It was remembering what he did not care to remember, and being alive to the knowledge that the others were all gone. The silence of his heart, the barren expanse of his soul, knowing that the world was a void entire, in which he would never see their faces again, or hear the voices of the ones who had understood that world in the same way he had. Anger, at being left behind, robbed of a finality, a stolen peace he had hoped to find in the crossover, the blissful rest of a good death.

It took some time for him to recognize that he had lost more than a fate he felt was deserved. There was another voice that he could no longer account for, no matter how he searched for it. Wolf had left him, and for the first time in over a thousand years, he was completely, utterly, alone.

108

HE WANDERED OUT OF THE hut into an eerie quiet. Goats and chickens were gone, had been moved to the plantation as a precaution. Or something more, as they had all been so certain that there was no turning back from the Place of the Fallen, no probability that Kusini and Ambakisye would return to their life here, and that reminder drove him once more to his knees.
He cried out in anger and despair, but the sky did not answer him.

He went back inside to escape the oppression of the heat, and noticed his clothing laid out there. He could not remember, but perhaps it had been there, on the chair, when he had awakened. Even his work boots, which he had assumed ruined and lost in the catacombs during his transformation, placed by the chair, dusty and dry from his recent travels. His pants, still marked by the red dust of this beautiful and forsaken place, and his knapsack with his few belongings, including his passport and wallet.

He turned his back on it all, curling up into a ball on the bed, and cried himself back to sleep.

He slept the night through and awakened again, in much the same state as the day before, unsure of his surroundings, and then remembering anew. Whether he was better for sleep or the slow process of acceptance, he did not know, but he found the strength to get dressed, and settled his knapsack on his shoulders. He borrowed a light-colored scarf from one of the pegs on the door and set out up the hill to the turnabout, following it down to the post road, where he looked outward to the distant mountain. He turned east and resigned himself to the long walk.

He kept to the road, stopping to drink from the Nalgene bottle in his pack, smiling when he discovered dried fruit and jerky carefully packed for him. He appreciated, and would miss these gifts, Kusini's small magics. The double handful of coffee beans was probably Ambakisye's contribution, or perhaps Mwana'jua's. He chewed one or two of them dutifully every now and then to keep his energy up.

He made it to Arusha, having strangely met no other travelers on the road, and when he arrived there, it was like stepping out of a dream and back into reality. People went about their business and it both saddened and angered him that they had no idea the sacrifice that had been made on their behalf. The damned and the pureflesh alike, unmindful, and it seemed to him uncaring. The anger was new, and he could not recognize that the problem of it was his.

He had no difficulty hiring passage to Dodoma, where he was surprised to discover that transportation had been arranged for him. When attempting to book flights home, he was directed back to the private airstrip where they had first arrived. An attendant asked him about his travel plans, but he was confused until she told him that the Vatican had made arrangements for any eventual return. When he protested he would not be going back to Rome, she explained that he misunderstood. Her instructions were to arrange his travel to the destination of his choice, no questions asked.

When it came time to pay, this too was waved off. "It's all taken care of, Mr. Severnoj," the attendant told him with a warm smile.

BBC World News

...and in other news, the BBC has learned that Azuma Himura, the controversial CEO of Rising Sun Industries, is missing, along with several members of her inner circle and her security detail. We have learned that the group recently left Japan on a private flight and apparently never arrived at their destination...

Japan Today Lifestyle

...but perhaps Ms. Himura has taken her money, and diverted to some tourist destination in Fiji for some well-deserved R&R, and she is sitting on a beach somewhere bikini-gazing as we speak...

CNN

...it was discovered that all of the servers containing research and development, military applications, and proprietary methodology, as well as the archives of past projects have been erased...sources close to the investigation suspect Russian or Chinese interference, or similar breaches in a large-scale corporate espionage attempt...it appears that no data was recoverable, and it is unknown whether an outside attempt to gain access triggered the data dump as a security measure...this is an immeasurable loss to the fields of Genetics and Bioengineering...no further information has been forthcoming regarding the whereabouts of Dr. Himura and her associates...in light of these developments, the Japanese government has expressed concern that she and her security team may have met with foul play...

BBC World News

...Rising Sun Industries was entered into receivership today...Dr. Himura's estate planning apparently called for liquidation of all assets, with proceeds earmarked for a number of scientific and humanitarian charitable efforts...the exact benefactors remain unknown, as the executors have successfully argued to keep the details of her will sealed...

Newswire

...In Iraq, the mysterious fireball in the desert outside of Tikrit continues to confound investigators. Iraqi leadership remain quiet about speculation as to

the cause of the explosion, with politicians in Iran and Afghanistan pointing to Western interference or an attempt to hide unlawful activity in the Middle East.

There have been vague reports of Israeli involvement following the apparent loss of a scientific team at an undisclosed archeological dig near the site of the incident. Satellite imagery from the time of the event is inconclusive, contractors citing unspecified malfunctions of image capture at the time of the explosion, but note a strange flicker of phosphorescence at that location just prior to the alleged equipment failure.

International recovery teams have been assembled to investigate, but early findings suggested higher than expected levels of radiation at ground zero, and experts are suggesting that this contamination will confound efforts to get any answers. It may be several years before it is safe to investigate fully…

109

HEAVY PREDAWN MISTS SHROUDED THE mountain, a cold breeze not strong enough to lift them from where they had encamped in the valley nevertheless moved them, making them dance a bit like restless ghosts.

Ichimonji Yuma snuffed the lamps at the *Wasureta Mono*, the Forgotten Gate of the Shrine of the Dragon Sect, in anticipation of the dawn. As she stood beneath the massive Shinto arch that marked the entrance of a place talked about in legend but not known to mortals, she heard a disturbance in the heavy vegetation on the side of the mountain below.

She had spent nearly one hundred years in residence here, so long that she did not remember her own name, did not know that she had been stolen away as an infant, thought to be lost to the *yokai*, but rather taken up in ceremony. Every time the Dragon Goddess required another faithful priest from the sect, twelve more initiates were found, unfortunates trained in sorcery, martial strategy, and the blood arts. Trained for one purpose: if chosen, they would be elevated and assume the role of the *Akai Hogo-sha*, and become members of the Crimson Guard responsible for sustaining and protecting the Dragon.

When the mendicant appeared on the footpath created by the creatures that inhabited the forest, she bowed, taught to expect these mishaps, and placed her hands behind her back, settling one on the handle of the *usugurai* hidden there in the folds of her robe.

When she made eye contact with the supplicant, she was surprised to see its shiny orbs, and she dropped to her knees, whispering, "Akenomyosei-san, *watashi no Shujin.*"

The Great Dragon merely took down its hood, revealing dark hair that moved independently of the morning breeze, and the face of a handsome young man of indeterminate provenance but indescribable beauty. Its attractive features were fixed in what appeared to be distress, and she could see that it was burned, and moved as though in some pain. "What is your name?" it asked her, its voice the voice of many, inside of her, and around her.

"I am *ushinawareta shisai,*" she replied as she had been taught, telling it that she was merely one of the lost priests of the Dragon Sect. "I have no name. I am no one. I serve at the pleasure of my master."

Akenomyosei nodded, and appeared pleased. She had been trained well, programmed to obey. She was also attractive. "I would enter the shrine at the Dawn Gate. This requires a sacrifice."

"Then it is provident that I am here, *Shujin.*" She produced her sword swiftly and silently sliced into her forearm, presenting it in offering. She made no noise as her blood flowed down over her closed fist and onto the ground at the Monster's feet.

"Your willingness is merely an invitation," it reminded her. "Passage requires something more. It requires your suffering."

"Take of me what you will, and I shall be fulfilled."

Akenomyosei smiled a terrible smile. He preferred this version of obeisance to the bastardy that Azuma had allowed in her guard. So suffer she did, and the Monster's hurts were much relieved by the time it had gained entrance to the secret shrine, its appetite whetted for more of what it required for restoration.

110

LISBON. Toronto. On to Anchorage. A private flight to Bethel, where Amaoke laid in provisions. River ice breakup on the Kuskokwim was still some weeks away. He rode upriver by snowmobile with some hunters, who dropped him at Kwethluk, and he went on from there on foot.

The days were getting longer and warmer, and the smell of meltwater pervaded the forests, but the weather was still harsh and unpredictable, and the wind out of the Kilbucks was as icy as the deep winter. Calendar spring would mean nothing here for another month, perhaps two.

The whalebone hunting lodge in the clearing on his land had weathered the past half century well. Understandably, it needed some repairs, but it would provide adequate shelter for the early days of spring, until the weather was warm enough to decide how to proceed. He considered building something more substantial than this sod house, but had to consider how to get it started and finished while the days were long.

His dreams were as vivid as ever, the wolf was hunting, its howls echoed off the mountain as it ran down through the trees, chasing a dark and nameless quarry. And Amaoke would awaken, but the wolf had departed, leaving him trying to remember something he had once known, once understood.

Weeks passed, and one day he woke to the thundering sounds of the river awakening, a reminder of spring, and renewal. The animals were on the move, finding mates, starting over. The cycle was beginning, and he would be able to start building in earnest. But it was not to be. He felt it in his soul, in the frigid darkness of his heart, the part that still felt something was as yet undone, felt he was yet unfinished.

He went for a walk in the woods and found himself in a familiar place. The cave was abandoned, had been empty of any winter inhabitant, quiet and cold at the entrance. He turned away, not having a reason to step inside, when the sharp caw of a raven scolded him from a nearby tree. He apologized to it, assuming he had interrupted its hunting, and started down the hill toward the water.

But it continued its exhortations, and its cries were strangely syncopated, almost in the rhythm of human speech. He stopped to listen, and when he looked up, the bird fluttered from the tree it was in to one nearer to him, alighting on a branch just out of his reach, where it studied him intently, those dark eyes shining in its bobbing head. It was much larger than average, and he was superstitious.

As if reading his mind, it screamed down at him from its perch, and flapped its wings vigorously. Air rushed over his face, and he knew. It was directing him, back to the cave. It kept up the racket until he complied, retreating back up the hill, and it followed, this time landing on the ground near the entrance to his old den. It was quiet, watching him intently, nodding as if he finally understood what was necessary.

What he found threatened to break him. The stone shelf now an altar, holding ulu, and spear, samurai sword, and cross. Arranged in a line, an offering. A reminder.

"No, no more," Amaoke sobbed, sinking to his knees. "I cannot."

He heard the crunch of footsteps at the entrance to the cave, and a shadow fell across him. A warm hand placed gently but inexorably on his shoulder. Peace enveloped him as power washed over him, Raven making itself known. The smell of warm feathers and wild celery smoke surrounded his Creator.

My son, you must. You are elder, wolf, shaman. You are the Noatak of legend. You are the Destroyer and the Protector.

"The Wolf has gone," he protested. "I do not know where to look for him."

He waits for you to strike the balance and accept that you are a god. You fear you serve the Other, but you have ever been imbued with my will, my promise, my purpose. This is no secret.

"I am afraid. It – he – is my friend."

And as you love Weston you must save him from himself. He is and is not the Morningstar. Only you can lift from him a fate he never wanted. You are the key to unlock his prison and free his soul. It is not only my gifts that compel you. You gave your word. No being who loves is ever alone; reach for me and you shall find me, for I am the miracle that lives within you.

111

THE CREATURE THAT CLIMBED UP into their forest was not of the pureflesh. It seemed unmindful of the night demons that swarmed to it, curious. It looked human but smelled of something not unlike the trees, not unlike the beasts of the forests.

A *yokai* in its own right, dressed like a man in flannel and denim. The relentless mountain breeze lifted its long hair, endlessly it flowed and danced, pointing toward the valley that curled away from the peaks. It carried an axe.

It knew of the secret shrine, of Akenomyosei's lost priests, hidden there on the face of the ridge, but never approached it, instead pacing out a perimeter some distance from its walls. Not disturbing the impenetrable gates, merely content to study them.

At night, it climbed up into the trees and slept, unmolested by the spirits that haunted the forests. Perhaps these wraiths did not mind it, or more likely, did not even notice it there. Perhaps they recognized in it the potential for balance, and renewal.

By day, the axe rang out, methodically clearing four great corridors between the trees, ash along the north, pine to the south, bamboo to the west, ornamental yew to the east. The timbers piled up against the inner faces of the clearings, those trees notched to lean inward.

It built a sort of cairn, choosing the twelve stones carefully, finding ones with special colors or qualities to build this primitive tribute. Then it brought fire, controlled and methodical, burning some sweet-smelling herb that did not come from those mountains.

Dancing and singing in a language as old as time, a language only that creature knew. Its magic elemental, the fire razed these corridors down to scorched earth, sparing the forest without, trapping the trees and shrine within. Each time its foot touched the ground a new prayer was born, trapping priests within, the others, elemental *kami*, without.

Had those hermit priests decided sooner to challenge the outsider, this shaman who dared approach their sacred home, it cannot be known what outcome. Their arrogance in deeming the creature insignificant in the shadow of their mountain sealed their fate.

The creature withdrew, taking its herbs, its axe, and its magic away. The dark earth it left behind grew no new growth, even rapid-growing bamboo shoots did not pierce the blackened soil.

A southerly wind brought a storm with no rain, the pressure building in an angry sky. Heat lightning arced down from the peaks, finding tinder, birthing a supernatural fire that consumed the last refuge of the Great Two-Headed Dragon and all of its remaining priests. The forest and mountain were spared by the shaman's prayers and his sacred firebreak.

When the rains finally came, too late to spare the shrine and its occupants, bamboo that sprouted from new soil reached once more for the heavens.

M

He has destroyed my last place of refuge, the first sure sign that he is still on the hunt.

It appears we have unfinished business, he and I, and perhaps we must spill one another's blood to resolve our differences.

I will, of course, offer him another chance to take his place at my right hand, to become the Destroyer I intended. He is an improvement on Forcas in so many unsubtle ways, a suitable replacement surely.

Death-Bringer.

I need not be particular about how such things are accomplished; I merely need to ensure that they are. Amaoke has certainly proven he has a talent for it, can easily be reminded of his taste for it.

This time, the collar I fashion for him will be permanent, ensuring suffering, engendering rage. He will pay for what he has taken from me whether he swears his fealty or not.

112

THE FIGURE SITTING QUIETLY ON the bed could have easily been mistaken for a child. The impossibly appealing features, creamy skin, sooty lashes on rosy cheeks, a cupid's bow mouth. The only blemish a slight wrinkling of the small patch of skin between the brows, the eyes moving beneath the lids, engrossed in a book.

A fairytale princess in an enchanted story, awaiting her prince. The fact that her surroundings were the cramped quarters of a Garden District carriage house in New Orleans was of little import. She was protected by a guardian more powerful than either of them knew.

For the prince she awaited was no longer the valiant, handsome hero he had once been; it was now the Dark Prince of prophecy. And the Beast that watched over her knew that it would come to claim its Bride.

And come it did, one evening in late spring, whistling up the walk. The faded denim, and a broadcloth shirt with blue stripes, the Converse sneakers on its feet familiar. No spectacles, no need, not thinking of the incongruity it presented now, this man with a child's face, the cherub still. Normalcy its new illusion, the brown eyes as warm as ever before, calm and sure of itself.

The patio door slid quietly, but there was no need for stealth, for its chosen knew it came. Came with the intentions of a lover, no longer accompanied by an evil host, invested as it was in its stolen flesh, apparently none the worse for wear having been robbed of the inherited wings. The dead travel fast.

But its first and best general awaited it, and having tasted of its flesh had grown hungry for more. The Beast rested among the shadows in the room, waiting for a moment it would recognize.

"I've missed you," the Morningstar said, coming to sit near her, and when she saw him she was more than a little sad, for this was not the Beloved she had chosen, despite the kind illusion he was trying to provide.

There was something about it that was too guarded and diminished, and it seemed unwell for all that it intended to put forth an appearance of health. Simulacra had never suited Weston, he would never have pretended with her. It was too close to a lie.

Carter was unsure what the Morningstar expected her to say, so she said nothing.

It leaned over, looking at her book as if it were interested, surprised to find it was not a novel, as it had first guessed, but the New American Bible. Proverbs.

"I prefer Psalms," it said. "But Proverbs is a close second."

"Weston loved Isaiah best," Carter replied, not to injure, but to remind it that she loved another. She didn't even think it needed her to love, didn't think it could care whether she did or not.

"I want you to be happy," it lied.

"That was Weston's truth, too," she said, sighing. "I can't pretend to love you."

"I think, in time, you'll get used to me. I'm still him," it said gently. "It doesn't have to be unpleasant."

"It has already been too unpleasant. *From the fruit of his words a man eats good things, but the treacherous one craves violence.* Wisdom for myself among my beloved Proverbs. Weston would never mark me, he would have no need to return and remind me," she sighed, deliberately provoking it, looking at Weston's beautiful face and knowing she would never get him back was causing her physical pain. To loathe something she once loved above all else broke her heart; to know what Weston had lost burned it to ashes.

It was uncomfortable, her words bothered him, and it was obvious there was something very wrong. It did not deign to reply to her, but the Scripture did not seem to bother it, which frightened her more than any of the rest of it.

"Are you burning incense?" it asked, the nose wrinkling, the voice betraying impatience for the first time.

"I like it, it was something Amaoke had lying around," she said, with a small shrug.

"What is it?"

"I'm not sure – wild celery, I think," she said, watching carefully to see if this would garner a reaction. There seemed no longer to be any division of divine and profane in it, what Weston had given it was protecting it from the sacred in a new way.

"I'm alone now, too," it told her, taking another approach. "I want us to be as we were, I fear that you are the only one that can fully restore me. Perhaps if we can be together, I will be more fully myself. You are promised to me. I can make you happy, like – I mean, I am still him." Repetitious.

"That would mean more if you said, 'I am still me.' To separate yourself from him tells me you never respected him, never loved him," she said, trying to resign herself to what was coming next, not thinking she could stand to be touched. She recalled Weston's promise to her. "Weston promised that I would be only for him, that for us to be together, he would never share me."

"He also told you that in this life, he would not give up the priesthood for you," the Morningstar said. "He rejected you outright. I shall not. Yet still, we must complete the grand design, you are destined to spend your eternity with me. You can make things more pleasant altogether, it need not be a noxious existence you fear, and I can be as you'd like me to be, but you must make the sacrifice. I can show you only him, keeping the other part of myself separate from us." More lies, more deception.

"I thought that you would know what it is to be loved first and best," Carter said, still trying to provoke. "And to lose that love. Surely time has not dimmed that memory. You were the favorite. Weston was that for me. For that, I could be a Bride."

"What do I have to do? What promises shall I make?" it replied.

"Only one thing," she told it, leaning back on the pillows, letting her hair spread out across them. She started to unbutton her blouse, exposing her skin, the smooth expanse between her rounded breasts. She watched its eyes, greed, lust, and nothing. She saw nothing of her Weston.

It leaned over her, ready to kiss her, ready to touch. Close, closer, their eyelashes almost touching. But still she did not offer herself.

And as she had known it would come for her, she also knew it did not realize that the flesh it now possessed with which to penetrate her was a trap entire and perfect, in its desire to consummate this evil union, it barely noticed when she slipped the cross over its head. Or perhaps did not care.

"I just want you to say his name," she said calmly, focusing on the strong forearms, strangely still more Weston than the rest of him. She couldn't take looking in its eyes, understanding that the Morningstar would never look at her the way Weston had. "It should be simple enough, right? After all, it's your name, too."

It opened its mouth to speak, and Carter saw something, just a flicker of something there, and it *was* Weston, but then he was distracted suddenly by something he was battling. Finally, he turned back to her, seeing her for the first time as she was meant to be seen.

And her lips parted slowly, inviting, wanting him, desperately saddened. Their kiss was far too brief, but so sweet that she knew it was Weston, and then he looked at her, that look that was just for her, and he whispered, "I am *not* myself. *Do it now.*"

Then he kissed her once more, holding her close, having seen the glowing eyes of the Beast, Amaoke lurking in the dim recess near what the Morningstar had thought its wedding bed. And the Beast came, as terrible a destroyer as nature could supply, trapping them there together.

New spirits had arrived, the *ayuq* opening the boundary between the living and the dead. Kusini, thrusting her spear down through the Monster's back, down and down, not stopping, impaling Carter with it as well, piercing both hearts on its course through lovers and bed to the floor beneath. Anchoring the holy couple to the earth and departing, the air expanding and then rushing away, like a sacred breath, leaving only the vacuum.

And the Bride had only a smile for her Prince, as it gazed in horror and surprise at the blood that now spattered those perfect lips. Carter reached up, responding to Weston's choking agony as his soul sought freedom from its prison, and made as if to whisper something to her Love, instead, with her dying breath, she drove home the Redeemer, under the ribs, this, too, finding the heart, setting free the soul trapped there.

The Morningstar cried out, a sound that could destroy galaxies, as its Bride became light, a light so astounding that the Beast bore the blindness it caused, and then she was no more, pulling love, pulling Weston behind her.

The Dragon was there, too, among the spirits. Azuma stepped forward, sinuous and insubstantial as smoke, with the sword forged in the mouth of Hell she collected another head, the last, the most important, and the separation of the flesh was complete. And just as quickly as she had appeared, Azuma's spirit dispersed.

The Wolf then did what it was engaged by all of nature to do. It harvested flesh, taking every bit into itself, methodical, savage but determined, swallowing all the darkness it could hold, before it, too, departed with the other spirits, carrying away its grisly meal, crossing to the beyond, taking the Morningstar and its evil out of reach of this world, the Wolf's howl of triumph echoing among the stars.

after

WHEN THE LETTER ARRIVED, SUMMER had taken a firm hold on the city. The heat was oppressive, but oddly, the rise in violent crime that typically accompanied it was absent. So, too, the increased admissions to her hospital service that went hand in hand with such extreme weather. The unassuming envelope had traveled through time to reach her, taking more than a month to arrive. The global stamp was cancelled by a postmark from Africa, Tanzania specifically, and Aleta's hands shook as she examined it because she could see that the handwriting was not Ama's.

She still had the short note he had written her the night he'd left her house after his accident. It was still tucked beneath the magnet in the center of her refrigerator door where he'd put it, where she could see it always.

Yet there was no viable choice other than to open it, and she did so with understandable apprehension.

Aleta,

I have elected to write to you by way of apology, and to provide you with some answers. I suspect as a fellow physician and scientist that there are some questions that are difficult to relinquish without the satisfaction of an explanation.

I originally ignored your request, thinking it routine in nature, unconcerned that the client wished anonymity, for such a desire is not unusual in genetics, especially given the insurance landscape in your country. Many patients do not want publicized results that may demonstrate an anomaly.

The results of the study were astounding; while I will not delve into the particulars of what was discovered, I will acknowledge that you have a special knowledge of the individual in question, and he tells me that you were a terrific counselor to him regarding the pros and cons of the process. His genetic profile was confirmatory of his reality, and I will go so far as to tell you that I have taken steps to ensure that those results are never known, irretrievable, unavailable for further research and/or mischief.

It may also comfort you to know that he was not alone; as you astutely guessed when we met, he and I were somewhat similar in our make-up, and even we two were not uniquely situated. If there is a purpose to all of this, it is simply to provide a means to an end that was not constructed by either of us. When I invaded your home and your privacy, it was to ask for his help; in my usual approach, I thought to leverage what you knew to get him to cooperate. I was wrong in doing so.

The apology out of the way, I wanted to share something interesting with you, should you ever find yourself in a similar predicament in the future. Understand that my reach and influence gave me nearly unlimited access to many things that most people think private and unimpeachable in their security.

I interrogated the financial footprint left by our mutual friend when he made payment for our evaluation of his specimen, and we were able to trace that money to its source. I did it personally and privately, which I hope will give you a clue about the nature of our related origins. I thought you might find the results of my investigation remarkably interesting, if only for your own edification.

Follow the instructions provided here to access my private server. They can only be used once, so take your time and look over the information that is harbored there. I purposely left out your unique password because I must maintain the server's integrity. Only you will know or be able to deduce this password, so I ask you to be deliberate and thoughtful in your attempts. You will only have three, after that, whether you have successfully accessed the data or not, the information will be deconstructed and destroyed. I trust you to keep your own record of what you see there, after you are finished, the server will be decommissioned permanently.

I did not let the subject know of this intrusion, nor did I make him aware of this correspondence.

I am sure you will understand my motivations once you have all the details in hand. It is clear that you represent the best of what he would hope for in a companion, and I am grateful that at least one of us can be remembered in our humanity by the living.

In closing, I will reiterate the advice of the Sorceress, which is simply this: Live the life you are blessed to have.

Warm regards,
Azuma Himura

AMAOKE BALANCED CAREFULLY ON THE crossbeams at the peak of the roof, pleased with his progress. The days were long, thankfully the summer had been warm, and he was on schedule to finish the exterior of the home and get a roof over it before the weather turned cold again.

He was alone once more, in some ways as alone as he had ever been, as in the time after his mother died, before he became aware of his special gifts. But this was not marked by the madness of that time, if yet the grief. His maturity allowed him a perspective hard-won and certainly he could appreciate it. He told himself he was not lonely, and did not spend enough time on reflection to decide whether he believed it.

He was a man, the wolf gone into places he could not yet follow, knowing they would meet again. He had been left with some of his augmented senses, a gift of Raven, an appreciation, something to serve him as he settled out the balance of his life here in his wilderness. Aches and pains were new, stiffness of a morning, but even these he gave thanks for, reminders of this gift of life provided anew.

The sound of the four-wheeler in the distance heralded the arrival of more supplies from Bethel, Harry Goodluck running the delivery out of Tuluksak. Amaoke kept at his task as the engine noise was still some distance off. He dropped off the beam, letting the harness suspend him so that he could secure the timbers properly. It would also make it more expeditious to get down when Harry arrived.

He was concentrating on the work of connecting one of the crosspieces when he heard the vehicle enter the clearing, so he didn't look away from the task. Harry shut the engine off and called a hello. Amaoke waved to acknowledge him. "Up here."

"Slow goin' today with that glass," Harry said.

"I'm just grateful for you," Amaoke said absently. "It's quite a service, these deliveries."

"Bethel sent along another package as well," Harry added, and there was something in his voice that Amaoke hadn't heard before.

"Oh? I don't recall an order besides the first group of windows." Amaoke glanced down toward where he'd last heard Harry's voice below him. The beam was obscuring his view, but he could see Harry's boots, and beside them, a second, smaller pair, on feet belonging to someone who needed aluminum crutches, their tips pressed into the dark soil.

"I think you'll want this," Harry said, sounding pleased with himself. "If it's a mistake, I'll just take it back with me." Amaoke understood just why Harry might want to.

"Down in a second," he said, letting out the rope and lowering himself quickly, his words cut short when he saw her again. Could it be he'd forgotten how unbelievably gorgeous she was?

He unclipped the harness and stepped out of it carefully before walking over to his visitors. Then he just stood there, like an idiot, staring at her. Her hair was pulled up on her head into a little pouf of curls, probably her concession to practicality for the trip. Her boots were perfectly chosen, her jeans seemed to fit well, and she had topped her cream-colored shirt with light flannel in off-white and cranberry. It was scary how she seemed to belong out here as seamlessly as she had in the city.

The wind had coaxed roses from her cheeks, and the sun had bronzed her a bit. She looked every bit the goddess in his wilderness, even more lovely than memory.

"*Well*," Harry cleared his throat. "I guess we should get this glass unloaded, eh? Before we run out of light?"

Aleta and Amaoke both turned to look at him as though they had forgotten he was there.

"Oh, boy," Harry muttered, shaking his head and smiling. He'd seen it before.

Amaoke remembered himself, and he and Harry spent the next hour and a half setting windows. Aleta fed them caribou jerky and boiled eggs from her backpack, and found some horseradish cheese and apples as well. She had a second thermos with honey-lavender lemonade that Harry tried and loved, so Amaoke left him to it.

When it was time for Harry to go, he said to Aleta, "You're sure you'll be okay with this one?" He jerked his head in Amaoke's direction. "You can change your mind, you know. Not every man is blessed with good looks like mine."

She surprised him by kissing his cheek. "Harry, you're a prince among men." He flushed and was completely undone.

"I've never known him to be without words," Amaoke said, trying to keep a straight face and failing.

Harry looked around the makeshift camp one more time and then back at the two of them. "You got a place for her to sleep?" he asked, looking sternly at Amaoke.

Amaoke just smiled inscrutably. "I'm sure I'll find one."

"Alright then, I'll be back next week with more glass and supplies," Harry said, starting up the four-wheeler and making a wide turn in the yard to pull the trailer out behind him. He waved and was gone into the trees.

Aleta was looking around, at the forest, across the meadow, out over the river. She glanced toward the mountains in the distance. "It's beautiful here," she sighed.

"How about a walk?" he suggested. "This is where I grew up. I once lived on this spot with my mother."

"This is your wilderness," she said, and he was glad she remembered. "Where your heart lives. It's fitting."

As they crossed the meadow toward the pines, she said, "You're getting grey hair."
She reached out and ran her fingers through the strands that flowed over his shoulder.

"Am I?" He looked at her questioningly. "I didn't know. No mirrors out here."

"Ama, it's so lovely. It's right," she smiled, giving him an unambiguous look of admiration. "It's distinguished. Makes you even more beautiful."

He could feel the heat in his face after she said it. "I'm pretty sure the forest knows beauty has arrived, now that you're here. Being outdoors seems to suit you." He stopped walking. "But I don't understand why you're here."

"Don't you? I just figured we had some things to discuss, considering I am the beneficiary of a five-million-dollar trust fund," she told him, with only a hint of a challenge in her tone. She sounded mostly amused.

"How did you-? Mmmm. Azuma, of course, meddling from beyond," he answered his own question.

"She was something," Aleta agreed, frowning slightly because he was confirming what she had feared of all of them.

"You could do a lot with that money," he replied, walking again, knowing she wouldn't spend it on herself.

He had almost reached the trees when she said, "And, Abigail told me to come."

He stopped, and turned back to look at her. "*What did you say?*" His eyes were intent now, and he came up close, as if he were suddenly having trouble hearing her. His expression was unreadable, and he was searching her eyes for answers.

"I said, it was Abigail's idea," she repeated herself, more timidly this time, because he looked distressed.

He turned away again, and took several steps into the pines before he said, "Abigail? Where did you-? Abigail *who?*" It was almost a demand, and this confused Aleta.

"It's just an old inside joke between my sister and I, a way to simplify difficult choices. Whenever we are having a hard time making a decision, we ask each other, not what Alaina or Aleta would do, rather what would Alicia or Abigail do? Abigail is my middle name, and the excuse I have for deciding to come, since Aleta wasn't sure. Like an alter ego, you know?" she explained, and it made sense to him.

Not just what she said. Because she couldn't know that Abigail had also been the given name of his beloved wife, Nanatha. But Amaoke recognized the blessing in this, the gift Aleta was giving him unknowing. The message that had traveled through time, had survived memory, delivered by an angel he'd not known he had been searching for. Permission to go on. To love again, as he wanted to.

He turned to the trees, raised his arms and face to the sky, and whispered, "Thank you."

"I'M SORRY I INTERRUPTED YOUR work," she said, suddenly shy. "I hope it's okay that I came."

He nodded. "I hope you'll be comfortable enough. You're more than welcome, but you're stuck here until Harry comes back next week."

"He told me," she smiled, and he could see she was thinking about something she wasn't ready to share.

"The house will get finished one way or the other," he told her. "Up here, there's no choice. The shell and the windows have to be done by end of summer. Everything else I can work on during the cold months, using whatever can be delivered here by first snowfall."

"Outside-in?" Aleta marveled. "I'm used to it the other way around."

"That's the luxury of living in a temperate climate," he laughed. "Besides, there isn't much else to do in the winter here; it will keep me out of trouble." He realized that he was inadvertently warning her about the disadvantages of his subarctic, off-the-grid lifestyle. She gave no indication she noticed, if she had.

"Would you give me a tour?" she asked, looking back across the meadow admiringly at the unfinished structure.

So he spent the better part of an hour explaining what he had already done, how the roof would be put in place once the final wall went up, how he had already started the water collection system, how he would make use of solar and wind energy for power. He made a rough drawing for her in the dirt at the bottom of the front steps, showing her how the interior would be laid out.

"The porch will wrap around?" she asked, looking at where the platform overlapped the three existing walls.

"Three sides," he nodded. "Eventually, I will put a deck in the back to overlook the trees and have storage underneath. I will probably tackle that next year."

"No railings?" she asked, honestly curious about his plans and trying to picture what it would be like.

"There'll have to be. I want to bring out the front at the top there, and it will need supports. I think I will try to fashion something out of willow or aspen; it's pretty, and the flexibility will allow for some kind of design. Toughest part will be figuring out how to get what's in my head put together in practice. It isn't as though I don't have time," he laughed.

"It sounds lovely," she said, and he could see she meant it. "I hope you'll invite me back to see it."

"No more party-crashing, then?" he asked, teasing, and reached out gently, briefly touching her rosy face, loving the way the elements kissed her.

She was still, relishing his touch, and she closed her eyes contentedly. When she opened them, he could tell she was on to something else; she looked determined about whatever it was.

"Can we talk about the money?" she asked, and he sighed.

"Do we have to?" he asked, knowing it was a rhetorical question. She wasn't one to give up on a subject so easily.

She laughed at his tone, trying to understand. "How about just this once?" Her tone was softer, and he could see she was more curious than serious.

"The money's yours. It's not mine anymore, what's there to talk about?" Amaoke said it reasonably, not challenging her, unperturbed, just letting her know what he was thinking.

"Well, yes, but – won't you need it...now?" Her question punctuated by a half-shrug as she turned from her perch on the step, indicating the house.

It was his turn to laugh, now understanding what was bothering her so much. Aside from him gifting her the money. "You mean, because I'm alive?"

But whatever was beneath her queries, she didn't find it funny. And what he said next didn't help.

"I guess they wouldn't tell you the rest of it, under the circumstances," he said, and she understood he meant the Bank of Montreal. "If I'd died, it would have been more."

He heard her angry exhale, all nostrils, an admonishment on its own. Aleta resisted the urge to swat him, infuriated that he could be so cavalier about something so emotionally charged for her. "What if I said I don't want it?"

"Then I would say you should give it away," he said reasonably, trying to understand what was making her so angry. He should have known it was a combination of exasperation and relief. "I expected you would anyway. I know you don't need it."

"Ama, I-"

"Listen, I have never had much use for the stuff. Would it make you feel better to know that I have spent more money building this house than I have in my entire lifetime? On anything? That I have put quite a bit into Alaskan Native charities, building funds, and other worthy causes? I am pleased to be able to do it. I don't need it for myself. It's a tool, Aleta. Too many people forget that. I'll use what I need, and the rest has to go somewhere. You were always the logical steward of my wealth. I said it before, and I meant it: you could do a lot of good with it." He studied his hands, wondering how to defuse the situation and not having a clue whether anything he said was helping.

Aleta's hand gripped his forearm, firmly. "I'm sorry. I should have just told you, but it is so hard for me to say it out loud. I would rather have you than the money."

"I'm here," he told her, allowing himself to hope that she wasn't simply celebrating his well-being. "You don't have to choose. It's enough to know that I was right."

"About what?" she asked him, still unsure whether he was teasing her.

"You."

That silenced her. How he could know something she was still so unsure about was an idea she had yet to accept.

"SINCE YOU'RE HERE, I HOPE it's okay to ask for your help," Amaoke said, wanting to dispel any residual awkwardness between them. "I know you're on vacation."

His smile was so endearing she could not help but return it. "Oh, I don't know," she said, warming up to tease him back. "I was thinking I would just get out my bathing suit and start sunning myself over there on the beach." She indicated the rocky strip that led down to the riverbank.

"I'll have to ask you to reconsider, ma'am," he answered. "I fear that would have a negative effect on the productivity of the work crew."

Aleta laughed aloud. "Of course I will help. I'd love to help. But I have no idea what I'm doing." She waved at the structure helplessly. "Construction is not one of my strong suits."

"I have no doubt you could learn it. But for now, you'll be perfect for what I have in mind," he reassured her. "Come on."

He took her down to the riverbank. "I'm thinking to use river stones to line my shower," he told her, squatting down and pulling a few egg-sized rocks from the sandy mud. "Can you help me choose a few…thousand?"

So she sat with him there in the silt, unmindful as she got more and more filthy, as they scavenged and dug for stones of a multitude of colors, and he told her the stories of each one, where it came from, how old it might be.

After a while, he helped her strip off her wet and dirty clothing, carrying her clad in her underclothes into the cool water to rinse off, ducking underwater with her, not surprised when she told him she was an avid swimmer, taking pleasure at her delight as he helped her balance on her own feet, feeling the water flow around her, something he knew she had never experienced. Pleased to see her relax, letting go of her fear of the unknown, letting her decide how tightly to hold onto him, watching her gain even more freedom.

He had to force her out, feeling her shivering start. "The river will be here tomorrow," he murmured against her hair, ignoring her protests. He carried her up to the platform of the house and wrapped her in blankets and left her to warm in the sun while he toweled himself off and pulled on dry pants and a hooded pullover. By the time he finished bringing the spare clothing from her backpack onto the deck to warm up too, Aleta was asleep, her curls dancing around her face in the soft breeze. Amaoke anchored her clothing with some of his tools and went back down to the water to haul the stones they had gathered up to the site. It was a start.

AFTER A DINNER OF FRESH-caught fish and dried fruit, they sat together near the fire, enjoying its warmth, peaceful and quiet. Amaoke got up occasionally to feed the flames, and offered Aleta another of her s'mores, but she shook her head. After some time, she started to talk, about herself for a change, which he knew was a significant gift.

"My parents raised my sister and myself to be self-sufficient; as much as possible we were treated the same way, and their expectations of us were the same. I'm not sure now that it was an ideal approach, since it ignored our fundamental differences, but it may have been a type of coping mechanism for them," Aleta began, looking out at the darkening yard.

"My mother was almost stringently fair, and I think she felt guilty about my legs – I suspect she still does. My sister never tiptoed around the issue, and these days, as I told you, she is even more direct in her observations."

She sighed, and then continued. "I think that I grew up with two realities, one at home and one in the world. At home, I was the same as anyone else, and everywhere else I was different.

"I persisted in my belief that if I ignored the second reality, it would allow everyone else to do so as well. Imagine my surprise as an adult when men I knew found me attractive, appreciated my intelligence, and with whom I had a great deal in common never asked me out on a date. I stubbornly held on to the idea that if I ignored my disability, the rest of the world could do so as well.

"I was wrong. Most of them couldn't get past the crutches, I guess, and I eventually had to face the reality that those who did were not some noble, rare species of male who could rise above external societal pressure and prejudice. They were often simply curious. They did and said enough to get me into bed and *then* leave, their behavior even more predatory than the others. Eventually, I gave up, and told myself I was content to have everything else, which was more than most people had anyway."

"It took a lot of courage to come here," he allowed, hoping she would say more.

"You have no idea. When you didn't come back, and I thought...well, you know what I thought," she said, not wanting to belabor it. "Then I find out you're alive, and it became so complicated, so fast.

"I knew my own feelings, but I couldn't understand what would keep you away from me. I didn't want to make a decision for you, or put you in a position where you had to face me if it wasn't what you wanted. I didn't even know if I would be able to find you.

"I've done everything in my life by the book," she said, and there was something in her voice that he couldn't read. "I never went anywhere without a clear purpose, without planning, without an invitation. But ever since I met you, I think I have known. And at some point, I realized that if I didn't put myself out there and find out how you felt, really, about me, or us, or what could be, I knew I would never have a moment's peace. Even if you were going to reject me, I needed the closure."

"I wanted you to have happiness without obligation," he told her. "I'm not the man I was, you see. The wolf has gone. I wasn't sure I wanted to burden you with all my…survivor's guilt, I guess it is. That's what I have been able to glean from the library anyway. I thought I needed to be alone. Turns out I was lying to myself."

"You're not a werewolf any longer?" she asked, and looked confused.

"No. I still have some of the augmented senses, smell, hearing, but other than that…this is all there is," he said, reaching his arms out wide. "We – all of us - went together, looking for an ending. The others found peace, and I got a kind of…well, I could call it limbo, but I suspect it is more like a retirement. Especially now, grey hair and all.

"Now, the wolf remains with me, but more like my totem, a spirit companion that will always be a part of me, but never again a physical expression. My wolf brother has crossed over. He'll wait for me on the other side. But please, let's not talk about me. I want to hear the rest of your story."

"I argued with myself for days," she related, picking up where she had left off. "Prayed. Talked to my sister about it and was so uncomfortable explaining these feelings to her. I was blushing, stammering, a total wreck. Alaina was probably thinking I had lost my mind, and she laughed and asked me what Abigail had to say about it," Aleta looked down at her hands.

Amaoke reached over and picked one up in both of his, and brought it to his lips. He held his mouth against her palm for several moments, and then twined his fingers into hers. She leaned against his shoulder and he rearranged the blanket around her.

"I controlled what I could, I am probably the world's worst outdoorsperson, but my dad helped me gear up. I told him I was traveling alone to Alaska, and his eyes did this funny thing, like he wondered what had happened to his daughter, but he took me to Cabela's and didn't say a word about it.

"And the only information I had about this place was in your chart, from the intake interview, the second one, anyway, and that felt questionably ethical and too much like stalking." Amaoke laughed out loud, and she gave him a surprised look. "What?"

"Nothing, nothing," he told her, thinking about his evenings under her backyard hedges.

"Ama? What is it?" She was alert to the mischief in his eyes.

"This is *your* story," he reassured her. "There will be chances to talk about many different things in the future. Save some of them for another time."

SOMEWHAT RELUCTANTLY ALETA BEGAN AGAIN.

"I got to Bethel and got lucky immediately. I stopped at the post office to ask how the mail got routed to this area, and the postmistress told me the plane for the day hadn't left. I thought she wanted me to ask the pilot, since he knew who lived up around Tuluksak, but when I walked over there to the airstrip, the pilot took my backpack and put it and me on the plane.

"She must have called him, or someone, and said she was sending me over there. He never said more than two words to me, and I didn't understand them, but he was very kind. He had your windows on the plane. I tried to pay him, but he wouldn't let me."

Amaoke nodded. "Mail service means something entirely different up here. And we all need each other to survive."

"Is that so?" She scrutinized him carefully. "I think it is because everyone seems to know you. I heard some interesting stories at the exchange in town, and in the community lodge. They put me in touch with Harry."

"Old men, trying to scare you with old legends. Or more likely, just wanting to keep you around, so they kept talking. And looking at you." She thought he sounded jealous, and she smiled a bit, tucking her chin into the collar of her jacket. "I'm surprised Harry agreed to bring you; I think the latest rumor is that I must be luring beautiful maidens out here and eating them."

"Harry told me you'd never had a woman out here," she said, a little too triumphantly.

"And what else did he tell you?" Amaoke growled it, as though he was impatient with these nuisances, but she could tell he was amused, the way anyone is when talking about the behavior of crazy uncles. Everybody has at least one.

"That he thought I'd be safer staying in town with him," she laughed, and Amaoke had to laugh as well.

"He would." He got up slowly and stoked the fire, turning back to rearrange the blankets around her and looking at her appraisingly. "Cold?"

She nodded. She was unable to get comfortable and she was tired, but she wasn't ready to give up this day. It was so perfect; it made her irrationally afraid if she closed her eyes it would be gone, like a dream.

"I can make tea, but nights here, it gets to a point where the best way to get warm is in the bed," he told her, helping her up and gathering the blankets. He pulled her close and kissed the top of her head. "Sleep will do us both good. Just be with me," he said against her hair, making sure she understood that was all it would be for now. He felt her relax, and give in to her exhaustion.

He handed her the crutches she had placed off to the side of the bench, and led her to the sod house, where he was staying while he constructed the more formal dwelling. He liked that she was curious about it, but this would be the first time she had been inside it.

Aleta was surprised at the layout. He'd built up the central fire hours ago, and the banked coals kept the space under the domed roof pleasantly cozy, despite the large smoke hole in the roof. The air was scented with pine and cedar, and there was a massive bed made of timbers, the posts at the four corners were taller than she was. It looked very inviting, with a modern mattress and linens, covered with handmade quilts and topped with animal skins.

"Did you build this?" she asked wonderingly, running a hand over the silky furs.

"I did," he said. "My one extravagance. I've gotten spoiled by modern beds, slept too much out in the elements and on the ground, I suppose. But I made a miscalculation," he admitted with a sheepish grin.

"What's that?" she asked, still marveling over the bed.

"Well, I wanted it for the house," he explained, laughing at his lack of foresight. "Then, once I built it, I realized it's too big to move, so…I guess it will have to be taken down and reassembled, or else I'll be building another one."

"It's amazing," she nodded, yawning and swaying on her feet. "You could sell a bed like this in the city for a mint."

"Let's get you into it before you fall down," he said gently, relieving her of her crutches and pulling back the covers so she could sit down. He slipped her jacket down off her arms and set it aside. Then he kneeled and pulled the laces on her boots, removing them before encouraging her to lie down.

"I'm keeping my clothes on?" she asked, surprised.

"For now," he smiled conspiratorially at her.

"Won't I get hot?" she asked.

Too late for that, he thought, but said only, "I think you'll see that the furs help regulate your temperature. Socks on or off?"

"On, I think," she said, settling in with a sigh as he pulled the furs up over her. "Oh, they're heavy!" she marveled.

He sat next to her for a moment, then leaned over to brush his lips against her eyebrow. "*Unnu alluataq,*" Amaoke wished her sweet dreams in his own language, like a prayer for thanks, hoping the spirits could hear it. She could barely keep her eyes open, and he watched her as she gave in to her slumber, then stood up and just looked at her, because he could.

Mine, he thought, hardly daring to believe it, knowing it was wrong to think it, unable to stay such sentiments. He'd decided, but he knew her life was elsewhere, and he was trying hard not to draw premature conclusions.

He finally climbed into bed himself, moved in close to her. She mumbled something incoherent when he pulled her close, but didn't wake. He closed his eyes and slept more soundly than he had in centuries.

UNLIKE IN HIS YOUTH, AMAOKE was up before the sun. He brought water up from the river, and started the fire in the sod house, wanting it to be warm for Aleta when she woke. He put water in the pot and hung it near the fire to heat.

He made his rounds, picking berries and wild celery. He put the berries in the ground, lamenting the sad state of the permafrost, and lay out the celery stalks to dry in the sunshine.

He ventured into the forest to salvage more timbers for building, thinking the strokes of the axe would be less likely to filter into a sleeping brain than the repeated blows of his hammer. He pulled bark off some trees downed by a recent storm and nodded. He could have Harry help him drag them with the Cat and they'd dry out fine. Some of the more manageable pieces he cut down to his liking, and moved these under his own power.

Half the morning had gone before she emerged, looking refreshed and perhaps a bit guilty. She smiled in greeting and made her way carefully over to the building site, where he was already up in the harness, securing timber crossbeams. The skeleton of the roof was taking shape.

"Would you like coffee?" he asked, loosening his tether and lowering himself to the ground.

"I'd love some," she nodded. "I can make it, though, if you tell me where everything is."

"No need," he told her. "It's ready. Check the thermos. Over by the tools." He stepped out of the harness and sat on the deck, facing the river.

"But you don't drink coffee," she observed. "It's sweet that you remembered."

"Well, before you give me too much credit, I've always kept it handy for when I have visitors. Harry drinks most of it. I drink it occasionally now, too, although I prefer eating the beans," he told her, watching the surprise on her face.

"You *eat* coffee beans?!" Aleta was astonished.

"Kusini's husband was a bit of a coffee nut," Amaoke explained. "He loved coffee, loved to drink it, cook with it, you name it. He even had a tea he made out of the green coffee cherries…or perhaps it was the ripe coffee cherries, I'm not sure. Maybe both. Ambakisye was very interesting."

"Wow, what was that like?" Aleta's face betrayed skepticism that tea from coffee cherries could be enjoyed, and it was too much like the face Kusini had always made regarding the tea.

"Probably not for everyone," Amaoke said, being kind. "Anyway, they had a friend who let us stay on her coffee plantation, and she gave me dry roasted coffee beans one day. I just liked them, that flavor is smoky and deep. She'd dump a handful in my pockets in the mornings after that."

"Oh, did she?" Aleta tried to sound casual, but he could hear the jealousy in her voice this time, and he realized how that statement might sound as though the relationship had been intimate.

He laughed, wanting to tease her some more, but felt some clarification was in order. "Yes, amazing woman. She was all of one hundred years old," he said, hoping it would give Aleta some relief.

It did, but she teased him back. "Only one hundred? What man doesn't find a younger woman attractive?"

"Keep talking like that, jailbait, and we'll need a chaperone out here," he told her, referring to her thirty-odd years, and tapped her gently on the nose. "Time to put you to work."

He put his spare harness on her, guessing, correctly, that she might enjoy the novelty of the experience. He realized, after she had shed her initial nervousness about the prospect of being suspended, that her relationship to gravity was different than that of most people. For her, it was a bit of an adversary, not necessarily the source of reassuring stability that it was for everyone else. For this reason, she took to the awkwardness of the harness more quickly than he had expected, more quickly than he had initially when he'd learned it on the construction crew. It held her securely, and she had freedom of movement for her arms, not needing to rely upon them for balance.

By late afternoon, they had arrived at a comfortable arrangement, hanging at opposite ends of the structure, working in rhythm. Amaoke would seat each crossbeam at her end, then secure it at the midpoint, and the two of them would nail it in place simultaneously. With Aleta's assistance he finished the basic roof support, and set the floor of the loft he had planned in a single day.

"Glad I don't have to compete with you for a job," he teased, bringing her down onto the platform gently. "You're a natural."

She smiled proudly. "It's so much fun being up there. No one ever let me do anything like that before." She was slightly breathless in her pleasure, and he was happy to see her this way, letting some of her guard down, having fun. "What's next?"

"Let's take a break," he suggested. "Most men my age take naps in the afternoon."

She laughed. "Swim first?" She was negotiating, watching his eyes. "Since there *are* no men your age, and the river is calling to me."

Amaoke could see she meant it, and her choice of words touched his heart because he could see she was falling in love with this place, which was more than he could have hoped for. It was certainly more than he deserved. He marveled at the pace at which she was shedding whatever sheltered life she'd had, was embracing this new kind of freedom. Perhaps it was something she had always needed but never found.

Aleta didn't tell him what she already knew. She wanted to be with him, but could never ask him to give up this life to come back to New Orleans. And she really didn't want him to, because it wasn't even what she wanted for herself anymore.

"I LOVE THIS PLACE. I always found myself back here over the years. But at the same time, I knew that there were things that would pull me back out into the world. Now, I just want to settle, and I thought that by finally putting a permanent building here…" Amaoke's voice trailed off, and he sighed. They had settled by the fire again for the evening, and Aleta was patient, waiting for him to continue. She passed him some more dried fruit. "I should have seen what the spirits were telling me. What man builds a house for himself?"

Aleta laughed at his expression, but didn't know what to say. It sounded like such an existential question from such a concrete person. She knew he was thoughtful, but something about hearing him say it like that was funny. "I don't understand."

"Sure you do, you're just too kind to psychoanalyze me out loud," he teased. "Some years back, I was in L.A., drifting. I took a job as a bouncer in a comedy club, and this comedian was talking about how men *would* live in cardboard boxes but then, well, I won't repeat what he said, but basically we have to have houses or women would be entirely uninterested in us. The fairer sex need houses."

"But what about that bed you built?" she asked. "Wasn't that for your own comfort?"

"Sure, but I could keep living in the sod house. I've done it for centuries."

"You're not going to get rid of the sod house, once the house is built?" she asked, and sounded distressed. "I like it. I could live there, with you. I don't need a house."

"Aleta." He said her name and she heard the skepticism in his tone. "Sure, during the honeymoon, before you realize how much I annoy you."

She narrowed her eyes at him and reached for his arm, laughing when he pulled away out of reach of her mischief.

"But I will keep it," he told her, achieving an impressively serious expression, and keeping a straight face. "I'll need a place to stay whenever you kick me out of the house."

"That's your version of sleeping on the couch?!" Aleta was still laughing, but not at him, not really, so he came close and put a stop to it by putting his mouth on hers. She was so still and so surprised by it that he thought something was wrong. Then she rested her forehead against his, briefly, before offering her lips once more, and he cradled her face in his hands and explored, gently, tasting her, taking his time with it, refusing to rush, not stopping until they were both breathless.

"I don't know if I'm ever going to be able to sleep without you next to me after this," she admitted in a small voice, and he knew that she sounded that way because she was afraid of the vulnerability she was betraying.

"I won't mind if you follow me out there," he whispered, holding her close. He didn't want to ruin the moment, but the conversation was presenting itself, and he wanted complete understanding between them if they were going forward. "Can we talk about New Orleans? And what happens when Harry comes back to bring more windows and take you back?" he asked, feeling her posture change subtly.

"Do we have to?" she asked, half-teasing and half not.

"How about just this once?" he suggested, following her lead and trying to maintain some levity.

"It's ground zero," she shrugged, and seeing he didn't understand, she tried to explain. "It is home; when I left for college, I thought I might not come back, but of course I did, because it was the path of least resistance. It's the devil I know. It's a place to hide, a place I got stuck in for a long time."

"Stuck? What about your family?" Amaoke asked her.

"Another excuse, another reason it is easy. Kusini told my sister to live her life, and I think maybe me as well, but I – it is so hard to remember that night. And then Azuma, she said the same thing essentially – *live the life you are blessed to have.*

"I think coming here was my trial run, break the pattern of doing things one way, to try and see how to do them another way. It won't happen overnight, there is too much to consider. I know I will have to think about how to make the transition, and it will take time. But I am already impatient for it, already planning what needs to happen.

"Mostly I think about the others, your friends, how they gave up everything, even you, all of you sacrificed so much. I remember when you left me you told me that to deserve me you needed to be willing to die to make the world better for me.

"I think about Kusini, and the way she looked when she said her husband's name, and Carter, and Weston, and what could have been, what they already had. Love is the answer; love is the gift. It would be a poor way for me to show my gratitude for such a thing by being stuck, not growing, not changing, not taking any chances.

"Not trying to love without worrying how it will end," Aleta whispered, putting her hand on his face. She was unable to see his eyes, the breeze was blowing his hair across them, the strands dancing against her fingers. "You told me once that I deserved love, I hope you meant yours."

Amaoke breathed deeply, filling his nose with Aleta's warm, spicy scent, letting it settle him. He knew that Nanatha would not begrudge him any happiness, but the selfish part of him had to admit that if the circumstances were in reverse, the thought of her with another man would have been distressing, at best. He also knew, deeply and instinctively, that the cycle of life was meant to bring new blessings even as it brought new difficulties, and had she survived him, he would have celebrated the idea that she could be deeply loved again, and cared for, and cherished.

He looked down at Aleta, returning his proper focus to her, saying a rightful prayer for her, thanking the spirits for the blessings she represented. She looked up at him, waiting, expectant. They never looked away from one another, never gave up eye contact as he picked her up and carried her into the little house, with the warm fire, and the big bed. Home.

Amaoke took his time with his kisses, even rolling onto his back with Aleta stretched out on top of him, stroking her through her clothing, feeling her respond. He took his own clothes off first, making himself the more vulnerable, before slowly and reverently removing each item she wore, kissing the cocoa-colored skin he exposed, learning about what she liked. Finally, she lay next to him in the sheets, naked and glorious. Flushed in the places his mouth had touched.

He positioned himself over her, and she turned her face up to his. Looking in her eyes, he asked, "Is this okay with you?"

Though she smiled a bit and nodded, he paid attention to his nose, which confirmed her arousal, but there was an underlying scent of fear. He placed a hand on her waist and could feel her trembling, so he settled back down beside her, but his erection was insistent against her thigh. So he pulled the sheet up between them as a reassurance, and reached across her protectively, placing a warm hand on her opposite hip and propping his head on his other arm to look down at her. Some of his hair flowed onto her body and the dark strands draped across her torso. Aleta held some of them in her free hand, looking at them lovingly, then turned her face up to him with a pleading look.

Amaoke waited a few moments to see if she would talk, but when she remained silent, he spoke.

"Did you know that most wolves' mating bonds last a lifetime?"

When she shook her head, he continued, "The beast in me only wants to protect you, never wants to hurt you, because of the love I feel for you. I will not be able to be with you like this if you feel forced, and especially not if you feel afraid."

She made a soft sound in her throat, part surprise, perhaps, and part grief. He knew that she had been hurt, and that created a fear not easily calmed. He settled down next to her, and held her, placing kisses on her neck and her shoulder, feeling her respond, and this time, when the sharp sweet scent of her arousal reached his nose, there was no fear to taint it.

In the silent spaces
Where the journey ends
I shall finally find my rest

Author's Note

This is a story driven by feelings. Love, renewal, family. Surprises and disappointments. Sheltering with your people before the storm. Finding friends you didn't know you had. The bittersweet agony of letting go, both for the characters and for me. A well-deserved and long-anticipated new beginning. It certainly reflects my journey creating this epic fairytale, and hey, 2020, anyone?

My family is now used to having to compete with my laptop for my attention during the creation of stories; their love and support are more than I deserve, and like the Collector, I count my blessings every day (and would defend them with a bloody sword).

I heartily thank Nici Flann for beta reading, challenging me, asking questions, and showing me what lifetime friendship looks like.

Thanks to Carrie Coslov, who asked me about Nanatha's given name a few years ago, setting me on the path to Aleta's big reveal in the epilogue of this novel. At the time, I told Carrie I was certain that Amaoke knew her name, he just had not whispered it in my ear. Yet.

Thanks to Becky Alwood, who helped me give myself permission to have Weston speak in first person. She's also responsible for one of the most critical one-liners in this book.

And to Elizabeth – editor, teacher, wordmaster – I extend my gratitude for making me a better writer and a better person.

Thanks to everyone who tolerates me referring to imaginary folk as if they were real people, past, present, and future. If you thought I was going to stop, well, you never really knew me.

About the Author

LJ Farrow is an author, poet, and optimist who writes fairytales about redemption. A Colorado native, she now lives in rural Indiana with her husband, two children, and one very angry hedgehog.

www.ingramcontent.com/pod-product-compliance
Lightning Source LLC
Chambersburg PA
CBHW060808120726
47909CB00006B/1832